TALE
OF THE
TAPE

TWO UNLIKELY HEROES
TAKE DOWN THE DIXIE MAFIA

ALAN ABLES

outskirtspress

DENVER, COLORADO

Tale of the Tape
Two Unlikely Heroes Take Down the Dixie Mafia
All Rights Reserved.
Copyright © 2014 Alan Ables
v3.0 R1.1

Cover Photo © 2014 Shutterstock.com/Stephen Finn
All rights reserved - used with permission.

Outskirts Press, Inc.
http://www.outskirtspress.com

ISBN: 978-1-4787-2398-1

Outskirts Press and the "OP" logo are trademarks belonging to Outskirts Press, Inc.

PRINTED IN THE UNITED STATES OF AMERICA

This above all: to thine own self be true,
And it must follow, as the night the day,
Thou canst not then be false to any man.

Hamlet Act 1, scene 3

Acknowledgements

Judy Whitcomb for inexhaustible enthusiasm and support

Captain Jay Stocks, USN (ret.)
for assistance in things aeronautical

Bobby Stevenson for conversations about driving a train

Bob Fehringer for encyclopedic knowledge about firearms

Tom Hughes and Steve Thompson for encouragement

And a multitude of mentors, teachers, shipmates, friends and
neighbors who have lifted, guided, inspired and endured

To Frank H. Ables, my father and a gentleman

Part One

Fall 1983

One

Flying long-distance alone was no big deal for a pilot with his experience, most of it in the old bird currently strapped to his body. He'd flown Fat Girl and nothing else for nearly twenty years. With skill and more luck than he would ever admit, he had handled every curve ball the old relic had ever thrown at him. Even so, what he was doing right now was not exactly brilliant. There was no work-around, no plan B, if and—more likely—when things started going south.

But, for Chris Cain, clandestine operative by choice, loner and survivor by nature, the mission always came first, even those with bad odds. For decades he had cheated fate by relying on his intellect and instinct to overcome the paralyzing doubts born of personal danger. So, bouncing along alone he shut his eyes, mopped his face with a towel he'd borrowed from the Mayflower Hotel on a rare debrief visit to Washington, D.C., and, once again, methodically check-listed the current reality. The committee debating in his head only agreed on one thing: panic never led to a solution. Losing control of options was always a fatal mistake.

The way he figured, his survival turned on three variables: the strength of the massive storm roiling off his right wing; whether or not his fifty-something and slightly abused body could weather the beating it would take once inside it and—most disturbing—whether he still trusted his judgment at all.

He'd always had the most confidence in his intellect. A member of the first class to graduate the newly established Air Force Academy, Cain knew he was sharper than anyone else in this or any other situation. The

1

fact that he was alone only heightened his confidence because he never liked working with a team, unless he was captain. Few, if any, shared his talent for leaning forward, anticipating, reading the plane and the bigger picture and coming up with a workable plan. The discipline to remain calm—even if just for a few seconds longer than anyone else—set him apart from other men. This acquired talent had kept him alive for decades of dangerous, often solo, operations against the worst odds. An inner voice which denied defeat saved his life more than once.

Cain's face was expressionless except for his steel-grey eyes deep set beneath heavy dark brows. This inventory troubled him.

He knew better than this. Even at a respectable distance, the energy roiling on the storm's trailing edge has jerked him around in the sky like a string puppet. He tugged the harness tabs crisscrossing his chest and around the waist of his shorts; they cinched him even tighter into the cracked green leather seat which felt like it was part of his anatomy. It was another reflexive, unconscious move, but it did ensure that he could at least keep his hands and feet on the controls once things got worse. Trying to control the plane only slightly younger then he was would take every ounce of strength left in his broad-shouldered and rapidly tiring six-foot frame. Even if he could, he didn't know what combination of wind and lightning, metal stress, hydraulic or electrical failure, fatigue or a lethal amalgam of any and all of those variables would set the odds of completing the mission. The definition of success is very simple: landing alive.

His pounding heart felt like it was climbing up his throat. He closed his eyes in a grimace and squeezed his thoughts into a one-word mantra: *control, control, control.*

His heart beat faster and a couple of sweat beads raced down his neck. His tightly-stretched t-shirt was already sopping wet. Is continuing the mission possible? And, if it isn't, why is he even considering it? Only one thought kept pulling him toward the edge of sanity: at what point exactly had he gone crazy?

The plane was chugging fuel as he flew low and slow to avoid detection, not that any radar could see him against the face of a thunderhead. He banked right to gaze at it head on. It had to be at least two hundred miles wide, wider than his radar could measure. It is a solid, impenetrable wall. Even with the added advantage of the fuel in a balloon-like bladder riding with more than a half-ton of illicit cargo behind him, there was neither the option of delaying much longer nor of flying around the black, vertical column of raw, immeasurable brute energy.

Turning the aging airplane again to the north, he looked at his hard hands; somehow they seemed to be attached to the airplane, not him. He saw them tighten on the yoke. As another strobe light burned a purple streak in his vision and sent the plane on another roller-coaster bounce that flexed the wings to the breaking point, only one idea shot through his head: *get the hell out of here.*

Again, he closed his eyes to concentrate.

His heart skipped as another blinding flash of white light, followed too quickly by a numbing explosion, punched him in the chest. He shouted a curse heard by no one; he was talking to himself as he often did, and it did release some tension. He inhaled the cool, humid air and closed his eyes as the plane vibrated. One more thought echoed through his head. It was the same, cowardly and sanctimonious pronouncement he'd heard forever from duller and weaker men: "There's old pilots, there's bold pilots, but there ain't no old, bold pilots."

Would it be his epitaph, chiseled below his expiration date?

With perfect hindsight he wished his co-pilot wasn't debauching on a remote beach near Tampico. But, it made perfectly good sense to leave him there: having another body aboard was too risky, even in the remote chance that law enforcement would force him to land, either in the States or—much more unlikely—on the much longer transits in South America and Mexico.

Only four hours ago, flying due east over the Gulf from northern Mexico, weather broadcasts warned of a fast-moving storm system roaring northeast from Texas and sweeping over Oklahoma and western Arkansas. Two hours later he penetrated U.S. air space, cruising at two-hundred feet south of Lake Charles, Louisiana. He had been noticed and followed briefly by a DEA King Air, but there had been no radio request for identification. Since then nothing in the broadcasts mentioned that the front was slowing. Now, his visual and radar observations confirmed that he wasn't going to fly over or around it. So, for the past hour he had burned much more fuel than he wanted to by boring holes in the sky behind the wide front, willing it to move on or even to break up just enough to leave a corridor to the mile-long abandoned military runway that he reckoned was about ninety miles beyond the storm's training edge.

He had spent well more than half his life as a pilot. He'd learned to fly the Provider back at Hurlburt Field, Florida. In Vietnam he flew it on scores of Project Ranch Hand missions spraying herbicides—Agents Pink, Green, Purple, Blue, White and Orange—to defoliate the jungles of the Mekong Delta.

Midway through his first tour he had been pulled from those duties and became a command pilot flying the White Whale, a specially outfitted C-123 used to transport South Vietnamese and American VIPs, including General William Westmoreland, commander of Military Assistance Command, Vietnam. He volunteered to extend his tour before returning for Special Forces training at Fort Bragg, North Carolina. At Westmoreland's request, he returned to pilot the White Whale. At the end of the year-long assignment he left the Air Force and began flying secret cargo and passenger missions into Laos and Cambodia for his new employer, Southern Air Cargo, a wholly-owned and clandestine subsidiary of the Central Intelligence Agency.

During the next two decades he lived in the Philippines, Chile, South Africa and Saudi Arabia.

When offered a large pay raise to transfer to the CIA's newest air cargo company, flying vastly different cargo for much more vague reasons, he had no qualms. He could afford to maintain a walled villa in old Cartagena, Colombia, and another home in New Orleans, deep within the city's fashionable Garden District, upriver from the French Quarter.

He'd flown Fat Girl or one her siblings for more than forty-thousand hours—probably more than anyone alive—in all kinds of weather, on nearly every continent, on long hauls and short.

Blinking away his trip down memory lane, Cain again looked around the cockpit with new eyes, the eyes of an old pilot who wasn't as sure about his or the Fat Girl's immortality as he once most certainly was.

His mind began to roam, split-second lapses from reality, but he couldn't shake off thoughts about how he had come to be in a spot like this.

He was a survivor, and he was lucky.

That luck began early. Abandoned by a troubled teenager who left him in a cardboard box on the steps of the convent at Ursulines and Charters Streets in the French Quarter, he was rescued by the nuns who named him Christian Cain. Through their love and charity, he grew from boy to young man, first within their cloistered confines, then in a nearby orphanage where priests and nuns nurtured him and cultivated the better angels of his soul. But, with shrinking resources to support him, he worked odd jobs on nights and weekends in the kitchens and back doors of the adjacent restaurants, bars and bordellos. He learned that New Orleans wouldn't exist without the Mississippi River and—just as it drains the North American Continent—the human flotsam borne with it. He tried to avoid the violence, perversion and crime that crept into the Quarter from Faubourg-Marigny and upper Ninth Ward neighborhoods. Close-at-hand observations of hope and despair, divinity and debauchery, of saints and sinners who often were one in the same, shaped and hardened the mind. By sixteen he was a born-again cynic, with an insight into the human condition well beyond his years.

Whoever his parents were, they at least left him with a quick mind. He'd devoured math and science at the Catholic high school, enough to be noticed by a wealthy and well-connected parish patron who took him under her wing. It was her influence that eventually secured his appointment to the Air Force Academy. He was proud of the appointment; with no equals, at least in his mind, Cain knew he truly deserved it.

At the Academy he made no close friends. All his energies went to excelling above his soft-minded and immature classmates. Afterwards he served his time, learned to fly, and when other opportunities came his way he never looked back.

The vomitous ambiance of French Quarter mornings he washed off the broken sidewalks bred a disdain of excess and the wealth that enabled the weak, degenerate and unworthy. The memories never left him, even when he wanted. But, they also imbued him with a permanent ambition for power. Through the decades he remained true to that belief. Big money for big risks fulfilled the dream. If he didn't die tonight, this would be the fourth time he'd made this trip this year, each time concluding a four-thousand mile adventure including cargo and passenger deliveries in overnight stopovers in Nicaragua and northern Mexico. The special delivery of cocaine behind him would net him more than other pilots did in a year and another large windfall for the sisters of the Urusuline Convent.

Now he wasn't so sure. He knew the next half hour could be more dangerous than any street fight or special operations mission, maybe even worse. In no particular order, he was pushing his skill, the plane and—what he hated more than anything—dumb luck. He was pushing the absolute limits. To land and walk away tonight, he'd need all the mojo he could dredge from his misty memories of his childhood on the filthy streets and the wild bayous.

* * * *

The reassuring vibrations that had lulled him for the past few minutes brought him back to reality. Flexing his firm grip around the u-shaped yoke which disappeared in those big hands felt good. Even if older, his arms and back were still strong. His legs were another issue: and they ached sooner than they used to, and four hours of constantly pushing against the rudder pedals was tiring, especially doing all the work alone. He remembered football practice step drills at the Academy; he hated them decades ago; he felt like he was running them again right now.

A flash of lightening ignited the sky, blasting away his mental inventory and leaving another gold-gilded purple wash in his vision, near complete in his right eye. As the concussion of thunder rolled on and on across the sky, he tilted his head forward, squinting at the radar with his left, less affected eye.

Might as well lay cold steel on my head and cock the hammer.

Again, he tried to concentrate on the bigger picture, anything but the hell surrounding him, but the reality was still the same. He was rolling the dice and betting his life. He was taking a very big gamble with some very crappy odds.

Taking risks—calculated risks based on a calculus of physics, logic and luck—had made him a rich man. He was the best of the best, or at least he had been until now, and just like everyone in the dark chain of command that put him tonight in the sky over the Oklahoma-Arkansas border, he knew that it was always all about the money. But, even that rationalization failed him right now. He was uncharacteristically, disturbingly uncertain, even regretful that greed would be the final temptation of Christian Cain.

It wasn't as though he feared death or much of anything or anyone else, but he certainly didn't see any reason to hasten the rendezvous. He despised weakness, especially suicide. He felt weak. He felt like a fool. Has he now gone too far? Was he about to add his name to a pathetic roll of losers?

Exhaling deeply, he looked over his left shoulder. To the west the panorama of a soft, tranquil, night lured his very soul. The forests, fields and gently rolling hills below were bathed in pale, peaceful moonlight. Lakes and creeks refreshed by the recent rains twinkled like diamonds thrown on a dark carpet.

Twisting to look through the starboard window, his heart sank into total despair.

Flying into that thunderstorm is insane, suicide by airplane.

Even subtracting the instinct for self-preservation, he knew he was right because he was never wrong. Any novice pilot—even a grossly overconfident one—could call this shot. If it could even be considered a betting proposition, the odds would be slim and none of living to tell the story. For men like Cain telling the story had always been a reward, maybe even more satisfying than the money from faceless espiocrats and narco lords who profited from men like him, surrogates paid well to take risks for them.

He did not want to lose control, especially control of his mind. Panic would raise the odds against him, even before the real game began. His eyes reaped all the physical, rational details from the faces of the instruments mounted below the windshield. With his legs and hands he jiggled the rudder and wing ailerons. Again, he closed his eyes and pushed forward against the harness and arched his back, twisting his neck to break tension and clear his head.

Then the veteran pilot and aeronautical engineer listened.

He listened to the airplane as though his life depended on it, because it did. From ten miles away the old crate creaked and groaned against the storm. The twin piston engines drove propellers that hummed with a steady pitch. Two more engines, jets slung under the wing outboard of them, added thrust. They harmonized with a throaty murmur. He listened, and he didn't needed instruments to know their RPMs and that he was running out of fuel, and time. But, the odd harmony was reassuring, disturbed only by the staccato rhythm of rivets popping and bulkheads moaning as they twisted under the punishment.

It gave him more time to think, to fully involve his senses of sight, sound, touch, for anything that would change the odds.

His rubbery face pulled into something like a cruel smile. He laughed at himself: *My Invictus: I'm the captain of my fate, the master of this freakin' crap shoot.*

* * * *

He didn't own the plane, but he might as well for all the time and interest he gave it.

By modern standards, the C-123 was not a particularly small aircraft, nor was it large.

It went into service 1949 and served through Vietnam. Its two

two-thousand horsepower eighteen-cylinder Pratt and Whitney radial engines are among the most reliable in aviation history; if that weren't enough, the two General Electric turbojets slung under the wings and outboard of them added even more thrust. It's "Provider" nickname was well earned in underdeveloped or undeveloped areas of the world, flying in what engineers euphemistically described as primitive areas of operation. Because of that, most of the three hundred of such planes built by Fairchild Aircraft were sold in Southeast Asia and South America. Its utility wasn't lost on the U.S. Air Force, who retired the last one from service in the early '80s.

Its high-mounted, one-hundred-ten-foot wing, much shorter but wide body, enabled it to carry heavy loads. Low take-off and landing speeds and raw power made it a hands-down favorite of pilots on unpaved and short runways. Stubby wheels held it only a foot or so off the ground, making cargo transfer very easy. It was perfect for tonight's flight; it was a drug smuggler's ideal.

The roomy, haze green aluminum cockpit was his command center, office and—on extended missions like this and many others—his home. He knew how everything in it worked; he'd be a fool if he didn't.

And he knew that despite the airplane's age everything was state-of-the-art, including a weather radar installed last week during a lay-over in the Florida Panhandle at Hurlburt Field, the center of the Air Force's special operations command. Only advanced military aircraft had anything like it, and this one was probably better. He knew that Great Circle Air Cargo got it from a non-commercial source, and he knew that source was the CIA, through yet another of their cover companies. In turn, they'd bought it as some fantastically inflated expense that would never be accounted to the taxpayer. Mounted on top of the instrument panel, directly in line-of-sight to the windshield, the round screen he studied glowed a dull grey. A brilliant green pencil-thin, nearly straight line ran from top to bottom on the screen's right side; it graphically showed him what he could see with his own eyes: the face of the storm off his right wing. The left two thirds of the screen was totally clear of any shade or lines; that was the ground-to-stratosphere calm from the storm all the way back to Amarillo. The radar was a real help, but it didn't tell him much more than he already knew, and it certainly didn't predict the future. Worst of all it offered no clues about the speed or direction of downdrafts and sheer winds that could tear his wings off or slam him into the forest below; even if it could, there was no way to anticipate what lightning could do to electronics. Flying blind is definitely suicide.

He retrieved a plastic bottle from a metal rack below the window on his left, pulled the stopper with his teeth and took a long draw. The water was tepid but refreshing. He looked again aground the dark cockpit as though begging the gauges and bundles of wires and cables that ran in shielded tunnels overhead and under his feet for some insight that he had missed.

A trunk-like console separated him from the empty seat to his right. The four florescent-red engine throttles of flat iron rose from it. They and a bright orange dinner-plate size trim-tab wheel inches from his right knee provided the only color. He looked through the windows in front, on both sides, above his head and below his feet. He hadn't missed anything. Only the fuel gauge had changed since his last survey, starkly proclaiming the undeniable truth that decision-making time was evaporating.

* * * *

The wing tanks were empty. Checking the level in the bladder, he figured three minutes for a go-no-go decision; after that there wouldn't be enough fuel left to make it. The good news was that there was fuel enough to abort to Fort Smith or Texarkana. That was also the bad news: it would be his first stop on his trip for a very long stay in a federal prison or—if he was lucky enough to escape—spending the rest of his life hiding from the men not amused by a lost cargo.

Christian Cain was a lot of things, but most of all he was a realist: the storm between him and that forsaken runway isn't going to go away before he runs out of gas.

Threshold: two minutes

It's a classic approach-avoidance decision, but that's nothing new to the aviation legend—if a shady one lately—of special operations in Laos, Vietnam, Cambodia and dozens of secret missions known only to a small circle of spies, high-ranking military and State Department officers and a handful of overly educated cowards in Washington, London and Moscow.

Chris takes a deep breath and focuses on the radar.

He twists his back and neck and stretches his arms and legs— especially his legs—and shifts his weight in the seat in which he's been marinating for hours.

He thinks about the runway. He knows exactly where it is. How was he going to get there alive?

The destination was remote because it had to be. It's perfect for smuggling. Surrounded by miles of national forest, there are no lights, radar, tower or even another human at the end of a radio transmission to relay conditions or, worse, to note the landing. Most importantly there are no customs agents, cops or witnesses.

Great Circle doesn't like anyone knowing where the plane lands, and know Chris is a pro. He doesn't care why he's not stopped along the way or who pays him on delivery. He doesn't care what or who he delivers or why. What they don't know but might suspect is that he might even take the risks for less money, just for the challenge.

Threshold: one minute

No guts, no air medal, major.

Banking to the right he throttles forward and checks another, smaller screen visible through the yoke handles; it shows two lines which will move apart or merge depending on the strength of three Loran radio signals broadcasting from transmitters about a hundred miles on either side of his direction of flight. The lines will intersect if he's on course, guiding him through the storm to the runway's exact longitude and latitude.

Lifting his eyes to study the pulsating mass ahead, it only glares back at him with ugly indifference; but, flicking his focus back to the radar, there is a hint of promise: a notch growing on the right of the radar's green line that now appears left to right across the screen, a break in the storm dead ahead. He steers toward it like a trapped miner would scramble towards daylight. The notch begins to grow deeper and wider; as it does his eyes widen. He bites his lips, pulling his face into a smile and pushes the yoke forward. The Provider drops below five-hundred feet at two-hundred seventy-five knots.

Bigger and brighter bursts are now mostly to his sides. Faster, he descends into the corridor. The plane feels like a toy in a washing machine on spin cycle. Winds from all directions jerk the airplane and the control surfaces. Rain is so intense, and droplets appear around the front windshield and from somewhere overhead. His knees and hips are absorbing sharper jabs from the rudder pedals. He squeezes the yoke even tighter to keep it from jerking out of his hands.

Increasing to three-hundred knots and dropping below four-hundred feet, there's no turning back. What's behind is just as dangerous as what lies ahead.

Crossing threshold

The air outside is cooler, and it's refreshing through his soaking wet khaki shorts and black Mardi Gras Krewe of Rex t-shirt. Sweat beads mix with the mysterious water droplets raining on his mostly bald head. He grabs the towel off his shoulders and wipes his face. It smells like hydraulic fluid, sweat and burrito, today's in-flight meal. Reaching overhead, he pulls on a St. Louis Cardinals ball cap to keep sweat, rain and hydraulic fluid out of his eyes.

His heart races, his chest rises and falls rapidly and his seat tries to throw him through the windshield. The gulps of warm water rise in his throat.

Feeling like he's bouncing down stairs, his neck muscles tense; being shaken like a rag doll, it's hard work just looking straight ahead. His shoulders chafe under the harness, cutting with every violent forward thrust. His legs are aching with dull pain. He has made one huge mistake.

Lightning is continuous. He sees only the Loran, pointing the way into total chaos; it shows the notch growing deeper about a half mile to his right. *East bound and down, loaded up and truckin', we gonna do what they say can't be done!*

He has done that more than once, much more often than those too timid to try.

Nobody lives forever.

Two

The obsessive little ritual is satisfying.

The key turns easily in the heavy lock, its bolt lands in the doorframe with a satisfying clunk. He smiles, nodding slightly at his reflection in the newly lacquered door, then ceremoniously stuffs the brass key into a vest pocket. With the gold chain draped across his ample belly, he stretches to his full five-feet, six-inches, and spins around quickly—almost in a pirouette—to face P Street, Northwest, Washington, D.C. Inhaling the crisp autumn air, he dances down four marble steps to the wide sidewalk and begins the ten-minute walk to his club.

The life of Nathaniel Langford Pierce is good, very good indeed.

Following a light sprinkle, the street is remarkably clean, the air fresh, even under the steady stream of early rush-hour traffic. Dressed in a grey Armani, brilliant white shirt, yellow tie and black Bruno Maglis, his quick, short strides soon lead beneath a canopy of yellow, brown and red leaves still clinging to the oaks and maples of DuPont Circle. Overhead, the last sharp angles of the setting sun sets them ablaze; the sidewalk below is carpeted by the sodden remains of their predecessors.

Turning down Massachusetts Avenue, random shafts stream between the mansions farther to the west, dramatically spotlighting the Indian chancery's Ghandi statue. For a few more moments the great peacemaker will walk to the sea on golden droplets of rain reflected off the ivy at his feet. Pausing to catch his breath, even after such minor exertion, contentment fills the little man's florid face. A more stark contrast in character would be hard to imagine, if Pierce were even capable of such self-examination.

The walk ends moments later. Pale blue eyes in the round face brighten as he marches to his right and puffs his way up the club's circular driveway off Florida Avenue and drinks in one last survey.

Lights now spill softly from the porticoes and tall windows of the stone mansions and wash onto the manicured lawns of the neighborhood's rich and infamous. Even the noise and congestion along the wide avenue cannot disrupt his vista of serenity. After all, this is his neighborhood. Its power and potential are firmly in his grasp.

As night fell his day was beginning.

Pierce knows well that the evening's countless tableaus—especially what he thought of as the political obligation he repays tonight—will be tomorrow's reality in the Federal City and beyond. Tomorrow countless acts, large and small, will be executed by this powerful, often self-proclaimed intellectual but always relentless ruling class, over those who give them power. It is this ruling class who will be chief beneficiaries of all law, regulation and foreign policy their self-interests can provide.

The scion of one of America's most prominent families, Nat Pierce is one of those power elite. Since moving to the nation's capital this has been his home, his battlefield, his kingdom. He loves it all. He loves Washington, D.C., and this walk always rekindles the flame of his one true, although twisted, passion, whose depth is unplumbed, even to him: masking his pathetic insecurities and grand deceits behind a façade of respectability. Beyond that, making a quick buck and living large, as his French-speaking New Orleans friends affect, was *lagnappe.*

* * * *

From the beginning, everything had fallen into place.

As the newly minted administrative officer, he arrived three years ago at his first posting in the U.S. Consular Office in Cartagena, Colombia. Briefings and position papers quickly dispensed within a few days, he immediately turned his attention to his top priority: furnishing quarters commensurate with his career aspirations and personal fetishes.

If any talent lay within, he knew that it was in setting traps to snare secrets, freely given or comfortably extorted, and turning them to his advantage. For this, lavish entertainment had always been his weapon of choice. The process only took three days after he met Don Jose Vasquez, scion of a coffee fortune and an equally novice diplomat. After graduating from the University of Miami, his career began in the Colombian Navy, a military organization which also serves as an exclusive club for the nation's elite. *Capitan de Corbeta* Vasquez served the past two years as a special assistant to the Colombian Chief of Naval Operations. The new assignment from the government in Bogota was unexpected, a major compliment for the young officer and, more subtly, his venerable family. He will serve out of uniform in the Administrative Department of Security, the equivalent of the U.S. FBI and the Immigration Service. His task is simple: become best friends with Nathan Langford Pierce, Administrative Inspector, Consul of the United States, Cartagena, Colombia. Further instruction would follow.

* * * *

Any excuse to display a supremely developed talent for hospitality is sufficient for the Colombians to hold court. They are masters, and the arrival of a new staff officer—even one of low rank—easily justified the diplomatic reception at the country's palatial *Club Naval*. It is a true jewel of the Caribbean, built on an isolated narrow point extending into the bay. The single-story, impeccably white-washed building is surrounded by gardens that slope imperceptibly into tall palms dotting the beach on three sides. Its lighthouse beacon is seen for miles at sea.

Spanish and South American brandies and wines were poured by smiling young naval cadets in starched, high-collar white uniforms. As though their lives depended on pleasant efficiency, they ushered guests to flower-draped tables of fresh seafood, roasted pork, fish and tropical fruits that filled the grand hall and spilled out on the manicured beach. Soft torch light lit the shadows cast by moonlight through the towering palms. In the bandstand, musicians played dance music to the beat of dark water gently caressing the beach. A tenor's voice lifted to starry skies on the gentle wings of the sweetly scented breeze.

The formal reception enabled some of the nation's leading business leaders and the country's military and diplomatic officers to meet the new diplomat and to mingle with more than two hundred foreigners, including the staff of every embassy and consulate present.

But, more than a few guests, including what seemed like platoons of twenty- to forty-something single women appearing at intervals from nowhere, possibly fashion runways, knew this was really a work site.

Tonight more than a dozen guests would listen with casual intensity to anything they could hear, gleaning bits of information which before dawn would be included in highly sensitive dispatches. Technicians would transmit them on scrambled radio frequencies to other faceless espiocrats reporting to work in intelligence agencies throughout the western hemisphere.

War is hell.

In the spirit of the evening, the newly anointed Don Jose Vasquez wasted no time finding his target, having already begun a dossier on the chubby little American and his family. Flattered, aroused and gladly succumbing to the irresistible delights of free fundador and his first encounter with innocuous looking but deadly Peruvian pisco, Pierce's spirits stirred deep within. He proclaimed his love of truth, beauty, the brotherhood of man and a pressing need for an appropriately grand property in which to pursue them all. As anticipated, the evening ended sooner than expected for the newly arrived North American. It was Vasquez who discretely poured him into his Alpha, depositing him minutes later at the U.S. Chancery. Don Jose then drove straight to his office and worked through dawn like a crazed real estate agent.

At the diplomatically genteel hour of ten, he phoned Pierce and arranged to pick him up for lunch and a specially prepared real estate tour. And, like all property agents worldwide, the first stops were at homes adequate but not impressive. Following a late lunch, the tour stopped at a spectacular Spanish colonial structure overlooking the harbor and the old fort which once had guarded the port.

Pierce fell in love.

Entrance off the cobblestone street was through a tall wooden door supported by massive iron hinges that spanned it. Equally ancient double carriage doors adjacent led through the thick outer wall on the villa's south side and into the outer, paved courtyard and car park. From there a tall archway opened in the stone wall. It led to a cool breezeway that separated the massive western outer wall and a garage on the right. The passageway opened again into the flagstone interior courtyard. Flowers surrounded a gently gurgling fountain at its center. Ivy and primrose clung to walls on three sides. On the eastern side, which the St. Frances of Assisi faced, wide teak stairs led to a landing halfway to the balconied second level. From there more stairs on the right led to bedroom suites; stairs to the left led to a living room over the northern wall. An elevated patio up two steps overlooked the city's old fort and Cartagena harbor to the southwest.

The brilliant white outer walls dominated the surrounding structures and were rivaled only by the *Castillo de San Felipe De Baraja*, the old neighborhood's other, more famous landmark, also built to withstand attack from land and sea. In the late Eighteenth Century the Vasquez patriarch built his home, with the same purpose. Original furnishings included cannon on the covered patio where Vasquez now anesthetized his guest with another shot of fundador.

Rent exceeded Pierce' salary, but such a trifle was not a problem for the aging trust-fund baby. From his research, Vasquez knew this already. He explained that the property had sat vacant for several years. Money was not a real concern for his family; the property would be available at a discount to someone who would truly appreciate it. That whopper was embellished by the even more theatrically told lie that his family believed it was their patriotic duty to assist such a promising friend of Colombia.

Pierce listened, said nothing and sipped the Spanish brandy. He graciously took advantage of another generous pouring.

This new resident, as those who built the fortress, wished to project a façade, if not the reality, of power and prestige that shielded life in its inner sanctum from prying eyes.

He wasted no time launching himself into the social and diplomatic circles. From the beginning, Vasquez became a constant presence. Beginning with the guest list for Nat's first party, his attention to detail never failed; indeed, in a few weeks Don Jose was soon functioning as an unofficial *majordomo*. Invitations soon became a hot commodity across a spectrum of interests, tastes and orientations. Both men knew that information is power; information, of all sorts, was the medium of exchange for the hottest ticket in Cartagena.

* * * *

Nat Pierce was a great listener, and he kept even better files. Those in his office only hinted at the secrets locked in the safe hidden beneath a false stone slab in the floor of the strong room immediately beneath of patio.

But he did share his official files, and during the coming months Diplomatic Security agents read some of them with great interest. At the U.S. Embassy in Bogota, the ambassador, one of few career diplomats named to such a posting, had been annoyed, then gradually more interested in the junior officer. With more favorable staff reports, he soon began thinking him less a self-indulgent liability and more as a valuable, if unofficial, source of intelligence on an unexpected variety of subjects well beyond the duties as an administrative inspector. After all, actionable intelligence had always outweighed the distasteful means by which it was collected. Much could be overlooked. In highly sensitive diplomatic dispatches to the State Department South American Desk in Washington he gladly took credit for timely and valuable information, also broader than his clearance level. The flamboyant little administrator was scoring information that traditional, even clandestine means, couldn't, especially about Caribbean business connections in the U.S. and government corruption in drug interdiction programs in South America and the Caribbean.

He also prospered, more than he ever had expected.

It was a full year after he arrived that he hosted his largest party on the eve of the July 20 Colombia Independence Day.

He had served a lavish dinner to more than a hundred invited guests seated at long tables in the inner courtyard. This time food and drink were underwritten by the U.S. government, as the Ambassador designated the evening as an official function. The guest list also broadened to include several cabinet ministers, seated with the Ambassador on the stair landing above.

Official status brought the U.S. Information Agency into the action. Pierce was absolutely giddy as local news media joined others from Bogota and as far away as Panama and Venezuela snapped his picture and recorded his video image. Some even remained to document the endless succession of patriotic speeches and medal presentations to a dozen citizens, bureaucrats and military leaders who had most notably served in some capacity or another, known mostly to the citation writers.

Learning well from his Colombian hosts, Pierce made sure that no opportunity to ingratiate himself was overlooked. In addition to the formal celebrations within, he served food and drink in the outer courtyard for drivers and aides who took turns guarding limos that made neighborhood streets impassable and to those inconvenienced neighbors.

After midnight, long after the dignitaries and media had departed, a six-piece dance band performed in the courtyard. The party was on cruise control; Pierce was now at ease enjoying his creativity. Finally, he was talking with the newly arrived French cultural attaché. Their eyes met a couple of times during the evening, but there had been no appropriate time for Pierce to establish what he hoped would be a regular routine with the tall, sensitive, aristocratically thin young man.

Don Jose ruined the moment, "If you please, my boss wishes a word with you."

Raphael Mendoza, deputy minister of ADS, waited on the patio. He was an ugly giant, albeit a well-dressed one, Pierce thought, pleased and slightly irritated by the interruption.

"I don't know what he had in mind, but I do know that he doesn't talk to people he doesn't like," Don Jose spoke confidentially in Nat's ear as they walked, smiling and nodding at knots of quiet conversations in the long living room and through the glassed patio doors, which he closed behind Pierce.

"*Señor* Mendoza, so happy to meet you. Very glad you could accept. It is an honor to host you in my humble home. I trust that you have enjoyed the evening."

"Indeed, you are a splendid host, sir, I have had a wonderful evening," he said nodding, smiling, swallowing Pierce's outstretched hand in his massive fist.

Mendoza towered above his host. He was older than nearly all of the men at the party. Pierce had ceased trying to guess the ages of Latin men, most of whom paid meticulous attention to their appearance.

"Please," Nat gestured toward overstuffed leather chairs and a round teak table between them.

"Mr. Pierce, I appreciate the demands on such a gracious host. I do not wish to take your time. Please allow me to come right to the point. I do not flatter—for it is not my style—but I speak directly and truthfully. My understanding of you comes from my trusted colleague, Don Jose, and also from others here in Cartagena. You are a gentleman and a faithful servant of your country. These are difficult tasks to perform well, and you do," he spoke slowly, his head tilted forward, unblinking black eyes fixed on Pierce. "I am confident that any sensitive, even delicate, information we discuss will remain so?" he continued, leaning forward to rest a massive right arm on the table, as if to measure his prey even more intently.

"I am humbled by your trust, and I am honored by your opinion. Of course, it is my obligation to abide with your wish."

"You cannot attribute what I say to me or anyone in the ADS. If you should, your claim would be denied, who knows just how ardently and to what unfortunate effect. If you act on what I tell you, you must verify independently, but I believe that in the end our nations – and you, yourself *señor* Pierce – will be very well served," he spoke, settling back against the sofa, a cold smile only a hind on slightly curled lips in the darkly tanned and deeply lined face. "Good," he nodded, then spoke without interruption, or even moving, for the next ten minutes.

Pierce wished he could make notes, but that would be inappropriate; his listening skill—even if impaired—would be sufficient. This man he had never met, whose manners belied the implications behind his words, counted on that.

"The consular officer assigned to your office here is assuming too much responsibility, and he is a fool and a criminal," was his opening, deadpan shocker. "Bottom line, Mr. Pierce, he is providing U.S. entry visas to certain citizens who Bogota did not wish to travel. Worse, our investigations can prove that your man in Cartagena is accepting bribes, amazingly small ones at that for such a vile act, to provide visas to drug traffickers."

With the face of professional revulsion that masked sheer joy, Nat replied, "This is shocking news, Mr. Mendoza. I am outraged and ashamed." He paused, "I have an annual audit, my first since arriving, scheduled of the consular section scheduled for next fall. But, the seriousness of this situation cannot be delayed. However, I do not have command of assets to begin a criminal investigation, you see my duties…"

"Your audit is of great interest. The ADS, my friend, will provide details only to you. Perhaps the timing could be advanced? It will be up to you, and I'm sure it will be no problem for a man of your imagination and ability to have such information surface within matters of your authority. We are men of the world, Mr. Pierce. This opportunity to exercise your competent leadership is given as a gesture of friendship and respect," he finished with a warm smile, his first.

As the giant spoke, Nat scoured his memory for what he possibly could have done to befriend the ADS or the Colombian government; throwing some great parties couldn't be the answer. In this Latin culture, Nat Pierce was an amateur. The answer came in the next sentences, as though Mendoza was reading his mind.

The narrative turned suddenly—oddly, Nat first thought—to the Vasquez family. What followed was a narrative: they were among the first Spanish families in South America; they built banking and trading companies, without whom Colombia may not have gained independence from Spain. Pierce got it: on Independence Day eve, how appropriate to speak of such an historic family. Befriending Don Jose had been a genius stroke of luck!

Less perplexed, he relaxed and continued to listen.

The Vasquez family, who enabled him to afford this mini palace, and their scion Don Jose, now his best friend and confidant, are still among the leading land owners in Colombia. Their *Monte Verde* plantations produce the nation's largest coffee crop; their export network, including their own ships, was unparalleled.

"These illegal visas, Mr. Pierce, these favors to their chief competitors, have put them at a great disadvantage, and it angers them and saddens many others."

The words "chief competitors" were numbing. The trap has sprung shut, and his immediate response was a barely audible gasp: traveling coffee salesmen don't need illegal visas. Nat Pierce is casually and confidentially discussing a drug cartel powerful enough to send the Colombian government on their errands.

"Mr. Pierce, here is a Swiss bank account number," Mendoza spoke as he delicately lifted a business card from his breast pocket and laid it on the table between them. "You will receive information soon about dates and visa numbers, the records you audit will not contain." With this, he rose and extended his hand. His dominance was not complete but well underway.

"No problem, Mr. Mendoza. These matters will be treated with all delicacy. Good evening to you."

* * * *

Events of the next few days fast-forwarded in a blur and ended with events that—even in his wildest imagining—he would not have dreamed possible.

The audit began July 21; Pierce apologizing that a fall wedding of a non-existent cousin in Boston had upset his schedule. Two days later Nat, in the privacy of his office, pulled a manila folder from his top desk drawer and pushed it across to the consular agent. It showed gaps in his records that did not seem to match visa numbers for three Colombians who had arrived in Miami during the past three months. Pierce didn't fully understand the details, of course, being new to the job, and had not gone farther back than covered by Mendoza's information. With deference to the fellow officer, Nat asked that if – at his convenience – he could simply drop a memo clearing up that small question in an otherwise ship-shape office, the annual formality was finished. In the afternoon mail delivery, the agent opened a small white envelope; it had neither delivery, nor return address or postage. It contained only a plain piece of paper, folded in two; on it were typed a long series of numbers and letters and the word, "Swiss." Nat had left the office early, on urgent business.

Rain fell early on July 25, subduing the mood in the consulate. While staff assembled for a weekly meeting even jokes around the conference table were soggy. Nat noted that the consular agent's seat was empty. Had anyone had heard from him? Maybe he raced last evening in the regatta? He owned a vintage, all spruce, teak and holly forty-foot wooden ketch, the envy of the yacht club. Maybe he ran aground at the *Club Naval.* Nat's quick wit got a good laugh.

The body was found by children playing on the long, concrete seawall along the inner harbor.

A polite police lieutenant explained to the *charge de affairs* that death was due to massive blunt trauma to the head. The poor man, he added with apologetic solemnity, apparently had been drinking heavily judging from the strong smell of alcohol on him and a broken Scotch bottle nearby. Such a tragedy, such a handsome, fit young man. He must have slipped and broke his skull and neck falling to massive, black rocks below. It had happened before. It was a tragedy; no foul play was suspected.

The stunned staff accepted the autopsy finding, albeit hasty by North American standards, without question. They knew that actual homicides were a rarity, even for such a large city, owing to its status as an unofficial demilitarized zone among rival drug cartels, all of whom enjoyed treating their families to the beaches and five-star hotels and restaurants. They knew the only danger around them was their own overindulgence.

Nat Pierce was not about to suggest anything else, even if he had strong suspicions. His report was already written, but he waited until the following morning before placing copies in the diplomatic pouches that would be opened tomorrow in Bogota and Washington, D.C.

* * * *

"Please join me, *me amigo*," Nat spoke cheerfully, a highball glass raised high in wobbly salute, as Don Jose walked beneath the canopy and sat with him on the patio. The sun would not set for another two hours, but the little man was well on his way. "Yes, such a tragedy. Such a tragic coincidence, but not worse than the tragedy of an empty glass! A Scotch, my friend, my kingdom for a freakin' Scotch!"

"What tangled webs we weave, and what amateurish mistakes are made by such fools," he responded. He poured fresh drinks, handed one to Nat and gazed down at the harbor. Turning back he raised his glass, "But, great tragedies begat great opportunities and greater rewards."

Admiring the look and feel of another round, Nat glowed in agreement.

The Colombian ADS agent settled in a chair, and the two men sat silently.

"What?" Nat finally managed. He set down his drink and curiously watched his colleague retrieve a long, leather wallet from his inside breast pocket.

"Just this for your inspection."

It contained a single sheet of heavy, gilt-edge bond paper. Two gold foil seals were affixed below signatures flourished large across the bottom. Several paragraphs of Spanish covered the page above. On close examination, he made out his name and, in several places, "*Monte Verde* Coffee Company North American Properties" in bold type.

"You have been of invaluable service to some great men and to my family. Even more significantly, we know that you will continue as a friend and colleague to those who admire your ambition and brilliant mind. I can only show you this document. It will never leave this country; in that you can rest assured. It designates you a protected trustee of the *Monte Verde*. Your very confidential and discreet services will involve ensuring the success of the company's trade office in New Orleans and— with even more sensitivity—other future, equally sensitive business interests. Through blind transfers within a series of business, trust and non-governmental organizations in no less than six countries in South America, Africa, Italy, France and the United States, this favors you with partial ownership in certain North American property. Your portion will grow commensurate with services provided. Other compensation will be made in gold bullion, never anything as traceable as a Swiss bank account," he chuckled. Again raising his glass, "To a friend and a valuable colleague. To prosperity and long life!"

* * * *

It had been seven years since he departed the consular office in Cartagena. His remarkable investigative skills that had saved the United States from international embarrassment were swiftly—and repeatedly—rewarded. Before his fortieth birthday Nat was the youngest man ever to serve as Chief of Operations, an office whose real function and duties were as murky and ill-defined as any in the federal bureaucracy, a perfect match for his own dark character.

Tonight those duties included drinks and dinner with the old colleague who had enabled it all.

The club's glass doors looked as though they were supporting the tons of granite above them. His gut tightened: even if he was a member in good standing for the past decade, he knew that he really didn't belong there. He didn't like to think about it, but somehow the thought seized him, at least momentarily, every time he visited.

The Cosmos Club is one of the most exclusive in the nation. For nearly a century it had been a gathering place for Nobel Laureates, Pulitzer Prize-winning journalists and lesser-known giants of American capitalism. Membership is augmented with brilliant academics and some of America's highest-ranking public servants. Just as his admission to Choate and later Yale, Pierce's entre to this Edwardian mansion nestled behind ivied courtyard walls came through his father's formidable wealth and – more importantly – his good name, nothing Pierce himself had earned.

"Good evening, Mr. Pierce," a smiling, aging Egyptian man in black tie and dinner jacket spoke as he opened the door and bowed imperceptibly.

"Of course; good evening to you," Nat managed as he avoided eye contact and stepped past him, then stopped two steps inside. Insecurities were neatly stuffed away. His mind focused. It was show time. He was center stage.

The room was large and sepulchral and smelled slightly of furniture polish and fresh news print. An ebony-faced fireplace and even wider mantel spanned most of the west wall. It was flanked by yellow sofas and a low, oval glass table. Leather-covered wingbacks filled the room behind him, on either side of the doorway. A wide passageway on the salon's north wall led to the club's main dining room and bar, and to the right marble stairs led up past the room's walnut-paneled walls and ancient tapestries to a ball room, banquet hall, library and the sleeping rooms on the floors above. More sofas fronted the east wall, behind a library table covered with current editions of the *Wall Street Journal, New York Times, Washington Post* and *Barrons*. Behind that was the entrance to the reception desk discreetly tucked behind a doorway through which the on-duty manager materialized to fulfill the slightest need.

If there were a casual observer in that atmosphere, Nat would appear to meld in seamlessly; the fact that he didn't belong there created a cavernous hole in him which he could never fill. But, it was a well-guarded secret insecurity. He believed that members knew nothing about his cheating scandal at Yale, and even if it were gentlemanly discretion would rule. Nat's life membership ensured the opportunity to mix with the great and influential, all of whom he disdained as naïve pawns to his appetite and ambition. This was his birthright, he believed, the entitlement afforded a main-line Philadelphia scion and third-highest-ranking career diplomat enthroned in the United States Department of State.

The truth was that Nat was a huge embarrassment to his family, but after more than twenty years and his impressive advance through State's Byzantine political hazards he had established his own persona. He had saved face with his family who had as much or more positive effect on his career momentum than him, and—even if he didn't know it—would never bequeath their wealth to him.

Nathaniel Langford Pierce was the quintessential bureaucrat who—through a series of skillful, successive, subtle and often blatant back-stabbing betrayals of his colleagues—had achieved a fearful reputation in one of the nation's most preeminent, corrupt institutions, a breeding ground for insecure sycophants, social climbers and much, much worse.

His career began soon after Yale's trustees received a million dollars in discreet contributions from his family's charitable foundation. As that generosity led to a diploma, similarly directed incentives—even more strategically targeted bribes—brought a position at a level far beyond his intellect, ability or character. And, just as others in State's shameful history since World War II, the bureaucracy quickly moved him into assignments where he could fail with dignity. However, to the chagrin of all involved, he not only took root but blossomed as an auditor within the South American consulate operations. There he had access to sensitive FBI, Diplomatic Security Division and INS documents; just as he had done for himself and male companions at Yale, he had quickly learned how to adapt State's culture to his own advancement. Machiavelli would have wept in envy.

* * * *

But, now it was show time. He walked down the carpeted hallway lined with a multi-million dollar art collection and stopped at the old café. He saw his target.

"*Buena tardes señor!*" Pierce' theatrical basso broke the silence as he stepped into the salon, took a mental roll call of those attending and turned immediately toward Jose Eduardo Vasquez, vice president of North American sales for the *Monte Verde* Coffee Co., Bogota, Colombia. Pierce was only too happy to accommodate a request from his old friend and colleague whose sensitivities, especially involving Interpol investigations, included never making official calls at Headquarters, U.S. Department of State.

"*Jefe, me amigo, buena tardes* to you and respects," Vasquez delivered with equal volume as heads at a half-dozen tables turned toward the unwelcome, overly theatrical interruption. Vasquez, Nat's Latin body double—except for a mane of silver hair—rose, and the two men embraced.

"Thanks for setting this up, old boy, you do have a nose for self-preservation," Vasquez murmured as Pierce' eyes fell on the two seated men, smiling at the tableau before them.

"Excellency, it is my pleasure to introduce my good friends of whom we spoke earlier, *señors* Gene Menard and Frank Gordon, both of your wonderful city of New Orleans," Vasquez spoke respectfully and softly, gesturing with his outstretched left palm toward the still-seated men.

"A pleasure, señor, your friends are my friends, welcome."

Pierce reckoned that both men were in their late fifties, perhaps older. The athletic-looking Menard was perhaps older, and slightly shorter than the six-foot-plus Gordon. Both were tanned, trim and well dressed in tailored dark suits. Menard was bald, and Gordon's hair was jet black and combed back. Their hands were rough and large. Pierce had made a career of reading people, usually to discover fear, the opportune of larceny or physical attraction. Through his well-perfected diplomatic smile, Pierce thought that this pair had the look of men who had spent much of their lives outdoors, perhaps near the water, as longshoremen—Nat thought—not yacht captains. He was much more certain that none of the guests were here without the expectation of a favor from him.

"Gentlemen, I think we'll be more comfortable in the rear booth," Pierce said, meeting eyes with Vasquez. He raised his arm and motioned the bartender to follow as he directed the trio toward three stairs to a platform and a high-backed booth beside doors to the courtyard patio.

"My pleasure, gentlemen, I've heard much about you from Don Jose, I'm delighted to meet you both," Pierce replied and smiled after drinks were ordered and the waiter departed. "I trust that you're taking good care of my second home at Vacherie while I'm detained on the nation's business in the Federal City." Now with an even larger theatrical smile and wink, "Yes, I do know what it means to miss New Orleans!"

Both men beamed, and Pierce was pleased. So far, so good. He breathed a little more deeply and wondered what was next. All he knew was that—typical of Vasquez' well-advised aversion to wire taps and public knowledge of his exact location—he'd called only at noon and spoken cryptically and uncharacteristically nervously of the men's interest in meeting. Pierce was not the least disturbed; his relationship with Vasquez had been handsomely rewarded during the years of their association, beginning with that opportune tour as auditor. He also knew that there would never be a day when he would turn down any request from the man or, as the case may be, any of his friends.

"We appreciate your hospitality. You must know that even if we've not met, your commitments are well known among our business associates." Gordon spoke, scanning beyond the little nook where they were seated, satisfied that nobody could overhear.

"They are determined men," Gordon's eyes now bored into Pierce, the brief statement having its intended effect. Pierce sat at attention, motionless, his smile frozen like stone.

"We also know that those who help them are generously rewarded, even for the little things that are trifles for us. With your attention to detail, logistics has been flawless. You've ensured that whatever problem may arise is quickly, discreetly solved. Faithful in little, faithful in much, I've heard them say more than once. As it happens, a small issue that for you is routine may mean the world for them. Who's to know?" He concluded, spreading his palms apart and leaning back as drinks are delivered.

"Mr. Pierce, we've been asked a very simple favor and must ensure that it's fulfilled," Menard spoke, his eyes having never left Nat's. "We wouldn't have troubled you like this, but you must understand the delicacy of our situation."

Nat felt Vasquez staring at him. His mind whirled trying to catalogue what request was so sensitive that it required this meeting, with players he'd never met.

"The time and attention of a man of your influence is invaluable," Gordon spoke as he turned to look at Vasquez, who took the cue.

"One of our freighters will arrive tomorrow night at our wharf in New Orleans. Even though this is routine, a trifle, there are certain considerations, certain anxieties associated with this particular docking. The urgency of their request has touched us all. To assuage their concerns, to guarantee their continued respect and reward, our request is very simple. We wish for you to personally guarantee—as you have so professionally in the past—that absolutely nothing about that arrival could cause even the slightest notice. Your presence aboard would be seen as a great gesture of friendship and commitment," Vasquez spoke, then paused as a collegial expression returned. "I can personally assure you that your accommodation of such a short request will be noted by the *Monte Verde* board of directors. Our senior partners in Bogota have expressed interest in allowing certain board members to expand ownership. Their understanding of the situation has been heartwarming," Vasquez spoke, nodding toward Pierce. "The Gulf Stream will leave tomorrow at noon. It's at your disposal for a return."

No more needed to be spoken. Nat's presence aboard was totally unnecessary, he knew. He had no choice. The effect of any reluctance, even a pause in accepting, was unthinkable.

"*Fiel en lo poco, fiel en lo mucho,*" Nat grandly gestured as he raised his glass and beamed around the table to his guests. Vasquez lifted his glass, and the others, slightly confused, followed. "Faithful in little, faithful in much," Vasquez finished the toast, speaking slowly to make sure they understood.

Nat tossed back the martini wishing he had four more within reach.

"Gentlemen, I will see you tomorrow. And, some day very soon, Mr. Gordon, Mr. Menard, I hope to host you at my beautiful *Bon Homme.*"

The professional bureaucrat, the manipulative coward his nation offered ignorantly to the world in its great name, was scared to death.

Three

Lieutenant Emma Lucas loves her job.

She even loves her commute which she would make today in the fresh, clean air following a steady half-hour rain. With the top down on her cherry red '64 Mustang, she drives through the dappled sunlight piercing the canopy of old oaks that stand like sentries along St. Charles Avenue. In a few minutes she'll pass through her home in the Garden District and into the French Quarter's quirky cocktail of charm and street hustle. The twenty-minute drive, never topping twenty-five miles per hour, will end amid the humble Camelback homes crowding the dingy, mean streets of Faubourg-Marigny.

Lucas savors every second of it and hopes it would also to clear her head. *Cheap therapy*, she muses.

She didn't know why or how, only that lately something like the Ghost of Christmas Past was a regular and unannounced visitor. As if she were viewing video tapes, her thoughts often drifted to her childhood, a time of hardships conquered by love. Why this sudden preoccupation? Was there some meaning in all this that she couldn't quite grasp?

Her life was good. There had been dramatic changes in the few years since she, her sister and mother had moved here with her. With the exception of her mother's death, most of that had been positive. It must mean something, she thought, but the disciplined, orderly mind of the Coast Guard officer, marine engineer and fiercely devoted guardian couldn't sort it out, at least not yet. It was a little crazy making.

Emma and her parents had been very close, out of love and

necessity. Her earliest memories were of close-knit family life helping in her father's small boat yard on the Ohio River at Paducah, Kentucky. The family lived in a barn-turned-residence next to the yard's small dry dock. The two-acre yard was truly a family business. Her mother was a sail maker and upholsterer. Her father a welder, carpenter, electrician and any other skill that brought repair contracts to his yard. Through example, her parents taught Emma and her sister the value of honesty and hard work. Her memories were built on that, even seeing the art and beauty blooming amid the dirty mess that such yards tend to be. By the time she could drive, she was an excellent welder, engine mechanic and painter and a passable electrician. She could write job specifications and price jobs to a profit. By the time she finished high school she was a maritime jack of all trades. She was her father's partner.

She was unusually tall, nearly six feet. Narrow hips and long legs provided an athletic, nearly boyish frame. She managed to minimize other, more feminine physical attributes. Not that anyone noticed, especially as she was always in overalls and work boots, her long chestnut hair stuffed into a welders hat. But, if anyone did get close enough, her face betrayed the disguise. She was stunning, with features both distinctive and delicate: dark brown eyes, upturned nose, a small mouth over a wider, square jaw. She was a beauty who successfully avoided detection and didn't see any reason to advertise.

At her parents' insistence, she had graduated with an engineering technology degree from the community college practically next door. The courses had been ridiculously easy for her, and she wondered if she'd actually learned anything new. But, a degree was a degree, and it helped with Coast Guard licenses when her father died.

She struggled to keep the yard afloat but soon discovered that whatever profits she could wrestle wouldn't offset her father's old debts and new, drastically higher taxes aimed at dislodging businesses from land coveted by condominium developers. But, sometimes good things do happen to good people. Through her reputation up and down the Ohio River, the Coast Guard found her. She was a recruiter's dream come true. In turn, she had found a secure home for the three surviving Lucas women who moved to Seattle, San Diego, Charleston and, four years ago, New Orleans.

Cancer took her mother suddenly; her deathbed wish for Emma to care for Lucy, then a brilliant student, now—with Emma's generosity—a recent Tulane graduate.

* * * *

Emma isn't distracted by her musings lately, more entertained and indulgent of them. But, she can't shake the vague notion that something isn't quite right. They hint at questions with no answers, certainly nothing that could be taken apart with logic. Had her responsibilities consumed the wonder of her childhood? Had this handicapped her as a woman? If so, how? And, what's with these flashes of memory—duties, challenges and constant vigilance—that don't even hint at some answer?

As the French Market passed in a colorful blur in her peripheral vision, the phantoms visited again, launching her imagination into the cosmos. Gripping the wheel too tightly, she checks the right side mirror to change lanes. Above the mirror she focuses on huge forklifts loading equally large cotton bales on a ship tied up at Governor Nichols Wharf. In an instant she is struck by insight so pure, so intense, so liberating, that her body tingles in waves and her breasts warm, burning with confusing passion. *Look at those men. They and their ancestors, me and my parents, everyone who ever lived, play out the same struggles. From the beginning of time it is the same plot: the struggle between good and bad, old and new, happiness or sorrow.*

She looked at the sweat pouring off their strong bodies. *Those men act out their roles, their lines paced by this oppressive heat, the threats of disease and storm in this lowland along the Mississippi. Am I no different? This isn't dress rehearsal; this is it. Why do I act like it isn't? Then the most disturbing thought. Are they more alive than I am?*

She jerks the wheel to miss a bicycle appearing during the brief inattention. There had been too much of that lately. With her heart racing, she imagines that on a day like this the cyclist's mind may be as far away as hers. But, she had hardly driven another block before the passing tableau again grabs her attention. This time it is the sight of four tourists wandering down Esplanade. As if seeing in slow motion, she realizes that they are self-consciously, even comically struggling not to stare at a young woman crossing the street. Emma slows to follow their pointing, then stops to let her pass. Emma knows her, who more worldly observers would describe as a high-class working girl. Emma had met her a couple of times at a mostly-locals French Quarter bar that catered to the military, political and media people who gravitated there. Her clientele were far above this neighborhood, and her presence probably meant that she kept an apartment nearby. Her lifestyle had more than piqued Emma's interest;

she had seemed so normal yet so different. Emma was surprised that neither in the short term nor over time, could she seem to pass judgment. The experience was unforgettable, and unsettling.

"Hi , Mary isn't it? What a day. I love your outfit!"

"Oh, hi, bay-bee. Look at you!" The tall brunette speaks, stepping closer to Emma's front bumper as a car passes. "And, you, too, darling. I'll let you borrow it sometime. But, cher, ever-e-won just loves a woman in uniform!" She flashes a smile across a big mouth. Reaching the curb, she spots the little audience. With hands on her hips she winks, wiggles her barely covered breasts in the tight green satin dress. "Sorry to hear about your mom. That's rough, I know. I'll be lookin' for you at Jims. We can talk more."

"I'll look forward to that," Emma smiles, "'till then."

By now the tourists are gaping open-mouthed at the amazing scene between a hooker and a khaki-clad officer in a classic convertible. Emma could practically see their thoughts as clearly as if they'd appeared in cartoon balloons over their heads. She once might have agreed with them. But, now somehow she knew they'd never know that the woman's dress, bearing and attitude conceal much more than they revealed or that those people would ever care to or grow to know. Her thoughts are clear, even startling. There is no empathy, no concern for the cause or effects— whether good or evil—of her lifestyle on the little girl Mary still cherished somewhere deep inside. The people were no more than narrowly focused scorekeepers of the rulebook whose broader revelations they never consider. Their call in the great here and now was all that matters.

What's the point? Am I different, just luckier, with more options for charting my course? In the last judgment, what scores higher: what we do or why we do it?

She couldn't resist tossing a casual wave and smile in their direction. As she accelerated away from the scene, she wondered why she felt more aware, alive and even happier than when she left home only a few minutes ago. It was as though she'd just avoided death. She drove on; she devoured everything with her senses: the smell of coffee, lilac blossoms, shrimp boil, the leavings of mule-drawn carriages; the brilliant colors on smartly restored buildings against the colorless decay of abandoned ruins around them. *I love it all! It's great to be alive!*

* * * *

Her new-found insights evaporate as she turns off the narrow street and stops at the tiny concrete guard shack. She flashes her identification to the young Marine who responds with a snappy salute and waves her on. She drives inside the high-fenced compound that surrounds three identical, green three-story buildings and slides the Mustang under the covered parking spot designated for the Command Duty Officer. For the next twenty-four hours she will be the first person called about anything happening on and along the river from its mouth at the Gulf of Mexico, upriver to Baton Rouge. She will be top river cop, watching over literally billions invested in barges, ships, towboats and every craft afloat as well as waterfront infrastructure and the lives of everyone in harm's way on and near the water.

Job security, she smiles shutting the driver door and walking in to the cool old building nearest the industrial canal. *As long as that river flows north to south there'll be a New Orleans, and they'll be needing a traffic cop.*

She opts to avoid the elevator and enters the freshly scrubbed stairwell still smelling of disinfectant. Arriving on the sixth floor she pulls the heavy metal door open and walks to her left, down the long grey hallway. She is pleased that her breath comes only slightly faster. She walks down the buffed grey linoleum flanked by greyer cinder block walls made only slightly more attractive by walnut wainscoting and expensively framed photographs of ships hanging from them. Entering a code into a keypad, she opens another steel door and enters the Port Operations Center. It is a large room indistinguishable from many others in the complex except for one magnificent feature: wall-to-wall, floor-to-ceiling windows overlooking New Orleans and about four miles of the Mississippi River. She drops her small duffel and purse into a wall locker, pockets the key and walks to the wall of glass. It is a million dollar view. Only the Trade Center at the foot of Canal Street, towering in the distance on the right, has a better view of the city and river, both so prominent in the continent's history.

From its origins near the Canadian border, the river splits North America into its east and west banks. America's longest river, the Mississippi and its principal tributaries—the Ohio and Missouri Rivers and the scores of navigable rivers feeding into them—literally drain the continent, from the Great Lakes to the Gulf, from the Appalachians to the Rockies.

The transportation and commercial possibilities of the river system is mind numbing. The advantages were obvious for a city at the river's mouth, at the end of this natural waterway system. But, the topography there is an equally awesome obstacle. From the river's delta to more than two hundred miles upriver, there is no high ground. Indeed, the continent's first inhabitants and later-arriving Europeans believed the area was actually an island. Establishing a city was nearly impossible.

But, it had taken root, and Emma Lucas is looking at it. On her right, the river seems motionless as it curls around skyscrapers backlit in the low golden glow from the west. It is darker closer to her, and it captures lights reflected from both banks. This is Algiers Point, the river's deepest point, just below the French Quarter. It is one of the river's most treacherous challenges. To the left the panorama fades to black. In the darkness the river turns again, even more sharply southward toward the web of canals where it disappears into the Gulf of Mexico.

ₗ At New Orleans the Mississippi's serpentine curves turn it to flow west-to-east. Gazing out the window, Emma mouth curls slightly into a smile thinking how she, like many newcomers, discover that the east bank is actually to the north, the west bank is south. Those gigantic bends are the literal geographic origin of the city. They inspired the Crescent City nickname given it by its more recent inhabitants.

Millions of gallons per minute surge silently past the city. Through the millennia the endless force has gouged the river to a depth of nearly three-hundred feet at Algiers Point, slowly building its banks to form the narrow band of high ground, the French Quarter, where the city began.

The river traffic is always heavy, and the current is treacherous and unforgiving. In the crowded highway ships and barges cannot see each other, even in clear weather. Experienced river pilots respect this stretch of river which for hundreds of years has remained one of oldest and highest volume ports in the United States, a reality not lost on the U.S. Coast Guard or its predecessor, the U.S. Revenue Service, major players in the maritime and international shipping industries, or for the Spanish, French and an assortment of pirates who took care of business before that.

* * * *

"Well, good afternoon, lieutenant," Commander Art Jacks speaks, glancing at his wristwatch as he glides through one of the bunk room doors as though he is in a hurry and walks toward her. "You're always prompt, I must say. Ready to relieve?"

Emma instantly assumes that Jacks, the command's executive officer and highest-ranking watch stander, has spent the afternoon sleeping. He'd probably given orders not to be disturbed unless the river suddenly changed direction. Rank has its perks, she rationalizes.

"Good afternoon, to you, sir," she speaks, managing a smile as she turns to face him. *I'm giving him a half-hour break and he acts like it's some kind of failure on my part*, she simmers. "Is there anything to pass along?"

After the collegial greetings, she listens as he speaks, essentially telling her that she shouldn't expect anything unusual. She has never trusted his judgment. As soon as he leaves she'd satisfy her own mind, quickly scanning log entries and "action" message traffic. *You get what you inspect, not what you expect*, she remembers, the truth proven more than once.

Petty Officer Lyle Rees busied himself during the formalities, listening and acting as though the officers weren't even there. As soon as the steel door snapped shut and locked behind Jacks, she smiles and turns toward her Petty Officer of the Watch.

"Good evening, ma'am," Rees speaks over his shoulder. He is seated at the long desk that supports an equally wide single-shelf bookcase. Several telephones, radio microphones and scanners that monitor the Port Captain, local police and fire departments are grouped in the middle. "I've entered your name in the log book, sign here," Rees slides the large ledger towards her as she sits, then signs his name underneath hers.

"Thanks, petty officer Rees. I don't want to jinx anything, but if the turnover brief is accurate, we're not going to have much to worry about. Nothing unusual in the offing: a few tankers tonight and early tomorrow through Southwest Passage, pretty light barge traffic and a couple of merchantman. One of them is scheduled to tie up at Piety, looks like about 0200."

"Sounds like a plan, boss. Standing by to answer all the bells and whistles." He'd never speak so casually to an officer and only to her in private. Like most others on the staff, Rees likes working with Lucas. She knows her stuff and is fair.

She respects his intellect. She is also awed by his talent and personality. In addition to being a first class sailor, he is a talented musician, playing trumpet with a couple of local jazz bands. He even filled in with the New Orleans Symphony Orchestra. In the past couple of years since he arrived at the command, he'd gotten Lucy and Emma stage passes or invitations to parties where he performed. But, the threesome of days past became a less frequent foursome with the announcement of his imminent wedding. The Lucas women were shocked by the announcement and wedding scheduled only a month later, but retained composure in front of him.

Lyle was clueless about the effect of his sudden marriage on Emma and Lucy. Nothing changed in his mind; Lyle, Emma, Lucy and now Ann, enjoyed the eye-popping world of the New Orleans jazz scene. Meeting big name musicians, an occasional movie star or an infamous Louisiana politician was a heady bonus; the locals called it *lagniappe*, something extra, the thirteenth doughnut in a dozen. In turn, the newlyweds were was always welcome in the Lucas' home. More frequently, the foursome was a near constant Sunday brunch presence at the Southern Yacht Club, where Ann kept a sailboat large enough to comfortably accommodate sleepovers.

Before the wedding, Rees had been closer, especially to Lucy. He had grown comfortable talking about his past. The women listened. From what they heard from him about Ann, her family and lifestyle, the marriage didn't seem like a great idea. But they kept quiet and shared in his excitement.

He'd been raised by a single mother, the daughter of one of Virginia's first families. Lyle assumed his father's last name. About a year later when his parents were married, his mother did the same. The family was not pleased with their daughter's belated choice, hoping that she'd never become officially attached to the professional yacht racer and broker. If relations with her family were cool before the wedding, they grew frigid afterwards. When the marriage ended four years later and she declined their offer to raise Lyle while she maintained her lifestyle in Tampa, the cut-off was complete. He grew up a victim and witness of her slow descent into alcoholism and drug abuse. She drifted from one seating hostess, receptionist, sales clerk job to another, always seeking a never-attained prosperity dangled by party-girl contacts among the rich and decadent. Growing up quickly, he soon resented the pride that prevented her family's help. He felt he was raising her, providing her a meal ticket for welfare, most of which she drank and drugged away. Unlike Emma, family wasn't the loving joy of life itself, rather a cynical obligation, a hustle and a bump for daily bread.

The youngster was intelligent, and there had been bright spots, mainly from a couple of saints employed by Florida Child Welfare. They made sure that he stayed in school where, against all odds, he excelled, even discovering something greater than himself in music and developing as a talented musician in the jazz band. He was street smart, too. With fake identification, he soon made reasonable money playing clubs and bars. But, he knew that what he saw playing for private parties wasn't discussed in polite company, and most especially the police. It most certainly pushed the envelope of acceptable or even legal behavior. He'd seen a couple of his friends jailed for drug trafficking and receiving stolen property. And, he didn't look forward to what seemed like more and more frequent police interviews. His practiced ignorance of the fencing, prostitution and drug trafficking he knew well was total jive, and something told him that he couldn't tap dance forever.

By the time he graduated high school, he'd grown to more than six feet. He wasn't robust or athletic, but trim, darkly handsome, with a strong jaw developed by years with the trumpet. There was even something like an entourage for his bigger gigs.

As if on cue, his father drifted back from Louisiana to check out the action. But, this time, fresh from a year at Angola on another fraud conviction, he arrived with a mind to do something different: be helpful. Stumbling on street talk about Lyle's inclusion on the vice squad's usual suspects list and the real possibility that a criminal complaint may soon have his name on it, he stayed sober long enough to suggest a quick way out of town: the United States Coast Guard. It wasn't as weird as it sounded, he reasoned: the duty would always be in the States, usually in a big city where pick-up gigs existed for the kind of musician and hustler he'd become. It beat hell of going to jail for receiving stolen property.

Indeed, it had worked out.

The discipline seemed simple to him: obey the rules, nobody's in your stuff. And, he actually liked being outdoors, on the water. Who knew? Maybe it was hereditary. Likewise, New Orleans had been a gold mine for the musician, in more ways than one. Last year the daughter of a prominent Alabama planter decided the handsome, talented sailor was her destiny. They were married a St. Louis Cathedral. The reception was a small gathering at the Monteleone where Daddy booked the grand ballroom and a hundred rooms. Lyle's parents never heard about it.

Four

Lightning and thunder roiled overhead, wind-driven rain scoured the black runway. The deluge dampened the sound of gravel crunching beneath tires of two pick-ups moving slowly across a parking lot and on to the tarmac.

The drivers were far from strangers.

Lamar Sparks had been county judge for fifteen years, and Coy Golden had been sheriff two years longer than that. They followed men whose similarly unchallenged status arose from one moral characteristic: an unquestioning devotion to the social and economic superiority of the five inter-related families who owned and operated Dodd County, Arkansas. For such prudent men, tenure was lifetime. With that one exception, their careers were unremarkable. And, until such time as one of the five families grew uncomfortable, these two would never face a Democratic Party primary challenge or—in this quarter of one-party Arkansas where November balloting tends to be redundant—a general election opponent. After late afternoon drinks in the judge's suite atop the courthouse on the town square, each eagerly awaited a very high-paying middle-of-the-night rendezvous. The only agenda item was reviewing local events to concoct a believable cover story should a spouse, deputy or curious citizen wonder what they were doing in the middle of the night way out there at Army Air Corps Park. Such a question was yet to be asked.

Later, each would steal away into the miserable night. Both knew that the generous cash payday for a half-hour drive and brief encounter with a cranky old guy flying a weird old airplane was worth the trouble. The easy money more than trumped any inconvenience and the remote-to-nonexistent danger of being discovered as drug traffickers. Neither knew or even cared about the larger significance of their actions. They shared a healthy lack of curiosity about it all, knowing that their high-ranking politician handlers in Little Rock shared this intellectual blind spot and lapse of conscience. From several years' always unwritten instructions about dates, times and logistics, Lamar Sparks and Coy Golden knew that there'd be no complications, either from state or federal agencies. Everyone got paid, well. There'd be no questions about their selfless and patriotic roles in very special, beyond-top-secret "national security operation."

Each drove to an opposite end of the southwest-to-northeast runway. They turned, pointing headlights to the southwest. Both lit roof-mounted blue and white lights rotating atop the county-owned trucks. Neither of them saw any need to talk on their VHF radios, either with each other or to the pilot of the plane they were to meet. Sitting alone, listening to the rain power wash around them, there was nothing to say that they or Chris Cain didn't already know. They'd done this dozens of times, and there was no need to alert anyone with a police scanner about what they were up to at this hour of the morning.

They waited. The plane was already more than an hour overdue. Separately, Sparks and Golden endured the storm and doubted there'd be a payday this morning. Judge Sparks knew that if there wasn't, he would get a new schedule during the next white-water canoeing trip, regularly scheduled by powerful politicians in Little Rock.

Unknown and most certainly unseen, Cain was only a couple of miles away, struggling to fly on a heading of exactly forty-five degrees and alternatively searching through the darkness, then back to the altimeter and those lines intersecting on the Loran. He never felt more alone. His eyes pierced the darkness for any hint of light, but there is nothing to see, no hint of hope. He tried to control his breathing, forcing deep breaths. He blinked hard but only for an instant. Searching the sky ahead he still saw nothing but lightning flashes; the good news was that now they were farther away from the wipers' slow, rhythmic beat. *Was it retina burn or is there something out there?* In a disappointing instant, he knew there was nothing but the glint from his glasses reflecting on the windshield. Focusing closer, he saw the ghostly image of a man who never doubted himself or his ability or his superiority over every man he's ever met, at least until right now. He shook the chilling thoughts away. The Loran lines still intersected. If he was wrong, tonight he would buy the farm in Arkansas.

He pushed the thought away. The rudder and yoke jostling him are reassuring, they feel good, real. They're something he can wrestle and win. It's the unseen, unknown he can't fight. Breathing very heavily and fast now, cold pin pricks sting his face and back and ignite in his lungs. He stares ahead at the man in the windshield, at nothing.

With his right hand he reaches down and flips open a chart locker between the two seats. This time his fingers wrap around a bottle. He uncorks it with his teeth and takes a long drag, sloshing most of it on his chest. The Loran still confirms that he's gliding toward the runway, but where the hell is it?

Where are the freaking lights! He speaks to nobody in the continuous roar of thunder. For a mille-second a lightning flash shows the bottom of the clouds overhead and the ground below. It's nightmarish. It was way too close. But, even if it leaves his retina streaked in purple, it is a visual reference.

Almost instantly, his worst fear comes true: another lightning bolt rips from somewhere behind and slaps the plane's vertical stabilizer and burns the ground too close below. Damn it all!

He is jerked left, then right. He struggles to look straight down; lit by lightning strikes he's able to straighten his glide path over the treetops. The horror is not complete: the instruments go dark; no more Loran, no idea of his altitude or speed. At least the rudder feels like it's still there, and he can control it.

Straight! Level! Steady! Damn it!

Flashing strobe lights—blue and white—appear directly ahead, with another pair barely visible behind them.

His eyes widen to grasp more. They are there! He's lined up on the runway, pulling back on the throttles. His head is up and biting his lips hard enough to bruise them. As an added bonus, the rain stops, and the last drops race to the edges of the windshield.

Chris knows that even if his descent is right on line he hasn't a clue about how fast the wind shear is gusting across the runway, winds that could pitch him like a straw into the forest on either side. He'll just have to deal with it as it comes, and it's coming fast. But, the odds are better than they were seconds ago.

With clear view ahead he sees the lights distinctly and in perspective to each other. He can connect an invisible line between them which marks the runway. Two blinks later a paralyzing blow to his chest freezes him with numbing shock: the lights are too far to his right. He's not lined up on the runway but on a parallel line adjacent to it. In about ten seconds—max—Christian Cain's long journey is going to end in a stand of loblolly pines.

As his final act, he thrusts his right hand into the throttles, flips on the jet afterburners just below them. Resolved, more angry than afraid, he pulls the wheel to his chest and closes his eyes. He sees Sister Mary Carol. She is smiling through the windshield.

Acceleration and the steep climb press him into the seat soaked with his sweat. The now much lighter airplane shudders and groans. It stops falling.

The instruments blink alive. Even in the violent vibration he finds the artificial horizon: he's gaining altitude. Another flash and instantaneous, deafening explosion. This time it's his right wing. The stall horn bleats.

He is going to crash.

His last desperate, albeit counterintuitive act will be to firmly, mechanically push the wheel and throttles forward. One, two, three seconds, he falls through two hundred feet, one hundred fifty feet. At eighty feet his airspeed increases and—like a miracle—an updraft lifts the wings over the trees north of the runway.

Slowly altitude increases.

Maybe Sister Mary Carol really is out there.

A top branch slaps the landing gear as he wills the plane upward again and into a sweeping circle to the left for another approach.

Christian Cain is flying. He begins to pray: *Hail Mary, full of grace…*

Powering into the west, he punched through yet another intense squall line. Then, arching east for another approach, lightning is joined by something else so loud, so terrifying that initially he can't identify. In a wide-eyed instant, he knows: hail! It's like a thousand machine guns rounds hitting his propellers and ricocheting off the jet intake fans and every square centimeter of the aluminum skin. It is also beating the windshield to its shattering point. The bullets of ice makes moving control surfaces more difficult and—even more horrifying—they could stop his engines. Even though he's still too far from the runway to lose speed, he throttles back anyway to lessen the impact. A pulsating white curtain of chainmail is slamming against the windshield. As quickly as it and the noise began, the assault ceases. He can see colored strobe lights.

The twinkle in a lover's eyes could not be more lovely.

Again, maybe for the last time, he lines up on the lights just two miles ahead.

On his second pass he knows the wind is pushing him from right to left, off the runway centerline, back into the crash course he just avoided.

I will adjust. I will overcome.

Dull pain shoots through his right leg pushing even harder on the rudder pedal. He now points the nose so far into the northeast that the still unseen runway approaches over his left shoulder.

With his head cocked left, he eases back on the throttles and with the practiced hand of a surgeon again gently pushes the yoke forward, literally flying the plane into the ground.

Crabbing forward with the runway now nearly under his left wing, he pushes the nose down. It looks just like a hundred other landings. He is not breathing.

Descending at a hundred knots through a hundred fifty feet, he angles the nose into the cross wind from the right; sensing its varying speed, the plane twists and wobbles slightly left and right but maintains a constant approach angle toward the runway.

There will be no more approaches. *Two strikes and you're out.*

One way or another, he will hit the ground.

...The Lord is with thee. Blessed are thou among women...

Roaring over the flashing lights just fifty feet below, he pulls down on the flaps, slowing to ninety knots, and throttles back.

With a pained yelp, the fat left tire strikes the tarmac. He practically stands on the left rudder pedal, twisting the airframe and slamming the right landing gear on the surface with a soul satisfying thud. The motion is violent, jerking him against the harness and snapping his neck to the right. The punishment never felt better. He has landed! His legs balance the rudder pedals to taxi down the centerline. It's over: he's steering the plane, completely under control, slowly decreasing speed.

Releasing his talon grip, he raises now numb fists over his head, splays his bloodless fingers to gain circulation and reclaims them as part of his anatomy.

The landing roll is smooth, gentle rhythmic and—after what he has just been through—practically orgasmic. He approaches the headlights, still a half mile ahead, savoring every second. He breathes deeply and grins.

He is alive. Nobody ever flew an airplane better. His heart beats again with the slow, steady beat of the athlete he was three decades and fifty pounds ago.

Two hundred feet from the conical headlights, he stops, then races the left engine and stands on the right rudder pedal. The plane pivots right, turning southwest toward the hell from which he's come.

Shutting down the engines, he takes the towel from around his shoulders, places the cap on the yoke and mops his head. One more swallow is an exquisite, warm reward from Johnny Walker Red, then it's back in the locker for the return to Mexico or perhaps another future final toast.

Cain has earned at least a few moments of afterglow. The rain has stopped. Savoring the silence, he looks out the left window at the airport's only navigation aid: an orange windsock, squeaking lazily in the now-gentle breeze following the storm front.

About a minute later, the two trucks approach. *Look at them. Those dumb yahoos don't have a clue about what's happened.*

He unbuckles the harness and peals himself off the seat. For the first time in six hours he stands, stretching to his full height, hands on the small of his back. He grasps an overhead handhold, takes all weight off his legs and—suspended by his arms—dangles his weight. He stands, then does it again. His back answers with grateful cracks.

Grasping the backs of the two seats to steady himself, he steps to the rear of the cockpit, turns and backs down the four-step ladder to the cargo deck. The cargo still rests securely beneath the wide green nylon cargo nets. With legs feeling again like parts of his body, he sidles past the fuel bladder and around the pallets of red and white ice chests. A few steps later he reaches the rear of the plane and pushes the red button that glows as the clam-like rear cargo doors begin opening.

He turns and walks forward and opens the crew door on the left side. He makes the small step to solid earth which never felt better under foot. A truck loaded with five fifty-five gallon barrels of aviation gas pulls under the left wing behind him. Without a word, the driver, dressed in a yellow poncho and nor'easter hat, had climbed in the truck bed and begins unrolling a black hose.

"Fill 'er up," he shouts merrily to the county sheriff.

Still sorting the gut wrenching terror of the past half hour, Cain can't help stealing a double take at the man, an officer of the law, fueling an airplane carrying more dope than has been seized by U.S. officials in the past five years. The corruption is reassuring. What a country!

Cain turns away and walks still stiff-legged to a spot just forward of the Provider's nose. Hands on hips, he stretches with another satisfying crack in his lower back. He becomes aware that he has a shadow; he's bathed in moonlight beaming now that the trailing edge of the storm clouds has raced away to the northeast.

Except for the purr of the fuel pump running in the pick-up, there's no other sound.

Chris Cain is a winner. The old pilot was totally, exquisitely alive, as only a man familiar with the face of death knows every sensual sight, sound, feel, smell, hunger and taste. He looks back at Fat Girl: no one else is ever going to know that if he'd held out a couple minutes longer this would have been just another routine landing.

... and blessed is the fruit of thy womb, Jesus. Holy Mary, Mother of God.

* * * *

The rain let up, then stopped. Judge Sparks turned off the wipers and sat in deafening silence, pierced suddenly by the rumble of engines in the distance. A split second later horror distorted his face as he realized the airplane materializing in the sheriff's headlights was going to crash into the truck. It didn't. In a half a heartbeat the strobes reflected off the wings and stubby fuselage zooming over his truck, missing him by inches.

Holy shit! Sparks growled as oversized balloon tires gripped the runway and began rolling towards him. With wide eyes and trembling hands, he drove to his left, off the runway, across a parking pad and under a large pole barn open on two sides. He made a u-turn, parking on the dirt and sawdust floor next to a low platform stage in the center. He walked to the grey electrical breaker panel and turned on overhead lights.

The barn and a playground behind it were the only permanent improvements at the Army Air Corps Park. The Air Force abandoned the training field and ammunition depot in the early '50s. When the sixty-acre site, runway and skeletons of a few outbuildings became county property in 1968, a much younger and lighter Judge Lamar Sparks championed its development. He had visions of it becoming a major lumber warehouse and shipping yard. Its location was perfect: the main Union Pacific rail line passed the runway, about a quarter mile to the northwest.

The unusually deep channel of the *Fourche Lafave* River paralleled the runway in a natural valley a quarter mile on the other side. But after a year or so of negotiations, the U.S. Forestry Service had not seen any need to harvest the hundreds of square miles of national forest that included nearly a tenth of the state and half of Dodd County. The vision dimmed, and with money and goodwill lagging, Sparks saved face with the dozen or so tax payers who really counted by creating Amy Air Corps Park. The main draw was boating and fishing. It was easily accommodated by modest investment in a boat ramp, dock and slips and a large boat house.

The barn catered to equestrian events favored by half of his benefactors and hosted small folk music performances favored by the other half.

The park is far from a destination, even among the locals. It is remote even by their standards, part of a fifty-thousand acre National Forest. The only road access is from the east along a fifteen-mile gravel road through the federal land from Buckeye, a settlement of about two-hundred, mostly part-time recreational cabin owners. A saw mill once provided jobs in the community of about a thousand before the National Forest locked them off the land in early days of the New Deal. It disappeared after the airfield closed about the same time an ancient granite quarry petered out. Hunting restrictions on federal land and an abundance of feral hogs and water moccasins in the sluggish river discouraged even the heartiest of the curious from exploring. All the same, in the five years that GCAC had operated there, Cain never made a landing or take-off toward the Buckeye settlement.

Owing to twelve-inch thick concrete construction possible in 1942 wartime America, the runway required no maintenance and remained in very good condition. After decades of disuse and lack of any attention from the Federal Aviation Administration or even the Arkansas Department of Parks and Tourism, it was just an anomaly in the deep pine woods. Few knew it existed; for those who did it was a billion dollar transshipment center for drugs, arms, people and a lot more.

"Who's there?" he jerked his eyes up and shouted into the rafters. There was no response. He froze and listened. The only sound was the receding thunder. As his poncho slid back down over his holster, he smiled and shook his head. He realized that the roof worked like a sounding board to amplify the now gentle rumbles. He felt foolish and old. Maybe what he'd just seen had really shaken him up. "Maybe that's why younger, dumber guys do that kind of stuff," he thought.

Sparks—like his colleague refueling—was in his early 60s. Both were overweight, the sheriff less so.

Rolling down the runway, Cain's thoughts shifted from flying to the more distasteful tasks with the men who awaited him, neither of whom he trusted. He imagined them both as incarnations from the mind of Tennessee Williams, once a neighbor to the nuns who rescued Cain off their doorstep. He despised everything about them. His revulsion was primal.

He dropped the towel from his face to see Sparks waiting on him. The old man still wore a green poncho; on him it looked like a tent. And, as relaxed as he was after the landing, just seeing the poster boy for sloth and corruption in this deserted and dark middle-of-nowhere airstrip primed his revulsion. Worse, he had little control on their turf. As much as he hated it, he knew that these two, who took very little risk and were well paid for doing practically nothing, controlled all the action now.

"*Buena dias, jefe*," Cain paused to make eye contact and take the extended right hand. "How'd you like the air show," he spoke over his shoulder before flopping down on the tattered Army blanket spread across the battered sofa.

"Mornin', major. Well, I guess you're into drama, you sure know how to make an entrance," Sparks replied to Cain's back. With a grunt he lifted his left foot on the stage, then wrapped both hands around his thigh and hefted up the rest his bulk on the platform. With more effort and accompanying sound effects he wedged his rump between the arms in one of the two overstuffed chairs facing the sofa. With his legs resting on a battered coffee table between them, Cain observed the human sloth with disgust.

"Thought I'd put on a little exhibition for you. Don't know how much entertainment you get out here," Cain spoke, attempting to hide his disdain. "Gotta say, the storm did make the landing more interesting. Otherwise, the trip up here to the 'natural state' your tourism ads tout can be pretty dull."

"No problem entering the country?" Sparks asked, pushing his soaking wet Stetson to the back of his head. Rain water drained into the rotting upholstery behind him.

"A DEA bird spotted me near Lake Charles and even made a show of coming close for a peek. They lost interest fast when they saw the Great Circle Air Cargo logo all over my tail. Dropped away like he heard his mother calling. It's still wired solid. GCAC must be paying their bills on time, those DEA weenies weren't seriously curious about anything.

Didn't radio for ID, cargo or destination. Just for grins I listened on their operation frequency. They didn't even make radio report that would confirm that I was ever there."

Motioning to a small foam cooler on the table, "Help yourself. It ain't spicy like you like, but it's better than usual. Cookin's a lot better since we got another trustee up from Cummins. He was chef or something at the Arlington in Hot Springs. Sent down for manslaughter."

Cain slid his feet off the table and reached for the cooler, lifted the lid and looked inside.

"Thanks, I'm glad the state's helping out." For the first time in hours, Cain managed a real smile, then began exploring the plate of fried chicken, potato salad, sliced tomatoes and warm biscuits and honey.

Sparks grunted as he reached into a much bigger cooler next to his chair and fished two bottles of Coors from the crushed ice. He began sucking on one as he handed the other to Cain.

"Just like mom used to make," Cain spoke with a mouth full and reached for the bottle.

"Here's to you, Inmate Relief Act and the good old U.S. of A.," Sparks said, raising his bottle, tilting the long neck in Cain's direction.

Cain, nodded. He took a long pull at his bottle.

"The what act?"

The Inmate Relief Act, was passed by the Arkansas Legislature at the request of the County Judges Association, which Sparks chaired. Known as the IRA, it enabled counties to keep inmates for the state, ostensibly to relieve overcrowding at the prisons and to save the daily costs of feeding and housing ever increasing numbers. In return their labor was used on public works projects in the host counties. In practice, for men like Sparks and Golden, the legislative intent was applied much more broadly. A favored few could pay for the labor. The proceeds—always in cash—enhanced the lifestyles and retirement accounts of county judges and sheriffs throughout the state.

Everyone was a winner with the IRA. At the state prisons skilled and educated inmates, especially from more wealthy families, could avoid the violent life of a prison. Again, with discreet consideration, very carefully pre-screened inmates need not spend much time with the general population before departing for a much more comfortable and accommodating jail, usually not too far from their home. Essentially, it meant that their time would be served on parole; the county jail cell was only an occasional dormitory. Within certain limits, they moved around the community, maintained relationships and enjoyed freedom like everyone else. On rare occasions the most trustworthy inmates were loaned out to some closely guarded business associates near New Orleans.

"It's the grease that keeps the wheels turning," Sparks responded with a wink and smile.

"Whatever, I'll drink to that, but it's your ass with that prison lash up. I get in the plane and leave," Cain said. "My friends in Louisiana will never be a problem. You've got to worry about whether those bonehead cons stay happy and keep quiet. All it takes is one ass-hole finishing his time, getting momma all worked up about it all, then talking to a prosecutor or reporter about what's really going down. Then, you're in a world of hurt." Pointing with the bottle toward the runway, "I'll take my odds over yours any day. At least I've got some control out there. I can always see it coming."

"Maybe so, major, but I doubt it. Their families are in play. There might be one who'd try it, but getting follow-on witnesses in our little town or testimony from a dead ex-con would be mighty challenging," Sparks replied squinting with distaste. His face darkened to an even more florid pink. Grasping the chair arms to lean forward, his red-splotched jowls wobbled as he snarled, "Big man-of-the-world, bastard pilot doesn't get it, does he? Who are our good, small-town people gonna believe: a venerable pillar of the community who's kept crime from their community as long as they or any of their kin can remember or some drugged-up, malcontent, pervert maggot? I know human nature, and I know what scares people way down inside where most folks never want to look, let alone think about. Those inmates got families, and they know the score. You know what I'm talking about, don't you? No, I'm not worried at all. I know the odds better than you, and they're better than yours. No pathetic loser inmate doing a life sentence three or six years at a pop is ever going to see me sweat. He sure as hell ain't gonna crap where he eats," Sparks replied. Pleased with himself, he leaned back. The distant sound of a motor drew their attention into the darkness outside.

* * * *

The motor, clearly identifiable now as a large truck engine, was approaching through the forest.

"Some of your honored guests arriving?" Cain nodded toward the a white, ten-ton panel truck now visible in the hangar lights and rolling very slowly past the open-sided barn, toward the parking pad. As the truck moved slowly toward Fat Girl, he saw the Great Circle Air Cargo logo, a green diamond with the letters GCA reversed in white and inscribed within a red circle. It was the same logo on the Provider's vertical stabilizer, on all company's single-axle trucks, smaller planes and a fleet of tow boats operating on the Mississippi River from Memphis to New Orleans and along the Gulf Coast from Mobile to Galveston. This wasn't the way things were done in the old days. Cain thought the advertising invited unnecessary scrutiny. But, over time he'd seen what it could do, not just for the DEA planes and military aircraft patrolling with them in the Gulf. There was real hiding-in-plain-sight advantage for moving drugs, guns, ammunition and some more recent, sensitive human and special cargos mixed in with legal freight, especially in areas like this where cops and customs agents may as well have been, or aspired to be, on the payroll.

Cain finished the last bite of chicken, drained the beer and rose to walk toward Fat Girl. Rear doors open and facing the plane, it began backing slowly and stopped under the plane's elevated tail section, inches from the cargo deck. The driver killed the engine, then climbed inside the airplane.

Entering the pilot door below the cockpit, Cain reached to his right, opened an electrical panel and turned on the interior lights. He showed the men, now inside the plane, how to loosen the netting and clamps that enabled large pallets to slide.

By now the sheriff had finished refueling and climbed aboard to take charge of the inmates, each outfitted with rubber boots and wearing bright yellow rain coats, trousers and hats.

"You three, get back in the truck and catch the pallet. You three push here, slowly," the sheriff ordered. Cain noticed the sheriff's empty holster. "There was no need to tempt anyone, anyone beyond his ability to resist," the sheriff spoke lowly to Cain. Without a word, the team obeyed. Remembering that he had a sawed-off 12-gage Browning shotgun, a Smith & Wesson .44-special revolver and ten thousand dollars in cash in the cockpit, he leaned back on the flight deck ladder. It wasn't comforting to think how easily he and the sheriff could be overpowered.

In less than five minutes the steel pallet loaded with twenty-four, two-foot square pine boxes, each fifty-pounds and stenciled "*Monte Verde* Coffee Co, Pure Colombian," slipped easily over rollers in the plane's cargo deck and on to similar floor in the truck.

The sheriff hopped down and began stowing the refueling hose. As the bigger truck pulled away, he backed to the cargo bay doors.

"Let's get this done. Give me a hand here," the sheriff said as he climbed into the bed of his truck and began pulling a metal footlocker from behind the empty fuel barrels. His Model 1911 .45 automatic was back in its holster.

This was the only part Cain didn't like. He had no way of knowing how much money was aboard or if someone in the stateside distribution chain was skimming. After all, none of them were exactly choir boys.

He had insisted that the trunks be sealed and banded. That was his principal concern as he and the sheriff struggled, each with one end of the trunk and dragged it inside.

"Who put the bands and cipher locks on?" Cain asked as he and the sheriff slid it forward and began strapping it to the deck close to the flight deck ladder.

"We found it at the boat house, just like this," the sheriff replied as the pair covered it with a heavy canvas and a smaller cargo net.

"They must be coming up the river."

Cain had a grain of respect for Golden as a man of some action. They made eye contact, silently communicating relief that neither of them, at least, would be suspected if some drug lord's consigliore decide the cocaine-to-cash account didn't balance.

Cain knew as little as Golden and Sparks about these transactions. They could only guess as the amounts inside the metal box bound with four wide, locked metal bands. Someone, they were aware, knew the value, to the dollar. They knew that the runners who assembled and packed the cash before flying to New Orleans, Mexico City and finally to Cartagena knew the flight would land on the Colombian coast two days later with just more than three million dollars in used, small denominations of U.S. currency. There, before the box left Fat Girl, they'd count the cash again.

"Here's the final load. Give me a hand with these two," Cain said, walking to the forward bulkhead; there two green metal 50-millimeter ammunition boxes were strapped to the deck. They were unusually heavy. Like the cash box, each case was sealed with two metal bands and cipher locks. Each man grasped handles on both ends of a box and slid them to the cargo ramp, across a narrow plank and into the pick-up.

"I don't think they're going anywhere, from here to the boat dock.

I'll ride with you and help you stow them aboard," Cain said, and both men climbed in the truck.

"This is the only part of this I don't get. That ain't no drugs in there, is it? And it ain't nobody's coin collection." Golden started the motor and looked back at the ammo cases. "Whatever it is, it's way too heavy for liquid. Maybe its lead, and he's starting a car battery factory down in New Orleans.

"Sometimes it's best not to wonder," Cain spoke. He lowered his head to mop his forehead on the towel he wore like a shawl.

The truck moved slowly from the cargo ramp, turned right across the parking lot and past the barn. They pulled on to the gravel road that led a couple hundred yards through the park, toward the river. As they drove Cain checked the side mirror and watched the big ten-ton cargo truck rock off the grass and on to the gravel road and drive away in the opposite direction, toward Buckeye and the state highway. He was relieved. Cain realized that sitting down felt good. He didn't feel as uncomfortable around the sheriff. But, he was tired, and he still had a long morning and a lot of flying ahead of him.

If loading on the boat goes well and Sparks shuts the hell up and leaves, maybe I'll get a nap, he hoped.

A minute later, the headlights panned a newly planked dock. Smaller boat slips extended into the river from it. At the river bank a ramp bridged the ten-foot gap between the road and the dock. A large pleasure craft was tied up at the far end. It was the only boat in the marina.

"Coy, I've got to admit, the idea of a four-day cruise at a blinding twelve knots sounds pretty good. A nice vacation, that. You ever get any farther south than the mouth of the Arkansas?"

"Well, no, maybe someday. The trip's kind of like yours. They say I gotta do this alone. There's nobody else to do the drivin', and that gets old. I usually catch a big cat fish or two trawling and keep 'em in the live well, but that's about all. Not much time to look around." Golden turned the truck around and began backing down the ramp, with Cain standing behind, directing.

Great Circle gave the thirty-five-foot Chris Craft Commander to Golden about a year ago, when the mysterious ammo can transfers began. Two men whose campaign ads he'd seen on television, delivered the boat the Golden. A state trooper had picked them up and delivered them and the produce of their two-day fishing trip back to Little Rock.

"They said it come from New Orleans; extra pay for the long trips down to the Mississippi. The wages of sin, the preacher might say, major. Works for me," Sparks spoke dully into the windshield.

Even more than that, it rewarded nearly three years of flawless operations at Army Air Corps Park. After all that time the operation had remained secret. Although cover stories were always ready, nobody—no lawmen not cut in on the corruption, no alert citizen, no curious reporter— had ever raised a question. This was always uppermost on their minds and those of the string of anonymous men from New Orleans who came to Buckeye a few days before each flight. They worked for the same men who somehow ensured the blind eye of several federal agencies who should be intercepting Cain's flights across the Caribbean from Mexico to Arkansas and the truck deliveries of the special Colombian coffee blend to restaurants from Cincinnati to Houston.

The Chris Craft Commander was a beauty, maintained like a painted and polished lady, built for comfort and long-distance cruising. The classic trawler featured a flying bridge on the top deck, another helm station, air conditioned salon and complete galley was below that. The lowest level included a stateroom with a marine head and shower. A large aft deck spanned the transom from port to starboard. Below, the engine room housed two enormous, spotless Cummins diesels and a specially fit four-hundred-gallon fuel tank.

Cain's eyes drifted away from the boat lying motionless in the truck's headlights. Something drew him farther down the dock, and he walked slowly. The few steps were eerie but also somehow serene. His sound of his boots on the dock echoing across the dark water, the basso belching of bull frogs along the bank, the humid and still air carrying the river's redolence, possessed him like some weird spell. He felt that he was entering, more likely intruding, in a sacred place. Golden watched, and neither man realized that they'd stopped, both staring at nothing in the still unseen mist that hugged the river. For a moment they stood like statues.

Sensing Cain's uneasy vibe, Golden snapped out of the trance, back to the business at hand. He shot a quick look at him and walked across the dock to unlock the boat house. He returned dragging a long, narrow plywood board which they anchored in the truck bed and gently laid it atop the boat's vanished wood railing. With ropes attached, Cain carefully slid the first of the ammo cases down the improvised ramp.

"You got it bad, don't you," Cain said, laughing as he finished and dropped aboard, "You don't even want to ding the railing! Can't say I blame you. Don't tell me, is this another job for your inmates, polishing and painting on a weekly basis?"

"Give me a hand with these hatches," the reply was terse. Cain was right, of course, and for some reason Golden was embarrassed to admit it or that it was so obvious.

Each tugged on a wide deck hatch, lifting them to expose the engines below. Golden slid into the tight space and turned to receive the first ammo can. He carefully tugged it into a metal frame welded beside the port engine block. When Cain lowered the other, he repeated the delicate task on the starboard diesel.

Neither knew what they were handling, only that whatever it was inside was securely sealed in these airtight, heavy canisters. Guessing was always interesting, but not as satisfying for a man like Cain for whom knowing answers was always better. At a minimum, he always wanted to know the odds.

Both men shared the thought, but neither said a word. They closed the hatches, climbed back in the truck and headed back to the barn for the morning's next major event.

Five

"Let's go through the SOPs in the watch books and clean 'em up. Standard operating procedures are worthless unless they're up to date with current contacts and phone numbers. I'll do the same with this stack." She spoke as she tucked a stray strand of hair behind her ear, reaching with her right hand for another three-ring binder across the desk.

Watch standing was a routine, mostly boring chore at the Coast Guard District Headquarters. In essence, it was a phone-answering and overnight mailroom service. The only unusual or very interesting part was reading the headquarters message traffic, telex radio messages retrieved from the command's around-the-clock communications center, always fully staffed and locked in a huge vault a floor below them. It was Rees' job to make the trip about every two hours. They would sift through the hundreds of formatted messages received continuously from the federal establishment, the Coast Guard and military commands around the world. Most of it was unclassified and could be seen by anyone. It usually was a mind-numbing iteration of ship arrivals and departures, the latest Notices to Airmen and Mariners about hazards on the river and weather forecasts, or the endless administrative details of an organization the size of the Coast Guard.

Regardless, it all had to be read, routed or dealt with efficiently. It was the assistant's job to sort it. But, Lucas helped plow through it. Both stacks were further sorted into large mail slots mounted in a floor-to-ceiling cabinet behind them. Unless she saw that some needed immediate attention, they would be picked up before dawn by appropriate staff.

The most interesting messages were those classified as Secret and Top Secret. There were never many. They usually were details of ongoing administrative investigations, generally from Headquarters Coast Guard, the FBI, Customs and any number of similar alphabet acronym national, state or local law enforcement agencies.

The real treasures, at least for Rees and anyone with the clearances high enough to read them, were backgrounders from the CIA, major military commands and U.S. Embassies around the world. They often contained details of events in the news, often with startlingly different facts versus journalistic accounts. She couldn't remember any that actually required action from the District, but standing this watch only once a month, she hardly saw even a small portion of them. The challenge was to read them and decide whether the content warranted interrupting the sleep of the District Commander or his deputy. Otherwise, she'd lock the messages in a walk-in safe and deliver them the next working day. On rare occasions when she'd seen news about an on-going investigation involving the District she had called the working level officer involved, usually an officer of equal rank, to give a heads up. This was the professional thing to do. It also tended to build close relationships among the junior officers. The smart ones, like Emma, would come immediately or arrive at work early to read-in before the front office asked questions they hadn't anticipated, let alone for which they had any answer. They, or at least most of them, would do the same for her. Thumbing through the first batch tonight, something told her that there probably was one, maybe only one, who wouldn't: Lieutenant Commander Art Jacks.

There was nothing specific that made her think so, but she felt that something wasn't right. She'd had a sixth sense about this sort of thing. She'd picked it up working side by side with her father. Like him, she knew how to read people, seeing what most others couldn't, just behind their eyes.

She knew that she'd learn more listening than talking. She was a practiced observer. She'd seen Jacks offer advice, especially to the newly arrived. When the command suffered some usually minor embarrassment, he'd volunteer a fix and discretely offer to mentor the inexperienced colleague. After establishing trust, Jacks mined them for information about anything and everything, mostly gossip. Lucas never spoke to anyone about Jacks. But, she wrestled with her reluctance. She knew that her background and personality may work against her. She had succeeded on her own strengths, not by finding flaws in others. Could someone like Jacks fabricate myths about her disciplined life as Lucy's obsessively protective guardian? It was possible, she thought, that she may appear unfriendly, different or even intimidating. She didn't really know because she didn't waste time listening to gossip; she knew that conventional wisdom was usually wrong. But, lately she sensed that, if not a mistake, it was a handicap not to be at least aware. It made her angry that purveyors never seemed to be ashamed or even suffer any consequence from their miscalculations. Being right only once seemed to justify their silliness. That and a nagging feeling that she was the object of their rumor and gossip was renting more space in her head than she liked. She didn't know what to make of the occasional odd looks, occasional smirks when she entered a room and had no idea what they implied. Should she take any serious inference from them? If so, why? She looked down at the open binder, picked up a pen and frowned that she was entertaining such paranoia.

She had recorded each message in the classified messages log, another of the three-ring binders that required attention through the night. She paused and stole a quick look at Rees, still sorting in a chair to her left. She felt guilty.

She liked him, and she liked spending time with him, even on watch. She looked beyond her reflection in the wide window, to the lights of the city shimmering on the river. The full moon was rising in the southeast. She wondered how Rees wound up on the watch with her; it was likely a coincidence, there were only about a dozen officers and maybe twice that many enlisted available. And, each watch stander could trade assignments to fit personal schedules. So, the odds weren't all that long that they'd be thrown together.

They met at a command picnic two years ago. Since then he had become a very welcome part of her little family circle. He was charming, and Lucy was smitten with him. Still, neither Emma nor Lucy could understand why the handsome musician and sailor, a young man with something of a shady past, would want to spend time with them. Surely, Emma thought, the rush of being on stage, the applause and the press of people all around, would be terribly exciting. That he wanted to spend time with them, inviting them to tag along, was beyond her, but he seemed to thrive in their presence. Emma had never spent so much time, or had so much feeling for any man other than her father. And, even if she enjoyed knowing him, she was also ever the guardian. Lucy was a little person, born with acondroplasia, the genetic disorder that made her stature short. She had always been Lucy's champion. Her newer role as guardian was natural, but she knew that her sister could resent too much mothering, especially now she was becoming a woman, and a beautiful one. She rationalized that it was her maternal instinct that scanned for any sign of a romance between the two; she didn't want to think there was more to it than that.

Four months ago neither were surprised when a third woman entered the group. They didn't warm as quickly, of course, as he did to the graceful, petit blonde with a theatrical Southern dialect. His invitations and visits had become less frequent, but that was only natural, they thought. But, a month later when he announced he was married, they were shaken, and more. Neither shared their real feelings, to each other or him, instead hoping that their expression of happy surprise masked them. But, it was Emma who couldn't let go. Watching him now, shifting through the papers beside her, she felt awkward and distanced, even oddly uncomfortable. She wanted more than small talk.

"How you doing with that? I can help," she spoke to clear the air and regain professional decorum.

"Oh, yeah, sorry. Just finishing," he spoke finally as if his mind also had been wandering. He cross stacked about a half dozen short piles of paper, walked to the mailboxes and fed them into the proper slots. "This is why they pay us the big bucks, lieutenant!"

"You 'da man!" Emma laughed as she swiveled for another guilty look at the tall man. "How 'bout supper?"

Lyle had hoped the suggestion would come soon, as it always did with Lieutenant Lucas.

"Hey, howzabout Jimbo's Port-O-Call? It's just across the street!" he gestured grandly in its direction, gliding back to the long desk. He opened a pencil drawer beside his chair. As if surprised by what he found, he said "Why, here's the menu right here!"

Like many eateries in the old city, the Port-O-Call was proof that looks are deceiving. Far from the beaten path, it was a locals-only enterprise; a lost tourist would not have given it a second look or even consider leaving their car parked in the neighborhood and venturing inside the paint-deprived clapboard shanty. For as long as anyone in the neighborhood could remember, food bought from a side window was as cheap as a trip to the corner grocery. Jimbo and his heirs were also proud to serve as an unofficial around-the-clock dining hall and after-duty watering hole.

The predictable details about splitting the tab followed the phoned-in order. With calculations finished, he departed with Emma's cash. By 8 p.m. he'd returned with warm seafood gumbo, beans and rice, French bread and the cold, impossibly sweet tea. He spread the feast on one end of the desk. Emma savored every bite, this place and time and her dining partner. More pleasure, and guilt; she didn't care. Truth was that she hoped that Lyle felt the same.

* * * *

She woke with a jerk from a deep, dreamless slumber and didn't move. She lay still in total darkness. The rough feel of a wool blanket on her cheek confirmed that she was in the bunk room. She felt foolish and reached to turn on the nightstand lamp. It was 1 a.m. A little embarrassed by her confusion and how good the two-hour nap felt, she stretched, splashed water on her face and tidied her hair piled on top of her head. Quietly opening the bunkroom door, she smiled at the sight of him across the room, drumming a pencil on a pile of papers.

"OK, I'm impressed. You not sleepy?"

Lyle startled at the unexpected voice. "Hey, boss. No, not really."

"Oh, wait, now I remember: you musicians thrive in the night."

"Maybe it's the coffee and chicory: bayou voodoo, turning me in to a wild man," he said swiveling around in the chair and waving his arms and fingers at her. He pointed toward the windows, "Look at the moon, I'm the original Wolf Man, the man who walks and talks at midnight; ah-woo!"

"No, you're just a piece of work," she spoke, hiding her amusement in mock seriousness, turning to open one of the half dozen tall grey metal lockers between the bunkroom doors. "I think it's time for me to move around a little. I'm going to make a tour, maybe catch the ship docking at Piety. Stay here and catch the phones or grab some fresh air?"

"No brainer, boss," Lyle spoke, throwing the last of the papers into mail slots. He retrieved overalls from his locker and began pulling them over his uniform. "I'll catch up on the landing. Got some gear in my car."

"OK, I guess, I'll set the phone watch in Comms," she frowned, turning away to retrieve the log book, dialing and entering the time of her request.

She descended two flights of concrete stairs and emerged at double doors that led outside to a covered steel walkway. It spanned the fifty feet between the building and the roof of an adjacent warehouse, then continued down its length. At the far end a long flight of metal stairs dropped steeply and ended on a commercial barge moored to the riverbank. In the brilliant moonlight Coxswain John Scott had started the engine of the thirty-foot launch where he and Lyle waited. Returning the coxswain's salute, Emma stepped aboard, and Scott handed her an orange life vest as Lyle cast off the dock line.

"Cast off, coxswain, stand by for further orders," Emma commanded, tightening the straps.

"Aye-aye, ma'am," the coxswain answered, spun the wheel and gently nudged the throttle. The aluminum boat, a trawler confiscated from a drug smuggler, struggled against the river current and quickly into the dark water.

The air was still, and it was warm, even at this hour. It felt good on her face as the launch gained speed toward the lights of the city ahead. The sights and sounds of the river were always fascinating; the steam calliope on the Natchez paddle wheeler returning from a charter cruise added to the ambiance, as did tantalizing aromas from restaurant kitchens preparing breakfast. Feeling the launch vibrate beneath her feet, she fixed her gaze on Lyle standing in the forecastle. Was he thinking the same thing she was? This moment was timeless; 1983 or a century earlier. Not much has really changed on this stage, only the players and their props.

Perhaps that was why she has grown so fond of New Orleans; she certainly wouldn't be the first seduced by the Big Easy, the City that Care Forgot. Her feelings were inspired not so much by the place, although that was a large attraction, but by the primal awareness it stirred.

The little inspection excursion is the ultimate perk for a woman raised on an urban river; but, it was more. She was in command; a woman in a man's world, and every bit as capable. As the launch plowed through the water, her senses caught and amplified every sensation. She smiled. *I get paid to do this!*

Watching as a tow boat with a dozen barges passed downriver, hugging mid-channel about two hundred feet to her left, Emma's euphoria evaporated. The situational briefing from Art Jacks had been a joke, perhaps worse: a trap to lull her into complacency and inattention. Instead of a routine night, traffic was going to be more intense than usual.

"You get what you inspect, not what you expect," her father taught her long ago. As soon as Jacks had breezed away, Emma's immediate inspection of radar repeaters in the command center and message traffic had confirmed that the ship channel would be jammed overnight from the Mississippi's Southwest entrance to the Gulf, through New Orleans and well beyond the thicket of refineries and grain elevators crowding the upriver banks. Much of the traffic would be northbound shipping from overseas. As the ships leave the open Gulf and enter the river, launches will dart out to them and deliver river pilots. The highly skilled, often third- and fourth-generation pilots' intense, high-paying jobs were to guide the ships safely to destinations as far north as Baton Rouge. Pilots boarding at sites upriver would reverse the process for the ships loaded with petroleum, grain or bulk cargo headed toward the Gulf and destinations in South America, Europe, the U.S. east coast and—via the Panama Canal—the west coast and Asia across the Pacific.

The river would also be jammed with an equal or greater number of towboats struggling behind as many as twenty barges lashed together as a single unit. They could be completing journeys that began in Minneapolis, Pittsburgh, St. Louis or in tributary ports such as Tulsa, Nashville or literally scores of small cargo docks from Pennsylvania to North Dakota.

All day, every day, the world comes calling on New Orleans, as it would during the next few hours. Any inattention, neglect, mechanical failure would create disaster. The catastrophic possibilities were endless. The absolute worst, most likely scenario involved just one inattentive or—more likely—incapacitated captain plowing into bridge pilings, crashing hundreds of vehicles into the river. Next on the hit parade in her head was the vision of multiple towboats, barges and ships colliding, transforming the waterway in to a slow-motion pinball machine. Sunken wrecks would close the river for months, possibly filling it with toxic material or bursting into noxious flames killing thousands downwind. Great for the tourist trade, too, she thought.

"Orders, ma'am?" the coxswain poked his head through a window and interrupted her well-practiced mental exercises.

"Upriver, eight knots, to Gulf Coast Steel," Emma instructed, joining him inside the pilot house. She checked her watch, then lifted heavy binoculars from a drawer and scanned the river behind. In the far darkness she saw only one set of still-faint red and green navigation lights just entering the long channel downriver. "Make a slow pass along Gulf Coast. We can lay off between the ferry landings. It's 0145. Port Captain says a merchantman will tie up at Piety sometime near 0200 or so. We can drop back down then and take a look. Head back to the landing after that."

"Aye, aye, ma'am. Just heard that the *Maria* has steamed past Belle Chasse, should be on time." Looking over his shoulder he steered left into center channel.

It would take only a few minutes to motor upriver to the Gulf Coast shipyard and floating dry docks directly across the river from the Canal Street and adjacent to the ferry landing at Algiers Point. The inspection wouldn't last more than an hour and cover no more than two miles. Lucas knew that observing the ship arrive at Piety Street Wharf was enough to justify it; but, she also had a small, hidden agenda.

Piety, only a couple hundred yards upriver from the Coast Guard landing, was home of the Colombian-owned *Monte Verde* Coffee Company's North American offices and roasting operation; as they motored past it on the right, she breathed in the delicious aroma, as she had on the way to work. Neither of the men spoke but exchanged a quick, knowing glance; they knew that their lieutenant was looking out for them. They knew that even their casual attention to the arrival of a company-owned ship would be rewarded. As soon as *Maria's* lines were doubled up, employees would appear and toss them a few pounds of freshly-roasted coffee. *Lagniappe*, Emma thought, returning to the weather deck and looking at the now brightly lit Piety Wharf, *New Orleans at its genteel best.*

Six

Sheriff Coy Golden reversed his route from the dock; they rolled slowly over the gravel road from which they had come. Both men peered through the windshield, concentrating on the dark tree line a furlong beyond the headlights. "Stop, turn off the lights and blink your searchlight, Cain spoke. Almost immediately, a pencil-thin red dot danced across Golden's, then Cain's eyes.

"There they are. Wonder how long the snake eaters have been lying out there," Cain spoke, smiling as two headlights appeared in the distance and began wobbling slowly toward them. As they turned off the gravel road and rolled toward the airstrip, the lights fell in behind.

When he parked beside the barn, Cain got out and walked to Fat Girl as another GCAC-marked truck backed slowly under the tail, inches from the cargo deck. The rear door rolled up, and Cain could see six sets of eyeballs in black-painted faces. The men were seated on about a dozen wooden cargo cases.

A fit young man but seemingly older than most of the others, stepped aboard and shook Cain's hand.

"Captain Simms, sir. Got six pax and about twenty-five hundred pounds for Nicaragua. With your permission our load master will secure, we'll rig the jump seats and wait for takeoff."

"Make yourself at home. Make it fast. I wanna get out of here, wheels up no later than 0445."

The men, dressed in mismatched combinations of black, red and green t-shirts, jeans, khaki shorts, knit and ball caps, running shoes and boots, quickly and silently went to work lashing long crates of rifles, ammunition and high explosives to the deck. Cain pretended not to watch, then turned away; they were pros who needed no supervision. He climbed into the cockpit to make ready and returned a few minutes later. The special ops crew sat on the deck, passing around sandwiches and soft drinks from a cooler, identical to the ones just unloaded.

"We left North Little Rock about sunset and haven't eaten much. This isn't exactly the kind of caravan you'd risk pulling into McDonalds with," the captain flashed a smile and extended a wrapped sandwich toward him.

"Thanks, I'll take you up on it when we're airborne." Cain nodded with a genuine, perhaps envious, smile. *These guys get younger and dumber every day.* He still hoped for a quick nap, but the idea of taking these highly-trained, highly-motivated warriors to a real fight in Central America gave him second wind. Working Special Operations had always been like a shot of adrenaline. Their blind trust in their mission and each other, betting their life for soldiers' pay, came close—but not quite close enough—to shaming him. He didn't like thinking that these young men probably sized him up the same way he did the sheriff and judge.

* * * *

"Happy days. The eagle has flown, gentlemen," Cain announced, stepping up on the platform where Sparks and Golden were seated on the sofa, beers in hand, feet on the table. The judge, still in his rain gear, looked like a ridiculous Humpty Dumpty hiding under a green tent. The mouth-breathing sheriff was last to set his beer down but did manage to catch the envelope pitched at him. The judge managed to jerk his back as his payment thudded on his stomach.

"There's five-thou in each one. Count it out on the table before I go."

The judge managed to drag his feet off the table and joined the sheriff who had already begun thumping the well-worn twenties and fifties one-by-one on the table.

Cain took a chair opposite them. *They and everyone in this hellhole deserve each other. How cheaply they're bought.*

"All here," Golden announced and turned to watch Sparks fumbling to finish.

"Same," Sparks confirmed.

Even if it wasn't his problem, Cain was relieved. He gripped the chair arms to rise. With this last bit of business behind him, he would have time to rest before taking off again.

"Well, 'till we meet again…" He stopped in mid-sentence, freezing. He riveted his eyes over their heads, toward the rear of the barn. When he moved, it was slowly. He held out his palms toward the two men to keep them still.

"Quiet," he mouthed and pointed.

Golden followed Cain's gaze and also rose slowly, drawing his sidearm.

The metallic snap of a round chambering in the .45 sent an unmistakable message. He cocked the hammer and rose to a firing stance, aiming with both hands. Cain and Golden crept along, their eyes settling on the only possible hiding place: a narrow platform of planks in the cross beams above them.

By now Sparks had wrestled himself off the sofa, eyes wide in his round face.

There was another creak. This time Sparks heard it too. He sucked air: it was the same thing he had heard and ignored earlier.

Instantly, Golden's aim swiveled left, and Cain quickly scooted farther away from him to get a better view of the twenty-four-square-foot plywood platform. He still saw nothing. If someone was there, he must be lying down, pressing himself into the boards.

He picked up an empty beer bottle. Golden saw the motion and understood what was about to happen.

"You got five seconds. Show yourself or I start shooting," Golden shouted.

Nothing.

The bottle bounced against the roof and sounded like an explosion.

"Don't shoot, don't shoot! Please don't shoot!" a high-pitched, trembling voice pleaded.

"Show yourself, hands up!" Golden spoke, moving next to Cain. "Move! Now!"

Two hands, two more, then two heads.

"Get down, one at a time," Cain ordered.

As a pair of blue jeans-clad, skinny legs slid over the side, Cain moved closer. When the intruder landed nimbly on the soft dirt, Cain grabbed a right wrist, twisted it under a shoulder blade and walked toward the Sparks and the light.

It's a kid!

He turned to watch as the second hit the ground. Golden frog marched him beside Cain.

Two kids!

They were fifteen, seventeen, at most. Golden patted them down; the boys were now scared out of their wits. The smaller of the two, the first one down, was shaking and getting wobbly. Cain eased the arm lock. His shorter and more well-padded, wild-eyed companion looked around; he made sounds like he was going to vomit. Neither took their eyes off the .45 aimed at them.

Golden handcuffed them together. Sparks looked on in total horror, and Golden, holstering the .45, scanned their faces and understood why: they knew exactly who they were. *In a rural county like this*, Cain thought, *how in hell could they not know each other?*

The mission was inexorably compromised. Unless he could diffuse the situation, right here, right now, he may just as well have crashed. If the boys couldn't be somehow and reliably co-opted into silence, the entire elaborate and expensive network he'd put together in the past two years would have to be dismantled. He didn't even want to think about the repercussions of that.

The possibility of something like this had occurred to him, and on those long fights he'd had time to make a contingency plan of action, something he had never discussed with the locals. The men paying the bills did not care.

"Sit down," Cain spoke firmly, pointing at the platform's edge, the judge and sheriff now standing behind them, out of their field of vision. In the moment they looked down to sit, Cain looked at Sparks and Golden, extended his palms again, signaling that should keep quiet. They were more than happy to pick up on the cue.

"You're really in a bad place right now, way over your head," Cain spoke slowly and calmly as a parent to a child. After a very long pause, "But, what is done is done. You guys are OK. Nobody's going to hurt you. Try to relax." he spoke softly, smiling and spreading his arms in a gesture of greeting. Golden and Sparks were confused.

"You've made a little mistake, that's all. By now you know you shouldn't be here. So, why are you?" Cain asked with a classic "good cop" smile, hands on knees bending toward them. Cain's body language and words were working: the boys, at least, were calming down, lifting their gaze from the sawdust floor. Golden and Sparks, still mutely staring at Cain, now looked like they were the ones in real trouble. They were.

Cain continued to control his anxieties, as he always did, always with good result.

"OK, why don't you just start from the beginning? Who are you, and why were you hiding?"

The pair shot quick glances at each other, then the heavier and shorter one spoke. "I'm Darrel Wayne Justice, he's Teece Longman. We come to coon hunt on the track last night, but it started to rain. We stayed in Teece's truck. When it let up, we started home but got wallered out down there on the south end. We figured there might be something we could use up here ta dig with. When we seen the sheriff acomin' we hid." He looked at Golden, "High sheriff don't allow no huntin' in the park. We heard that big ol' airplane out there, then the lights come on. We seen it was the judge. We'uz scared, so, we stayed hid." He studied the sawdust at his feet, "Then you found us."

"We didn't shoot nothing, honest, you can look in the truck!" Teece blurted out, prompted by the short silence after Darrell Wayne's explanation.

"Well, that sounds reasonable. I'm sure that's true. With all that was going on and in your shoes, I probably would have done the same. We trust them, don't we?" Cain spoke with animation toward the judge, straightening up, hands now on his hips.

"I don't think we need these cuffs," Cain announced, turning his inquiring gaze to the sheriff, tilting his head toward the boys.

"Judge, we got any more beer? These boys have had quite a scare. They could probably use a couple!" Sparks and Golden looked at Cain as though he was holding a gun on them, but—neither knowing Cain's plan nor any other option—both played their rolls.

"Bring one for me, too," Cain said, placing his hands on the boys' shoulders, guiding them to the two chairs.

"You boys just gave us a start," Sparks, even though he did not know where it was going, was quick to join the tableau. He managed to smile, handing each a bottle and one for Cain, one for himself. Cain signaled for Golden to remove the cuffs.

Bundles of nerves and amazed that one powerful man was freeing, the other serving them, the boys drained the bottles in a couple of long gulps.

"Good grief: how long were you guys the Dodd County chug-a-lug champs!" Cain spoke in mock amazement. Nervous laughter erupted from all four. With right foot on the stage, he grasped his hands and leaned on his elbow and continued the plan.

"Look here, boys. I can't tell you much, but what we're doing here is top secret, actually beyond top secret. By that I mean, that the judge and the sheriff are helping the U.S. government with a very important project. It's a very secret project. People's lives could be lost if word of this gets around, to anybody. That's why we were so jumpy when we found you. Like it or not, you two are now part of something that you cannot understand, at least not right now. Now, listen very carefully: neither of you can ever, ever speak about what you've seen tonight. I mean never, and I mean to anybody. If you can do that, and we'll know if you don't, you could join the team. Frankly, we could use some help around here." Pulling a solemn face, "And, you'd be helping America. Otherwise, we could put you in jail, nowhere around here by the way, to keep you quiet for a very long time. Nobody wants to do that. I think you're the kind of guys who can be trusted. If you want to help, you'd be getting a lot of money, more for keeping the secrets than anything else. If you can do that, and we'd know if you didn't, there may be a lot more work and a lot of money for you." He held his arms wide with the closer, "What do you think? Can we count on you?"

Cain was a born actor, and his lies would have made any con man weep in envy.

Two more beers are drained, with gusto, and as if on cue the sheriff brings two more. By now they were relieved, relaxed and—as Cain observed—totally naïve. The judge had settled back on the sofa, a bystander trying to figure out Cain's strategy and why—by the look on his face—Golden already seemed to know.

Darrell Wayne's maturity, capacity for alcohol and patriotic avarice prompted his acceptance; hook, line and sinker. He turned to Teece who belched and blinked dumbly back at him.

"I'm proud to serve my country," he slurred, turning the wide eyes of drunken enthusiasm in Cain's direction, "You can count on me, sir!"

"Great! I'm glad this is going to work out. You've got the right stuff. Welcome aboard."

Cain led the handshakes all around, goofy high-fives with Darrell Wayne and Teece.

Cain left the little celebration and walked toward the side of the barn where he stopped, "Hey, Darrell Wayne, give me a hand out here with some more beer. This'll be your first assignment; we're going do some celebrating!"

Cain slapped the boy on the back as they emerged in the moonlight, walking a few more feet to the sheriff's pick-up.

"Look behind those barrels. There's a case of long necks in there somewhere."

As the boy faced the tail gate, Cain stepped close behind him. He slapped one hand on his forehead, the other at the base of his spine. In one precise motion, he twisted violently toward the boy's right shoulder and slightly down. From the crunch, more felt than heard, Cain knew he hadn't lost touch. Almost effortlessly, he had broken at least one of eight high cervical vertebrae at the base of the brain; which ones didn't matter. Judging from the limp and breathless body in his hands, he knew the damage was high enough to bruise or tear the spinal cord somewhere between C3 and C5 vertebrae. Either way, seventeen-year-old Darrell Wayne Justice of Buckhorn, Arkansas, was dying of asphyxiation or was dead already. Cain lowered the body to the grass. Fewer than fifteen seconds has elapsed since they'd left the barn.

"Teece, give us a hand out here. Old fumble fingers here is worthless!"

The lanky youngster pulled a puzzled look toward the summons. A rubbery smile replaced it as he politely tabled his beer, found his feet and eagerly trotted into the darkness.

"Huh…?" he muttered as his dilated eyes focused on the body, then froze in confusion. His last awareness was of two large hands wrapping around his head, then an impossibly loud snap, then nothing. Teece Longman, sixteen, of Rural Route Two, Dodd County, Arkansas, was dead.

"Coy!"

Golden arrived first, then Sparks.

"What the hell?" the judge gagged in horror. "What the hell!"

"They won't be telling anyone what they saw tonight, judge, they're dead. And, you can thank me for cleaning up the Dodd County gene pool!" Cain laughed, slapping the gasping Sparks on the back.

"Have you lost your mind! You're crazy! We could have kept them quiet! How in hell are we going to explain two dead bodies?"

"Calm down and try to think, fat man," Cain snapped back. "It's the only way out, and nobody's going to know what happened. Do you really believe that you could have kept them from talking, like your inmates? You can hold on to that dream, old man, but I don't think so. That chain gang can be scared because they've at least got some brains," Cain spoke as he unlatched the tailgate and let if fall open. "These kids didn't, and—trust me—they didn't think they had anything to lose. They'd take your chump change, alright, but they'd talk to anybody who'd listen. If they walked away you might as well have told your buddies in New Orleans that you're tired of living," Cain said as he stepped toward the two bodies. "Give me a hand, Coy."

As Sparks alternately stood and stared or walked in circles and muttered to himself, he and Golden heaved the limp bodies with grotesquely twisted necks into the truck.

"What are you going to do?" Sparks managed to ask in a near whisper, his eyes wide in his bloated face.

"It's after four now," Cain looked at his watch. "The Missouri-Pacific left North Little Rock more than two hours ago. We've got a little time. We get them back in their truck with a bunch of the empties. We'll pull it on the track." He looked north and pointed, "By the time it rounds the turn it'll start putting on speed, should hit sixty when they hit it. Broken necks aren't going to look unusual when they find the pieces."

The judge looked at the bodies, rubbing the back of his neck with a trembling hand. "I guess it's all we got. It will work?" he seemed to beg Golden, hugging himself, then dropped his arms to stand like a plump statue. Returning from the edge of panic now and embarrassed that the other two knew it, he tried to speak with some authority, "You all take care of it. I'll head on back to town," adding with a bit of swagger, "Coy, we'll talk this afternoon after you get back from the tragic accident." Sparks slapped Golden on the shoulder, then turned to Cain. "See you next time. Appreciate your help." Cain ignored his extended hand. Sparks dropped it as though he was adjusting the poncho. "Glad you're on the team." He turned and waddled away."

Cain cinched his jaw so tightly it might have dislocated and followed him with his eyes. It was not too late. He fanaticized the headline: *County Judge, Teens, Killed in Truck-Train Collision.*

* * * *

Cain pushed the throttles steadily, then rapidly forward. Seconds later the plane broke free of the earth. He climbed steadily into the breaking dawn.

In the park below, the drone of engines faded away. The quiet stillness of the dawn, broken only by a chorus of birds greeting it from the pines and old oaks fronting the railroad, had barely returned before the earth began to shake. Right on time, the four-hundred-thousand-pound Missouri Pacific diesel-electric locomotive rounded Ozark Curve and wailed two long, a short and another long horn blast as it approached the gravel road north of the park. Freight cars stretching for a mile and a half began accelerating as the grade increased. The brakeman handed a cup of coffee to the engineer and he took a sip, gazing down the rails ahead in the cone of light piercing the darkness. It was going to be another boring, long run, he thought, checking the gages just below his windshield.

His face froze in horror. He dropped the cup, seized the emergency brake with both hands and swung it to his right.

The sensation of impact was no more than a bug on a tractor-trailer rig as the locomotive plowed through the '62 Chevy pick-up. As the engineer reflexively pulled the engine brake handle down, in the corner of his eye he saw a vehicle of some sort – at least a big part of it – flipping past and flying toward the trees. Five minutes later and more than a mile down the track, the train rolled to a stop. The engineer and brakeman began the long walk back to the other brakemen in the caboose. They joined in sweeping flashlights into the forest on both sides of the track. As the sky glowed gold behind the hills beyond the river, they discovered a truck frame. The differential and drive shaft weren't far away. As the first shafts of golden morning struck the treetops, they came across the crumpled truck cab, its doors nearly touching, about fifty yards away on the other side of the tracks. Inside were two human torsos: one appeared to be a young man. There was no head on the other. Walking a line from the truck to the point of impact, they found hunks of muscle, a forearm with hand still attached and legs still attached to an exposed pelvic bone. Farther up the track was the missing head, mostly a skull scalped clean, sitting upright as though placed in the gravel. The eyes were open, staring into the Army Air Corps Park.

The engineer relayed the details to the Dodd County Sheriff's Office and, considering the isolated location, was impressed with the quick arrival on scene. Sheriff Golden was shaken but calm, icily professional. Almost immediately he traced the truck's owner. Within an hour his detective work had paid off with positive identifications of the bodies, solemn notifications to next of kin and a sad conclusion: a teenage drinking party gone tragically wrong.

Not long after noon, a Chris Craft Commander drifted from the dock at Army Air Corps Park and into the river. Its pilot made steady progress down the *Fourche Lafayve.* By nightfall he had tied up on the Arkansas River at Dardanelle. A day later the yacht would rendezvous with a southbound towboat out of Memphis and transfer two very heavy ammo cans to it. Two days later Great Circle lines towboat would arrive unnoticed at a private dock at Vacherie, Louisiana.

The mysterious cargo would disappear.

Seven

Nathaniel Pierce sat alone.

Leaning on his elbows, his stubby fingers massaged his tired eyes. Leaning back, he lifts his head and focuses on the long table in front of him. It is covered with a thick white tablecloth embroidered with a gold "MV" at each corner. Eight Windsor chairs are tucked beneath it, bracketed by two more on the ends, including the one he occupied. Pulling a lighter and silver cigarette case from his white linen jacket, he lights up and takes in the lime green walls and ceiling and the deep, brown carpet. He exhales a cloud of grey smoke into the room which seems smaller than it really is, probably because of a low acoustic ceiling.

The décor, Pierce approvingly notes, is tasteful, with the exception of the long, stainless steel counter and cabinet built into the wall behind him, below a service window from the adjoining galley. To his left are two black, basketball-sized portholes framed by navy curtains on brass rods. A large oil painting of the *Monte Verde* plantation house covers most of the opposite wall. Farthest from him a glass china cabinet occupies most of the rear bulkhead, behind facing leather sofas and a low table. He nods approvingly: the walnut furniture was probably Nineteenth Century, complemented by matching wainscoting crafted by the ship's Norwegian builders. Tasteful, Pierce thought, much better than he'd imagined and a welcome contrast to the tar paper shack on a rotting dock at Pilot Town where a helicopter dropped him to board the motor launch.

The launch had sprinted out to match Maria's speed and maneuvered close enough to touch the two-hundred-fifty-foot merchantman. As a crewman grappled the launch, Pierce reached for his free hand and stepped over to a small platform at the bottom of a steep staircase. A bright light from above him lit the side of the ship, and he began climbing, each footstep synchronized with a white-knuckled, hand-over-hand pull on the cool aluminum railing, sticky with sea salt. At the top, Captain Rudolph Garcia observed worriedly, telepathically willing Pierce along. In a few moments he greeted Pierce' brave smile and sweaty palm with a warm handshake and escorted him through a heavy watertight door, down a long central passageway, turning left again into the wardroom. With no prompting, Pierce took a seat while a red-jacketed steward produced coffee and warm pastries. Behind a forced smile Pierce was making a mental note: never do this again.

Garcia, like his employers, spoke nearly accent-free English and was a gracious host in the best Latin tradition. Lean and in his mid-fifties, he looked the part: deep crows feet trenched the corners of his black eyes; a salt-and-pepper beard matched a mane of sculpted hair. Four stripes of gold braid crowded the shoulder boards on his short-sleeve uniform which was only a shade whiter than Pierce's hand-made linen suit.

The officers had duties as the ship entered the channel, Garcia explained, and—even after hundreds of transits—there was nothing routine about dodging barges and towboats on such a busy river. Assured there were no problems with the passenger and nothing more required, the captain departed for the bridge. Pierce sat and watched the door close. The wardroom felt even more inviting: the hastily arranged and long day of travel and the mental exercise of endlessly spinning "what-ifs" had tired Pierce more than he expected. A few minutes alone was perfectly alright. He walked to the mirrored china cabinet and adjusted his red satin tie. In a few minutes another officer would return and escort to the bridge where he'd watch Capitan Garcia dock at Piety.

Even if this command performance is just an exercise in hand-holding, his mind cannot turn off. Nobody would question the cargo manifest; but, if they did it certainly does not include a man traveling against his will, unencumbered by passport or visa or an even an identity known to Pierce. *What then?* In their brief conversation, Garcia had replied that his special passenger had been no problem. No problem. Pierce turned the phrase in his head. That was the only reply South Americans ever had to any direct question they didn't want to answer. Why should the captain be any different or honest? But, Capitan Garcia—in deference to Pierce's status, he deluded himself—had volunteered some details. The mystery passenger guarded by the large man standing in the passageway outside has been no problem because he couldn't be: he has been sedated for the three days since the ship left Cartagena. Why is he sedated, with what, he wonders and pushes away the thought. Is he lucid enough right now to walk off the ship, or will he be carried?

What a pain, I give headaches, I don't get headaches. Screw this.

Ever since his meeting only yesterday at the Cosmos Club, he has been rushed, off balance, growing more paranoid about the very long odds of disaster. Satisfied with his tie, he slicks back his thinning hair and raises his left wrist with a quick jerk to check his Rolex: 2:40 a.m. for his body, 1:40 a.m. New Orleans. No wonder he is tired and jumpy. But, in only an hour or so he will flee from this non-chore and escape upriver to *Bon Homme* for a long weekend as gentleman planter and host extraordinaire at his Vacherie, Louisiana, plantation.

I'll wake up in my four-poster, take coffee on the verandah, feast my eyes on the majestic old oaks and forget this ever happened.

"*Uno mas, por favor.*" Pierce passes his cup through the galley window to the steward. He claws another cigarette from its silver case. A weary Nathan Pierce looks back through the porthole. *Only a little longer.* He wanted to run away.

* * * *

The *Monte Verde* Coffee Co. is a well-respected presence on the New Orleans waterfront. The owners hold a twenty-five year lease and paid ahead. They maintain the wharf and warehouse far beyond the Port Authority's expectations. The contrast between it and the others at irregular intervals along the shore or side-by-side closer to the city is immediately noticeable. Even tourists on the paddle wheel excursion boats passing daily fix on the bright green roof and shiny red sides of the long structure.

The company's PR strategy is one of good citizenship, which is periodically acclaimed in Port Authority publications and gushed over in the *Times-Picayune* business section. The National Association of Port Authorities has highlighted *Monte Verde* in their monthly magazine, noting their addition of mercury vapor lights that promote safety and enable around-the-clock cargo handling. As it was intended, such goodwill also brings some favors that enable *Monte Verde* to use Piety for more than shipping and receiving. During the past four years the Port Authority has waived fire regulations and allowed *Monte Verde* to convert the warehouse into a factory, including gas-fired roasting ovens, packaging lines and external, covered conveyors for loading trucks. The Colombian owners also installed their North American headquarters offices at one end and – more discreetly – a half dozen luxury apartments in space reclaimed above the factory floor, facing the river. Architectural magazines have touted the business-government partnership throughout the world.

* * * *

Maria steams through English Curve, a nearly circular oxbow in the Mississippi, and arrives at the straight range of water that runs all the way to the next curve at Algiers Point, three miles ahead. Capitan Garcia looks through large, deck-mounted binoculars on the starboard bridge wing and immediately sees Piety, bathed in golden light. His tanned face is a mask of confidence, as he turns to his honored guest. "Take a look, we're almost there, *jefe*." Motioning with both palms toward the binoculars, Garcia ceremoniously steps aside as Pierce bends to look. "We could land blindfolded, the smell of the coffee roasting would guide the way."

A smirk, what passed as a smile, crosses Pierce' face in the darkness, and he exhales deeply. *Not much longer.*

* * * *

"Wow. This is just un-freakin'-believable," Lyle speaks to no one, not aware he has spoken the words aloud. He was standing on the wide after deck, a video camera balanced on his shoulder.

"What's up?" Emma turns her head quickly and looks back from the pilot house. With engines idling as they drift in the current, his words carry in the relative silence.

"This new camera is just amazing," he replies a little louder, self-conscious that she has heard him talking to himself. Still standing with his back to her, he focuses the camera on the Interstate 10 bridge passing overhead and begins turning slowing and dropping aim to his right, to the darkened waterfront. "I can practically shoot in the dark. The automatic aperture goes from low-light to no-light. The exposure is constant. The color's perfect. Focus remains constant. It does all the work!"

"I'm so happy for you. Would you like to be alone?" Emma said, wishing she hadn't. "I saw that suitcase, or whatever that is, and I started thinking that the honeymoon was over mighty fast. Is that the camera you were telling me about at Lucy's graduation? Don't point it at me!"

"OK, yes, still married. Last week was the first time I shot it." He swings the heavy camera off his shoulder, cradling it back in the case. "I'm going to edit the tape and give her something really professional. I mean no kidding. This is really a big-deal, professional. It's the kind of equipment TV shows and documentaries use," reverently adding as he admires his possession.

"Haven't heard about any bank robberies lately. I'm assuming it's a gift. The wedding?" Emma looks away quickly, as though distracted. She'd done it again and was embarrassed by the brazen probe and subtle, judgmental comment about his new affluence. Scanning binoculars toward St. Louis Cathedral, Emma hopes that he hasn't heard the question. She hopes that he doesn't know how confused and uncomfortable she and Lucy have been for the past three months. Once close friends— almost family she ruminates—now relegated to the status of poor, distant relatives, they had been miserable at one of the most fabulous bashes of the season. Every set of eyes that caught hers could see nothing but two strangers lurking on the fringe of a generous celebration of love, or something like it, perhaps nothing more than hollow, passionate ambition. "*I wonder what Mary's doing right now.*" She frowns into the warm air and shudders. Again, she thinks: shame on her.

Rees kneels on the deck beside her, gently settling the case into a waterproof locker. He stands and joins Emma's scan downriver. "Ann must have shown him the piece I did on the band."

"There she is. Pass port-to-port. Lay off toward the west bank," she orders suddenly, happy to change the subject back to reality.

"Could have been something I said. We're not talking Sony or Panasonic. It's a freakin' Ikegami EC-35," he spoke like a proud father. "He got some kind of deal in New York, Ann said. Seriously, we're talking about five digits, big five digits, more than you and me together make in a year." His enthusiasm dropped a notch, "Technically it's not even mine, 'cause we weren't married when he got it. She has got a good head for money. It's already added it to some insurance policy she has on her boat or something."

Emma bites her lips and looks at him, showing only a little

annoyance. In disbelief, shock, pity or something else, she says nothing as the launch picks up speed.

A quarter mile down river, *Maria* has left center channel and is slowing to a crawl about two hundred yards off Piety. As it crabs almost imperceptibly closer, the launch makes a j-turn and approaches from behind.

"Do you mind if I shoot the arrival?" The video might be kind of interesting," Lyle enthusiastically beams, anticipating her indulgence.

"Sure, be my guest," she answers, overcoming more thoughts about him and the camera and everything else that now make the inspection tour a little tedious. There was nothing that required any of his attention. "Why the heck not?"

Now facing into the powerful current pushing around Algiers Point off to port, the coxswain backs down the throttle and, as she had instructed, stays in position about fifty yards behind the ship's transom.

The ship's far-aft superstructure rose four-floors above the main deck, a design feature allowing maximum space for cargo hatches forward of it, all the way to the bow. Zooming in, Rees focuses on it, then pulls the view back to include the vertical transom below it. As tape rolls through the camera, the single watertight door opens at deck level and four men exit. The line handlers disappear on the starboard side.

"Can't really get a good look from this angle, but still great video. I'll try to get all the approach and docking. Maybe a nice gift for the captain."

He was right. Docking at Piety St. Wharf, especially at night with fewer visual references from the bridge, would not be as easy as it may appear. Slowing against the invisible and powerful current, the ship angles slowly and steadily upriver. Coming within a few hundred feet of the shore, Emma knows that too much left rudder sends it sideways into channel traffic; too little drives it the other way, accelerating into the wharf and more than likely several feet through it.

Rees is videotaping a perfect approach. Any pilot would be pleased to have documentation of his seamanship.

The door opens again. Backlit by interior light, a dark figure jerks his head left and right, then stumbles and falls. Standing again, the shadow steadies on the doorframe and looks back inside before stumbling toward the rear railing. Lyle has filled the frame with the action.

"Heads up, lieutenant, top of the transom. Check it out. Something's up."

Even in near total darkness the camera records a man, barefoot and in underwear. He staggers back toward the superstructure, rips a life ring off a mount, runs toward the railing, climbs over it and looks down. As another silhouette appears in the doorway, the man at the rail jumps feet first into the black water forty feet below. The camera follows. Only the life ring is visible, nothing else.

"Holy shit! You see that!"

"Dead ahead, coxswain, man overboard, fifty yards off the starboard bow," Lucas shouts. In the time it has taken her to speak she has stepped from the pilothouse, pulled a throwing line from a deck mount and is rushing to the bow. "Standby to recover!"

"There he is, a hundred feet, ten degrees off port," Rees zooms in on a head that has suddenly appeared. Still unseen except through the light-sensitive lens, Rees can see that the swimmer is flailing wildly, his words oddly unintelligible, their terrorized meaning unmistakable. Swinging the boat and steering to follow the camera lens, the coxswain accelerates. The propeller wash splashes against the ship's transom but by the time the boat has moved forward there are no more cries and no sign of anyone in the water.

As Emma shines a search light ahead, voices erupt behind. Lyle swings the camera up to focus on two men, both dressed in white, looking down at them from the ship's port bridge wing which is now brightly lit.

"*Alli, alli,* there!" the bearded man in uniform shouts as he leans far over the wing railing and points toward mid channel. Zooming in, Lyle video tapes the portly man beside him, also dressed in white. The man's mouth is open, saying nothing, and his eyes look like they're going to pop out of his head.

Lyle swings the camera to follow the captain's arm.

"There, lieutenant," he shouts from behind the eyepiece. The swimmer is floating face up, pushed to the surface by a reverse in the percolating undertow.

"Got him," Lucas responds urgently.

Knowing that the river won't repeat the miracle, Rees quickly lays down the camera and snatches another life ring and line, plants his feet and heaves away with one powerful twisting motion. Within seconds of the first, the second miracle occurs: the ring lands with a thud, square on the swimmer's chest; as if shaken awake by the impact, he hooks an arm through it and grasps the line with both hands.

"All stop, coxswain, swing to the stern. Rees, help me haul in."

Emma speaks calmly passing by the pilothouse, impressed by the athletic throw, and takes the helm to make sure the boat's prop won't cut the line or the swimmer. Scott joins Lyle on the dive platform, and the two men begin a slow, steady pull. Within seconds they have their hands on the swimmer.

"On my count of three." Lyle firmly grasps the swimmer's right hand and forearm; the coxswain wraps his arms around the legs.

"One, two, THREE!" They begin tugging at the nearly naked figure and struggle to heave him on to the dive platform, thankful that he is not a large man. After two attempts, he lies on the swim deck, gasping for air. Rolled on his side, he coughs up several mouthfuls of water. He manages to sit up and on wobbly legs helps the men move him into the pilothouse. Panic returns again, and with the eyes of a wounded animal he looks from one man to the other, drawing his knees to his chest. He is quickly wrapped in a blanket, which calms him. Emma, at the helm, looks down and knows that the man is going into shock.

"He's conscious. Breathing's shallow." Lyle reports, as though reading her mind.

"Emergency, emergency, emergency," she speaks slowly and forcefully into the VHF radio, aware that any vessel on the river is monitoring the emergency channel, most assuredly including the crew aboard *Maria*; even if English is a second language for them, it is the only internationally accepted language of maritime disasters. "Coast Guard NOLA has retrieved man overboard *SS Maria* arriving Piety Street Wharf. Victim is breathing. No vitals available." With just one radio transmission from the Coast Guard boat, everyone on the river, including those on the bridge of *Maria*, the emergency room at Hebert Naval Hospital, Coast Guard Headquarters and police and fire departments on both banks are aware of the emergency. "Coast Guard NOLA proceeding to Hebert dock, ETA approximately three minutes, 0210. Request Hebert ambulance." Placing the microphone in its cradle, Emma hears amplified voices, not from the radio but nearby. Her hand on the throttle, she hesitates to look out the window toward the ship. The two men in white are the only crew she can see; those on the lower deck from where the man jumped have disappeared. The one in uniform, the captain she supposes, starts shouting through a bull horn.

"Avast! Avast! We have a doctor aboard. Do not leave the area. We are standing by to provide medical services. Tie up now at Piety Street Wharf. Stand by to hoist aboard. Avast!"

"Coast Guard NOLA hailing *SS Maria*. Coast Guard NOLA hailing *SS Maria*."

"Hebert hailing Coast Guard NOLA. Be advised ambulance standing by at river landing."

Frowning with disbelief, Emma throttles away, gaining speed as the bull horn fades beneath the engine's roar. *Idiots!*

Trying to shake off the weird request from *Maria*, she focuses on the flashing ambulance lights as it backs down the dock, only a quarter mile ahead on the west bank and casting red beacons across the choppy water. She throttles back as the two men stand on deck with mooring lines. The *Maria's* lack of response is perplexing, then makes her angry.

"Roger Hebert, arriving." Reversing engines, the boat's bow wake washes over the low dock as the two men leap on it and secure the boat. Even before the boat has stopped rocking from the quick arrival, two paramedics are aboard and have strapped the patient on a stretcher. Emma begins to breathe normally, standing aside with hands on hips as the ambulance speeds away.

"He's going to make it, guys," Emma speaks, her eyes following the ambulance's short drive to the emergency room, only about fifty yards up the ramp. "Fantastic teamwork. You know it doesn't happen like this all the time. We're good all the time, but sometimes we just get lucky."

Darker thoughts return as she turns to look toward Piety Street Wharf, bathed in golden light spanning the dark river. *Maria* is also brilliantly lit now. Crewmen unload as though nothing happened.

Why?

The ship's lack of response is negligence, inexcusable, punishable under international maritime law. Like a thunderbolt it struck her: *they heard my voice.* Barely able to speak through her clinched jaw, she jumps back into the boat and spits into the radio, "Coast Guard NOLA hailing *SS Maria*." A pause, no reply. "*SS Maria*, be advised patient arrived 0215 at F. Edward Hebert Naval Hospital, Algiers, for evaluation. Repeat: patient arrived F. Edward Hebert Naval Hospital, Algiers, for evaluation. *Maria* hail Hebert on this frequency for status and updates. Coast Guard NOLA clear."

Even if they had a doctor aboard, what kind of idiots think the Coast Guard would opt to stand by and watch them try hoist him aboard rather than deliver him to a hospital five minutes away?

"*Maria* to Coast Guard. Understood. Crewman at Hebert Naval. Will comply with your instructions for follow-up. Captain Garcia salutes

Coast Guard superior seamanship and assistance. *Maria* clear."

"Well, isn't that just special!" Emma speaks, not entirely she spoke the words or only thought them in amazement.

"Stop pointing that thing at me, Rees!"

"Didn't get a thing: the tape must of run out. I'm not sure how much I got. Sorry, lieutenant, but the look on your face," he smiles, happy that he has gotten a rise out of her.

* * * *

The sudden realization that Rees was literally focused on her, even with all that was happening around them, drove everything else from her mind and lit off the same emotions as her drive to work, hours before. She couldn't think of anything to say, or was afraid to, but was relieved that the anger flushing her face moments earlier now disguised a blush.

"Good thing for you, Rees!" she recovers with a hearty laugh shared by all three.

"Matter of fact, I've got an idea. Come with me to the hospital and bring the camera. You have more tape? If that guy comes around, maybe someone could prompt him to make some kind of statement. That would be a pretty good supplement to our incident report."

In the emergency room the attending physician greets Emma with a handshake, a grim smile and words of thanks for doubtlessly saving a life. As they walk to a recovery room, the doctor tells Emma that his examination of the approximately forty-year-old man found only bruised ribs, probably from a fifty-foot belly flop into the river. He is fairly certain that the man is drugged; there are needle marks near his shoulders. With the huge difference of being alive and minor exceptions for the bruises on his face and skull and skin irritation on his wrists and ankles, the patient is not exceptionally different that many others pulled from the river. Also like those pulled dead from the muddy waters, the patient doesn't offer a story about what has happened to him. In shock when he arrived and—as the doctor expected—probably under influence of some drug, the patient has only mumbled a few words, and those are in some Slavic language, perhaps Russian, the doctor guesses.

Emma and Lyle pause in the doorway. A nurse is hooking up an IV drip, and the patient is calmly but intently watching her attach it. As Emma walks to the end of the bed, he looks at her as furrows grow deep in his brow and fear lights up his widening eyes. Emma stands motionless. She smiles. The agitation passed, and whether in fatigue, comfort of a pretty woman's face or both, he lowers his head to the pillow and stares at the ceiling.

Emma walks to his side, sits on a stool and speaks gently as she touches his arm, "Sir, do you speak or understand English?"

He manages to roll his head slightly toward her and frown. In heavily accented Russian he says, "Aingleesh. *Я не говорю по.*"

Emma smiles and nods slowly. Turning her head toward Lyle and the doctor, she speaks softly, "I'll take that as a no. Petty Officer Rees, ready your camera, but don't crowd him. Stay over there. Move slowly. I don't want to startle him." With a wink she adds, "You do have tape in it, right? Start now."

"Are you Russian?"

"*Я Россия,*" he responds, nervously cutting his eyes to meet Emma's, then at the camera a few feet away.

With theatrical exaggeration, Emma smiles and extends her right arm and uplifted palm toward the camera. She then draws her left palm toward his face. Nodding and smiling, she bows toward him. With both arms spread wide, she steps between the camera and man and looks left and right, pantomiming a connection between the two. She turns again towards him and extends both palms.

He begins speaking. For the next ten minutes he tells a fantastic story. Nobody understands a word of it.

Eight

Alexi Zotkin is not afraid. He feels safe, and his mind is clearing, the fog is blowing away. The light over his bed is too bright.

He is happy to be warm, under a heavy blanket, even if he is only beginning to grasp what's going on around him, another strange place. He is sleepily aware that wherever he is now, he's not in danger; there's something reassuring about this place and these people.

His brain still struggles to process the strobe-flash images of horror, but they're receding into the brilliant light. Alexi studies the serious but friendly faces and the muffled voices echoing around the room. He tries to focus: a woman in some kind of military uniform, a man in a white jacket, another, younger man dressed differently and pointing an object at him. It's only slightly frightening, but making more sense. Why can't he think clearly?

It was these people—he remembers a boat and an enclosed truck of some sort—who brought him here.

His eyes widen again in horror as he remembers going under the dark water, gasping for breath, a peaceful drowsiness, then little else. He was drowning, now he's not. His head and chest hurt.

He can't remember much of anything before getting free, running outside, then jumping off the ship. *Whose ship?*

Cold panic overtakes his still feeble senses, even if his body doesn't have the energy to react. There is much he doesn't know, but the concern on these faces is unmistakable; something, even just out of his intellectual grasp, tells him that he can trust them.

As much as he tries to focus, his eyes bounce around the room, then stick on "U.S. Coast Guard" embroidered in white letters above the chest pocket of the woman's blue overalls.

A moment of clarity: *English, that's English. They're speaking English*, his mind is wakening. With maddening effort his senses sharpen. *I must be in America, or at least someplace controlled by Americans. Americans*!

His eyes widen with the recognition and meet hers. She is attractive and responds with an even bigger smile. It is the smile of an angel. Twice she turns slowly toward him, each time engaging his eyes with hers. He follows her gaze; it is a camera.

Why a camera? What frivolous nonsense is this?

His vision sharpens slowly, revealing more. As if jolted by the defibrillator hanging on the wall behind him, he jerks his head off the pillow. Propping himself with his elbows he squints at the camera, then at the pretty face so intently studying him. He's in some kind of hospital.

She places another pillow under his head and smiles.

Speaking the only word she knows in Russian she slowly leads his gaze with her hand toward the camera. "*Da?*" she says again, now moving to stand beside Lyle.

Tension drains from his face and is replaced with a slight smile. With an understanding nod, his toothy grin emerges. He speaks, rapidly at first, then continues with a calm, deliberate narrative.

He tells a fantastic story.

* * * *

Alexi Zotkin, age thirty-two, is a nuclear technician. He is a citizen of the United Soviet Socialist Republic. He is not a Party member, but he, his wife and three girls live well in a comfortable Moscow apartment. For the past seven years he has been on the scientific team which has built three underground nuclear research laboratories in the rugged mountains northwest of Tehran, near the Caspian Sea. Prior to the assignment to Iran, Alexi built and operated nuclear reactors aboard Soviet submarines and maintained nuclear warheads. In Iran he is assisting Iranian scientists in transforming yellow cake into fissile material, building centrifuges and processing spent nuclear fuel into conventional and non-conventional nuclear weapons.

The last thing he recalls with clarity is three weeks before his six-month shift was to end. He is sick at work and passes out. He awakens, perhaps as much as a day later judging from the stubble on his usually clean-shaven face. His ankles are bound together. He is freezing and realizes that he's clutching a blanket to stay warm, lying on the floor inside a small, circular and noisy, vibrating metal structure. He is disoriented and confused.

After some time, again he is not certain how long, he is aware that he is in an airplane.

Happy that he is at least aware of his surroundings, he tries to stand.

A large hand seizes his arm. He manages to raise his head to see a large, dark-featured man who speaks to him in Russian. Over the noise he tells Alexi that his family is well cared for. There's a small sting in his shoulder, caused by another man holding his other arm. He remembers voices; Russian, definitely, farther away in the noise maybe Spanish, English? Another long sleep.

A violent bounce jars him awake, as it has three, maybe four, times before. Then, no more noise, no vibration. The plane has stopped. But, this time there is no more injection. Instead, two men lift him to his feet and guide him toward a large door. With an unsteady step down to the surface, he's guided into the blinding sunlight. The air is heavy, moist and hot. Supported mostly by his arms, he manages to shuffle along as two men walk him to a flat-bed truck. Sitting side-by-side, the trio faces the rear. A hat is placed on his head. One of the men gives him a bottle of cool water. He drinks, chokes, then drinks again. In a few moments the trucks moves. His eyes adjust to see an oddly shaped airplane grow smaller, then disappear as the truck bounces gently into shadow. A tunnel of dense foliage closes around him.

In a few minutes the deep shadow suddenly explodes in bright sunlight. As far as he can see, small trees or shrubs are planted in rows on hillsides rising gently on both sides of the dirt trail. A lurch throws him against the man to his right as the truck turns sharply, then stops. More steady now, his escorts walk him towards a long, single floor wooden building, across the rough boards of wide porch and inside to a chair in what looks like an office. It is furnished only with a wooden desk, tall cabinets and a long table. On both sides and onto the porch, long louvered shutters extend like awnings over wide windows. A single fan rotates overhead; even in slow motion, it manages a cooling breeze.

A rough plank door opens behind the desk, and an older man steps through. He is cleanly dressed with a loose-fitting Hawaiian shirt over brown trousers and high riding boots. He tosses his wide-brimmed straw hat on the rough table and mops his brown face with a handkerchief. He fills a large glass with cool water from the spigot of a tall crock on the table and—pulling a chair to sit knee-to-knee with Alexi—hands it to him. Alexi drains it. The man soothes closely cropped silver hair with both hands and watches. He nods, expressionless and says nothing. He pulls a small photograph from his shirt pocket: it's a color photo of Alexi's wife and children smiling at the camera. Across her chest, his wife holds the October 15, 1983, edition of *Pravda.*

"Cooperate. All is good with them," translates the man who has accompanied Alexi from Iran. "No questions."

A smaller man brings a tray of food—roasted chicken and beans— and places it on the table and departs.

The older man walks to the table and places the photo next to the tray and points at it.

Ravished, Alexi falls on the food. With every bite his eyes he also devours the photo, feebly searching its meaning. He is aware that the old man is leaving. Outside Alexi sees him mount a big horse and gallop toward the jungle. Someone jerks him to his feet and half carries him through a door. The room on the other side is very big. It is piled from floor to ceiling with enormous, bulging bags. The odor is rich, earthy.

"Rest here," he is commanded. With no further encouragement, he falls on a cot beneath one of the long widows spanning the length of the long room.

Groggy but stronger, he awakens in a dark room which even in the darkness he senses is much smaller. The air is still, and the earthy smells are gone. Struggling to concentrate, he feels a steady vibration and an almost imperceptible rhythmic motion. This is not another airplane, he realizes. He sits up and realizes that he now aboard a ship. His head hurts.

He is locked in the small, windowless room furnished with a comfortable bed and a small, enclosed compartment with a wash basin and toilet. Before dawn, at noon and at twilight a guard takes him down a narrow hallway, then outside around what he realizes are two cargo hatches in front of the tall superstructure where he is locked away at the rear of the ship. There is nothing but the vast, cloudless sky and blue ocean to see and no hint of where he is or is going. He still has no idea why he is a prisoner or where he is being taken. He has not seen the man who escorted him from Iran. Perhaps he is long gone.

⸸ The walks end in much larger room furnished with a long table, chairs. A painting of a large home in some sort of jungle nearly covers one wall. Two leather couches and a very large glass display case occupy one end of the room, but he never sees anyone except the guard lounging there. Even with uncertainty and fear, he savors the walks and the good, if unfamiliar, food served through a service window by a small, speechless man dressed in a red jacket.

On the third night the tray includes a small paper beneath his plate. It is a photo of his family, transmitted by radio facsimile to this ship; in the heavily contrasted black and white image, his wife smiles. Is that a bruise around her left eye? He cannot be certain looking at this smeared copy. This time she holds an Oct. 22 edition of Pravda. His oldest child holds a small hand lettered sign: HELP THEM, PAPA. The two youngest hold hands and look at their mother. The picture is indoors, someplace Alexi doesn't recognize.

He walks to the porthole. Darkness has fallen. The ocean is inky black. But, in the eastern sky a full moon is beginning its assent, its pale light shimmering low across the water towards him. *Does this pure light embrace my family, my home? Can they see it now? Will I ever see them again?*

His mind is clearer during the next days. It is time to face facts: his family is in as much – even more – danger than him. He is an expert in nuclear materials and explosives; whoever kidnapped him must know that he cannot build a bomb alone, but they know that he had made some pretty nasty alternatives for the KGB. Even if they release him after his service, he knows what happened in Iran before the Soviet nuclear scientists arrived: no safeguards, carelessness or worse, led to scores, maybe hundreds of excruciatingly slow, painful deaths. He cannot understand. He has done no wrong; he is innocent. He fears that he has no future. But, when's he no longer useful to whoever has kidnapped him, worse fates await his wife and precious girls: death is better than life as Siberian slaves or prostitutes in Asia. With sudden rage he beats on the porthole glass with his fists and screams like a soul cast into hell. Still screaming, he's pushed stumbling into his stateroom and hears the door lock behind him. In a few minutes the door opens and two men thrust him face down on his bed. He feels the sing in his arm and falls into another deep sleep.

When he awakes, three faces are staring down at him.

The one with the youngest features waives the other two toward the door. A curly, dark beard covers handsome Eastern European features. Pulling a chair close to the bed, he thrusts a red leather wallet close to Alexi. It holds a KGB identification card that matches his face. With the same voice Alexi heard days, perhaps weeks ago, he speaks softly.

He apologizes for comrade Alexi's treatment and explains that both men are chosen for an historic mission, one that—with Alexi's full cooperation—will change the course of history. Taking as much time and care as Alexi requires, he will create a lab to his specifications to convert nuclear materials into dirty warheads fitted into artillery ammunition. Realizing that the work will take time, his family will join him at the lab site, which the ship was now approaching. Upon completion, all will be heroes of the USSR, their future assured in the glorious new world order firmly established in North America.

Alexi rises. With pride he takes the KGB man's hand in friendship, grateful for this opportunity, humbled by the faith the Premier and all of the USSR has bestowed upon him. Moments later the door is opened, and a handsome shirt, suit and shoes are brought in. With a warm embrace the KGB man and the guards leave him alone to dress as the ships prepares to dock in the place called New Orleans.

Not one word does Alexi believe.

Hearing no one outside, he steps cautiously into the passageway, then walks quickly towards a door to the ship's small rear deck.

Opening it slightly, he can see a brightly lit dock and men walking on it only a hundred meters to his left. He steps through the door and walks to the rear railing, only a few meters away. Even though it's dark there, there's nowhere to hide, only one place to go. He turns, sees a life jacket locker, but before he can fasten one around his chest, he looks up and sees the KGB agent leaving the wardroom. Their eyes meet, and each is frozen in astonishment. The agent moves first, charging towards him. Still unsteady from the sedative, he manages to close the door. He turns and stumbles into a fire extinguisher. It is heavy, and as the door latch moves, he struggles to hold it with both hands over his head. Summoning some primal instinct, Alexi drives it down as a head appears through the door. Hearing and feeling the sickening crunch, Alexi knows he has killed. There's no time to react; another man is running toward him.

With only seconds before the agent's body is seen lying in the doorway, Alexi staggers, his back against the superstructure, with no idea what to do next.

He is a killer. He will be killed. He has destroyed his family.

He runs to the railing and stares into the black abyss, seeing only their faces. He jumps overboard.

* * * *

"Are you Lieutenant Lucas?" the tall, crew-cut man asks as he strides into the recovery room. He shows Emma an Immigration and Naturalization Agency badge and identification, Emma sees an automatic pistol tucked into his waist under his dark blazer. Through the open door behind him she sees two more men. They're more casually dressed, in jeans, black polo shirts and windbreakers with "INS" stenciled in tall yellow lettering on their backs.

Motioning with his head toward the open door he says, "Could I please have a word with you?"

A few steps down the hallway, but still within sight of the recovery room door, he begins. "I'm agent Todd Burlingame; these are agents John Parker and Frank Hayes. We're with the New Orleans Division."

"Pleased to meet you all," Emma speaks and shakes each offered hand. "What can I do for you?"

"Emma, if I may, I can't tell you much. As a matter of fact, I don't know much more than what I'm about to tell you," he says with less serious and more approachable demeanor. "But my orders are as clear as they are brief: we're to take custody of the man you pulled from the river." Seeing her expression, he continued, "And, no, I don't know why. Driving over here I can only guess. Based on what you've seen and done, we can only assume that the swimmer didn't want to wait around for whatever welcoming party had been set up for him here. The call came from somebody aboard the ship. All I know from the DO is that they seemed mighty happy you happened to be where you were tonight," he finished with a broad smile spreading beneath penetrating blue eyes. "I am aware that whoever is interested in him is way up the food chain, and it ain't us, if you catch my drift."

Emma scanned each face, then focused on Burlingame, "Well, they sure as hell didn't respond to me. If somebody's heard anything from them it's more than I've got. There's nothing I know other than we fished him out and he's alive. No idea why he was in the water. I could be wrong, of course, but I think there's something not quite right on the *Maria*."

An awkward moment passed in silence, finally Burlingame asks, "What's with the video camera? What's that all about? Has he said anything?"

"Actually yes he has, but we haven't understood a word of it: he's speaking Russian or some Slavic language. One of my crew just happened to have the camera. After the swimmer calmed down we got him to start talking. Again, we don't have a clue. He seems to be pretty intelligent. I'm either good at charades or he catches on fast. He got it that—even if we couldn't understand—the camera could, once a translator sees it. I hope it'll help."

"Super, it might be valuable in the right hands," Burlingame replies, confused but regarding her with more respect, and suspicion. "Good, heads-up thinking."

With names, badge numbers and phone numbers exchanged, they cross the hallway.

"Rees, the INS will take it from here," Emma speaks, placing her hand on his back. They're also impressed with your video. They'd like to take it, too."

"Thanks, Emma, call me if you need anything else for your report, but I'm not sure there'll be much else," Burlingame responds, looking down at Alexi. Lyle hands him the cassette. "We'll get a medical release and move on when the doc says it's OK. You guys have done a fantastic job tonight. Many thanks. You may have done more good than we'll ever know. Who knows? I'm thinking the usual 'atta-boys' will come 'round sometime soon. Could be a pretty good, career-enhancing day, lieutenant."

Burlingame left the two agents in the room with Alexi and walked toward the wide emergency room door. For some reason she didn't understand, Emma followed him. From there she saw him walk to a black Ford SUV only a few feet away. He spoke to a short, fat man dressed in white linen. He was pacing, smoking a cigarette. A moment later, both turned and saw her looking through the glass door. The nervous man caught her eye. He practically dove inside the SUV. Burlingame, holding the door for him, turned to look toward Emma. The expression was no longer so friendly. As the SUV backed away, she wondered who the strange, well-dressed passenger was. *Why hadn't he come inside with the others?*

* * * *

As the launch races back across the river the acceleration lifts the hull and Emma's spirits with it. She can hardly contain her happiness. She grabs quick glances at one, then the other man standing on either side, their faces lit in instrument lights. Her mind is already composing her report and the award citations for them. She drapes her arms on their shoulders, "Not a bad night, shipmates," she shouts louder than necessary for them to hear her above the engine's roar.

A minute later she and Lyle prepare to loop mooring lines through the dock cleats. Watching him complete the little task, then step off the boat, she says playfully, "Like it or not, I suppose that I'll have to change my attitude about that damned camera of yours. It may be the key to unlocking what really went down."

Lyle smiles. "It's like the lyrics we worked on down at Tipatina's. You liked it, remember? You just repeated one of the lines."

She was stumped. Even if she would never forget the thrill of being a real insider, of watching him at jam sessions with his musician friends, the music was only background, the lyrics even less memorable. He can be such a child sometimes, she thought.

With hands on his hips he shifts weight from left to right and sings, "Ooh, ooh, ooh, she's got a new attitude! I'm betting it'll go somewhere with the right artist."

"If you say so. You do know that I worry about you, don't you?"

Only a little less unserious, he steps closer, places his index fingers to his temples and frowns with deep thought, "Ah, yes, the tale of the tape. Who knows what that guy was saying? Will the truth emerge? Tune in next week." Dropping the pose and pulling a mock serious pose, he continues, "And, by the way, ma'am, I'm supposing you've got the magic, official U.S. Government claim form to reimburse me for that rather expensive video tape you just gave away!"

Nine

The morning sky grows from grey to the sun's white-hot glow. Even barely above the cloudless horizon, it heats the humid morning and portends the slow boil of midday. The city wakes early as the rhythm of life resumes on the river at its feet and along the bayous snaking into the flatlands for hundreds of miles.

Emma Lucas is oblivious, seeing only her words on paper rolled into the navy blue IBM Selectric. The monster snaps and rattles with each stroke. In successive detail, the engineer's mind animates every moment of the previous night. She leaves nothing about the patient's chain of custody to question; noting the names and points of contact for the INS agents, she begins an official curiosity about the mystery man at the emergency room parking lot. Whatever, if anything, is discovered, Lieutenant Emma Lucas, USCG, has covered all the bases.

Two hours earlier, with his clerical duties finished, she had ordered Rees to rest. Knowing better than to argue, but still puzzled, he left her alone. She didn't want him looking over her shoulder at the award citations recommended for him and the coxswain.

The tropical office day begins and ends early to avoid work in the oppressive mid-afternoon heat. As staff begin arriving, Lucas has already been awake for more than twenty-four hours, an adrenaline rush driving her tired body and mind.

"Quiet watch, lieutenant?" The booming voice brings her back to the four walls of the duty room. She looks over her shoulder to see Captain Jack Clark, district commander, holding open the door to the Port Ops

Center, beaming a smile that brightens the room and Emma.

She and everyone else under his command regard him with great respect. To her thinking, he is the best example of a leader and a gentleman. This is his twilight command and caps a thirty-year career.

Reflexively, she springs to her feet. As he strides towards her with his hand extended, she self-consciously tucks away strands of hair that have fallen around her face bent for the past two hours over the keyboard. "Yes, sir, just another great Coast Guard day in the Crescent City, another chance to excel!"

"Of that, lieutenant, I have no doubt whatsoever. Sounds like you've done us proud. Congratulations."

Wondering how much he knows and how he learned it, she continues, "I'm just finishing my report, sir. I'll bring it in as it comes out of the copier. There are some interesting twists. I can also provide some background, if you wish."

"Fantastic, see you in ten minutes. There are some twists I can tell you about, too."

Entering his office a few minutes later, he accepts the blue three-binder, opens it and begins reading. He waves to a chair in front of his massive partners desk. Anxious to provide even more detail, she instead summons the patience to sit in silence, allowing her boss time to read. Hands in her lap, she looks at the plaques and photos hung on the oak-paneled walls. The occasional turn of a page and a ship chronometer ticking are the only sounds until her stomach woke to realize that breakfast is being served next door in the officer's dining room. The aroma of sausage, toast and coffee are overpowering; her stomach sounds like it is about to walk in there without her.

Embarrassed, she squirms in the leather chair, trying to disguise the rumble. Captain Clark looks up, with a little wink and smile. With his eyes already back on the report, he continues, "Go ahead, take a seat at my table. I'll join you in a minute. I want to finish this. We'll continue over breakfast."

* * * *

He is a trim man, not muscular but fit, and as she matches him fork for fork and outdoes him with the side of biscuits and gravy, she knows why. She wonders how a man of fifty manages to stay in shape; only on occasion as she seen him in the gym, and he does not participate in group runs. He eats like a bird, she observes.

"The ComSta called after you reported in from Hebert. From what they said, I couldn't see any reason to slow you down, so I didn't call. The business with the video camera may be a real stroke of luck, at least for the INS. Getting the swimmer to talk, whatever he said, was genius. I was not aware of your skills at interrogation, and acting. I don't know of many other officers, perhaps no other officers, who could have pulled that off."

"Thank you, sir, you are very generous. The watch standing crew made it happen. I've noted that the camera belongs to Petty Officer Rees. It was his initiative to carry it aboard on the inspection tour. I hope that I've that I've not overstepped with the commendation recommendations. They're at Tab C."

Placing the binder down and leaning back in his tall swivel chair, he continues, "Actually, that's the only part of your after action that I find lacking."

Her heart sinking like a rock, she offers, "Sir, I can revise and expand…"

"No, don't misunderstand. What I didn't see was a write up for you," his wry smile and words an instant relief. "What's with the INS in all of this? On the way in Bob Higgins rang me up on the car phone. He was asking me what I knew about the guy you pulled from the river. I don't think we know, even now, but whoever he is somebody thinks he's important enough to get contact the INS duty and their boss out of bed. Bob seemed rattled, not like him. I don't know how screwed up they must be over there if he's calling me, asking what I know about phone calls his duty officer is receiving at 0300 on his unlisted home number. Have you seen any message traffic from them, or anybody, about transferring custody?"

This was all new to Emma, and her brain percolated. She came up with nothing that might shed any light. "No, there's been nothing, routine or classified. I'll double check before I'm relieved. Anything Top Secret would have come up flagged. I don't get it."

Several officers were drifting in and taking seats at nearby tables.

"Grab your coffee, and let's continue in the office."

He closed his private entrance to the dining room and asked Lucas to shut the door to his outer office. Taking a seat across from her at a round conference table, he continued, "Fine, but I don't think you'll see anything, unless it arrived since we sat down. INS has nothing. Could be verbal, that is not common, far from it, but it does happen. I'm just guessing, but it looks like the swimmer is someone of interest, at least to the people who know things that mere mortals don't.

"He was in his skivvies, no identification, when we got him aboard?"

"Yes, noted in the report."

"Bob said his guy did ask for return-call verification and got it. Get this, it was a secure line at the State Department Ops in D.C. They confirmed a code word the caller left. End of statement. Satisfied that all the codes and secret handshakes were legit, his guys followed orders."

"Yes, sir, they were at the hospital. It couldn't have been more than a half hour after we got there: agents Burlingame, Parker and Hayes. I included their names, badges and POCs in the report…"

"Yes, I saw that. I don't know what else you could have done." Emma's heartbeat slowed. Her head was heavy with lack of sleep, but the conversation kept her alert. "If I may ask, sir, what were the orders? They told me they would assume responsibility for the swimmer."

With deliberation, Captain Clark returned his mug to the table. "I see in your write-up that the *Maria* didn't actually assist with the rescue, not even when you were practically under their transom." He stood and walked behind his desk. He lit a cigarette and opened the binder. "You say that somebody aboard kept shouting that you should return the man aboard."

"Yes, sir, and if I may speak freely, it blew my mind. I was too busy at first with the rescue to notice anything happening on *Maria*, but by the time we had the man aboard the captain and maybe one or two other men were out on the bridge wing shouting at us. By then the crew had started lowered a basket stretcher over the side. I couldn't believe it, but they wanted to man back aboard. My decision, as you know, was to proceed to Hebert. It seemed the only logical decision. As we left the area and after we arrived at Hebert landing, I radioed a Channel 16 distress and got nothing from the ship. I thought it odd, and I did note that they did not seem to be monitoring."

"It doesn't seem likely, but I suppose it's possible. But they were still not tied up. Somebody was on the bridge and could have heard the radio. There's that and their instructions to return the swimmer. Good grief, why? That's nuts. As far as they knew there were asking you to return a corpse. Well, the only thing I know is that the INS did exactly as the State Department, or whoever it was, wanted: they hung around the hospital for about a half hour after you left." He reached to a stack of pink telephone messages on his desk. "Bob called about fifteen minutes ago. It may surprise you—or not by now—that the last they saw of our mystery man was at Piety Street Wharf where they, following someone's orders, dropped him off.

Emma looked at the captain in open-mouthed disbelief. "You mean they just drove there and said 'good-by'?"

"Looks like it. Emma, I don't know what has or is going down with all this." He looked at the large clock over the outer door. "You've got to be very tired by now. It's going on 0650; go ahead and turn over the watch. I want you and Rees to secure and get some rest. I'm sure this will clear up during the day. I'll take it from here. By that, lieutenant, I mean go home and get some sleep."

Emma rose wearily to her feet. "Thank you, sir; I'll pass the word to my crew. I'll be in quarters if there's anything else you need," she replied, hoping that he would hear what she was really saying: please call if you hear anything that makes more sense of all this. State Department?

He walked to the door and opened it for her. As it swung open, Emma could see Commander Jacks, the executive officer. He is draped on the secretary's desk, angling for a good view down her well-filled blouse. Clark shook Emma's hand, then turned to see Jacks, now standing. In more an announcement than conversation, he spoke, "Fantastic job, lieutenant. I speak for everyone in this command in expressing my thanks for a job well done."

It had been a good morning. The praise in front of Jacks was icing on the cake. Emma flashed only a hint of a smile as she strode across the room and headed straight for the operations center.

Lyle was waiting, and they walked to the elevator. Inside, she told him what the captain had said, and added her own words of thanks. He didn't ask, and she didn't say anything about the swimmer's return to Piety.

"I like the part best where he said, 'see you *mañana!*'"

The doors opened. As they walked into the parking lot, heat slapped them like a wet mop. Lyle stopped abruptly and began fishing around in a gym bag. "Oh, I keep forgetting. This is the tape of the graduation party. Tell her congratulations."

She pitched it in the back seat of the Mustang.

With an impish grin, he said, "I hope she enjoys it; there's nothing incriminating on it, only some good music and a couple of beautiful ladies!"

* * * *

The phone buzzed on Emma's desk. It was the captain's secretary. "The captain would like to see you."

Emma welcomed the summons. It has been a full day since she left his office. There was nothing on her desk or in her in-box about the rescue or follow-up questions. "I'll be right there. Did he ask that I bring anything?"

"No. There are a couple of gentlemen visitors. Maybe it's about the rescue."

Taking only a few seconds to straighten her khaki blouse and trousers and smooth her hair in the topknot she improvised to fit under uniform caps, she scooted into captain's outer office a minute later. It was exciting to be a part of the meeting with a couple federal agents who—for all she knew—could be involved in an international incident, an incident in which she had played a key role.

The door to the captain's office was open. Standing in front of his desk, he saw Emma arrive and beckoned her to enter. "Gents, I want you to meet Lieutenant Emma Lucas. Emma this is Jack Foxworth and Ron Mills. They're with the Diplomatic Security Agency."

The pair stood. In turn, each shook her hand firmly and offered polite smiles. They seemed very young, she thought, and dressed casually in short-sleeves and denim, probably not too far up the chain of command. She was right.

"Jack and Ron are wrapping up details about the rescue. They were here yesterday. At their request, we gave them the watch log book and your report for copying. I just wanted them to meet you, in case they had some questions that you could answer."

There was a knock at the door. The secretary opened it slightly and said, "Petty Officer Rees is here."

"Oh, yes, send him in. Sorry, nearly forgot you wanted to see him, too."

Introductions out of the way, the captain asked everyone to sit as he returned to his desk chair.

"Thank you, captain. It's nice to meet you both," Jack spoke first. He wore a dark crew cut, was darkly tanned and slightly taller than his partner. "We understand that both of you have been off duty until this morning. From your report, lieutenant, it seems like time well deserved. Congratulations to your both. We appreciate the opportunity to sit down with everyone involved, with the exception of the third crewmember, John Scott, who we understand is on leave at his home address in Pass Christian?"

"That's correct," Clark responded, not sure how they knew that.

Ron, slightly shorter than Jack, muscular and even more serious than his partner, replied, "That's fine. We'll catch up with him later."

"I think that each of you may have some questions about why there's so much interest in the details of the rescue," a bit more formally as he looked at each of the Coast Guardsmen, Jack continued. "I am authorized to tell you that the investigation, now under the auspices of the U.S. Department of State, is now a classified matter. Although you and others have been involved in the physical rescue and hospital treatment, and those encounters are totally routine and open, we must inform you officially that the larger issues surrounding the incident are considered matters of national security."

Lucas, Clark and Rees sat motionless, each managing quick eye contact with the other. Lyle, compulsively not serious, caught Emma's eye and wiggled his brows in mock shock.

Roy opened an attaché case and retrieved some papers. "These are non-disclosure affidavits," Jack continued as Roy dealt one to each. "Sir, you've seen these before. Signing them is just a formality; I know that each of you holds at least a secret clearance. Captain we know yours is much higher. That notwithstanding, your observations, the log book and report, the video tape you surrendered to the INS, records at the Hebert Hospital, are now officially classified as Highly Compartmentalized Information. With the exception of your man on leave, we have collected affidavits from everyone. In reality, all this means is that you are not to discuss anything you saw or any information that may be written with anyone except agents of the DSA. I repeat, you are not to discuss with anyone, including your Coast Guard chain of command, except the DSA or other federal investigators or operative accompanied by a clearly identified DSA agent."

All three began reading the document, beginning with a paragraph at the top which could be interpreted as broadly as it was brief. It began with "I, the undersigned, and ended with "…under full penalty of the law." The only specifics, if they could be considered that, mentioned an "incident involving Coast Guard, Navy Hospital and INS personnel, on the aforementioned date and location."

"We will witness at the places indicated, below each of your signatures." Roy explained as he stood and offered a pen first to Clark, then Emma and Lyle. After Jack signed, Roy returned the papers to the attaché, placing them beneath the un-holstered Smith and Wesson .380-caliber automatic.

"It may be somewhat awkward should colleagues, spouses, etcetera, who are aware of your rescue ask, but I think you are all aware of the severe, judicial and extra-judicial penalties that can be brought against anyone breaking the agreement you've just signed, and from the very highest levels of our government. It will be up to each of you to find the best way to avoid further discussion," and after a brief beat, "or criminal disclosure." Again pausing to look individually at each of the signers, he concluded, "Very well."

The visitors signaled that their discussion was complete by rising, thanking each with a hand shake. Roy opened the door, followed Jack through, then pulled it shut behind him.

The three sat in silence. Emma couldn't read the captain's face. Whether it was shock at the turn of events or the annoyance of being treated like a schoolboy in his own office and in front of her and Rees, she was not certain. He looked at the door, then to his hands folded on his desk. Finally he looked at her, "Lieutenant Lucas, Petty Officer Rees, I cannot add anything to what you've just heard. I've never been involved in anything like this. Both of you listen closely: these guys mean business. Each of us has just signed a very serious document which I believe originated with some people we'll never know anything about, other than they're way above our pay grade. I can assure you that I'm going to do exactly what I signed. My advice is for you both to do the same. It's obvious that you two rescued a man from drowning, everybody knows that; but, it's going to end there, and it's going to begin right now." This time he stood to signal that the meeting was over.

Eyes fixed ahead as they walked through the outer office, they walked down the blue-tiled hallway, straight to the elevator. Neither spoke. The doors opened on the roof. Alone, they walked to the south edge of the building and—side-by-side—rested their elbows on the wall. The river stretched for miles below them.

Lyle spoke first, "Wow, this'll be something to tell the grandkids about! Spooky dudes!"

Emma winced and stared at nothing, "Maybe great-grandkids is more like it." She was conflicted: elated to be part of something so very important; disappointed, even frightened by the open-ended, perhaps life-long commitment, and the horrible price for even an innocent slip. She worried, not about herself, but for this man standing beside her: the talented and happy musician, the street-smart hustler who had survived his environment to become a good man whose friendship she treasured, who had stumbled into an easy, passing fancy of a marriage, trapped—at least she believed—by the promise of wealth and status. Trying to turn her thoughts back to the documents, to his future, she looked up the river to the city, then back at Lyle. "Maybe we'll both forget all this before then; it will probably be better if we do. Lyle, you're a dear friend, to me and Lucy, these guys aren't playing, they're deadly serious. They're like those people you knew back in Tampa, only with the law behind them if we screw up. Look at me. You and I are never going to talk about this." They were alone, and he was so close, his brown eyes full of childlike confusion. With desire and an unsettling hunger, she wanted to hold him and kiss the handsome face and those lips. She wanted to say more, much more. He would never know truth that she guarded, now as dearly as the documents they'd just signed. Her heart was breaking all over again. But, she knew that she needed something else. Finding inspiration from his wit and endless energy, she turned away, again resting her elbows on the hot, weather-darkened, concrete wall. "And, if you ever hear me blabbing away, just kill me. I'll do the same for you."

* * * *

Hearing a tapping of shoe leather on the linoleum, she turned from her desk to see the captain standing in the open door. She must have looked startled, and Clark smiled until she could lower the phone and put the call on hold. "Emma, stop by when you're free."

"Yes, sir, should I bring anything…"

"No," he interrupted, comically waving his hand side-to-side towards her playfully wrinkling his nose, "it's not about that. Something new," he added with a warm smile and disappeared from view

He was still in the outer office when she caught up, only a few moments later. After they filled coffee mugs he shut the door and joined her on the sofa. After she declined a cigarette, he lit up and exhaled a great grey cloud toward the low ceiling. "How you doing?"

He had not shown her a lot of attention before, certainly not over coffee in his office, but she supposed the day had also shaken him a little. He did seem a little stressed. *Who wouldn't?* "Well, I suppose it's fair to say that this has not been a routine day, or week, as far as that goes."

"That's the truth. I'll drink to that," he raised his mug and studied her. Emma looked straight ahead, her hands in her lap.

"Lieutenant, something has come up," he started, then quickly turned to look straight at her and smile, "something very good, I should add quickly. I don't know how much more either of us could take today. That's why I'm really knocked out by an opportunity that came up, just a couple hours ago. It's an opportunity for someone with your kind of record and at the right point in a career."

Emma was hearing with her eyes as much as her ears; Clark seemed happy about whatever he had to say, but she could see strain beneath.

"The Coast Guard has a medical emergency with the detachment at Adak, Alaska. We're looking for a temporary-duty volunteer to assume command until it can be sorted out. It is a larger detachment and a tough assignment, but there's a real plus for the volunteer: he, or she, will immediately pin-on lieutenant commander." He lowered his gaze, smiled and spoke, now more softly, "Should the officer not return to duty within a month or so, the rank would become permanent."

She couldn't seem to breathe normally and took another sip of hot coffee to revive. Adak was probably the most remote posting in the Coast Guard.

"I've been looking at your service record since I got the call. You'll be promotion eligible in about eighteen to twenty-four months. I think this is a fantastic opportunity for you, one which couldn't come at a more opportune time in your career. I also know that Coast Guard Headquarters in DC is allowing me to select the officer, maybe a perk for being one of the oldest surviving captains around," he laughed and leaned back before taking another long drag. I also cannot think of anyone more qualified or deserving of early promotion than you."

She was one of only a handful of women officers, and women, like her, who were qualified to take operational command, were even more rare. Although she had an excellent record, promotions had slowed. Intellectually, she had accepted that; she had asked to stay longer than normal in New Orleans and at earlier assignments so she could care for her sister and mother. She knew that the extensions alienated her from other officers, perhaps making enemies of some, but it had been fair enough trade off, she had rationalized, for fewer promotions and pay increases. With many years ahead, this offer was startling in its possibilities: it may even restore her place on the promotion ladder for commander. An image of Art Jacks shot across her mind.

"Well, what do you think?"

Emma realized that she had been silent with her thoughts. It was a lot to think about. She wished that she had more time, so she decided to stall, "Sir, it sounds almost too go to be true. What are the chances of this turning into a real assignment? I mean, what's the nature of the medical emergency with the commander? Was there an accident or something?"

Clark's smile faded. He looked toward the ceiling as he spoke, "I don't know the whole story. All I know is that he's in Anchorage, for evaluation."

"Evaluation?"

"Substance abuse, I'd guess. That had happened before on Adak, usually among the Navy community there, which is much larger. It can be extremely stressful for some people. In a place like that the strong get stronger, the weak get weaker. It's impossible to know the cause and effect. I get the impression from the call I got that he was drinking a lot, even got arrested by the local sheriff of a place inhabited by a thousand or so sailors and Marines whose only recreation is seeing who can get drunkest fastest."

"Is there a good chance he'll be returning?"

"I wouldn't bet on it, not in this case. Seems he showed up pretty well tore down at the Navy Birthday Ball. He apparently decided that the Naval Air Station commander's wife was really his style, asked her to dance, then started ripping her gown off. He may not be truly crazy, but—between you and me and the NAS skipper—sending him back would be fatal, really. I think it's a lead-pipe cinch that within a month or two, the Coast Guard's newest lieutenant commander will be on permanent change of station orders."

As the sound and image of all that filled her head, he continued, "And, just as important, even more so in the bigger picture, there are thirty men there. They're enduring the same hardships, operating in some of the worst weather and rough seas the planet has to offer, all while trying to stay sane in a place where there is practically nothing else to fill day after day, night after night, but more work. Makes Kodiak look like a day in the park. They deserve better than they've got with that guy, whatever the cause of his breakdown. They deserve good leadership. They deserve you."

"What's the timing on this?" She knew she couldn't refuse.

"We need someone immediately," he said, turning away from her and stretching an arm to his desk to retrieve a single sheet of paper. He slid it across the little table and laid a pen on top. "It's up to you."

There were no more words. Far away a tow boat blasted its horn as it toiled in the hot afternoon sun illuminating the flags behind the massive oak desk and the paper in her hands. Once again she looked at the serious man, the stern face that she respected and trusted. After a moment's pause, she picked up the pen, and she signed.

Ten

"What in hell is going on, Nat?" Gene Menard screams, exploding in rage as he slams the door behind the dazed bureaucrat. His face is purple, the veins on his forehead are pulsating. At age sixty-five the man is still a body builder, and he still is intimidating, even more so right now. A white polo shirt is stretched across his broad chest and Chinos hug the wedge-shaped man's narrow waist. "Somebody better be fixing this and damn quick, my friend." He punches the air with an index finger aimed at Nat. "Dead or alive, somebody—some-freaking-body—better be figuring out how in hell to get him back here!"

As the words of *Monte Verde's* North American manager flail at his back, Pierce sidesteps him and retreats, mostly stumbles, through the thick brown carpet towards the bar. With trembling hands spilling a good amount, he manages to pour two fingers of Pinch and drains it. It burns into his churning gut. He stares at the top of the bar, then turns quickly. Menard has taken a few menacing steps toward him, but has stopped, knowing that he needs the pathetic little man even more than before. With fists clinched at his sides, he is shaking with anger; his eyes are slits in the round face on the massive head of slicked back, black-dyed hair. Struggling to keep from strangling Pierce he manages instead to hiss, almost in a whisper, "If you don't come up with some solutions to this little problem, you over-educated, pampered little jerk, you soon won't have any more problems to worry about!"

"And, I'll tell you something else that needs to be figured out: how he could just jump off that stinking ship at absolutely the worst time possible. You say he's come all the way from Iran, taken weeks, and your morons let him blow the whole deal right under our noses!" Nat can't believe the words have come from his mouth and somehow summons the courage to continue, "By the way, do you see any feds here? There's not even a customs inspector out there. Are you wondering why? What if the yahoos from INS and Customs had been standing around for the past fifteen minutes? You think maybe we'd be in up to our eyeballs? I've lived up to my end of the bargain."

Menard returns the glare and says nothing. Nat breaks the standoff by turning back to the bar and picking up a phone. As it rings, he spills another drink into his tumbler. "Give me space to sort this out, at least make a plan."

Menard walks toward the bar and snatches a cigar from a humidor. He lights up as Nat mumbles what sounds to him like gibberish. A few seconds later he is calmed to hear comprehensible sentences spoken authoritatively to someone on the other end. He blows a cloud of grey smoke toward him and walks across the conference room to peer out a wall-to-wall window at the *Maria*, only a few feet away.

He hangs up and finishes the drink. Menard is still looking out the window, motionless, hands on hips, cigar chomped in his angry mouth. "I've set the wheels in motion. Within the next hour, maybe a little longer if he's dead, we'll have custody."

"For your sake, for all our sakes, I hope you're right. You've got a good track record. You've never failed before, you better not now. The stakes are way too high."

Even Nat was surprised that the words seemed to cast some calming spell on the pit bull of a man. "I'm going down to check on the unloading," he spoke almost civilly, still not returning Nat's gaze. "Stay on it, my friend. I'll be in my office. No need to call Carta right away. You've got a handle on this." He jerks his chin up, straightens his beefy shoulders and walks to a circular stairway to the warehouse below. Gripping the railing, he stops at the top and looks back. "What was it back in Carta, oh yeah, 'no problem,' right?" In another puff of smoke he was gone. Those two words were also a code, with power even more subtle than those he had just spoken to State Department Headquarters. Sweat beads on his forehead and a cold chill seizes his spine. He remembers his rise to power with *Monte Verde*: the visa fraud in Colombia, his colleague's unfortunate accident.

The ringing phone shatters those images, jerking him back into his present gut-wrenching dilemma.

He hears the voice of INS agent Todd Burlingame, "I've been asked to call this number and provide assistance…"

"Yes, yes, you are speaking with Verdant, Mr. Burlingame," Nat cut him off. The code name said everything the caller needed to hear. "You know where I am. Two questions: do you understand the sensitivity of your assistance? How fast can you get here? The call lasted ten seconds. Ten minutes later Nat heard footsteps climbing the steel staircase. The big man appeared, stopped and looked to see that they were alone.

Nat had turned off the lights and spoke from the darkness behind the bar. There was no need to show his face. "Sit down and listen; there will be no notes, now or ever. I'll make this very simple: a 'John Doe' was pulled from the river less than an hour ago; the Coast Guard has taken him to the Navy hospital; we do not know his condition, even if he is still alive. His identity and presence here now officially HCI, which is now and probably always will be limited to only a few individuals in Washington, D.C. You're here because involving other operatives will expose means and methods and the real possibility of retaliation from some very disagreeable people. It's why your Regional Director has been contacted and secure voice transmission have been made to your duty officer. Here's all you need to know: using all discretion, including disinformation, you are authorized to identify yourself to hospital and possibly Coast Guard personnel and take custody on authority of the INS. This man is considered dangerous in the extreme; deadly force is authorized—and expected—should he attempt escape. Do not return here without him. I repeat, Mr. Burlingame, you will not fail because you cannot fail. Do you understand?"

* * * *

Alexi Zotkin, dressed in blue hospital scrubs, robe and slippers, arrived an hour later at Piety Street Wharf, exactly five minutes after Burlingame's call. He suspected nothing until he arrived at the top of the stairs where two men stepped from the darkness on both sides and penned his arms behind him. Burlingame started toward his shoulder holster until he recognized Nat's voice, "We'll take it from here."

Burlingame watched Alexi muscled through carved teak doors and turned to look at Nat, seated at the end of the long conference table between them.

"Well done. All concerned in your chain of command will be contacted later today for proper disclosures and all. Please join me," he said pleasantly, rising and walking toward the bar. The red light glowing softly on the urn was the only illumination in the dark paneled room. "Tell me what's gone down since we left the parking lot."

The INS agent served himself, and Nat walked to the window and parted the draperies, just enough to scan the wharf. The artificial yellow light spilled across the long table behind him. The sight of his Chris Craft Commander now tied up at the bow of *Maria* pulled his face into a satisfied smirk. "Any problems?"

"Like I told you at the hospital, it went off OK, no questions at all. But, I've never seen a video camera before; maybe something new for them. I stopped it when I arrived. The guy was talking in some foreign language; they claimed nobody understood anything he said. Anyway, we got the tape, no hassle: 'National security' and our badge numbers was all it took. The doctor and this coast guard woman seemed happy, didn't make a scene."

"A damn video tape? Why the others with you? This is extremely sensitive." Nat spoke tersely and kept his face turned away to hide his anger.

"It would have looked weird, INS working solo on a custody case. We don't do that," he answered and laid the tape on the conference table. "This is it."

The effect on Nat couldn't have been any more terrifying if it had been a ticking bomb. He jammed his hands in his trouser pockets and tried to control his voice as the draperies fell shut. "You've got names?"

"Absolutely, a woman, lieutenant Lucas and a sailor. A third Coastie was out in their boat. That's the only thing that was in any way unusual, other than seeing a woman officer. There aren't too many of them, at least not that I've ever seen driving boats around. They left right away. We left Hebert maybe a half-hour after you and drove straight here, green lights all the way. Even the Quarter's dead at this time of day. Your friend was no problem, just sitting in the back seat looking at the scenery like he'd just got here from Mars."

A video tape! Pierce clutched the edge of the table to steady himself. He turned back to the window. Below two men walked their wobbly prisoner toward Menard's yacht. He followed them aboard. Moments later the craft nosed into the big river and sped upriver, past the city.

* * * *

By mid-morning Pierce is fighting off a full panic attack. He was struggling to keep his brain from spiraling off its axis: bad luck on top of bad luck, at least one, perhaps two, serious witness, official records, a video tape and, who knows, maybe news reports. There were too many moving parts.

He spoke of none of this to Menard, and in the hours it took his partner to motor upriver to Vacherie with Alexi, his plan had jelled.

The boat boy refueled Nat's Commander, and as the oppressive heat began to fade, he piloted the antique wooden yacht from the open-air flying bridge. Far below the engines purring. Passing breeze cooled his face. The trip would take him far past the city; day would dim to twilight along the way. He would pass scores of moored barges and miles of industrial development and—at occasional intervals between the stacks and tanks—the more interesting anti-bellum mansions that had outlasted the onslaught of the Twentieth Century.

Not until he climbed up the ladder to his dock and walked through its boat house did he see his beloved *Bon Homme* framed by a furlong corridor of old oaks. Like golden topaz set in the mansion's cream and green trim, the porch lights glowed softly across the wide porch and gallery. Cicadas buzzed dully in the stillness, and fire flies blinked silently beneath the massive Spanish moss-draped oaks and far into the darkness on both sides of this magnificent promenade.

* * * *

He pushed sheets of paper into the fireplace and watched each one burst into flame, then ash before feeding in another. Before leaving the city, he repeatedly dragged a powerful magnet over the tape and had viewed it twice from beginning to end to ensure there was no image left. It was the last thing to enter the barbeque pit on the back verandah.

The two Diplomatic Security agents had interviewed everyone involved, taken records from the hospital and the Coast Guard and gathered non-disclosure statements. Nat was relieved to hear of the doctor's move next week to the Bethesda Naval Medical Center in suburban Washington, D.C. That was a real break. Unless he spoke Russian—which he didn't, the agents reported—he would never be a threat. After a few shifts in the big-city emergency room, he would forget the strange patient, why he was there, or where he had gone.

The news about the Coast Guardsmen was not so assuring. Nat believed that the disclosures would keep them silent; but, there would also be doubt. There was no way of knowing if any future queries and absolution from their statements of secrecy would lead back to him and the people he feared. If there were weak links, this was it. The most troubling was the rudimentary psychological snapshot of the off-duty sailor they'd tracked down in Mississippi. They'd found him in his neighborhood tavern, and inside of ten minutes knew that, even with his best intent, this confiding, low-intellect would never resist bragging.

The other two were also troublesome, especially the officer. Her report officially linked the *Maria* and lack of response and possible civil penalties. He knew that she would not forget the panicked attempt to have her return the drowning man to them instead of saving his life. She wouldn't forget. *Why did she make the tape?* As the cassette tape melted, he shuddered. *Is there a copy?* His paranoid mind was working overtime; that was impossible, he rationalized. *But, why in hell had she made it in the first place?*

Only one player lifted his funk: the Coast Guard District Commander. Captain Clark was his ace in the hole, a team player, a regular guest at *Bon Homme*. And, if the implications of that weren't enough, through the years he had received favors for his less-than-diligent inquiries into *Monte Verde's* cargoes and crewmembers arriving and departing the New Orleans waterfront. He knew the score and the players who had very long memories.

Neither city or parish police had been involved; it had been Coast Guard all the way, so there was no public record, even in the microscopic type the *Times-Picayune* used once a week to chronicle police responses. Four days later a story did appear in the paper's state edition, but only three men knew its real significance:

Fisherman's Body Found
Third This Year in Bay St. Louis

(AP) -- Mississippi officials recovered the body of a man in Bay St. Louis. He is identified as John Scott, 38, of Pass Christian, Miss. The body was found floating about 5 p.m. yesterday in Cutoff Bayou, at the south end of the Diamondhead Airport, according to

Deputy Sgt. Lisa Mason, Hancock County Sheriff spokesman.

Mason said two fishermen saw a partially submerged 14-foot flat-bottom boat adrift as they left Cutoff Lake. The body was recovered from undergrowth along the Bayou's north shore, at the southern end of the Diamondhead Airport runway, about a mile from Bay St. Louis.

"This is a tragic accident. Judging from the amount of water in the boat, it looks like he fell overboard and couldn't get back in," Mason said, "Foul play is not suspected. Unfortunately, it is possible that alcohol was involved." Mason said this is the third drowning reported this year in the waters of Hancock County.

Police said the deceased lived at the Pearl River Mobile Home Park. He was on active duty at the U.S. Coast Headquarters in New Orleans.

Captain Clark heard the news about six p.m. the night before. The Hancock County Sheriff's Office called the CGNOLA duty officer who searched the dead man's service record and called his counterpart in Seattle. By nine p.m. a somber Coast Guard lieutenant drove in a misty rain to a motel-turned-apartment building near the docks in Tacoma and knocked on the door. Scott's wife, estranged, it turned out, unwound from her client long enough to slip on a pink terrycloth robe and answer it. Defensiveness and indignation quickly melted to joy as the she heard the sad news. Only then did she invite him inside, graciously throwing an empty pizza box on the orange shag so he could sit and unpack paperwork from a briefcase.

By now a cautious man in t-shirt and shorts emerged from the bathroom. He rubbed the grieved widow's shoulders as she signed to collect her dearly departed's life insurance. She even managed a tear.

The next-of-kin notification lay on top of the routine overnight messages on Captain Clark's desk as he arrived early the next morning. He was reading it as his private, secure phone line lit up. His booming greeting was instantly electronically scrambled and encrypted. A slight echo of his breathing reverberated down the line, indicating a connection, from somewhere, but he heard no reply. A few seconds later a voice he did not recognize spoke slowly. "Be a shame to get two more NOK notifications, worse to see a career end so badly, so close to the finish line," the monotone voice sounded mechanical. "Check your resources, captain. The answers are right in front of you." When the line went dead his hands shook so badly that he used both to cradle the hand piece.

In the time it took to steady himself enough to pour another cup of coffee from a silver pot into a gold-rimmed cup, he knew the fortunes of Scott's fellow heroes would also have to change. Their lives and his depended on him finding a way to remove both from New Orleans and from their friendship, immediately. *Resources in front of me?* Like a madman he began tearing through the pile of messages on his desk, scattering the papers, hardly comprehending anything he read. He did it again before it hit him like a lightning strike. His eyes wild with animal fear seemed to pop out of their sockets as they scanned two sheets of paper lying side by side: an emergency with the command on Adak; the other a seeming frivolous request from the Navy for individuals interested in music. He sat stunned, looking at them as if they were the last seats on the last lifeboat off the Titanic. *How did they get here?*

He collapsed in his leather chair and covered his face with both hands, then jerked forward nervously scanning the office, even behind his chair. He jumped up and snatched the blinds shut. He felt like somebody was watching him. He tried to breathe deeply, regain control, but he was panicking like a child lost in a house of mirrors. Scott's death was no accident, nor were the caller's threats and knowledge of his very private life and the contents of the messages on his desk.

Captain Jack Clark was terrified. He hated himself but he knew what he must do.

Eleven

No one is ever ready for Adak, Alaska.

It lies about two-thirds of the way down the Aleutian Island chain, a path of giant stepping stones from North America to Siberia, separating the Bering Sea from the Northern Pacific.

Emma, like everyone else, is arriving by air. From that perspective the island is breathtaking. Brilliantly lit in the sun's low angle in the northern latitudes, Mount Moffett offers the first glimpse of the tiny green island. Its snow-capped peak shines for hundreds of miles in all directions. Seen like this from inside the sturdy Reeve Aleutian Airlines Lockheed L1011, she begins to doubt the horror stories about life there; camp-fire stories, exaggerations to scare the uninitiated, she thinks. But, as the twice-a-week shuttle begins its landing descent—more a dive—brilliant day quickly becomes an eerie grey semi-twilight. The old workhorse of a plane begins shaking violently, shoved around by the unseen crosswinds. Most of the passengers begin gripping armrests and stare at the cockpit door, expecting some explanation. None comes. Seconds later the pilots among them wonder why the airplane is not losing speed, but is accelerating. For what seems far too long there is no visibility at all. Those brave enough to keep looking suddenly see a carpet of lush, green tundra that ends abruptly atop cliffs over rocky beaches. Wind-driven waves crash ashore, fading from deep blue to green to white spray launching skyward. Two miles south the sea becomes a gentle wash across a pebbly beach. This is the base of the runway, now alternatingly visible through left or right windows, depending on which way the aircraft fishtailed to maintain a landing approach. Silent prayers are answered as the airplane bounces, once, twice, then violently twists straight down the runway outlined in strobe lights piercing the odd darkness of noonday twilight.

White knuckles on talon fingers relaxed, many dig in again as a wall of rain suddenly blasts the plane from the left; the sizzling noise intense, unnatural. At the same moment downtown Adak is barely visible through the rain streaked windows. There's not much to see: maybe ten or fifteen bare metal structures built low to the ground behind some airplane hangars anchored to the earth by steel girders and cables. Tall grass lashes left, then right and back again as if parted by some frenzied, unseen brush. Trucks, bull dozers, metal shipping containers, oil drums and assorted junk punctuate at odd intervals along the taxiway.

Relieved when the plane rolls to a stop, Emma and her fellow passengers carefully pick their way down the wet metal stairs, grasping handrails to maintain balance in the wind. With nothing to hold at the bottom of the stairs, several are knocked off their feet on the wet tarmac before all are herded through driving, horizontal rain toward a small door in the side of a large storage building. Gamely assuming, incorrectly, that the weather is some freak occurrence, they spread out and gaped around the cavernous space. At the bottom of the high metal wall at the rear they see people standing, most smiling and waving through a tall chain link partition. Above them is the only color in the barn-like structure. It is a brightly colored, amateurishly painted mural: between green and brown palm trees and grass skirted dancers, two-foot tall yellow bamboo letters outlined in red proclaim, "Welcome to Adak: The Pacific Island Paradise."

In a few minutes those happy campers will board the L1011 for the return flight to Anchorage. After two years, each will be free from Adak's relentless assault on their bodies and minds.

With the exception of McMurdo Antarctic research station, the newcomers are now in the most remote, inhospitable and, with the exception of combat, dangerous U.S. military duty location in the world. This is Adak, Alaska, where the weak get weaker, the strong get stronger, and the leading cause of death is suicide.

The dangers, seen and unseen, predictable or not, are constant. Williwaws, highly localized storms with straight-line winds of more than a hundred twenty knots, appear without warning; they can literally suck the breath from a human body after tossing it around like a rag doll. An unfortunate step on a patch of thawing tundra can swallow the offender in the peat-like substance below, and then close without a trace. But, earthquakes top the list. No less than a dozen shake the island daily. The Aleutian Islands lie atop the Pacific Rim of volcanoes between two tectonic plates that are in constant apposition. No one knows when survival may depend on running to higher ground at the base of Mt. Moffett, itself a volcano. Earthquake sensors along the chain may give a half-hour warning of an approaching tsunami, long enough it's hoped to make the fifteen-minute dash for life. The dangers and the unspoiled, brutal beauty of this forgotten island coexist in a netherworld where even the sun is a rare visitor, seen about a half-dozen times a year through the angry clouds ceaselessly screaming overhead.

Hundreds of years ago most of the indigenous Aleut population deserted Adak and the westernmost islands. Their remaining descendants were massacred by Russian fur traders in the Eighteenth Century or relocated by U.S. forces to escape the Japanese who had taken the western end of the island chain at the beginning of World War II. For hundreds of years the only constant inhabitants were enormous rats descended from those who jumped off Russian sailing ships, sea lions, seals, otters and the fox and caribou brought there for sport after the war.

The modern human population is all military, their spouses and children. The sailors' vocation is tracking Soviet submarines exiting USSR ports and transiting south from the Arctic Ocean and Bering Sea into the northern Pacific. The full-time surveillance is provided by Navy patrol aircraft that constantly fly over millions of miles of ocean, from the Bering Strait south to Midway Island, east from the Kamchatka Peninsula to the U.S. Pacific northwest coast. Others on Adak listen for passing submarines on highly sensitive acoustic microphones laid on the ocean floor. A contingent of Marines guard buried stockpiles of highly classified munitions.

The Coast Guard's mission on Adak is directly tied to the wretched weather. The Aleutians lie along this unique demarcation between some of the world's most powerful forces, where frigid Arctic air and water from the north assault the warm Pacific's relentless Bamboo Trades current from Asia to North America. The result is nearly constant rain and snow. Continuous howling winds drive seas that can defy measurement along the rhumb line connecting Asian and North American ports of call and through some of the world's richest fishing ground. The Coast Guard is on Adak to try save the seamen who invariably will be caught in one perfect storm after another.

The day Emma arrived nearly a month ago, she joined about fifteen hundred highly trained servicemen and women on the tiny island, unknown and unseen combatants in the long Cold War.

* * * *

"There's a call for you, ma'am, from off island," mumbled Emma's clerk, a phlegmatic skeleton who never smiled. He stood dumbly in the doorway to her office, then shuffled away. During her first weeks on Adak she had not understood the significance of an "off island" call; now she realized her privilege: as a commander she had direct access to one of about a dozen dedicated phone lines. Although she didn't mind waiting like everyone else for a connection for a weekly call to her sister, she did savor this perquisite. Talking to the "outside world" any time she wanted was almost as good as leaving the island, even if the trip had only been in her head. But, this call from Captain Clark in New Orleans would erase even that small comfort.

"Everything is fine here, Emma," he began, knowing that his tone was ominous. He also knew that she wasn't a particularly social creature. Even when she was just down the hall from him, or even in the dining room, she wasn't one for small talk. He knew that just calling her now was awkward, so he pushed ahead. "I got a call this morning from the Naval Investigative Service, followed-up with an official message. Are you alone?"

She stretched the phone cord as she walked around her desk and pushed the door shut with her foot.

"I don't know what this is all about, and I'm sure there has been some huge mistake. But, this isn't routine, it is serious, at least from what I can tell. I'll just lay it out as simply as I can: they've opened an investigation involving you. I wanted to give you heads-up before you saw the official notification."

The walls of the small, low-ceiling, windowless room closed in on her. She suddenly held the phone with both hands as she hurried back behind her desk and sat. There was a pause, and the captain didn't fill it. "What?" she managed to gasp as her small world suddenly grew even more threatening, the storm outside now matching the one raging in her head.

"NIS said there are allegations about your associations, people you know here. They got your name during a couple of interviews, from people they're looking at. Listen, it's probably another case of the young Sherlocks adding two and two and getting five. Try keep it in perspective; they're just casting a net. These are only allegations."

Like the fateful earlier conversation over coffee in his office, she didn't know what to say. "Captain, I can't even imagine what you're talking about. I don't have any idea…"

"I understand. They certainly didn't tell me anything. I wish I were joking, but there's nothing funny about this stuff. Get hold of the message, it's probably being released right now."

"Allegations of what!" What on earth are they talking about?" she leaned on her elbows, eyes closed, supporting her head with one hand on the phone, the other on her forehead. She spoke loudly, almost yelling, then regained control as she realized that she was nearly shouting at this man she trusted and respected. "Sorry, sir."

"It's alright. Your reaction is understandable. Don't worry about me. The NIS investigations are into smuggling, drug trafficking and prostitution. The message only notifies me that a member of my command is under investigation. There are no specific charges, only mention of people you know here. All I know is what I got from the phone call."

"I hardly know anyone there. You know me. I can't believe this."

Emma, I know you and who you are. You're a damned fine officer and human being. You're certainly no criminal. Everyone knows that's the truth. I have no doubt that once they check things out all of this will go away."

His words calmed her. She lifted her head, sat back and took a deep breath. Tears welled up.

"But, there's something else. Even if they don't find anything to support their nutty ideas about some crime, they're also starting a personal background investigation."

"I suppose that would be routine if my name had come up like they say it has." Emma frowned at the opposite wall and listened closely for his reply. Hearing nothing immediately, she continued, "Sir, my clearance was reviewed, what, not even a year, eighteen months ago?"

"I mentioned that, too. I'm afraid this'll be a brand new game. They'll probably squeeze these dirt bags first; people they already know are criminals and liars, into what you may know about them, which could be a positive for you."

"What dirt bags? What do you mean, 'first'?"

"Get hold of yourself, this is where I'm afraid things are going to get nasty." He paused, disgusted at what he had done to destroy her good name and career to save his own. "Emma, they claim you may be unfit for service because of your moral character."

The statement hit her in the chest; she learned forward and held on to the desk with her left hand to steady herself.

"This is the part that disturbs me the most. Those claims are hard to prove…"

"What claims, for Pete's sake!"

"…but they're also hard to disprove, especially if they're anything at all they can tie to you. He wouldn't say how many, but he said they've interviewed some people you've met socially, I guess. They say they've also got two sources here at the command who can corroborate…"

"What in the world are you talking about, sir," she shouted again, now not caring how it sounded.

"They are willing to corroborate situations, your associates and your habits that would verify immoral sexual orientation."

"Oh, captain, no!" she sobbed, her voice choked as tears filled her eyes, "no, no!"

"Emma, I'm sorry," he spoke truthfully but without repentance for his secret slander. "I know who he's talked to here. He had to tell me that," he spoke with faux sympathy. "I tell you this as a friend and as an official responsibility. The two individuals here know that they cannot have any contact with you until this is cleared up. When NIS talks with you they'll tell you the same."

While he spoke her mind spiraled out of control, in ever widening circles that led nowhere. She was not a social animal. She didn't have conversations at work, or dates. Until well after her mother's death she and Lucy, and certainly not alone, had rarely had so much as a dinner and drinks on the town. When she and Lucy had gone out it was usually with Lyle to one of his gigs. Her mind went into higher gear: she didn't have any enemies, at least that she could recognize as such, she'd never had any trouble with anyone, and she had been left alone to do her job and take care of her family. What kind of moron or jerk or whatever could imagine some weird, secret, illicit social life in all that? The outrage was nearly unbearable. She lifted her head and wiped her eyes, "Who, who on earth could say such horrible, untrue things about me?"

"Emma, I cannot even begin to understand how you're feeling right now, and I'm sorry. Please hear me: I'm passing the names along so you won't be blindsided when you seem them in the message and have to deal with this all alone."

"Yes, sir," she spoke then covered her mouth with her left hand to keep from crying out.

"NIS says they've talked to Commander Jacks…"

"What?" was all she could manage in a hoarse whisper, her eyes widening in shock.

"And, there's one more: petty officer Rees."

She didn't remember much after that. She couldn't even remember how the call ended, or if she'd even thanked him. Her heart and soul had been ripped from her body. Nothing made sense. There was no thread of sanity she could grasp. There was only shock and disbelief and unbelievable pain and despair. *Lyle? Why?*

She ran to her private bathroom, threw up and cried. Has he lost his mind? Had he no awareness, even at the most superficial level, of the friendship and love she and Lucy shared with him? Is this why he suddenly cut them from his life and wound up married to a stranger? And, even if that were somehow the case, he had never seemed angry or hurtful afterwards.

She washed her face, fell on her side on a sofa and cried quietly into her knees hugged to her chest. The death of her father, her mother, had not hurt like this. She was betrayed, forsaken, alone, helpless and thousands of miles away, where even a phone call is not guaranteed, now even forbidden. *Damn Adak, Lyle, my pathetic life!* Wisecracks about the island as a penal colony, a place where hope is abandoned, were horribly, mockingly true. She was the condemned. She actually considered bursting through the door, running across the tundra and jumping in the sea.

The intercom buzzed.

She sat up and dried her eyes. After a deep breath she pressed the intercom button, "Yes?"

"Ma'am, the comms center says they've got a secret message 'for your eyes only.' With your permission, I'll send someone to sign for it."

"That's OK; I'll go get it myself. I, I could use a break."

"Aye, aye, ma'am, but it's pretty rotten out there, but it may be easing up some. You might want to wait. You sure you don't want me to drive?"

The brief exchange somehow brought her back to situational reality, one in which she was still in charge. The awareness was somehow a relief. It turned her senses again outward to the unending assault of wind and rain on the old building, not much more than a temporary shelter when it was built decades earlier. She looked at the foam core dropped ceiling. The guys who built this thing lived in tents. She was grateful for the luxury of just being sheltered from the storm.

"No, it's OK. I'll wait for a break. What's the number for the tower? I'll check with them before heading out. Thanks anyway." She copied the number on a note pad, then dialed it.

At least the storm is something here and now.

Emma stood behind the closed door before opening it. All eyes swept towards it as it opened into the big outer office, the headquarters of a remote Coast Guard detachment, the only one commanded by a woman. She passed first between rows of desks, then farther into the space used as garage, workshop, warehouse, command center, bunkroom, galley, lounge and gym for the twenty-man detachment. More than a couple remembered that the prior commander's closed door had been one of the first signs of a mental break up and retreat from them and, in the final days, any grasp of reality. Emma sensed this and called each by name as she passed.

At the far end she stopped and looked through the small window welded into the wide sliding door. Straight ahead the long pier disappeared as though draped with a heavy grey curtain. She saw her father. She remembered how hard she had worked at his side, the faith he had in her. She remembered struggling after his death to keep her family together. She saw the pain wracked, emaciated face of her mother, the look on Lucy's face at graduation. Maybe she had seen worse times, even if right now she couldn't remember any. "First things first," he'd always said; he'd never given up, and she wouldn't either. *Damn Jacks and Rees, I'm not a quitter.* She would go on, and she would fight, until she couldn't.

* * * *

"Em, I love you," was the only thing Lucy wanted her to hear, and she knew she had to say it quickly.

Since Emma arrived on Adak six weeks ago, she had learned that the connection could drop away at any moment. In frustration the sisters had learned to edit, speak quickly, to say the most important things first. "Actually, there is a lot of news here, but all of it is about as weird as everything else, but I do have some good news."

"Great, give me the good news first, I need it."

"I've got a job. I'll be starting next week at the New Orleans Police Department as payroll and audits accountant. Mr. Hebert must have put in a good word."

"Lucy, that is absolutely fantastic; you're making my day, week, year. Way to go, kiddo! I'm so, so very happy, Lucy. Don't underestimate yourself, though. I don't have any idea if he spoke to anyone about you. I can certainly understand if he didn't. He has a lot on his plate. Either way, Roland is solid gold, a rock. How's he doing?"

"I haven't seen him in weeks, maybe once at church right after you left. He must be on something intense. You know how he gets."

"I hope so. It's nice to see bad people get what they deserve." She cut herself off; there was no need to say any more about exactly which bad people she'd like to see punished. She changed the subject, "The last interviewer did ask if I knew anyone with the NOPD. When I mentioned his name it was like everything changed, everything seemed to be going my way. We spent the rest of the interview just talking about the city, how the police need good people. They called me the next day with the offer."

"I am so proud and happy for you," she spoke with real joy. She lifted her eyes from the picture of a happy family made long ago, worlds away, and to the long runway she could see from the windows of her Spartan room. The low clouds were a lighter shade of grey, what passed for a beautiful day there. "My sister, the cop!" Emma's laughter quickly brought tears; she was so far away, so far removed. She ached to hug her sister and to feel something in return.

"The other news is about Lyle. I'm sorry. I don't know how to describe it, good or bad, just pretty damned interesting and just about as goofy as everything else we know about him lately. Em, he's gone!"

"What do you mean? Oh, Lucy, please don't tell me something has happened…"

"No nothing like that, I mean he and that witch of a wife or whatever she is don't live here anymore. I don't know the details, but as I was walking last night, those two nurses who live below him were having their evening cocktails on the porch, like they always do. They called me over to join them. Get this, he's transferred to the Navy or something like that, and she didn't go with him."

"The Navy?"

"That's what they said. All they knew for sure was that they'd heard some serious fights from upstairs. Right after that they didn't see her car parked there anymore. You know how those two are: they could get a mute to talk. Next time they saw him he was helping movers pack his stuff. He told them he was on his way to Pensacola and was going to be commissioned and in charge of a band someplace. Here's the kicker: he told them that she had left him, was living with that Jacks son-of-a-bitch, pardon my French. No love lost there: he always looked at them like they were freaks or something. The bastard even had the balls to ask if they'd heard from you. Can you believe that shit?"

"Lucy, your language."

"I'm sorry, Em. I don't know what to think. If you ask me all of this is pretty damned interesting. Everyone acts like a bunch of trailer park trash and it's you who's being investigated as unfit and send to the ends of the earth to rot. Right, Emma Lucas is the problem! Sorry, it just makes me mad, and I don't know what to do."

* * * *

The legal officer was a nervous young man who looked to be about sixteen years old. If he had graduated from law school, she estimated, it could have been last week. He and an officer from district headquarters in Kodiak, arrived on the Reeve shuttle from Anchorage and went directly to her office. Their arrival was unannounced. Like everything else in the past two months, Emma knew nothing. She had not even been asked for a statement.

Immediately after she seated them and closed the door, the legal officer placed his briefcase on his knees and opened it, pulled a single sheet of paper from a thin manila folder and laid it on her desk. Staring at it and avoiding eye contact with Emma, he said only, "You can sign at the bottom."

Her face tensed, then burned red with anger as she read the single paragraph: her resignation. The officer was there to witness her signature.

All she could see before pushing it away was the horizontal line on the page with her with her name typed below it.

"I will not sign this," she managed to say calmly, even with her heart beating like a trip hammer. She literally saw red but managed to say no more as she crossed her arms on her chest. She clenched her mouth shut to avoid telling the little man just where he could stick it, then looked at the mute witness who seemed to be glassily looking at nothing, somewhere above her head.

"Will that be all, gentlemen?" she asked, hugging herself even tighter.

"By refusing to sign, you are officially denying any charge in connection with illegal activity at your previous command and the accusations, documented by witnesses, about your moral fitness to serve. Is that your intent by not signing?" he spoke mechanically to the paper while tediously replacing it in the briefcase and snapping it shut.

"If you're through, I have a command to run," she stood. The legal officer was now smiling. *What a twerp!*

"Please be seated, lieutenant," the Coast Guard commander finally spoke. "By your refusal to resign, it is my duty to inform you that the investigations, criminal and moral, are now complete. I can inform you that the investigations begun two months ago in New Orleans have produced no definitive evidence, no documentation that you are or have ever been involved with criminal activity. Likewise, I may now inform you that the questions raised in depositions from alleged witnesses in New Orleans about your moral character are dismissed, without prejudice. I regret the way this has all come about. My job here was to witness your signature and—failing that—to attest to what I saw. You should know that my official report will indicate that I saw the reaction of a wrongly-accused officer, on all counts."

Emma could hardly believe what she was hearing, and her suspicions about what would be said next were quickly confirmed.

Even the boy lawyer brightened. He continued with his best serious grown-up face, "As you know you have been prohibited contact with personnel who have deposed against you. That restriction is lifted. However, I would advise you to maintain that separation, which probably won't be too hard from here and considering the circumstances," he smirked. "If I were your counsel, which I am not, I would advise you to try forget the personalities and any idea of vendetta against those who have brought witness. They also have rights, and you would be well advised to avoid personal contact, indefinitely, as the case may be."

She began imaging what she would like to do to Lyle Rees, Anna Rees, Art Jacks and any of the faceless, nameless jerks who had made her life a living hell, when the commander began to speak.

"That's probably pretty good advice. Maybe time will heal some wounds. Meanwhile it's better to leave the scars alone. I'm sure that this is the news that I'm sure you've wanted to hear since this all began," he continued. "Official orders will follow when I get back to Kodiak. You'll be the permanent commander here, to complete the full twenty-four months, time on station already to be counted against the total. As of today you are authorized to wear the rank of lieutenant commander, with concomitant responsibilities, privileges and pay. Congratulations, commander, and good luck."

She didn't know whether to laugh or cry, kiss the commander, slap the prissy little lawyer or run down the pier, leap into the icy ocean and drown.

"We'll see ourselves out," the words reached her brain in a detached echo. She did manage to stand as the good-cop, bad-cop pair vanished through her office door. The commander, she thought, winked as he pulled it shut behind him.

Part Two

Five Years Later

Twelve

"Well, sir, that's a lot of booze," Chief Petty Officer Mark Jones frowned at the clipboard and passed it to his new boss. The two men were drenched with sweat, standing in a ten-by-ten-foot, low ceiling storage compartment. A single light bulb protected in a steel cage bolted to the ceiling provided the only light and an unwanted source of heat. There was no ventilation. Fumes from fresh foam green paint on every surface made the stifling atmosphere even harder to endure. As Jones used his t-shirt like a towel and wiped his face, Lieutenant Lyle Rees scanned the inventory. He had to trust its author—after all, he had no idea what was really inside any of the sealed cardboard boxes—and he wanted to escape to fresh air topside. Jones beat him to the punch; he bent deeply and in the same move stepped over the shin-high door threshold. He stretched to his full six feet four inches and sucked in a deep breath. The air wasn't much better, but even if it smelled of paint and cleaning fluid, it was at least cooler and a little fresher outside the tomb-like little room.

"One dandy weekend liberty: thirty-two cases, three-hundred eighty-four fifths of firewater," Jones spoke from the narrow passageway. He squatted, stretching his aching back by clasping his hands on the door transom to support his weight. He stood again, then stepped back inside to stand at Lyle's side, as though his boss needed help reading the figures. Admiring his work and trying to speed up the inspection, Jones ran his finger down the inventory sheet he had created, "Got it broken down to Scotch, bourbon, vodka and gin. Most of it's Scotch, twenty-two cases. Yep, that's apparently the great lesson learned from all these cruises. Our Latin colleagues apparently love the stuff. Who knew? Scotch whiskey is the elixir of Western democracy. Yessir, and the good ol' U.S. Navy is pourin' some good stuff: Johnny Walker Black mostly, mixed in with some eighteen-year-old Jameson and Bushmill. Way over my pay grade during by drinkin' days." He again pointed to the page, "I broke down the really expensive booze within the overall category of Scotch, see?" Hands on hips, he stood looking into the heavy gage chain-link cage built floor-to-ceiling, wall-to-wall across the rear two thirds of the room, then stooped deeply through its door for a final look. The cardboard boxes of liquor were stacked shoulder high, lashed tightly by nylon cargo nets stretched across them. Less attention was paid the boxes of non-breakable, far less expensive gifts—t-shirts, Frisbees, painters caps—stacked in boxes outside the cage, between the watertight bulkhead door and the chain link wall.

Until he arrived a month ago at Roosevelt Roads Naval Base, Puerto Rico, Lyle knew Jones only through reputation. After putting him and the other fourteen *Banda de Americas* members through six-hour-a-day rehearsals, he knew that the conventional wisdom was true: the old chief petty officer could do his and Lyle's job with ease. He also assumed that the trombone he played had been attached at birth.

The musicians were selected from Navy bands on both coasts to perform under Rees' direction. Jones would be second in command and right hand man, responsible for the daily care, feeding and—if needed—mothering of the other band members during the seven-month circumnavigation of South America. Other than that, the only thing Rees knew about Jones was that he had been in the Navy for nearly twenty years. He looked older that most men of that rank because he was. Jones' last comment hinted why: he'd been busted more than once.

"You're not a drinker?"

"No, sir, it didn't work out for me," Jones replied, quickly getting back to business. "You'll need to sign there at the bottom, sir. Me and the campus cops eye-balled it from the truck to the deck, down the after ammo hatch and behind the cage here. The boxes are factory glued and sealed. It's all been double counted from here to the delivery truck. Nobody's fooled with any of it. It's all there."

Lyle pulled a ballpoint pen from his soggy khaki shirt pocket and signed.

"Even if they wanted me to sign for it, it's better if you do," Jones volunteered. "I'm no cherry chief. I've put it on three times, this time for good. Haven't had a drink in five years. Lieutenant, I've also been in the Navy a long time, and I know what it's like to be at sea. It took me better part of seven years to stop drinking, for good, I hope. I don't need the temptation this offers an old drunk. No offense, but if I had the keys to all this and it came up short, the officers would be on me like a duck on a June bug," he drawled with a comfortable smile. "It probably wouldn't make any difference if I'd taken any or not. Been there, done that, got the t-shirt." he spoke softly, then studied the deck, thinking he may have said too much.

"Enough said, chief," Rees replied. "Regardless, I'm happy both of us will sign this and every other inventory from now on," Rees added, looking him in the eye and returning the clipboard to him.

Jones placed the clipboard outside the doorway and retrieved a small brown paper bag. "Here are the locks; one for the bulkhead door and the other for the cage." Jones used a pocket knife to liberate the locks from heavy plastic packaging. He placed one through the hasp on the cage door and locked it, the other he handed to Lyle. Both men ducked into the passageway that dead-ended at the storage room door and led ten feet in the other direction to a ladder, up to the daylight of an open hatch. As Jones stretched his long arms through his khaki shirt, Lyle pulled the steel door shut, inserted the other lock through its brass hasp and pushed the lock arm into the body. It shut with a heavy click.

"There's two keys for each lock. I'd really appreciate it if you'd follow me topside and watch me throw the two extras overboard."

"What?" Rees was confused by the request, then followed him up the ladder. Standing in the tropical heat, he was perplexed and squinted into the older man's sharp, almost skeletal face, then he got it. "You got it. Sounds like a plan."

They walked the few steps across the black deck that led to the back of the ship and stood next to the jack staff where the U.S. flag was lying limp in the mid-morning sun. Lyle placed the two extra keys in Jones' right palm.

"Thanks, boss, watch this." He turned and dropped the keys overboard; both men saw them plink below the surface. "Somebody's gonna be really crazy and mighty damned determined if that want to get to that booze," adding with an impish smile, "And, they'll be rolling you for a key, not this old drunk."

* * * *

Lyle stayed behind after the chief saluted and walked away. He pulled his blue ball cap from his belt at the small of his back, a sailor's constant hat rack, and stood beside a cleat wrapped with the thick rope that bound the ship to a bollard on the dock. There was lots of activity as the ship prepared for the long voyage.

To his left, where a long brow rose from the dock to the forward quarterdeck ten feet above, sailors in white t-shirts and bell-bottom denim formed a human chain, twisting left and right to relay cartons off a truck, up the brow and inside the destroyer. Farther forward, a crane dropped a cargo net of supplies near the forecastle. The odor of petroleum, oil and lubricants wafted from somewhere on the harbor side. Sea gulls circled overhead, anticipating a feast on food spillage. He propped his foot on the cleat. The concrete dock ended on his right where low, white-painted buildings sprouted from the jungle. Behind them verdant growth rose into the impossibly azure sky. The hustle, the color contrasts, smells and sounds of shouted commands: he loved it all. It was an intoxicating prelude to heady adventures yet to come.

Life had been very good to him, lately of the United States Navy. He had advanced quickly, faster than even he had imagined since his commissioning. Even so, it had taken him several months to really believe that it was him upon whom fortune had smiled so graciously after his sudden departure from New Orleans. Even now, five years later, it still seemed too good to be true. He never thought that his experience as a performing musician would ever net him anything but some extra spending money and ladies who'd help him spend it. Now he was one of only a handful of Navy officers whose sole purpose was directing bands, all at large commands around the U.S. and the world.

His life lay in the future, and only occasionally did he ever think about old times. His short marriage, Emma Lucas and all the dark events in New Orleans seemed a very long time ago. If he officially had to forget what he'd seen and done that night with Emma, why couldn't he just as easily forget the other stuff? Besides, everything that had happened since was just too good to jinx it all with a bunch of memories. Bad *mojo*.

About the time he was finishing Navy officers' "knife and fork finishing school" at Pensacola, Florida, he received a wad of cash from her father to ensure he would divorce without contest. If Commander Art "The Jerk" Jacks made her happy, the money more than compensated; good riddance to a mistake he'd never make again. Besides, traveling around the world playing music, who needed a wife?

But, if he had any regret, it was Emma. They shared some good times. He could let his guard down with her and Lucy. They were both so different, so trusting. He didn't like thinking about them or what he had done. Maybe some of the things he'd sworn to were true, he rationalized. Who could know, or care? She was a little strange: looking out for her sister all the time. She was a good looking woman; he had certainly noticed. Out of uniform, with her hair down, in a tight-fitting t-shirt and shorts, she was even approaching a knockout. But, she had no life. Even when she went with him to gigs, she spent her time talking with other women; most of them—he knew—were hookers. *Of course, you had to wonder.*

His deposition was a no-brainer; his only doubt was whether the promises made in exchange for it would really be delivered. She might have been a little hurt, but she was the forgiving type, he imagined. She had done alright after all, with a command and all that. What real pain could she have suffered? Last he heard—maybe two, three years ago— she had retired and had become some kind of a hermit, living in Alaska.

The flag stirred with a gust of wind from the sea and cooled his perch. It cleared his mind. If he helped get her there, and she liked it, what harm had he done? She would probably thank him, he deluded. If he ever thought about returning to visit New Orleans, the thought quickly passed. Los Angeles, New York, London, Tokyo or—most recently— Rome and the Mediterranean and whatever lay ahead in South America, weren't bad alternatives. Anyway, you can't recreate a party, his mother always said. Don't stop thinking about tomorrow; she'd evoke the wisdom of Fleetwood Mac. Always look out for number one. He walked back inside, to the coolness of the ship, and sadness accompanied him. He'd been on tour in Asia when he heard she died. He didn't know where she as buried.

Lyle had no reason to regret or look back. The commander of the Atlantic Fleet selected him, personally, to lead the sixteen-member *Banda de Americas* show band. As such he was a key player in the very high visibility diplomatic and naval outreach. Even if the stated purpose of the *Uno Americas* joint exercises was military cooperation and goodwill between the U.S. and various South American countries, its real value was political intelligence gathered mostly through a series of carefully coordinated social events for the a-listed high rollers in each country visited. In his previous tours, Lyle had excelled in ways he would never know, most likely not even suspect. There was no end to official Washington's curiosity about Soviet and Chinese activity in the Western Hemisphere. From the days of Teddy Roosevelt's Great White Fleet to the beginnings of the Cold War when the annual *Uno Americas* deployments began forty years ago, the Navy has always been closely linked to the nation's diplomacy. The mostly ceremonial war games with host navies and academic-looking seminars had only one real purpose: subtly remind participants of the U.S. Navy's power, dominance and deep pockets for friends. The gossip about neighbors provided real-time information about who had been naughty or nice. This year Lyle's *Banda de Americas* would prime the pump. He was a real player.

* * * *

The ambition was less grand for the seamen who would steam their ships into the new vision of an even more tightly bound Anglo-Latin brotherhood. *Uno Americas '88* was inspiriting, but their "*pina colada* cruise," fit their hopes much better. He visited each of their ships with a slide presentation, complete with audio samples of the rock-and-roll show his band would perform. When the lights went up, every man seemed ready to shoulder the awesome responsibilities Lt. Rees so earnestly told them they would assume as U.S. ambassadors of goodwill abroad. But, their faces beamed with joy when he spoke about the operational schedule: there'd be much more time in port than at sea. The imaginations of these hard-working and adventurous young men were filled with of visions of grandeur, usually involving sensual young ladies drawn to their wealth and sailors' universal and legendary eagerness toward liquidation. As the deployment grew close, the *Wall Street Journal* delivered to the officers' wardroom, most especially the Money section, would soon find its way to the mess decks. It would be an unusually rare seaman who couldn't converse about the conversion rate from their cash payday dollars to pesos, reals or Bolivars. They meant to take advantage of every possibility.

The older veterans among them also knew that life at sea also held a welcome reward. As the tropical summer faded to autumn and the five ships left the northern latitudes to steam across the Caribbean into the South American spring, there would be no rough weather. As the flotilla sailed counterclockwise around the continent, the only inconvenience would be a few colder days and rough seas as they made their way around Cape Horn's entrance to the Atlantic; good times awaited in Argentina and Brazil.

* * * *

Lyle had his expectations, too, beginning pleasantly with a mini-vacation during a two-day lay-over in DC. A couple nights of bar hopping in Georgetown were a great way to cure jet lag. As he had for his first band tour through the Philippines, Japan and Korea and more recently England and Italy, he would sit through the usual lecture of country-by-country facts. This series would be delivered by a low-ranking intelligence officer, probably the only person at the Pentagon, or anywhere else, who really cared about their content. The briefings were a formality, but the hand-outs were great, ample—Lyle had learned—for making brilliant cocktail conversation. On long days shipboard, he knew there'd be plenty of time to digest the information about history, culture, economics, ethnic makeup, government structure and the myriad details about each country. As before, he would be charming and sound like a scholar.

But, there was a new angle this time: his second day was free until a late-afternoon meeting at the State Department, followed by a reception at the Cosmos Club on the city's embassy row.

Lyle enjoyed sleeping in after a long night. He still had plenty of time to call on the director of the Navy Band by mid-morning and share lunch with him at the Washington Navy Yard officers club. The food was excellent. The barely disguised envy of headquarters staff was even better, for as heady as life in the Federal City surely was for those whose job was to make it all even more exciting, this deployment was a tantalizing fantasy. Lyle would have no real boss, only the pleasure of entertaining and enjoying the adulation.

Dressed in summer whites, his feet barely seemed to touch the sidewalk as he walked to the Metro. Foggy Bottom was only one transfer, three stops and a short walk away on a beautiful mid-summer afternoon. He exited at the Federal Triangle and walked proudly past the White House to the Vietnam Memorial. In the coolness and dappled sunlight swirling on the giant bust of Albert Einstein, Lyle turned off Constitution Avenue and walked the final block to the State Department. A visitor pass awaited him, and he followed directions to the third floor conference room. He found the door open, but there was no one waiting. The room was huge and much more ornate than he'd expected to find in a U.S. government building. The State Department lived well: light oak floor-to-ceiling paneling, heavy blue curtains on windows overlooking the

National Mall and an impossibly long, polished oak table anchoring two dozen pleated red leather chairs. A massive gold and crystal chandelier hung from the ceiling twelve feet overhead.

"Our Navy is on time and ahead of schedule, how marvelous," she spoke, both hands extended to take his as she exploded through the tall double doors. Lyle turned from a window to see a woman in her early thirties. She was stunning. She looked like she'd stepped from a Vogue layout on power dressing for success. Her above-the-shoulder platinum hair was cut in a pageboy. The white linen suit was sculpted so tightly that he wondered if there was anything beneath it besides the rock-hard, perfectly shaped body. He failed to notice that she had smartly complemented the outfit with red low-heels and a matching handbag that swung slightly at waist level, supported by a gold chain draped over her left shoulder.

She marched quickly and confidently to close the space between them. He admired the well-toned legs and fanaticized about how they could move in such a tight skirt. He accepted her warm hand and looked into her bottomless blue eyes. He was more than willing to hear anything she had to say.

"May I call you Lyle?" she asked as she led him to a sofa at the back of the room and took the chair behind a coffee service on the low table between them.

"Of course." This day just gets better and better, he thought.

"I'm Maggy Brown," she smiled. "On behalf of the Undersecretary for Public Diplomacy and Public Affairs, welcome to the State Department."

"Thank you, I'm pleased to be here and meet you," he spoke dramatically, as though he were on microphone. Whatever her official duties were, Lyle thought as he watched her pour coffee for them both, it must involve distance running: she was fit and tan, her crossed legs now showed even more of her thigh. Self-consciously, he lifted his vision to the delicate hands that extended a cup and saucer to him, then back to those eyes.

"That's one of the reasons we helped select you to lead the *Banda de Americas*," she said with perfect Castilian Spanish. She smiled and sat gracefully back in her chair.

For the first time today, he was a little confused, even a little off balance. *What "we" other than the U.S. Navy had anything to do with my orders?*

"You're an observant guy, Lyle. I'll bet that you have very adequately sized me up by now. If you had your video camera I doubt that it could make a much better picture of me and this room than the one in your head."

Lyle was embarrassed, then confused. *My video camera? How'd she know that?* "Well, I'm sorry, I didn't mean…" he stammered and leaned nervously forward.

"Oh, don't be embarrassed. We and some other people in Washington have read your after-actions from Asia and Europe. Friends and colleagues filled us in about you. You have a good eye for detail. I guess that's not too unusual for musicians. You don't miss much, and neither do we. That's what we're looking for."

These after-action reports had seemed so boringly routine, just meaningless, make-work paperwork he had always assumed. He attached no brilliance to them; more often than not he complained about having to write them in the first place. *Did these people, whoever they are, know that?* Suddenly they were significant, read by invisible people lurking around the room. *What else do they know about me? Who did they talk with to find out?* His face was burning as though he had been slapped. He couldn't have felt more vulnerable if he were sitting there naked.

She measured the effect of her words in his face and let the moment play out. She brought her cup to her lips and returned it to the saucer on her lap. Even through his well-developed poker face—one born of the stage presence cultivated by performers like him—she saw what she had hoped: curiosity and composure. Her handlers knew, as did she as a field agent, that coolness under pressure was a rare talent, a combination of intuition and control. Whatever mishap on stage, from his reaction the audience would think it was part of the act. "Sorry, I can be a little too much to the point sometimes. Relax. Bottom line is that we're on the same team. That's what all this is about," she placed her cup and saucer on the table and smiled as she rested her hands on the chair arms. "Uncle Sam signs my paycheck, too. Here's the big picture: if we and lots of people like us do our jobs right, there are people way above our pay grade who will know it and how to fit it all together. You're among friends, Lyle. I am glad to meet you."

He felt his heart start beating again. "OK, Maggy. You can understand that I feel a little over my head right now. Can you break it down a little for me?" he asked, tilting his head forward and folding his hands in his lap.

"Not a problem. Let me begin by telling you that you're well thought of, or you wouldn't be here. I can also assure you that the Navy is on board with all of this; I don't think I have to do more than simply remind you of how you were chosen for this assignment. Enough said. If what you'll be asked to do could even be described as extra duty, it doubtlessly is career enhancing. Sorry, there's no money involved. Essentially, you are going to have the opportunity to help certain individuals and organizations outside your Navy chain of command."

"Essentially?"

"Good question. Most of it's just talking with some embassy staff, cultural affairs, maybe some others. If they want something specific they'll tell you. The worst it could be is a written report; they'd tell you where to send it and things like that, but you're not going to be asked to write *War and Peace*, OK? And, there's not going to be anything outside your responsibilities as band officer. Worst case is just a little extra from time to time, maybe, and I understand there is plenty of that between ports."

"Wow. Are you sure you've got the right guy? Music is my life, and I'm loving what I get to do. What you're saying is kind of startling. You must know I'm a little dizzy right now." He took a deep breath and tried to calm down. "I'm a little overwhelmed that you know so much about me. I mean I know it's possible, no secret, but I sure as hell don't imagine that anyone even knows my name, let alone at the four-star level. Makes a dude a little nervous."

"Can't tell from here, Lyle," she smiled, "believe me, you're up to this. If a lot of folks didn't think so you wouldn't be sitting here right now. Relax, go with it."

"What about my chain of command? I mean, who's going to know, or is anyone else going to be aware…"

"That's where this gets a little complicated, which may be a little different for you at first: nobody's going to know. If and when you do something for us you'll never mention it. I think you've had some experience with this sort of thing before. New Orleans was it?" she asked with raised eyebrows.

He now was at a complete loss for words. That paper he signed five years ago had never come up with anyone. He had hardly ever even thought about it, and that was good, he thought, because there had never been any need to. A lot of life had replaced those memories. He had not forgotten everything, of course, but the details were less clear. An image of Emma flashed through his head. Why did Maggie remind him of her? He'd pushed it aside. Not speaking about it, which is what he had sworn to do, eased any temptation to do so, not even now. Obviously, Maggie knew something. "New Orleans was a great duty station. I haven't been there in a very long time."

"Still got friends there?"

"No, not to speak of. Seems like a million years ago. I've been busy since, always trying to look forward." He knew that she knew much more about him, but just how much? His palms were moist. "Anyone in particular I should look forward to meeting in South America?"

"Yes, but nobody you've ever met, not in New Orleans, or anywhere else," she added quickly with a blank expression.

"Who will be helping, if I may ask?"

"You may not. Look, here's the bottom line: we are aware of the non-disclosure, but, of course, not of the details. That's how it's supposed to work and how you'll keep playing it. Once you begin down there, you'll get another to sign, specific to that situation. I don't see this as any problem, in any way, for you. Again, trust me; we'd know if you'd ever had any problems honoring the first one." There was no mistaking the tone of her voice or the sudden professional hardness around her eyes. The look was sobering: if he ever had some fantasy about finding a new playmate, this woman was not the answer. He got the same gut feeling with her as he did with the spooky Diplomatic Security agent with Emma and Captain Clark.

"You'll meet a lot of cultural affairs officers as you go around. And, there will be an individual who you'll most likely see from time to time. I'm guessing he'll introduce himself early on, in Puerto Rico or on your first stops in Venezuela or Colombia. He'll be specific. All you need to know is that he or someone else he'll introduce you to will have requests, maybe even travel with you and the band, on occasion. They'll come and go from your group but never mingle." She paused to read Lyle's face. "Don't make this harder than it'll be. If anyone, including your band, should ask questions, just say they're part of the embassy security team. Trust me, they'll be good. To the rest of the world, they'll look like musicians, or security or whatever the team leader wants them to be. You don't have to worry about any of that. Just give a hand when you're asked. They'll wear some kind of uniform, usually, or not, and carry instrument cases that look just like yours. Relax. You'll be a lot more comfortable with all this as you go along. By the time you get to Peru or

Chile and start up the east coast, this will all be second nature to you."

"And, all of this and whatever else the CA officers want I'm supposed to do without my admiral or his chief of staff knowing?"

"Lyle, trust me, it's not going to be a problem for you, maybe someone else, but not you. Believe me, these guys are pros, and they know how to avoid making things tough on you. You do have some escape: the man I told you about can fix things and communicate at a level your boss will understand. My best advice is for you to remember that this isn't a license for you to morph into James Bond. It's a reminder that there are some questions you can't and, more important, won't answer. All you have to do is stall, probably no more than a day." She smiled and stood, "I'll bet you can tap dance longer than that!" She looked at her wrist watch, "Enough heavy stuff, my friend, we've got a reception to attend. I want to introduce you to some very interesting people." As they walked toward the tall double doors, she added with a friendly nudge, "Heads up, big guy: they also know a lot about you, so don't freak out, just enjoy the evening. Believe me, you'll never regret knowing these people. Honestly, they're fans and are looking forward to meeting you." She slapped her hand between his shoulders, "Relax, sailor!"

* * * *

The destroyer USS Aldrich, flagship of *Uno Americas,* ran fast across the Caribbean and began four days of war games with the Venezuelan navy. Eight days after leaving Puerto Rico, the flotilla of five U.S. ships tied up in the port of La Guairá. Essentially passengers while at sea, the band had been more than ready for action. They enthusiastically began the labor intensive logistics behind their music. That involved carrying a ton of instruments, amplifiers, speakers, dress uniforms and the allotted liquor up to the deck, transferring it all to a chartered truck and bus, then riding for an hour into Caracas.

The winding road led continuously uphill from the dingy port where they peered out the bus windows at their shipmates invading the roadside bars, past the grinding poverty of grim shanty towns clinging to the sides of steep hills and finally into the wide boulevards of the capital city. As the cool, sunlit day turned into late afternoon, their sprits lifted when the two-vehicle convoy arrived at the Venezuelan Officers Club, a green marble palace in one of the city's most affluent neighborhoods. They would work like stevedores for two hours, then shine like the pros they were during their first command performance.

The U.S. Cultural Affairs Officer was waiting for Lyle and explained the game plan. After the formal reception for diplomatic and military brass, he would take to the stage and launch into the band's well-rehearsed hour-long show. As the hour neared midnight the party would grow with the arrival of lower-ranking officers and platoons of beautiful, apparently party-starved and unattached women. The booze and carvings from slow-cooked steamship rounds of beef cooked for days in the ship's galley would flow even faster now as the intelligence operatives and Lyle worked the crowd, tirelessly listening to every word spoken. The band would play requests and dance music as long as *el jefe* and his guests remained.

It all went as planned.

A couple of hours before sunrise, as conversations end and the last guests leave in newly formed pairs, the band tears down, reloads for the reverse trip to the Aldrich. At the local U.S. Embassy and in Lyle's stateroom reports are written and cabled to D.C. and U.S. embassies throughout South America.

Tomorrow will be another day. Like clockwork, the CA Officer will arrive aboard the flagship before noon with formal invitations for the U.S. admiral, his staff and Lyle to attend social events in reciprocation of the previous night of U.S. hospitality. With only minor variations, this will be the well-established rhythm for every port visited in the next seven months, the duration of *Uno Americas*.

The exception arrived a week later in Cartagena, Colombia.

* * * *

"*Señor* lieutenant," the nun's soft words started Lyle, and he turned with a jerk to see the fragile little figure draped in white. She had stepped silently behind him and stood quietly until he finished a long pull on a bottle of cold water. He stood under the high-raftered, open-sided shelter, large enough for the band and orphanage staff. More than a hundred children sat in the sun on the grassy lawn outside. They were joined by a hundred more people, neighbors from unseen dwellings in the surrounding jungle, who were thrilled by the hour-long show. As usual, the band lingered with the crowd, shaking hands, chatting as best they could and giving away small trinkets marked with the *Uno Americas* logo. The tear-down for the two-hour drive back to Cartagena began shortly after their nuns led the children back inside the orphanage.

"Sorry, Sister Rose, I didn't know you were there. How may I help you?"

She greeted his polite reply with a smile and a slight nod. There is a man, one of the orphanage's benefactors, who wishes to speak with you. Follow me, please?"

She led him toward a gathering of better-dressed people standing inside the wide gate through the wall that enclosed the main building and others in the two-acre campus. She didn't stop. Through the gate, they turned left and toward the end of the tall stone wall. A few steps later the nun stopped in the shade at the edge of the jungle and pointed toward an opening in the low growth beneath the tall canopy above. "He waits just inside, he is a very good man," she spoke, taking his hand in both of hers. "God be with you and your musicians," she spoke, this time with a broad smile, and walked back toward the gate.

"That was just fantastic, dude. What a show," a friendly voice spoke from somewhere very nearby on what Lyle now recognized was a narrow path, barely two feet wide. Lyle walked a few feet down the path which turned sharply to the right. He nearly bumped into three men who materialized from the dense undergrowth. They were dressed in camouflaged fatigues and Timberland hiking boots. Each wore a web belt with a pistol and ammunition pouches. The two older looking men also had short, metal-stock machine guns slung across their chests. A very small, Italian van, covered in mud, was parked behind them. "Thought I was in Vegas," the voice boomed happily in a heavy Southern drawl. He was standing a few feet in front of the others, and—to Lyle's amazement—lifted his arm in a casual salute, his fingers touching the brim of his red Boston Red Sox ball cap, pulled down over his forehead. The rest of his face was barely visible, covered by a close-cropped black beard and wrap-around sun glasses. "I'm pleased to meet you."

Instinctively, Lyle returned the salute. "And, you are?"

"We're your biggest fans," he laughed in reply. He was younger than Lyle, although he wasn't certain. He is very athletic, shorter, perhaps a body builder judging by how tightly the fatigue shirt fit around his chest and shoulders. Lyle guessed that he was in his early thirties. He dropped the salute and extended a hand which Lyle shook in return. "Names are a liability. I'm sure you understand. But, here's a name to get things rolling: how 'bout Downtown Maggie Brown, the queen of Foggy Bottom? I'll bet you haven't forgotten her, shipmate," he laughed again.

The meeting from what seemed very long ago and far away from a narrow path in a dense jungle and this unexpected rendezvous now came together. "Well, thank you very much. Yes, I remember her, very well. Who wouldn't? Pleased to meet you. I believe that I am now at your service. What can I do for you?"

As though satisfied with the conversation, the two older men turned their attention away from the pair. They moved behind the van, scanning the undergrowth before opening the rear doors. They were big men and moved with the grace of big cats stalking prey. The ball caps, sun glasses and beards were the uniform of the day, Lyle thought.

"Want a beer? *Dos cervezas, por favor*," the younger man spoke over his shoulder. A moment later he turned, to snatch one, then another can that came flying over the roof.

"You can call me Al," he said, handing one to Lyle. "What a hoot. Didn't expect Simon and Garfunkel to sound so good. Your lead singer does a great job."

The cold beer tasted wonderful.

"Step into my office," "Al" spoke and led Lyle to sit with him on the van's rear bumper. The other two men had disappeared, again.

"Like Maggie told you, there's not a lot to ask of you. It's a real skate. That's the good news. The better news, depending on how you look at it, I guess, is that you can start immediately. We need help tonight at your diplomatic reception."

Lyle pulled a pen and a small notebook from his breast pocket.

"No notes, Lyle. And, it's not going to be that complicated, just pay attention," he paused to take a pull from the can, "like you always have." Gazing down the path behind the van, he continued, "We need some close-up eyeballs on Admiral Georges Lopez. He's the Colombian navy's director of ops. We hear that he has been sick, and that's what is most interesting. If that's true, he probably won't hang around long. You'll have to start checking him out just as soon as he arrives at the Naval Club."

"Unless he's dying, maybe not then, telling if someone's sick from looking probably isn't my strong suit."

"Understood. Just find him quickly and stay close. There are a couple of things you can see that some medical types can mull around: whether he stands or sits; if he stands, how long and whether or not in stands still or rocks on his heels and toes; what he drinks, if anything; when he arrives and departs and with whom. The rest is old news for you. Try keep track of who talks to him, especially anyone not in a uniform. Try stay close enough to at least pick a word or two. Language skills from misspent youth in Tampa are going to come in handy down here, it's one of the reasons you're here."

He stood to face Lyle, "Here's the most important chore: just make sure than when you introduce yourself he knows you're the band leader. Play it by ear," he paused, then leaned closer, "Remember exactly what he says to you after that and the specific words he uses. Relax, big guy, just assume he's a music fan. Just do it, don't think about it; that's the quickest way for all of us to get into some pretty deep, dark holes. OK?"

The medical observations were something new to worry about, but the rest, as "Al" said, were the basis of reports Lyle had written scores of times before. "Who gets the report, how?"

"Never mind who, big guy. Write it, then seal it in a business envelope and hand address it to the Cultural Affairs Officer, Bogota. Drop it in the in-port secure diplomatic mail pouch; call the CA office with a message about your schedule or something. Then slip your typewriter ribbon over the side." He reached inside the van, and pulled on a large, black object towards the door. Lyle moved to one side as a black drum case, the same kind his drummer was using, bumped against him. "Last thing: I need a ride to town."

The musicians lay or sat smoking in the shade beside the road in front of the orphanage. "Embassy security," Lyle said to the chief Jones as the band boarded. Their new passenger waited, then slung his apparently heavy drum case in the rear door and climbed in behind it. Most dozed off quickly, waking as the little convoy slowed to make its way along the city streets. As they approach the city's walled fort near the waterfront, Lyle's passenger tapped him on the shoulder, "I'll get out here." The bus jerked to a stop on the shop lined street. The passenger climbed out the back door.

Lyle looked at the rear window as the bus pulled away. His passenger and case disappeared through a short door to one of the two-story stone buildings flanking the narrow cobblestone street. The sign above it was painted in large gold letters against a red background: "*Monte Verde* Trading, Ltd., Cartagena, London, New Orleans."

Back aboard Nicholson at 3 a.m., Lyle scanned his report:

Subject arrived at 2145, and I was able to introduce myself immediately as band officer. He stood for about fifteen minutes and sat much earlier than other flag or general officers. He frequently seemed to rock forward on his toes and back on his heels. Subject spoke with other officers and briefly with two civilians who approached him (names/ descriptions below). On these occasions he rose and walked unsurely to the patio where I could not overhear unobserved. Each conversation lasted about five minutes Subject and his aide departed at 2300. Upon departure he approached me directly and alone. In English he said, "Your music is well made. Your hospitality is golden. Your Scotch is exquisite. Your colleagues and you will have no problems from now on." Note: Subject was not observed drinking liquor, only two glasses of red wine.

* * * *

This is going to be a snap!

Thirteen

Bon Homme is an antebellum beauty. The stately, painted lady fronting the Mississippi River is also a working plantation, at least on paper, but only a very few people, mostly the men gathering there tonight, have any idea exactly what happens there; not all of them know everything.

The rest of the world will remain clueless, if the owners have their way. They invested in the property four years ago, spending a fortune to buy more than a thousand acres of the rich delta land that surrounds the historic plantation house. The mansion's part-time resident became a partner. His contribution to the clandestine enterprises involved discouraging any, especially official, inquiries about those same activities. He has earned his keep. More than once he has intervened to smooth over matters, the exact extent and even the nature of all his actions, still unknown. Bribes from his partners to a hand full of local sheriffs and deputies, prosecuting attorneys and judges followed the Dixie Mafia paradigm. Of late, they terminated local queries, most likely involving missing persons, freelance opportunists and wanna-be thugs who have vanished like morning mist over steamy bayous.

Unlike Oak Alley, its famous neighbor only a couple miles upriver, the mansion and its vast acreage are not open to tourists. Little to nothing is known about the exact nature of business conducted there. The lost, confused and curious are quickly escorted away by polite but humorless men who seem to appear from nowhere atop tall horses. The guardians' duties are split between monitoring cameras and motion sensors from a converted mews and maintaining a stable of thoroughbred race horses.

Even the guardians never approach the grounds around the big house or the nearby out buildings at the end of a mile-long runway. Those security details are performed by other men arriving and departing from the dock or late at night aboard Great Circle Air Cargo flights. Other laborers and their guards are shuttled from somewhere upriver. They handled the surprisingly small cargos arriving on towboats and barges.

Inside this tightly controlled cocoon, life is truly grand for its gentrified owners. This afternoon is no exception.

The last golden rays stream through the mansion's tall west windows, past green draperies on burgundy walls and reflect off the thirty-foot polished mahogany dining table. Platoons of red jacketed wait staff flit like butterflies completing final touches for another gala evening. Their employer is confident in their nearly magical abilities, proven during dozens of similar events. Satisfying him has grown their fortunes, mightily. Still, a half hour before his guests arrive, he will stand at the top of the wide second-floor stair landing and bang a gong. Before the echo dissipates into hushed silence, those below will stand side-by-side on the south side of the central hallway. They'll wait as he descends the grand staircase to begin his inspection of everything from seating arrangements, silverware placement, the brilliance of crystal goblets, wine and water classes, to the cleanliness of clothing, carpets and fingernails.

Until then, Nat Pierce has retreated to enjoy moments alone on the wide gallery that wrapped around the mansion. The humidity and heat of mid-summer is easing, if only slightly. A heavy perfume of magnolias and honeysuckle replaces the aroma of dark, moist soil, crops of soybeans and cotton roasted in sunlight. A deep breath is intoxicating. He closes his eyes and opens them suddenly; he wonders if even the dead buried out in the dark fields may not also be aroused by it. He walks to the front gallery and looks north, toward the dock. In the sunset, it is glowing brighter beneath basketball-sized green, gold and purple Japanese lanterns. His guests will arrive aboard their own launches or on his yacht dispatched to *Monte Verde's* Piety Street Wharf to gather them.

Hundreds more, smaller lanterns hang motionless, suspended from the leafy oak tunnel leading from the river landing to the broad expanse of the front porch. There young men and young ladies in Nineteenth Century costume will greet them with juleps and mimosas and lead them up the brick steps to white linen-covered tables of *hors d'oeuvres,* wine fountains and antique bars at each end. On the gallery above, a string quartet will play Mozart, Beethoven and Handel.

These parties—a continuing series of victory celebrations for him—are all the talk among certain of the Big Easy social elite. The expense of the gatherings are tokens of his partners' appreciation for his loyalty and most effective services, complemented by his unprecedented rise to power in official Washington. He has succeeded beyond their wildest dreams. He is now third in command at the Department of State, with the newly created title, Principal Deputy of State for Immigration and Commerce. He reports only to the Secretary of State, among the guests who will soon arrive. And, even if his guests will not know, his partners are celebrating yet another payday for the man without whose protective favors their enterprises—legal and otherwise—could not have flourished. Tonight they will wink to each other as they toast their "golden boy."

They will speak heartily about the ice chests of fresh Gulf shrimp and snapper transferred from a passing Great Circle tow boat earlier today. The venerable hosts will neglect to mention the dozen kilograms of pure Colombian cocaine packed beneath the ice. They will also omit the two very heavy aluminum ammunition cases that were taken directly in a golf cart from the dock, delivered about a quarter mile away to the restored sugar cane barn which now serves as a laboratory and workshop.

A few hours before the guests arrived, the unlikely stevedores—Gene Menard, *Monte Verde* North American manager and owner of the Great Circle tow boat fleet, Gulf Coast Services ship chandler Frank Gordon and Russell Anderson, legendary criminal defense attorney—followed in a second golf cart and parked on the aircraft parking apron by the large barn. Menard removed a single ingot of solid gold, and a few minutes later the trio met Pierce in the library. Nat accepted their gratitude with grace and slid the ingot into the safe hidden in the floor behind his mahogany planters desk. He poured four shots of fifty-year-old Scotch.

"To the golden boy," Anderson led the toast. They would repeat it often tonight when they are joined by United States Secretary of State Jennifer Cotton.

"'Til then, gentlemen," Pierce responded.

* * * *

"Be it ever so humble, there's no place like home, especially if it's a five-million-dollar plantation on the mighty Mississippi," Anderson spoke as the two men walked back into the parlor from the front porch where they had just bid goodnight to most of his last tipsy guests. They stopped just inside the tall French doors and looked down the length of the long room in front of them. "Just look at that, my friend," he gestured with a nod of his head.

Nat followed Anderson's gaze. Secretary Cotton, a short, moon-faced matron, managed to look feminine, even voluptuously attractive in a light blue silk dress. Still, her girth more than amply filled an overstuffed wingback chair. At her left elbow, Menard and Gordon sat on a sofa facing the fireplace, bursting not with flames but verdant ferns and palms. She rested her fat hands demurely on the armrest's antique lace doilies and beamed her intense smile. Menard leaned closer toward her to add intimacy. She nodded in approval and smiled more broadly as she noticed Nat and the legendary attorney approaching.

"I never would have imagined anything like this," Anderson spoke as the two began moving toward the Secretary. "Gene, Frank and I moved here twenty years ago. We were outsiders. Were we outsiders, alright! Worse than that: all of us were damn Yankees! And try this on for size: I was from New York, a solo lawyer trying to start a practice from itch! I didn't even have a license to practice here. And, look at you, an east-coast bond baby who couldn't even keep a job with his own father!"

Nat concealed an inward cringe by pretending he didn't hear the insult. His partners could be brutal, as he well knew but wished he didn't. Of Croatian descent, he was short and muscular, and looked more like a miner than the silk-stocking lawyer he had become. Born to first-generation immigrants in lower Manhattan's garment district, he was well acquainted with men like Nat, and he cared for none of them. He had very little respect for Pierce, and it was obvious.

"Well, no doubt about it. The place has never been the same," he managed as the pair walked slowly and nodded to other guests being led gently but purposefully toward the landing.

The three men had moved to New Orleans in the mid-1960s, within three years of each other. Anderson came first, and his success was the most traditional of all. Already a well-known—and famously de-debarred—New York defense attorney, he had arrived in disgrace. He began his new career by passing Louisiana's torturous twenty-one-hour bar exam, only one of the peculiarities on a long list of the state's unique legal features. The courts are governed by French and Spanish Codes, not English Common Law, like every other state in the union. Anderson knew that Judges, especially in civil cases, have much broader powers of interpretation and set aside legal precedent with a well-mannered judicial whim. The same latitudes apply, although less formally, in criminal proceedings. The arrangement enables subjective latitude, and with good reasons clients hire lawyers they believe are part of the inner legal circle. He hung out his shingle on the third floor above a bar on Royal Street, directly across the street from the French Quarter police station. Clientele he knew best—criminals, large and small—followed quickly.

In less than three years Anderson and Associates grew to include admiralty law practiced by a half-dozen full partners. Much more in keeping with the principal's new status, the firm occupied the entire nineteenth floor of the World Trade Center at the foot of Canal Street. Russell Anderson was president of the Orleans Parish Bar Association, counselor of record for no fewer than four ocean shipping firms also located in the building and was chairman emeritus of the historic Ursulines Convent Orphanage. His status with the Southern Mob was less celebrated.

Menard and Gordon were transplants from New Jersey. They had taken less direct routes to the city and—until the past few years—had kept a much lower pubic profile. Menard had lived in Mobile for a couple of years; Gordon has settled initially in Memphis, then Mobile. Their paths to success were similar and much less respectable. From the beginning they had shared the same lawyer and discrete banker, long before arriving in New Orleans. Both owned antique stores in an unallied chain of pawn shops that stretched from Charleston to Fort Worth, Nashville and Charlotte to Birmingham and Tampa. Suspected of fencing stolen goods, especially very expensive antiques and jewelry, police in several jurisdictions throughout the south had watched them closely.

In the Dixie Mafia pattern, Gordon and Menard adapted. With perfect timing, they would close the business in question and move to another city to begin again. Although charged frequently, their skillful attorney avoided their conviction for a variety of crimes, most commonly receiving stolen goods, burglary and—more often in later years—murder for hire and extortion. Some of their business associates had not been so fortunate, but remained loyal—and silent—while in prison. Loyalty ensured that their families never suffered financially during their absence, a fact lost on no one, especially those they recruited in incarceration.

Even with the relentless FBI pursuit of organized crime that had jailed dozens of Italian Mafia on the East Coast, their confidential prison informants never provided solid leads to Menard or Gordon. Those who entertained favors-for-information offers mysteriously died at the hands of other inmates. This had become epidemic, especially inside the Louisiana State Penitentiary, and the Feds backed off. Rumors about the *Bon Homme* Plantation remained just that.

By the time the men moved to New Orleans, reports about a growing crime syndicate known either as the Southern Mob or the Dixie Mafia always included their names. They were persons of interest in a growing number of murder-for-hire schemes, more recently and the deaths or disappearance of four judges and a sheriff and his wife in Tennessee. But, they were only suspects. To the frustration of state and federal law enforcement, the men had avoided their grasp, and the breadth of their relationships – business and otherwise – had risen to empire. The trio of kindred minds soon blossomed into even more publicly known endeavors: most notably the *Bon Homme* Plantation, LLC.

In 1975, the *Times-Picayune* featured them in its Sunday business section. The long article glossed over their histories and focused instead on their success, power and exemplary corporate citizenship. The final paragraph summarized:

"From their vantage point high above the river, these visionaries see much more than the geography. Yes, they are new to our beloved city, but like those who've migrated here for more than five hundred years, they have translated their vision and labor into the success and economic opportunity they are more than willing to share. They envisioned a revitalized port, the centerpiece of New Orleans' expanding economic influence throughout the South and Latin America, and helped build it. They saw a need for more employment opportunities in New Orleans and created the enterprises to lead the way. They saw the need in our community and responded by underwriting, literally rescuing, the centuries-old Ursulines Orphanage. In business, citizenship and charity, these men believe in the unlimited world of the possible, and they have brought it to the banks of the mighty Mississippi. They came, they saw, and they conquered our imaginations and our respect."

* * * *

"I'm mentioned as a gubernatorial candidate; I'd win, too, without a Republican opponent. With the support of the people who tucked up under the dinner table tonight, I could win in a walk!" Anderson held the snifter to his nose, swirled the brandy inside and sipped.

"No argument here. What the hell, all of you are on the Louisiana Democratic Party Executive Committee; you practically finance the whole damned thing. Why not call in a few favors?"

❧ "I know, I know. It's a nice idea to play with, but there's too much scrutiny involved, even in Louisiana." He sipped again, then looked at Pierce and leaned closer as he spoke, "Dixie Mafia, all those skeletons, eh?" Anderson enjoyed watching him jerk like he'd been shot.

"Nat, what a delightful evening. I'm just blown away by what you've done with the old house," Cotton spoke as though she had not heard the exchange. Each took her hand as she offered like a queen to courtiers. "I remember daddy bringing us up here when I was a little girl to deliver some absolutely beautiful furniture. If memory serves, I'd almost bet that your dining table was a part of that delivery."

"Madame Secretary, you do have a great mind; yes, that dinner table and chairs were part of the estate," Nat spoke like a proud father.

"Maybe next time you're in town you could stop by and look the family's old store records. Granddad and his father were fascinating, meticulous, as you can imagine, about the origins of everything they bought and sold. We've got a lot of it on computer data bases now. If we don't, it's in some of the giant old ledgers up in the attic. We're really proud that Rue Royal Collectors remains a principal source about art and antiques traded here for more than a hundred fifty years. My heart's never far from that place; it's quite an anchor sometimes. Believe me, some days more than others, I daydream about returning and burying myself in that passion. Just being here tonight makes the desire stronger. Nat, thanks, so very much, for inviting me."

"The pleasure is all ours. I trust that you will not be a stranger to my humble home."

She looked at the men on her left, then at Anderson. Her eyes fixed again on Nat, "I don't like to mix business with pleasure, it seems so vulgar, Aunt Blanch used to say." She paused and smiled at the men fawning around her, "As a matter of fact I don't even want to think about business in this beautiful place," she laughed and all followed suit as the emerald broach around her neck shifted to be swallowed by fleshy cleavage. No one wanted to get caught looking.

"One great perk of being Secretary is the helo that'll pick me up for the ride home. I've got about fifteen minutes. I beg your pardon, gentlemen. Nat, is there someplace we could talk?"

"We can speak privately in the library."

"Please, stay where you are, we'll make ourselves scarce," Anderson spoke. Menard and Gordon were on their feet by the time he finished. In turn, they took Cotton's hand, not sure if they should shake or kiss one of the rings on her stubby fingers, and walked upstairs to wait on the gallery. Nat rolled shut both sets of the massive pocket doors that separated the central hallway from the parlor and sat on the sofa opposite her. Madam Secretary put on her game face.

"Nat, there'll be some big changes after the election; I'm afraid I'm one of them. I don't have to tell you that there are strains between me and the President. This just in: it's really not fair. The Mid East is a crap shoot. Best that can be done is kick the can and hope nothing happens to make things worse, and if they do that somebody, not us, gets the blame. That, my esteemed Principal Deputy Secretary of State for Immigration and Commerce, is about as creative as anything ever gets in DC. Everybody in the White House is just holding their breath 'til November."

Nat neither knew where this was headed nor how he should react, if at all. He rarely spoke alone with her, there was always at least one other person present. *What does this have to do with me?*

"That's the bad news, Nat, old boy; the worse news is that it affects you too."

Nat was frozen, a little more at ease as she smiled and continued.

"You're a classic example of a guy who's a victim of his own success," she scanned his face and smiled again. "Relax, that's a joke. What I'm saying is that there are very few, if any I've ever seen, who's had a career like you've enjoyed. You've played your cards close to the vest, and you've won." She propped on her elbows and the broach swung off her breasts as she pulled the chair closer and propped her forearms on the desk. She continued in a near whisper, "You're in the top three, fella. If there's a régime change you could be in the crosshairs. You've got a damned fine job, but it's new; there's no political appointee precedent, not yet, at least. I just want you to know that's how I see it. If worse comes to worse and I'm out in January, or sooner, I want you to know that I'll do my best to ensure that your position is protected as a careerist, non-political appointee." She scanned him again and sat back, "You can smile now."

Of course he'd thought about all this before, but to hear it from the

Secretary, sitting in his parlor, was a heart-stopping shock. Where would he be, what was his future if he could not pull strings for his partners? His guts felt like jello. She knew what he was thinking. "Yes, I have thought about the future. You have been wonderful to me. I hope that you feel I've lived up to your expectations."

She studied him for a moment, then continued, "Beyond my expectations. But, we don't own these jobs. I could be wrong, but I doubt it: I believe you understand that we make best of them, during and after. Smart folks start looking for the exit as soon as they enter. Life goes on. It will for you and me here in New Orleans, whether one or both of us begins a new chapter." She stopped, turned to look at the closed doors behind her and beyond Nat at the glass doors leading to the porch. She lowered her head and stared intensely at him from under her eyebrows. "This is a non-versation, I'll deny everything you've heard, and you'd better do the same. The way I see it, I've only got a couple of options: one, he or his hand-picked successor is elected and I hang on or don't or, two, the Democrats take over and I'm fired. Whatever comes down, I don't want to break up our team."

Her last word was punctuated by the beginning of a distant, barely audible roll of thunder. A storm was moving in from the Gulf, and Nat's gut.

"I understand the first option. I think you know how much that would mean to me to work with you for another four years. I'm a little uncertain about option two."

"Short and sweet, sweetheart: trading money for lost power is the best survival plan ever. If I leave government I'll be coming back here to take over Rue Royal. Expanding dramatically, into the Caribbean and father south is the way ahead. Who knows, maybe a chain across the south." She again leaned forward, now squinting, "I was born at night, but it wasn't last night, kiddo. Commodities and merchandise import and export, jewelry and precious metals trading, modeled on the rather infamous duty free port of the *Monte Verde* Plantation. I've heard anything's possible in such a magical place." Her garish, red smirk looked like a ghastly slash between cadaver-like cheeks, "I've heard stories about lead being turned in to gold here! Alchemy, isn't it? I think you and your playmates know exactly what I'm talking about. We both know that's the only reason you're where you are today and why I've given you a license to exploit—sorry, I meant to say explore—explore every legit or appropriately discrete opportunity you can winnow from

Latin America. What I'm talking about is the beginning of a beautiful friendship. It's why, beginning next week, you'll be promoted again, into a job that as of today doesn't even exist. You're going on the President's weekly briefing calendar from now on. You're going to be his special advisor for South American business development."

Pierce was dumbfounded, and she could see it.

"Don't worry; I'll convince the chief of staff and all his whiz kids on Pennsylvania Avenue and the assorted varieties of K Street bandits that you're the hottest item since old Ben Franklin. And, because your new post will require you to spend most of your time in New Orleans, obviously the best place to pursue your new additional duties, you will be my personal liaison to him for Republican National Convention next August in the Superdome. You'll commute from out there," she spoke, looking over Nat's shoulder, toward the dark runway.

Another faint rumble rose in the distance. Closer, he could hear the low-pitched, steady thump of a helicopter approaching.

"Your briefs, the one's that'll be filed with his National Security Advisor and me at State, will lay a paper trail from him, his inner circle, whoever he trusts, to every little scheme, every shady character you boys have met. If he's still standing next January, those little tidbits just might keep me in office. I almost don't care; he knows that I've got friends on both sides of the street. But, if both sides let me down, you, my very dear, sweet Nat, are going to be Rue Royal's entre into fascinating things you and your partners are tapped into in Colombia and who knows where else. You see, sweetie, I know an awful lot about you gentlemen planters and your very interesting friends. Need I say more?"

The helicopter was approaching. "Your career, meanwhile, is off to the races. Hell, who knows, you may own the racetrack before long! You and I, my friend, are a lot alike; we're going to come out on top. It could be the beginning of a beautiful friendship!"

Cotton's security officer appeared on the porch and knocked gently on the glass door. Pierce jumped up as though he'd been electrocuted. A minute later they sat side-by-side behind the agent as he drove the golf cart. Lightning flashed far away in the southwestern sky as he assisted her to her feet and gently squeezed her hand; she responded with a hug. She smelled like an expensive whore. The noise of the turning rotors would have covered her words, but she moved her mouth near his ear she said only one word: "Deal? Best friends forever?"

Of course, it was a deal.

The fat little bureaucrat had come a long way since that first posting in Cartagena. As the helicopter's prop blast tore at him he watched the olive drab and white Marine helicopter rise, turning slowly so he could see Cotton waving from a large window beneath "United States of America" painted above it. Seconds later it disappear into the darkness. He held his arm up, slowly waiving his hand from side to side, long after it was pointless. He stood alone, lit by the amber landing lights. As silence reclaimed the night, he drove up the pathway toward the big house. The pale footlights passed rhythmically, hypnotically. Images flashed before him: grotesque pictures of that unfortunate, amateurishly corrupt visa officer years ago in Cartagena, his weirdly bent neck, his bashed and bloody head. He thought about what was buried out on the plantation. He chased the terror: tomorrow he'll wake in his four-poster, take coffee on the verandah and feast his eyes on the majestic old oaks in the morning sun.

But, the happy thoughts didn't work this time: he was being squeezed from both ends.

Nathan Pierce was sick with fear.

Fourteen

UNCLASSIFIED//
ATTENTION INVITED TO
ROUTINE: PERSONAL FOR CTF28 PASS TO SUBJ
R ZZ0556Z JUL 12 PSN 885472M24
FM SECSTATE WASHINGTON DC
TO CO CTF28
CO USS ALDRICH
INFO USCINCLANTFLT
SECONDFLT
USCOMSOLANT
USSECSTATE SA EMBASSY DISTRO
NAVY CHINFO

ZEN/OU=SECSTATE/OU=ADDRESS LISTS(UC)/CN=AL
BT
UNCLAS
QQQQ
SUBJ: UNO AMERICAS/CTF28 PA/UNCLASSIFLED/PLEASE
    PASS TO

LT CARLYLE REES, USN
    1. AS UNO AMERICAS ENTERS 40TH ANNIVERSARY
       DEPLOYMENT,   WE   SHOULD   NEVER   FORGET
       SIGNIFICANCE/IMPORTANCE   OF   NORTH-SOUTH

AMERICA STRATEGIC/CULTURAL LEGACY/
COOPERATION.

2. ORIG AWARE OF BANDA DE UNO AMERICAS-88
OUTSTANDING PERFORMANCES, ESPECIALLY
NOTED IN DIPLOMATIC RESPONSES, MOST
NOTABLY FROM US AMBASSADORS VENEZUELA/
COLOMBIA AND IN INFORMAL COMMUNICATON
WITH HOST NATIONS. IN ADDITION TO
PROFESSIONAL EXCELLENCE, ORIG INFORMED
OF SUBJ OFFICER'S POSITIVE AND SUPPORTIVE
INTERFACE WITH EMBASSY PERSONNEL AND HOST
NATION NATIONALS.

3. ORIG REQUESTS CTF28/USS ALDRICH/
ADDRESSEES CONTINUE PROVIDING ALL
REASONABLE ACCOMMODATION TO ENABLE THE
BAND'S CONTINUED EXCELLENT PUBIC AFFAIRS
AND DIPLOMATIC ACHIEVEMENTS, WHICH TO
DATE FAR EXCEED EXPECTATIONS.

4. WELL DONE. PLEASE PASS PERSONAL
CONGRATULATIONS AND BEST WISHES TO BAND
LEADER, LT CARLYLE REES, USN, FOR FURTHER
CONVEYANCE.

5. US SECSTATE SPECIAL ASSISTANT TO PRESIDENT
FOR LATIN AMERICAN AFFAIRS SENDS.

BT
#3328
NNNN
UNCLASSIFIED//

"Attention on deck!" Chief Jones commanded sharply to the little knot of young men standing in the already hot morning sun. The band quickly arranged itself into two lines facing him and the lieutenant.

Even though the sun was barely above the horizon, it bore down hot on their backs. Such is morning in the tropics, and the little formation on the after deck enjoyed the breeze on their faces as the USS Aldrich raced westward through the deep blue ocean around them. Spirits were high, even under duress of such an early muster.

"Attention to Secretary of State message. To: Commander, Task Force Two Eight. Subject: Uno Americas, CTF 28 Public Affairs. Pass to: Lieutenant Lyle Rees, USN."

When he finished the only sound was the flapping canopy overhead. After a theatrical pause he turned to Rees, "Lieutenant, I've been around the Navy for a long time, but that beats any 'atta-boy' I've ever heard of." He looked toward the stunned band, paused again and continued, "You got pictures of somebody naked or somethin'?" The little gathering collapsed in laughter and high-fives.

"No, chief, just some four-oh shipmates in this band. Please, stand at ease."

"This is really about you, men. I mean it, it really is ALL about you. I don't know what to make of it, and I'm not even really sure where this comes from, but it's sure better than being put on report; the little after-the-show party back in Cartagena comes to mind. You know what I'm sayin'?"

More laughter, hoots and whistles.

"Apparently that one slipped below the radar. Can you imagine what kind of message we'd be getting if whoever wrote this happened to be driving by that little café? Petty Officer Lee, what was her name? Seriously, I'll tell you what I like about this: everything. We are a band, and we're team players on this deployment." He took the paper from his chief, "And, somebody pretty far up the chain, not even in the Navy, is paying close attention," he said, waiving the message in his right hand, "this is proof that you just never know who."

"Sir, if I may, what's the take up on the head shed?" the chief asked.

Before Rees could reply, as if responding to some hidden cue, a deep voice boomed on the ship's public address: "Lieutenant Rees, lay to the flag bridge. Lieutenant Rees, lay to the flag bridge on the double."

"Well, chief, I guess I'm about to find out. Great work, men."

All eyes followed him as he turned and walked through the open hangar and disappeared into the darkness.

Farther forward and up four ladders he stepped through a raised door jamb and entered the quiet coolness of the combat information center—the ship's electronic nerve center—then onto bridge through a door on the other side of the darkened room. The watch officer was there, but not the Commander Task Force 28. Seeing Rees, he cocked his thumb toward the bridge wing where Rear Admiral Steve Erick stood alone in the sunlight, scanning the horizon with binoculars.

"Sir?" Rees shut the door behind him and stood a few feet behind the rail thin veteran dressed in perfectly starched and ironed khakis. He was instantly embarrassed by his limp version of the same uniform.

"Morning. That's Panama, lieutenant," Erick spoke without turning, "Take a look."

He passed the binoculars and squinted to continue his unassisted gaze at the distant shore line. "Interesting message traffic today, Mister Rees. From what I've read between the lines, what you're seeing up ahead is another excellent change for you and that band of yours to grab some more glory." He continued, now resting his right elbow on the grey steel blast screen and turning toward Lyle, still pretending to see something through the binoculars.

"What do you think, Lieutenant, should I vacate flag quarters and get 'em ready for you. Doesn't look like I'm the top dog running this show, does it?"

If Rees hadn't seen anything through the binoculars before, he was now both blind and mute. If Santa's sleigh and eight tiny reindeer had appeared he wouldn't have seen them either. He held the attentive pose to buy time, standing like a statue for what seemed like a minute before he could recover enough to speak. By the time he managed a reply his eyes were as big as the lens now held at his chest. "Sir, I, no way, what I mean…"

"It's OK. You didn't write it. I'm pulling your leg," the admiral turned toward him and threw his head back in a laugh. "But I'm glad that I can be of some assistance, lieutenant. It's definitely a keeper, to say the least!" Erick slapped him on the shoulder, "But, coming from some weenie at State Department—even a great big weenie—may or may not be a recommendation for promotion in this man's Navy!" Rees felt faint and also leaned against the blast shield.

"Who the hell is this guy? Have you ever met him? You must have done something he or somebody in his chain really liked."

"Sir, no. I'm completely blindsided by this."

The old sailor jerked his head quickly toward Rees and squinted from beneath brushy grey eyebrows, "I see. Follow me below. Let's talk about it."

The two men walked to the rear of the bridge wing, then descended a steep exterior ladder to a small landing a deck below. The admiral opened the heavy steel watertight door, "After you."

Inside the command suite, he rang a buzzer and seconds later a man's head appeared through an interior door.

"Coffee, please."

Erick motioned for him to sit in a leather chair facing his desk and said nothing. He picked up a paper Lyle assumed was the message and began looking at it. He frowned and said nothing until the white-jacketed Filipino steward served efficiently and departed. Lyle was happy to have the cup and saucer to divert his attention as the silence lengthened.

"Honestly, sir, I am a bit lost in all this," he blurted out. "I've never met anyone at State at that level. I don't know who he is." They weren't complete lies.

Erick sat mute, then cocked an eyebrow, "Continue."

"I got briefed at State before leaving DC. It was routine. Since then my only connection has been through the cultural affairs officers in Venezuela, Colombia and—through message traffic—the officer in Panama. I've tried to turn-to for every request. It has involved some long hours, but—again—my men are not standing underway and it seems only fair that we turn and burn ashore. I believe that's what we're here to do."

"I don't know either, and you're right," the admiral said as he leaned back in the blue leather chair and rested his feet on the carved oak desk, the only piece of flammable wood on the ship. "But, one thing I learned a long time ago about stuff like this: when they're passing out tarts, take a tart. Don't say you're not hungry or that you're avoiding sweets or anything else. Even if tarts make you want to puke, just take the damned thing, say 'thanks' and smile; stand there holding it like you've never seen anything as freakin' wonderful, admiring it like it's some kind of treasure." Erick returned his gaze from the portholes and back to the very uncomfortable subordinate. He looked again at the paper, "This is a little strange. Actually, lieutenant, it is a lot damned strange, but it's better than a sharp stick in the eye. That's the good news. We'll take the tart."

"Yes, sir."

He stood, signaling that the meeting was ending.

Rees placed the still-full cup on the coffee table and began to move toward the door. He removed his hand from the door knob when Erick spoke. Lyle was standing at attention. The meeting was not over.

"One other thing, Rees; I don't what you to miss the point. You understand this little jewel ups the ante, and I don't know how much. But, I'm a realist, in a very real world. I hope for the best and plan for the worst. This is good, no doubt about it; but, my sixth sense of impending doom tells me that there's more here than meets the eye. There always is." He spoke louder after each pause. "I'll bet my next paycheck that this probably is prelude to more requests for more and more as we make our way around. Every U.S. embassy in South America was on distribution. Every prissy, second-team, wanna-be diplomatic sycophant from Panama to Brazil got it. Unless they're completely brain dead, it planted visions of glory in their heads about what we can provide to promote their careers. Everyone from here to Commander in Chief Atlantic Fleet may be the victim of your own success. Your happy gram has elevated our visibility from here to who knows where, in front of who knows who, and I don't like it one little bit!" Veins throbbed at his temples.

"Yes, sir."

"My official, reply to CINCLANT and Second Fleet is that we're just doing an outstanding job. That's the good news. The unspoken, bad news is that it has raised the pressure on everyone, and I've got somebody looking over my shoulder, somebody who probably talks to the President. We're probably on the hook for who knows what. A word of instruction," he continued, pointing a finger as he emphasized each point: "You bet everybody's working hard, but nobody but you is getting 'atta-boys' from some suck-up Presidential advisor in DC. They—me included—don't have a clue why. I'm taking it on face value. You're a smart guy, Rees, and you've got it right: all anybody in the wardroom sees in you is a transplanted Coastie who doesn't know jack shit about being a naval officer, who doesn't stand watches, who wakes up when we hit port and goes off to toot his horn for the high rollers. Don't let this go to your head, but if you need help, tell chief of staff. There's too much at stake now. If you drop the ball, I drop the ball. Keep me informed. Last word, Rees, don't screw up."

"Aye, aye, sir."

He stepped back outside on the steel grating, pulled the door shut and stood for a moment before climbing up to the bridge wing, gripping the steel railing with every step to steady himself. He took a few deep breaths and watched the blue water stream past under an only slightly less blue sky. His thoughts, the admiral's voice, were racing around his head so fast that he could hardly latch on to any one idea to examine.

He wasn't sure if he'd been chewed out or congratulated, maybe both. *What's the big picture? It's a cinch the old man knows a lot more, he has to. But, if he knows about his off-the-record, unofficial contacts and requests, why didn't he say so?* It would go a long way to untie the knots in his gut. *I didn't bring it up, because they said not to.*

The only option is to continue serving two masters; one offering high praise and promise, the other assuring support, even if he was angry about it like he was about everything else. But, he had walked out of the command suite with his rear end still attached to his body; that's not usually the case after one-on-ones in there. Not only that, he had some advantages and status far above his rank. *Is this the reassurance from Maggie Brown?*

He picked up the binoculars. This time he could actually see the green mass of Panama growing closer, still not much more than a thin green line separating two shades of blue. He put them down and rubbed his face with both hands. With the warm breeze on his face he came to a conclusion: even if the two big players didn't seem to acknowledge the other's presence, or worth, they did agree on the desired outcome. He was providing what both wanted. He'd need to be careful in pushing for too much from the admiral, but—bottom line—he was in a good place. He was a real player in something much bigger than he'd ever imagined.

Life in the fast lane, he smiled, *bring it on.*

* * * *

The transit through the Panama Canal's series of lakes and locks, like most everything involving South American ports, went slower than planned. He was worried by the time the small flotilla tied up at noon, two hours late at United States Naval Station Rodman, but there was still ample time to unload the band for the short ride to the commander's quarters at Fort Amador.

Tonight the highest visibility event of the deployment to date would take place. None other than Presidential Manuel Noriega himself, supported by his extended entourage of ministers, advisors, military brass and officially sanctioned thugs, was official host. Foreign diplomats, notably from Colombia, Ecuador, Venezuela, Peru, Nicaragua and the U.S., dozens of staff, wives and special friends, would swell the crowd to more than three hundred.

His mind drifted to the congratulatory message from Washington. He stopped pacing the wardroom carpet to enjoy the thought.

All the other officers were busy now as the ship approached the U.S. Naval Station, Rodman, Panama. As usual, Lyle was useless. He knew that nobody would be on the signal deck above the bridge. He dashed from the wardroom and up three sets of ladders to emerge on the ship's highest deck. From there he scanned the crowd trying to pick out the cultural affairs officer who, as in all ports, provided marching orders and support for the band ashore. Already behind schedule, he hoped he or she wouldn't follow the usual diplomatic custom of being fashionable late, having embraced their hosts' attitude about time: *mañana* he had learned, didn't mean tomorrow; it just meant "not now." His stomach churned. He needed good old North American on-time, ahead-of-schedule efficiency. After the morning's events, he was ready for anything.

Earlier messages from the embassy had laid out a light schedule and much smaller audiences than in Venezuela and Colombia. A couple of the performances were scheduled in places that hardly made the geographic atlas in the ship's library; the long trek to the orphanage deep in the Colombian jungle came to mind. The band had accepted his mantra, "We don't pick the gigs, we just play 'em," even setting it to music on the long bus rides back to the ship.

Then he saw it: two trucks and a small bus, each with large signs reading "U.S. Navy Band," on their windshields, were parked on the wide concrete dock. There were even two air conditioners atop the bus. *That's a new wrinkle. Movin' on up!*

As Aldrich crewmen began heaving the three-inch manila lines and warping the six-hundred foot ship to the dock, he descended to the band's storage room. He stopped dead in his tracks: Chief Jones stood smiling at him. Behind him a half-dozen seamen, not the band, were carefully dragging equipment from the storeroom and man-handling the bulky cases in fire brigade fashion from the storeroom, down the passageway, up the vertical ladder and through the ammo hatch to the main deck. Chief Jones read the startled expression and spoke through a broad smile, "Our shipmates here are taking our gear on deck and to the truck. All we gotta do is call them away when we return for the reload. Don't make no difference what time," he laughed as much as he spoke the words. "Unless you say otherwise, I'll have the band stand by in the bus."

"Absolutely, chief, that's what I had in mind," he answered, trying to hide his surprise, as though he knew how—or why—this was happening.

The two musicians stood in the shade of a warehouse door and watched the work party finish. The cultural affairs officer had not made an appearance.

"Got to hand it to you, boss. I reckon that the message and—I'm guessing—your chat on the bridge worked out nice? We can sure get used to this. Let's just say good morale is even better," he winked and slapped Rees' back.

The band was loaded and boarded the bus in about a third of the time Lyle had planned. The three-vehicle convoy pulled away and drove toward the tall pines ahead. Lyle sat in the front seat beside his chef and took in the exotic view. From the ancient Spanish portico, all the way to their destination a half mile away atop a hill at the fort's western end, Fort Amador looked more like a country club than a military base. Well-dressed golfers strolled along fairways and greens. In the foreground the less affluent sweated through limp t-shirts and ragged shorts as they pushed mowers; a few used scissors to manicure grass along the edge of sidewalks around the golf course bounded by the compound's low, immaculately white-washed, mission tile roofed buildings. Neither group seemed to notice the little convoy rolling past over the narrow concrete road stained darkly by decades of tropical heat and rain, past acres of mimosa-shaded lawns.

Humid air outside the bus fogged the windows. Lyle wiped it away as they began climbing up a narrow road that led steadily upward to the military compound's highest point. Near the top they were stopped by soldiers, serious men with machine guns slung over their shoulders. One with a clipboard quickly pointed toward a parking lot behind the palace just ahead. It was the official residence of the Panamanian Army's Chief of Staff.

Rees and Jones sat as the band members filed past them. Spirits were high. Even though they were always happy to leave the ship—especially after a week-long transit from Colombia—and start contributing their talent. Their enthusiasm was palpable. The feeling appeared even stronger now as each spoke to their leaders, jumped off the bus and gathered around the equipment truck like they were capable of levitating their equipment off it and on to the stage fifty feet away.

Rees and Jones had hardly joined them before a dozen soldiers appeared. "*Capitan de corbeta Rees*, we offer assistance, yes?" a soldier saluted, then turned toward the truck. Lyle returned the salute and winked at Jones who took it from there. Moments later their gear seemed to float across the lawn, handled as though it were so many cases of high explosives.

Lyle climbed to the front of the wide stage, stood beneath its white canvas canopy and watched. Judging from the smell of freshly-cut lumber, it must have been built expressly for tonight's show. It extended from the mansion's wide marble steps, out over the lawn. On three sides, red, white and blue bunting hung from the stage floor to the ground. Giant Panamanian and U.S. flags hung as backdrop from the mansion wall behind. A camera platform about sixty feet straight ahead would ensure that the magnificent scene would be well documented.

The game had definitely been kicked up a notch, or twenty.

"Yep, boss, we could sure get used to this."

"When they're passing out tarts, chief, take a tart."

"OK. If that means don't be lookin' a gift horse in the mouth, I'm with you, boss. At this rate we'll be through with sound checks in no time. If it's alright, corporal says they'll drive us back to the ship to shower and change. Hell, if the guys weren't so keyed up, we'd have time for a siesta, at least I would."

"I trust your judgment. Just make sure everything's ready to go. Bring 'em back in time for a speed rehearsal, then keep 'em out of the way. When in doubt just smile a lot; remember that *gracias* is always a good response."

In less than an hour the stage was ready, amplifiers where laid, mixer levels were set and all was in order, earlier than ever. Rees dismissed the musicians to the chief's care. About two hours before the show, they'd return in sharp white jumpers. He watched the bus until it descended beyond view beneath the thick growths of pines and mimosas fringing the hill. He inspected the set-up, happy that his band, rested and fresh, would perform their best in this magnificent setting. He smiled, *somebody in DC is watching*.

There was nothing left for him to do, not even worry as he usually did. He was current on paperwork, having risen before dawn. With little to think about, he realized that he wouldn't sleep again for at least another twelve hours. Who cares? It was late afternoon, and he should be tired, but he wasn't, far from it, as he stood alone. *I'm getting paid for this!*

The Pacific Ocean stretched across the horizon on his right, verdant, dark green foliage extended as far as he could see in the other direction. In front, to the south, the tropical metropolis of Panama City clung to the gentle hills. The canal lay motionless about a mile away. Closer, squads of gardeners, florists, caterers, carpenters, electricians milled around purposefully but not too quickly in the growing oppression of afternoon heat. Some soldiers were parting the bunting and doing something beneath the stage. In the shade of trees where the lawn dropped away, other men in cream *guayaberas* or brown uniforms stood and watched it all, him included. Their purpose, like those under the stage, was less clear.

He was ahead of the curve, at least right now, and it felt good. He felt strong, even taller somehow as he filled his lungs with the fragrance of salt air and freshly-mown grass. He pushed his white hat back and wiped his damp brow. Nothing but pleasant thoughts filled his head: the musicians are fantastic, any one of them could be working in Vegas or a recording studio anywhere. He had an experienced, exceptional chief to keep them in line. This night would be the best yet; it would still be young when they finished to be swept away by swarms of admiring and exotic women who'd treat them like rock stars. Then there was this morning and all the little things happening since; maybe it was just the start of a chain of events that would catapult his career beyond even his wildest imagination. The stars were aligned, as his mother would have said. For the first time since leaving DC, he felt that he had a firm grasp on everything and no place to go but up.

Take a tart.

A heavily accented tenor voice spoke quietly and politely. "A cool breeze is worth a lot of money on a hot day like this, yes?"

The delicately delivered words spoken precisely with an aristocratic Castilian Spanish dialect, landed softly on Lyle's back. He turned to see that they came from a young Latin man standing very close behind. He was dressed in white linen with a red silk handkerchief exploding from a breast pocket. He looked at Lyle with genteel politeness and toothy smile beaming from beneath a neatly trimmed black moustache. Lyle noticed a hint of lilac.

"Welcome to Panama," this time with a courtly nod and extended right hand which Lyle accepted. "My name is Alberto Dias, but—as your band delightfully performs so well—you can call me Al," he giggled, pleased with the play on words.

"Thank you, *señor*, you've seen our show?"

"Let's just say I'm familiar with your work. Unfortunately, my duties have kept me at a distance, but your talent is well noted. And your assistance—what is the musician's term, improvisation—with my colleagues in Colombia was flawless. And, your observations of Admiral Vasquez were thorough, better than could have been hoped. Your professionalism is credit to your naval service."

Releasing Rees' hand, his face became only slightly more serious.

He read Rees' face, then tilting his head back, he spoke, "We hope the recent and most official expression of confidence from your State Department was well received? That was our intent."

Rees tried not to look stunned. He remembered that Dias hadn't spoken of his title. Not wanting to appear uniformed, he resisted the urge to ask . But, his comments clearly placed him squarely in the loop, if not official State Department, then at least somewhere in someone's diplomatic or intelligence cabal. After all, he would not be wandering around this place if he weren't.

"We trust that the official recognition will pay rich dividends; that it will give you, shall I say, greater freedom, opportunity not afforded otherwise." He paused, but before Lyle could reply, he looked back toward the preparations in the distance, then back. "Beyond the pleasant generalities of the message, please understand this: your performance tonight will be admired by many friends. They salute you and will work to reward you as the cruise works its way around the continent. You will have no problems." He looked toward the Pacific, "We hope you enjoy your week in our gracious and ancient country. We anticipate that your reputation will only improve and that you and your band take time to enjoy what it has to offer, seize opportunities," he smiled, very broadly this time. "The English pirate Morgan once said this was the greatest mart for silver and gold in the whole world. May it be for you, too, but on much more peaceful terms, yes?" He again extended his hand, nodding slightly. He turned and seemed to float in the direction of the palace.

The strange, although somehow reassuring little exchange soon merged into the mind-boggling events of the following week. The most pleasantly distracting and unexpected development was with the news media. It was as though the newspapers, radio and television broadcasts were edited at the Palace. Turns out they were. The band catapulted from official acclaim to assume celebrity status in the Panamanian news media. In the five days that followed what local media labeled a "command performance," their shows in Panama City drew thousands. "Rock and roll diplomacy," as the headlines proclaimed, was a screaming success. Pictures of smiling U.S. and Panamanian military officers, vowing renewed north-south hemispheric solididarity, splashed across the front pages. The band's final performance was broadcast live.

Even their shipmates got it; as the flotilla departed Rodman officers and crew responded with new respect. The word had spread quickly: nobody wanted to miss out on mingling with the hundreds of impressionable young people drawn to their once-despised-now-famous passengers. A Navy jumper was a ticket to paradise. The band's schedule, especially after Ecuador and for the large cities of Peru and Chile, was a must-read item on the mess deck bulletin board.

Two weeks at sea was almost a welcome relief. After war games with Colombian and Ecuadorian navies, the Aldrich tied up at the end of a long pier in the small port city of Manta. Only a handful of embassy and naval staff met them. There would be no screaming crowds to mob them; this time their audiences would be found far inland, close to the Colombian border, deep in the jungle and far to the east. Each day they traveled farther to hamlets—not much more than clearings fronted by mud and stick huts packed beside dirt streets—inhabited by a sobering sight of filthy, half-naked children, wandering poultry and open sewers. An army truck carrying a diesel generator and a half-dozen soldiers followed them to provide the single 120-volt, 60-cycle electrical circuit to power the amplifiers. If the faces looking at them in amazement were any indication, Lyle and the band may very well have arrived from Mars. And, if the steadily growing number of soldiers trailing along was any indication, they had arrived in a place just as alien to these North Americans, where life was primitive and—judging from the fearful reaction to the soldiers—cheap.

"We'll be staying there tonight." He broke the news to the band as they watched their escorts hustle equipment off the truck and on to a concrete slab in what looked like a village square. They were good at it by now. "I know, I know, it's a dream come true." He pointed toward a clearing, barely visible about a mile away on a hill above the village. "They're setting up a tent for us, a field kitchen, even showers. We'll have all the comforts, even some Ecuadorian home cooking. It's too far back to Manta. That's the good news. The better news is that we're free tomorrow. We can sleep in and take it easy. We'll be back in time for liberty in Manta 'till we leave day after tomorrow."

He was as stunned as they were. He had no choice other than putting on a happy face. This had not been the plan. It changed before dawn this morning with the arrival of an embassy staffer from Quito, a good two hours away by plane. Awakened by the quarterdeck runner, Lyle was confused: pre-dawn is not the usual starting time for anyone, especially from a U.S. embassy drone. He slid his legs over the side of his bunk. What could have changed so dramatically that it required a face-to-face briefing? He shaved and dressed quickly, puzzled but anxious to put a face—he hoped a pretty one—with the name on the messages he'd exchanged with her during the past several weeks. These cultural affairs officers, he had learned in Venezuela, Colombia and Panama, had been knock-outs, selected—he supposed—for their good looks as much as anything else. A sailor knows better than most that a pretty face is a great way to start any day. If he had to be awake at this time of day, at least there may be some reward.

He quietly pulled his stateroom door shut and stepped into the passageway and waited for his eyes to adjust. Aboard all Navy ships, lights are turned off from sunset to sunrise; dim red lights provide just enough light to move safely and ensure that opening an outside door won't reveal the ship to potential enemies, even during peacetime operations like this. The aroma of coffee and fresh-baked bread propelled him. He stepped into the wardroom.

His fantasies crashed with one glimpse. A fifty-something woman dressed in baggy grey sweats sat on the long, green leather sofa. There was nobody else. Her dead-looking grey hair was pulled into a ratty pony tail, and she wore no make-up to soften her bloated face. She looked and greeted him like she'd been up all night, which she had. She did manage a handshake, fell back in a chair, then went straight to work.

"There are reports of roaming groups of outlaws along the border with Colombia," she spoke quietly, looking around the room, catching his eye only briefly. "The government is sensitive to all this, but don't like to admit that they really don't control their own territory. Staying up there overnight saves face for them. There will be plenty of security. They feel much more confident about securing a perimeter for you than providing a rolling target stumbling around the wilderness and attracting outlaws of every stripe."

Lyle had noticed that two trucks had trailed along as the usual bus-truck convoy pulled away from the dock and rolled through the little seaside town and into the foreboding, dark wilderness to the east.

* * * *

The old chief was an early riser and had been since he got sober. He believed that it was one of the benefits; it added at least two or three productive hours to his day, and—most recently—it also helped him to stay ahead of the much younger men in his care. Today he was up even earlier than usual, awakened by the sound of a motor struggling up the muddy road to the little hilltop encampment.

The sky above his mosquito-netted cot was still dark, but jungle birds sensed the approaching dawn and were beginning to sound off, even though daybreak was still at least an hour away. He heard someone start a cook fire, and in a few minutes he smelled coffee brewing. That was the final straw; he was fully awake. He threw back the netting, slipped on flip-flops and threw a towel over his shoulder. He was not exactly a dashing figure in his boxers as he padded the few yards across the packed dirt and walked toward the campfire. He scooped up a mug of hot water from a boiling pot, a little puzzled that whoever started it and brewed the coffee was nowhere around. Spindly, pale legs carried him into the darkness where a board was wedged between two trees to make a shaving table. He placed his mug on it and—even though he couldn't see his reflection—hung a small mirror from the tree on the left. He lathered up. It felt good; shaving, even using the braille method to guide his razor in the pre-dawn darkness, was a simple pleasure.

The sky was slowly, almost imperceptibly, growing brighter and paler above the thick branches when he heard two, maybe three men talking in Spanish from the darkness on the other side of the clearing. As his eyes adjusted, he saw that two of them were pulling a tarp off the back of a truck, the one he assumed he'd heard struggling up the hill. He thought little of it, concentrating more on the tricky act of shaving by feel. Finally wiping foam from his neck, a sharp clap drew his eyes back toward the two trucks parked side by side. Two soldiers had dropped a metal ramp between them.

He squinted hard, harder once he saw what was happening; the men were taking boxes from the newly arrived truck and loading them next to the band's equipment on the other. He started edging closer then stopped dead in his tracks. From behind a tree he saw that the boxes were actually drum cases, not just any drum cases: they were the exact same shape, size and number as the band's drummer. The only difference was their weight: they were heavy; it took two men to handle each of them. Five cases moved across the little bridge. What happened next was even more confusing: the two men quickly wiped down each of the cases with what looked like small bath towels. From where he stood about thirty feet away, he could smell gasoline. Finally, they pushed the cases next to the bands' and retied the cargo net over the expanded load. It was much lighter now, and fearing he'd be seen, Jones crouched farther down behind the tree and low undergrowth. From there he saw them throw the rags into a trash barrel. He didn't move again until the men climbed back in the truck. It lumbered down the muddy road.

* * * *

"You've been reading too many mystery books, chief." Lyle spoke calmly, trying to mask his true reaction to the story. Unlike past arrangements, nobody had told him anything about this. And, for the first time, nobody would accompany the mystery cargo, then jump off the truck and disappear. For the first time he was worried about just what was inside the drum cases that took two men to handle. Whoever did this had simply loaded and disappeared. This was too much. Should anyone want to inspect the load, he'd own whatever it was inside, something not lost on his chief.

"Sir, we've been through this a couple of times back in Venezuela and Colombia. I'm OK with all that. If it's some kind of diplomatic courier stuff like you said, that's cool, and all that's way above my pay grade. But, damn it all, what's going to happen to those cases when we get back to the ship? Those cases are sealed and locked. You get what you inspect, not what you expect. My name's on the manifest, too, and I don't know what the hell I'm signing for."

Lyle thought before answering his visibly upset deputy. He'd never seen him like this. As usual, they sat together on the front row of the bus. Lyle stared straight ahead and tried to think. He had to remain calm and come up with something reasonable that would sound logical, to both of them. "I understand your concern; I agree. I don't know exactly what's happening with this. We've got some time before we're back in Manta. A lot can happen between now and then, and I'm sure it will; it always has," he spoke, trying to convince himself of something, anything.

The three-hour drive over what passed as roads flew by, but worry made the trip even more nauseating. Both men had periodically looked at the truck following them, as though looking at it would provide a clue.

By the time the bus reached the first pavement on the outskirts of Manta, Lyle jumped to his feet and ordered the driver to stop. With both hands clamped tightly over his mouth he climbed over Jones and barely cleared the door before losing his breakfast in the gutter. Resting both hands on the side of the muddy fender and spitting out the last remnants, he palmed tears from his eyes. He looked back toward the truck.

He blinked away more tears in disbelief. It wasn't there.

He quickly stumbled toward the front bumper and looked down the road. For the half mile ahead the only thing moving were a couple of bicycles approaching from the opposite direction.

"Where's the truck?" he looked up the stairs at the driver. The young soldier's puzzled response was a palms-up, shoulder-shrugging, "*Que?*"

Jones managed to make himself understood in fractured Spanish. "He says he's taking us to the ship. The truck, he thinks, is going to the airport first, then meet us there."

The two sailors looked at each other. Lyle jumped back aboard. "*Pronto, pronto!*" he shouted and pointed toward the windshield. The bewildered armed teenager sped away.

* * * *

"Don't worry about the damned paperwork. I'll deal with the watch officer when we get back." Lyle accelerated, and the jeep bounced over the pot-holed lane, nearly launching Jones, and careened turned onto the asphalt highway. About a quarter mile past the spot where he'd left his breakfast, they saw a sign pointing toward the airport.

The street ended abruptly at the entrance gate. Behind it were two hangars and perhaps two dozen steel cargo containers scattered on either side of them, most stacked two high. Lyle was relieved that nobody was tending the gate and that nobody was in sight. Jones pushed it open and Lyle drove through. Aware that they conspicuous in their uniforms, he wheeled quickly to the right, stopping amid the containers. From there they could see a tower and some low buildings on the opposite side of the runway. They scanned what they imagined was about half of the airport, but the truck was nowhere in sight. They crept toward the edge of a container on their left and peeked around it to survey the rest. They jerked at the explosive racket of an un-muffled motor starting. They saw the truck parked no more than thirty feet away, between them and a hangar which looked like it was held together by rust and fading green paint. The motor was from a farm tractor attached to the nose gear of a weird looking airplane. The tractor pulled it from shadow to sunlight. The old looking airplane wobbled like a clumsy duck on the uneven tarmac until it was about a hundred feet from the hangar door.

"That looks like some kind of old military cargo carrier, but this don't look very military," Jones said. "Oh, crap: he's driving straight toward us!"

The tractor had uncoupled and was approaching them. The two men ran closer to the fence and hid on top of a twenty-foot steel cargo container. They had barely reached the top before the motor stopped. They lay frozen in silence. Raising his head just enough to see over the edge, Lyle saw the tractor parked next to their cargo truck. The driver—who Jones recognized as one of the two men he'd seen during his pre-dawn shave—climbed in and began backing toward the plane. Simultaneously, a wide cargo door opened at the rear.

"What the hell, commander? They're going to steal our equipment!"

"I don't think so. Follow me. I think I know what's going to happen." Jones followed Rees as he lowered himself to the ground and ran to their original vantage point. They peered around the container and saw the soldier and a civilian, a much older man—a North American, it appeared to them—lift the tarp just enough to expose the drum cases loaded in the jungle. The soldier wet a rag with gasoline poured from a two-gallon can and wiped them. The two men strained to drag them off the truck and across to the cargo ramp. From there the old man pushed them over rollers built into the cargo ramp and followed them inside. The truck driver threw the rag into a barrel by the hangar door and climbed back in the truck. The sailors again ducked as it passed on the other side of the container. The truck picked up speed and exited through the gate. Jones watched it down the street; it turned onto the highway, toward Manta.

In the opposite direction, the clam-like doors closed slowly. Moments later billows of black smoke erupted as the right, then the left engine began turning the huge propellers. He studied the round logo painted in green and gold on the otherwise bare aluminum tail: Great Circle Air Cargo. The ancient-looking aircraft began to roll.

"Get down!" Lyle hissed toward Jones, "He'll see us when he taxis by."

The sailors knelt behind the jeep until the airplane lumbered past to their right. A minute later it squared up on end of the runway, revved its engines and began its take-off roll. It gained speed rapidly, rocked back, almost striking the runway with its tail, and leaped into the cloudless blue sky. It banked toward the north and soon disappeared in the glare of the blinding noonday sun.

Fifteen

Arms spread wide, palms up, he shouted "It's alive! It's actually up and running. Can you believe this?" The big man could hardly contain himself. "They're gonna be as connected here as they are in the five-sided puzzle palace."

Emma smiled wryly from behind him; his enthusiasm was contagious, and that was one of the things she liked most about him. She laughed out loud, imagining that at any moment this bear of a man in a blue and white Chicago Cubs sweatshirt and pants and heavy-soled brogans might break into dance. In some ways, some very subtle ways, she knew that this meant more to him that it did for her and the business. Seeing him happy, this man who she has admired and to whom she owed so much, was priceless. She affected her country bumpkin pose, hanging her thumbs in the corners of her denim bib overalls and frowning at several hundred- thousand dollars of equipment, "But, can it pick up Lawrence Welk on Saturday night?"

"We're bouncing off a satellite for Pete's sake," he spoke emphatically. "Still blows me away. The world has turned. Those kids from Langley probably can't even imagine how primitive a lash-up we had back in the good old days. Scrambled, encrypted, x-band, y-band, sliced and diced, and it all runs on a car battery! Compared to this sat-com gear, we might as well have been throwing carrier pigeons into the prevailing wind out on Adak and hoping they'd land somewhere on the mainland in a month or two." Joe Degorski chuckled, "Listen to me, I sound like one of those old geezers I used to laugh at when I was their age."

The owner, proprietor and mortgage note holder of Lucas Lodge and her principal assistant owed much, to each other. If he expected a salary for all he did, it would cover his duties as carpenter, plumber, chef, fishing guide, security chief, housekeeper and counselor. Today the list grows to include secure satellite communications technician. He and Emma had just climbed up the zig-zag stairs, nearly a hundred feet up to the lodge's broad porch. They caught their breath on the plank deck that spanned the amber-stained clapboard lodge. From there they had waived as the rugged and roomy single-engine de Havilland Canada DHC-2 Beaver broke free of the lake. The work horse of Alaska bush pilots since the early '50s climbed into the air, making a wide circle and wobbling its wings in a farewell salute.

The two CIA technicians aboard were happy to be returning to civilization as they knew it. They had been there for two days, working around the clock—together at first, then in alternating six-hour shifts— to install the electronic gear. Joe stayed awake the whole time, building a closet and asking questions. They were scheduled to stay for another day to instruct in its care and maintenance, but their star pupil, the retired Navy master chief, had devoured the manual and everything they said. Emma was again awed by the insatiable curiosity and razor sharp mind of the former Navy SEAL whose career was cut short by a bullet. A steel pin replaced his shattered left knee.

She had learned a lot from the round-faced, balding Pole ten years her senior. Of all the revelations, one stood out: looks are deceiving. He carefully weighed physical exertion, owing to the pain of the crippling wound; when he did act he moved with precision, no motion wasted. He spoke little, but everyone knew to listen when he did. His loyalty to Emma was unshakable; she had been a rock during his wife's slow loss of a debilitating battle with cancer.

Mastering any skill that would ensure the lodge's success had become the passion of his remarkable mind and talent for everything from field dressing game to photography, gourmet cooking and even performing on an electronic keyboard. This Renaissance man, Emma thought, may be her very own resident genius.

They served together on Adak, and he followed her into retirement on Lake Illiamna, another remote location, albeit only two-hundred-seventy-five, not twelve-hundred miles southwest of Anchorage.

Surrounded by rugged mountains, there are no roads and probably never will be. For Emma it is a combination of paradise, challenge, vindication and a livelihood.

She studied the backside of her best friend and partner who had helped her dreams come true. "If you say so, but they must believe you've got a few ancient brain cells left, old man. It's you they're counting on to keep it up and running 'til it's needed. Last I heard Lucas Lodge was not listed as a major defense installation, complete with millions in operation and maintenance money. If it's not workin' when they get here it's not going to be a pretty sight!"

Emma left him to tidy up. Her steps echoed on the wood floor as she walked out on the chevron-shaped deck jutting toward the lake. The sunlight warmed her face. She never tired of the view. More than twenty miles across the richly blue water the jagged mountains on the south shore stabbed the sky. Its eighty-mile width extended to her left and beyond the horizon on the right. The empty silence was exquisitely serene. The impossibly brilliant and pure colors filled her senses. She allowed her mind to drift.

She loved this place and the way it made her feel. She had felt this way, so very long ago it seemed now, about New Orleans and her life there. She saw their faces. She remembered Lyle, and, just as suddenly, puzzled why and oddly uneasy that somehow he was thinking of her. Too strange, she thought. *This is renting too much space in my head.* So much had happened since then. She still couldn't come up with a single explanation, only that—somehow—she was inadequate. But, she is a different woman now. The thought passed, replaced with a sense that it was her father who was nearby, as she felt often during the past years of building and establishing the business. It was as close as she would ever be to the misty memory of working beside him at the old boat yard on the Ohio. Had he somehow returned from the grave to bring the pair together to rebuild the old, but roomy lodge attached to the mountainside behind her? Actually, he had.

When Emma was in her teens, he worked in Dutch Harbor as a mechanic on ships of Alaska's fishing fleet. The money had been very good, she remembered, enough to finance the boat yard that she and her mother had been left behind to hold together. Concerns about her mother's fragile health and unwarranted fears about how Lucy would fare in such a remote place, kept him from moving the family. But his stories about the Last Frontier thrilled her, and she never forgot them. Her orders to Adak and brutal beauty of that isolated island did not diminish her romantic ideas; the people she met there, men like Joe, opened her eyes to her own potential, in ways she never imagined. She happily shouldered the burdens of those brave enough to dream and ignore anyone who says they shouldn't try. Alaska is a place where actions speak louder than words: the serious and steady succeed; pedigree, swagger and a big mouth don't amount to much. Lucas Lodge had never been a sure thing, but—after only two seasons—she was in the black. But, that also could change; should she join the rank of losers, she knew it wouldn't be because she feared pouring her heart and soul into her dreams.

In a very real way, it was her father who got her started. He had left a good name in Alaska and had won the respect of good people, in many walks of life: fellow mariners, bush pilots, fishing guides and even a couple of politicians. During her unprecedented four years, and four winters, on Adak, Emma made frequent trips to Anchorage and met some of them, most notably the miner who built the remote cabin. As his wealth vanished, the cabin fell into disrepair. About the time she was helping Joe get through his loss, the idea of teaming with him began to take shape. Both were retiring and too young to drift or sit idle. When the down-on-luck prospector offered a family discount, she took the plunge.

Joe and Emma possessed all the mechanical and technical skill needed to operate a remote business, where everything is do-it-yourself. Even if neither knew anything about the mysteries of advertising and marketing nor had any experience in the commercial world, it didn't matter. Even in Alaska, Emma was bit of a novelty: a woman-owned, remote fishing lodge, complete with air service and an expert fishing guide. She learned to fly, quickly, and racked up hundreds of float-plane hours, ferrying material and supplies while the pair rebuilt the lodge and dock.

The need for marketing disappeared. Word of mouth, especially from some high-ranking sources, spread quickly; the general in command of the Eighteenth Air Force at Elmendorf was among her first fans. He became her biggest promoter. Two months later he became the head of the Central Intelligence Agency, and in only a few weeks she was booking groups of two, sometimes and many as eight. A heady array of Washington-based government leaders slowly filled her June-September booking calendar, but only if she guaranteed that no other guests would be present. Lucas Lodge evolved into a secure conference center for the nation's powerful, a mix of senior general and flag officers, members of

Congress and cabinet-level and deputy secretaries. The lack of creature comforts—sleeping in bunk beds, four to a room if required—didn't deter those eager for off-the-grid and off-the-record conversations Lucas Lodge provided.

Joe and Emma gladly adapted to their clients' routine. Guests usually arrived separately, ferried from Anchorage on closely timed flights. The hosts felt for the security details and various disgruntled horse-holders, most of whom were left on the shore of Lake Spenard, the float plane base in Anchorage, watching their boss disappear with a woman whose security clearance paper trail was far from usual. Joe's was quite the opposite and eased the minds of the bodyguards who made the trip for at least a cursory inspection of arrangements. After dragging bags up the long stairs, they would scan the two-story structure, noting the rifles, shotguns and pistols in the glass case beside the wood stove and ammunition, dynamite and blasting caps in storage below in the bunk rooms. Each would study Emma and Joe, matching their faces to official photos mined from security files back in DC, then have no other option than flying back to Anchorage and awaiting a coded radio call to return.

Arrangements at Lucas Lodge stretched the rules. Emma and Joe knew this and felt the discomfort of those who had to trust them. Joe built an addition on the shack that served as an office at Lake Spenard where her Cessna 182 docked. Like the other private float plane docks scattered around the lake, the structure was tiny. But, nestled neatly beneath three small birches and a young spruce and surrounded by a tiny but neatly trimmed lawn, the shack—about the size of a single-car garage—was weatherproof. The red metal roof sat atop yellow walls and also protected a front porch and deck that ended as steps down to the dock. Having learned long ago how to brighten up a home in the middle of a dingy boat yard, Emma placed cedar flower boxes down the sides of the deck and planted them with blue and gold pansies. To accommodate growing numbers of planes and accompanying staff, Joe upgraded the power of the VHF radio and built a bump-out addition that doubled the shack's footprint and served as a meeting place for the agents. Joe even installed an intercom for delivery orders from Cubby's bar and restaurant about a hundred yards away.

* * * *

In Washington, D.C., knowing more means surviving longer.

Trading in secrets and embarrassing personal details is the coin of the realm, an endless font to nurture extortion, promotion and respect among like-minded minions. Rumors of secret trips to Alaska by intriguing combinations of very high-ranking individuals aroused curiosity, especially among the non-participants. As always, the uninvited—especially the most highly developed paranoids among them—were quick to identify patterns. As the presidential election calendar neared the nominating conventions, the feverish desire for intelligence far beyond its legitimate interest was rising exponentially.

Conventional wisdom among the seasoned old timers who had survived under administrations from both sides of the aisle was reassuring: the two-term President Frank H. Lehman was popular, and his rumored hand-picked successor, former director of the FBI Hayes Abbott, was sure to receive the Republican nomination at the convention this summer in New Orleans. With a weak field among a lack-luster stable of potential Democrat candidates, Lehman—now dean of Pepperdine University's law school—was odds-on favorite.

But, others among the Capital City's most powerful criminals—including the Principal Deputy Secretary of State for Immigration and Commerce—knew that an Abbott administration spelled disaster.

Lack of any real attention from the well-meaning but detached Lehman Administration had enabled Nathan Langford Pierce and his partners to grow their fortunes and influence among the DC ruling class. The Republicans established an anti-crime reputation by winning widely publicized convictions, mostly of old Italian Mafia dons and capos on the East Coast. The real effect on organized crime was minimal: these were fading criminals and syndicates. They were well past their prime, no longer competitors with the money and political influence growing exponentially within the untouchable South American drug cartels and—to a lesser extent—Middle Eastern suppliers.

The Dixie Mafia fell neatly between the cracks. They operated in large Southern cities and in the rural counties surrounding them, where law enforcement experience—especially with homicide and organized crime—was weak to non-existent. Members often established legitimate junk and antique businesses, like Secretary Cotton's Rue Royale Collectables and *Monte Verde* in New Orleans, as fronts for selling stolen merchandise, most often to other members of the network. When suspicions were aroused, the operators simply closed shop, moved to a new location or curtailed illegal activity for a while. Local police soon lost interest. The feds never looked.

Members usually had served time in state or federal prisons, where the most violent of the violent were recruited; Louisiana's Angola prison was a prime source. The Southern Mob had no chain of command. Consequently, whoever had the most money became default leader. Only one tenet held the loose-knit mob together: never talk to the cops. Upon release, often arranged by *Monte Verde's* powerful criminal defense attorney, these men—with no familial or country-of-origin connection—simply began making money and gaining control of illegal revenues through murder and influence peddling that the three men in New Orleans and Nat Pierce in Washington, D.C., had brought to a fine art. From the 1960s to '80s the Dixie Mafia, if it ever identified as an organization, looked like a traveling band of criminals involved in residential burglary, theft and robbery. That suited them fine.

The FBI had made no connection between the Dixie Mafia and its businesses in South America and Iran, the lucrative trade in narcotics through the deep South and only passing knowledge of the emerging flow of gold-for-plutonium that was fueling international terrorism. Only the National Security Agency and the CIA were involved; about the time Pierce joined the ranks, unofficial Washington had sought creative counsel in trading arms-for-drugs in Nicaragua. Chris Cain, former CIA agent and now convenient cut-out, had put the network together.

For the cartels and their more-than-willing partners in the States, well-publicized prosecutions of the Italian and Sicilian mafia had been an unexpected gift, *lagniappe* on top of the previous eight years dominated by Democrats who had perfected the use of narco dollars to buy candidates and elections and hobble law enforcement. The Dixie Mafia offered a perfect paradigm. Former FBI director Hayes Abbott had been crushed eight years ago by mobbed-up politicians, but the tenacious Texan had never left the field entirely. His election would be a sea change: there would be renewed momentum to investigate real organized crime, wherever it led, and with real effects.

* * * *

Now, neither Pierce nor his partners were being invited to the party, they didn't know what plans were being made. Nobody was leaking; there was no information, and that was more than scary.

The palace guards were nervous. At the U.S. Department of State, with its world-wide sources of information and battalions of careerists who rarely or only temporarily rotated from Foggy Bottom, the paranoia index was off the charts. Pierce was under pressure.

"This is some kind of a nightmare. It just can't be true," he barely contained composure; his voice rising in a shrill whisper as he slammed his palms flat on the table, drawing frowns from tables across the quiet room. He calmed himself enough to look pleasantly at a familiar face taking a seat at the bar. He continued staring intently at the man seated across from him and continued through clenched teeth, "I thought we got rid of this bitch years ago. You told me you handled it. I left it to you. You said you'd taken care of the problem, trashed her, sent her to Siberia or some damn place to go nuts or freeze to death. How in hell does she show up again, damned near a decade later? Not just showing up, mind you, but hosting people who could put us away for the rest of our lives!"

Gene Menard gripped the arms of the chair and surveyed Nat. He never liked him; he was weak and effeminate, but he always delivered. He paused before speaking with an overly polite expression taken when talking to an idiot, "You may remember that I did have a long-term solution in mind. It was you who chickened out. It was you who got all runny after the accident on Bay St. Louis; some nobody, drunk sailor nobody cared about. You freaked out. He's not a problem now, is he? But now you say there's a big problem. How interesting!"

Nat sat back and stared at nothing across the Cosmos Club lounge, nothing in its ambience offering the usual comforts. He had learned a lot from Menard and the others: cover your tracks, never leave a witness. But, nobody imagined in their wildest dreams that this woman would survive and—more than that—have the ear of the people she does now. *Her signature on that document meant forever. She was straight. She'd never open her mouth; even if she did nobody would give a damn or even believe her.* Now she's shown up as some kind of a key player or at least someone who has the ear of the men who could relieve her of the oath and pursue it wherever her story led them. Hindsight is perfect, he mused, pouring more of his Gibson cocktail.

"The woman was different from the other sailor, the musician," Gene spoke again. "All three signed the statement. The stupid kid couldn't keep his mouth shut, so we had to shut it for him. The other one, the musician, was a piece of cake," he spoke with a slight smile. "He didn't have any problem doing what he was told. Saved his life, he did. If it weren't for him, the whole ship-jumping thing would probably have blown up quicker, especially when you lost your nerve about the woman. She was the straight arrow. Now look at her." Menard leaned forward on his elbows, "It'll just be a little more complicated now, that's all."

The room was spinning. Nat gripped the edges of the table to hold on. He checked his response before speaking. He knew so little, but what she knew would lead an investigation straight to that night on the river and raise questions about *Monte Verde* and his partners, then him. Then, even if questioning did not involve him—after all, he was never seen on the ship or anywhere else—he couldn't count on remaining anonymous. They would all go down together. The room seemed to turn faster. He began lifting his martini glass; he needed something to slow down his mind. "What about the other guy?"

"Smart kid, that one. He knows how things work in the real world. May live to a ripe old age. I saw him a couple weeks ago."

"What?" Nat choked, almost spitting across the table.

"He's leading some kind of a sailor band. I was in Cartagena at the annual board meeting. You were too busy, remember? We got invited to some big shindig where he was playing. When you were losing your nerve, we scrambled to get them to pamper your sensitivities. We leaned on his bosses, a couple of your ass-hole buddies in New Orleans. They got him to dump on her with some lesbian BS. Those military types are strange; the bent ones especially like going ape about where people get their jollies. He got rewarded like we arranged, tooting his horn for the Navy or some such shit."

"You're telling me that they're tracking that jerk after all this time? Why?"

"After New Orleans there's good reason you don't know. It's all in the details, Nat. Come on, you ought to know by now: those guys don't forget anything, and they don't turn loose of anyone."

"But, he's nobody."

"New Orleans scared hell out of them. Still does. You, my friend, had better never forget that. Difference is that they know how to turn people, communicate, know what I'm saying? Especially the willing, and make sure they never try flip. From the vibes I got at that party, I got the impression he's a player, cooperating in transportation. Small stuff, but on the team."

Both men studied each other across the table.

"She's gotta go," Menard mumbled the last word.

Sixteen

He walked a few steps on the oily gravel and stood beneath a metal-roofed lean-to running the length of the hangar. He motioned Rees to join him behind a stack of oil drums. Looking like he was in pain, he managed to speak softly, "I don't know what's going on here, sir. And, to tell the truth, sir—no disrespect intended—I'm not sure you do, either. All this," he jerked his finger, first at the sky where the plane had just disappeared, then toward the empty hangar, "is just too much. You may be dealing with some cosmic big picture and all that officer bull, but—again, with all due respect—I don't give a damn. I may be clueless, totally out of the loop and ignorant, and I might have been born at night, but it wasn't last night. I sure as hell know one thing for sure: whatever all this is, it is officially scaring the hell out of me; no good's gonna come from it. You outta be scared, too. For example: what the hell are we doing here? You're in over your head, boss. You're playing with fire." The stick-thin man was trembling with suppressed rage, struggling to keep from grabbing Lyle by the shoulders and shaking him like an errant child. His eyes were bulging out of his skeleton-like face, and his breath came in deep gasps; he looked and sounded like he'd just run a mile. He'd never spoken to an officer like this, especially this one. He tried to remain respectful to his boss and—in his mind, right now—a staggering reckless young man.

"Look, chief, you've got to understand…"

"Understand, nothing, sir! He jerks a trembling finger and presses it against the gold anchor on his collar, "This is what I understand.

My life's invested in this. It's all I got, now and when I retire. I'm not about to throw it all away over whatever's going on here and back in Venezuela and Colombia and whatever the next spooky crap's gonna happen." He leaned closer and bracketed Lyle's head between his hands, "I don't know how deep you're in, or even if you actually have a clue, but take my advice, sir: it's time to get out. Both of us are seeing stuff way beyond our pay grades," he was surprised by the pleading, almost whining, tone in his voice.

Lyle knew he was right: it was well past time for a reality check; that reality was written on Jones' face, with undeniable intensity. Lyle had nothing. He looked away, searching for anything that might give a next step, then back at the bug-eyed chief.

"I've got an idea," he spoke and stepped toward the trash barrel. He dug the rag from it and spread it on the gravel. "Why did he do it? Why wipe the drum case?"

Jones picked up the burgundy shop towel; it was moist with gasoline and crusted with grime. "Because there's something on or in the case they don't want anyone to see or smell. All we can see is different colored dirt. Some is red like in the jungle and lighter, maybe off the roads. But, you know there's more going on here. He smeared gasoline all over it; didn't look like clean freak to me. It ain't much, but maybe this can give us some ideas, even it's only what it looks like: a rag soaked in gasoline. Let me hold on to it. I've got a buddy with NIS who could test it find out what this other stuff on it is."

"Hold on, chief, I'm not sure I want to make this is federal case, starting tripping alarms and trying to explain our sudden interest in dumpster diving for dirty rags."

Jones looked at Lyle, again stopping himself from strangling him. Instead, with mock courtesy and restraint he practically sang, "Oh, my, of course not, sir. Why, that won't be a problem at all." Satisfied that Lyle got it, he continued more seriously, "He's been down here a long time. He's working with NIS and DEA, who knows who else, at a crime lab. Got his stuff together, I guess. They extended his tour, and you know the Navy just loves homesteading. It won't be no federal case. It won't be any kind of case at all. Whatever he finds will be totally off the record." He leaned closer, "And, you can count on that, sir. But, we both know that was something in that case and the others we've been riding around with from time to time. And, I'll bet my next paycheck that none of 'em are going through customs wherever in hell that plane was going."

Both knew there was risk involved; he also knew he had no choice.

"We'll cross the next bridge, if there is one, when we get the results. I hope I'm totally wrong, boss, but we've can't go on like this."

* * * *

The Aldrich, the *Uno Americas* flagship, left Valparaiso, washed in early morning sunlight as commuter traffic was reaching its peak. Within hours the warship would rendezvous about a hundred miles off shore with the other ships of the small U.S. flotilla. The navies of Chile and Peru and the United States would join them later to begin two weeks of naval war games.

Jones left the rag with his friend who returned immediately with it to the lab in Santiago. Results would wait, discreetly, until the ship docked again. Lyle wondered just how much Jones might have said; he hoped not too much. He'd followed instructions so far; now he feared that Jones and his friend might reveal, even accidentally, too much about his involvement in whatever he was doing. *Just what, exactly, am I doing? Has the old hustler been hustled?* Street smarts from his youth in Tampa told him so. He was a long way from home, and he never felt more alone. In addition to strangers along the way, now he was trusting the discretion of yet one more. His gut feeling would not be denied during the first days at sea. He couldn't come up with any scenario about that scene at the little airport—or any other of the other incidents—that didn't make him wish none of it ever happened. He was into something deeply, and he was beginning to suspect just what. *What would happen if I confided in the XO?* No: he had been warned against that, more than once. He had no choice: he had to tough this out, keep up his stage presence, dazzle 'em with footwork, hope for the best when it was all over. In a few days he would have some answers; either way, he promised himself that he'd never do anything this foolish again, regardless of promises.

Four days before the Aldrich was scheduled to return to port, word filtered throughout the ship that fleet command had changed their orders; they were to detach from the flotilla and follow two Ivan class Soviet submarines that had been transiting for a month from Asia, across the southern Pacific and up the west coast of South America. Such surveillance was routine—one of the tasks at which the U.S. Navy excelled, almost a courtesy between the world's two largest navies to test how well each potential enemy could shadow the other. It also offered a diversion to a real-time, real-life situation which the Anti-Submarine Warfare officers and crewmen relished over purposefully losing silly war games to their much inferior South American counterparts.

A collateral diversion soon became apparent to the crew: the tracking would take them across the Equator, and the captain had agreed to host the traditional crossing-the-line ceremonies he had postponed several weeks ago when they first steamed into the Southern Hemisphere. Because he had the least to do underway, Lt. Rees was in charge of the day-long initiation and induction ceremonies, playfully-to-cruelly run by King Neptune's Shellbacks for the new Pollywogs.

His band would provide the entertainment for the evening's talent show and drag queen beauty pageant, judged by Rex Neptune himself, embodied by the Aldrich's humorless captain. It was a task to be relished, and Lyle immersed himself, with Jones at his side, also enjoying the diversion. It was good to see him laugh.

Initiation day began long before dawn, amazingly cold, even at the Equator. The pollywogs were rousted from their bunks and herded to the forecastle to be cleaned with a fire hose. After a cold breakfast of jack mackerel and eggs, served in plates on the deck and without utensils, the pollywogs—still in their skivvy shorts—spent most of the morning on their hands and knees, gingerly picking their way in a circuit around the rough non-skid surface on the main deck. By mid-afternoon, with the tropical sun at its hottest, they crawled on their stomachs down long canvas troughs of garbage that had been ripening for days. This time the hosing was welcome, but even that small comfort was soon destroyed. Still dripping wet, they crawled in a long, undulating line from the fantail to the forecastle, where the most obese chef sat clad only in a diaper. With their tongues, each pollywog dug a cherry from his greased belly button, trying repeatedly until swallowing the totally disgusting fruit.

With the humiliating formalities complete, the sailors cleaned up for an evening "steel beach" party, complete with grilled steaks and—with a professional band aboard—the much anticipated talent show and pageant. The grateful performers had been spared most of the days' indignities to rehearse and assemble their wardrobes: mop-head wigs, balloon bosoms, even panty hose and make-up. Don't ask. It all was a screaming success, and on the mess decks below and in the wardroom, the band and Lyle were celebrated shipmates. As the mid-watch took over morale aboard USS Aldrich was probably as good as it would ever be.

Hours later, it all crashed with one announcement: head count was one short; Chief Jones was missing.

Led by the ship's master at arms, the ship's police chief, the crew turned the ship upside down in minutes. He was last seen around 0100 in the Chief's Mess, watching a movie with several other chiefs who reported that—for the first time in weeks—he'd been laughing and joking with them. Sometime between 0100 and 0700 he had disappeared, and by now everyone knew where: he'd gone over the side. They also knew that even if he'd been the water only since morning muster, he would have perished in the icy cold Humboldt Current that streams past the west coast of South America. Hypothermia would have killed him within minutes. Even if the ship returned to look, the chilled water would have pushed the body far below, never to resurface. *Why did he do it?*

Only minutes later the balding and paunchy master at arms knocked on the wardroom door. He entered, scanned the knot of officers and immediately caught Lyle's eye. Without speaking, he walked to Lyle and laid two u-shaped bolts on the table in front of him. "They're from the band's storage room door, sir. Cut with a hacksaw where they held the strong locks."

Lyle, the ship's captain and the admiral followed him below. They stopped to examine the metal filings on the door transom, then stepped inside. Lyle lifted the clipboard off its hook and looked at the chief's accounting form and his signature beside Jones', dated the evening they'd gotten underway two weeks ago. The master at arms saw that one of the cardboard boxes had been sliced; it took Lyle only a few seconds to know that the inventory was off by exactly one bottle of vodka. The men made their way through the narrow passageways, down two decks and entered the chief's tiny stateroom. The door was unlocked. Without hesitation, the master-at-arms stepped to the bunk and pulled back the mattress. The bottle of vodka was empty. It was all too obvious; nothing could be more apparent, Lyle thought, as the master at arms handed the evidence to the captain. "Suicide, sir; didn't see it coming. Real shame, sorry." He spoke softly, looking at Lyle, then the floor. "We'll get the doors fixed right away."

Wind chilled by the icy current which claimed Jones' body slackened in the long Equatorial sunset.

Lyle stood alone on the hangar deck, his eyes fixed thousands of miles away, toward the other side of the world, beyond far-away lands and strange peoples, where the sun is disappearing. Streaked with brilliant reds, yellows, then orange and purple, the western sky slowly fades, giving way to the ink-black darkness above. But—on a cloudless and moonless night like this—darkness does not long prevail; it soon yields to the majesty and awe of star rise. The phenomenon begins slowly. Gradually, the delicate light from billions of stars—light that began travelling towards him millions of years ago—graces a waiting world. For the men navigating the little flotilla tonight, the demarcation between infinite space and the black sea around them will be breathtaking. Most—like Lyle, like those who since antiquity have gone down to the sea in ships—will never forget the beauty and mind-numbing awareness of how small each is before the vast, eternal universe.

As he has several nights, Lyle watches, and thinks with an uncommon, silent reverence. With his only earthly tie the gentle rocking beneath his feet and the cool caress on his face, for a fleeting moment he wishes he could disappear into those stars and never return. But, he can't. He needs real answers.

The night's transcendent moments pass too quickly; tomorrow brings another difficult, tiring day. The admiral, chief of staff, master at arms have questioned him, almost continuously. Without saying so, they have sensed something lacking in his responses. Lyle answered with silence about what he didn't know, but only suspected. What was the rest of the story? Lyle wanted to know, too, but he couldn't tell them, at least not until he saw those test results.

Later in the day the Aldrich received a message that saddened Lyle even more. A check of records at Commander-in-Chief Atlantic Fleet, Norfolk, showed that Jones had no next of kin. The Servicemen's Group Life Insurance would be paid, as he had directed, to the Sailor's Home in Gulfport, Mississippi. Lyle was almost happy that there were no remains for internment in some pauper's cemetery.

The sadness was leading to depression. He left the cramped little office, realizing that he'd been there all day, after speaking only briefly with the band sometime around mid-morning. He'd probably screwed that up, too, he thought. The men had looked like zombies; few questions were asked, little was said. The next senior was the keyboard player, in Lyle's estimation completely unprepared to assume responsibilities.

With a sense of failure and despair Lyle retreats again that night to the helicopter landing deck behind officers' quarters. It is the most expansive space on the ship. It affords panoramic views of the dark ocean behind and on both sides. The only sound is the constant whisper of water parted by the warship and churning into its wake. IIn the past days he found himself there often – day and night – looking for as much peace and solitude as possible among six hundred men crammed inside the floating fighting machine. He finds neither, only more doubts. He knows that the trombone player was a recovering alcoholic; but, he seemed to have it together: he led Alcoholics Anonymous meetings aboard. He needed a reason for Jones' death: that it was not suicide was the only thing he knew for sure. Whatever happened, it must have to have something to do with that rag back in Santiago. Jones spoke nothing about it to anyone aboard the ship, Lyle knew. *What was on it? Had his friend or someone else seen too much?* All he knew for sure was that someone was willing to kill over whatever it was, and they are aboard the ship right now.

He wasn't sure how long he stood there before becoming aware that the ship was beginning to pitch deeply. The Aldrich, and Lyle, were headed for rough seas.

* * * *

The rare Pacific storm punished the ship and tortured Lyle's thoughts for three more days. Then it was over. The ship's crew had functioned brilliantly and so had the band; with little to do but stay out of the way, those who weren't sea sick had volunteered to stand the watches of their shipmates who were. Lyle used the time to begin rewriting arrangements to cover for the missing lead trombone player. Every bandsman had been trained to compose and eagerly joined in rescoring the music. When the storms subsided, they spent hours daily rehearsing. The work was cathartic.

The final days at sea passed slowly. A week later as they gathered on deck, ready to perform ceremonial martial music and the Chilean national anthem for the greeting dignitaries, Lyle studied their faces. They had overcome. They stood, instruments at the ready, quietly watching the long, low sandy beaches, backed with tall palms and high-rise hotels and condos growing closer. *Vina del Mar*, Santiago, Chile, will be a welcome relief, from physical danger and emotional stress. Their eyes told the story: they were eager to resume, to show their stuff, to hear the applause, to move on, even with a grueling schedule of performances.

As the destroyer neared the dock, the band struck up Sousa's *Hands Across the Sea* march, the admiral's favorite. But, by the time the last lines were doubled, it was obvious to all they had played to a ragged audience of line handlers and longshoremen. No one cheered the starched and shined sailors manning the rails of an equally scrubbed and painted ship fresh from a storm at sea. Only one Chilean Navy officer, dressed in a gold-braided comic-opera uniform, came aboard for the official greeting, not the usual platoons of efficient-looking adjutants and aides and gaggles of well-dressed matrons eager to grace the wardroom with engraved invitations to receptions and formal dinners. Lyle was puzzled that no cultural affairs officer accompanied the lone Chilean naval representative, eager to deliver another demanding schedule of band engagements.

Before calling on the admiral in his stateroom, the visitor left a note on the quarterdeck; it summoned Lyle ashore. At the bottom of the brow a young midshipman exited a black sedan and opened the door for him. From the driver's seat no explanation was offered; an open palm was the only response to Lyle's questions, even about their destination. They motored in silence for a few minutes down the wide beach boulevard before the young Chilean wheeled beneath a canopy of crisscrossed palms and into the polished cobblestone drive of the Chilean Navy Officers Club. The car jerked to a stop.

They walked quickly beneath a bleached canvas-covered sidewalk, through tall, varnished wood doors and along a white marble hallway. Seated alone in a darkly appointed small withdrawing room, Lyle was left to wait.

Ten minutes later a middle-aged, dark and well-built man in an expensively cut grey pinstripe suit entered, took Lyle's hand politely and sat in a chair behind a bare dining table. He gave no name. He produced only a sheet of paper and began reading from it. Lyle felt like he may be arrested. In thickly-accented English which Lyle struggled to understand, the news is presented: there is great concern by the government about a plebiscite vote scheduled in three days. It will be a national referendum to determine whether or not Augusto Pinochet will remain in power for another eight-year term or end his sixteen-and-a-half-year military dictatorship. The vote, he reads carefully, was arranged quickly. Bottom line: to put it politely, nobody wants U.S. presence there, especially the dictator who now sees the long-scheduled visit as a political liability among the left-leaning nationalists. Lifting his eyes only once to see if Lyle is taking it all in, he announced that the government of Chile is not thrilled with the visit of U.S. Navy ships and certainly not the prospect of a Navy band drawing crowds at public performances. All engagements have been cancelled and the U.S. Embassy so informed—at this very moment—by messenger. Finished with the narration, he slides the paper across the desk towards Lyle. He remains expressionless.

Lyle is aware that he is sitting at attention, as the strange little man continues, this time without a script. With elbows on the table, he squints and speaks through a snarl; tensions between the government and the U.S. embassy are further heightened by rumors about the death of an American sailor. Rumor from diplomatic security, he explains with a sudden out-of-context smile, is that the vaunted U.S. Naval Investigative Service believes that the death aboard USS Aldrich is connected with the trafficking of narcotics. This, he continues with absolute disdain, is not acceptable to the people of Chile. He adds that evidence, testing of the sailor's clothing retrieved before the destroyer left port, has confirmed these facts. The implications for the United States and the Navy were obvious. Similar discussions are being held, as he speaks, with the admiral aboard Aldrich, who is being informed that the port visit will be overnight, only long enough to accommodate refueling and provisioning.

Lyle sits stunned, recovering enough to stand as the man rises and abruptly marches out of the room.

During the brief ride back to the port Lyle's thoughts are an incoherent blur. In need of time to think, or at least not wishing to confront the admiral back aboard the ship before having time to form a plausible reply, he asks the driver to stop the car; he'd like to walk the last mile. The driver accommodates, keeping him in view while creeping along the curb from about a hundred yards behind.

What explanation will the admiral and the ambassador ask about the smuggling charge, about his and the band's implication in what he knows are totally confused, but—it is becoming clear—plausible accusations? He doesn't know what to do; he doesn't know how to contact CIA operatives who he assumes must know exactly what's coming down and exactly where Lyle is walking at this moment. His imagination begins to get the best of him; he sees faces among beachgoers who quickly glance away from him. The walk along the beautiful strand has the opposite of his hoped-for effect: he's growing more tense and afraid. *This has gone on too long. Nothing's going right, and there's no way this is going to end well.* Turning a corner and seeing his ship resting at the pier, he freezes: whoever ordered Jones' death could arrange his, too.

He pauses at the bottom of the brow. Hoping for the best, some kind of rescue or resolution, he slowly begins the steep climb. With each step he convinces himself that he'll survive by doing what he has always done: resisting panic, lasting just a little longer, making his own rules about right and wrong. Somehow he'd survive like he'd done since his childhood with his mother, with the cops in Tampa, as he did after the ship-jumping incident in New Orleans. He had always come out ahead, rewarded for his toughness, for grabbing the next best thing, never looking back. Taking care of number one had always worked for him, just like it did after he tipped Tampa cops about his mother's contacts with drug networks, as it did when he lied about Emma. His head came level with the quarterdeck. The rationalizations didn't provide comfort.

He was sweating. He was losing control; it couldn't be panic. He knew it was the guilt; that he could handle. Since he could remember, guilt had been a constant companion. It began with his mother. She wasn't like other mothers. She took from him, from men she met. He had tried to do the right thing. He'd said enough to get her committed to a drug rehabilitation program. The promise was golden: it would be a new beginning, she'd love him like a mother should, and he would love her. She was gone a long time, but finally there was a graduation, roses, loving embraces. Three days later she was dead of an overdose.

Stepping onto the quarterdeck, he saluted the officer of the day. Jones had been innocent; he had overcome his demons; he just wanted to retire, enjoy the immortality of teaching as a school band director. He steadied himself and opened the steel door. Cool air rushed past. It chilled his face and his thoughts. He tried, but couldn't push her away. Emma had been a saint, even more, to him. She was happy. She had loved her job, she loved her sister; everyone who met her knew it. At least she is still alive.

"Oh, Rees, the chief of staff said he wanted to see you as soon as you came aboard," the OOD spoke before Lyle pulled the door shut. He'd walked several steps inside before his brain got the message.

Captain Edward "Dog" Hidalgo is a short, athletic man, charismatic, fluent in Spanish, courtly and hand-picked for this diplomatic goodwill tour of South America. He is a smooth operator, outshining the ship's captain in social graces, fully expecting flag rank as a reward for this deployment. Expensively raised in San Francisco by Mexican parents, he was hand-picked by the family's Hispanic congressman to attend the Naval Academy; his father's political contributions didn't hurt at all. The assignment to this deployment and a surface ship comes as preparation for the aviator to be selected to command an aircraft carrier and eventual promotion to admiral.

"Oh, come in, Rees!" His enthusiastic greeting confused Lyle. "Another great Navy day, huh?" he spoke seated at the desk which took up most of his large stateroom. He looked up from a pile of papers and turned off the goose-necked reading light. Motioning for Lyle to sit down on the red leather settee that converted to his bunk, he swung around and began, "Don't let any of this get you down, shipmate. I don't know where all this NIS bull is coming from. Sounds like *el jefe* and the boys are trying to gin up some crap to hurt our feelings and embarrass the old *norte Americanos*. That's all it is. Your chief's got nothing to do with anything: drug smuggling, for Pete's sake! Pablo Escobar you ain't!"

The room stopped spinning. He liked what he was hearing. Maybe he should talk. Hidalgo was offering him a mug; he accepted it, mechanically.

"The steward makes this from beans I bought in Colombia. It's good stuff. This is the only pick-me-up I can offer you aboard the good old hotel Aldrich," he smiled, leaning forward to retrieve a sheet of paper from a separate pile and handed it to him. "You and the band and yours truly got to get to the airport by 1500."

The immediate priority message had been received an hour earlier, just after he'd left the ship. "In consideration of and in response to the late-developing diplomatic developments in Chile," it read, "... situational awareness requires that U.S. assets depart with all deliberate speed to await further instruction. Task Force commander authorized direct liaison with Unified Commander and Department of State."

"Skip down to paragraph six," Hidalgo said and pointed at the paper. Lyle hoped Dog hadn't seen his hand trembling.

"Originator recognizes value of unique assets embarked. As discussed with State Department and U.S. Embassy Asuncion, Paraguay, embarked band will depart via contract aircraft, arriving Asuncion. Report for operational purposes to U.S. Ambassador. Task Force COS to accompany as Senior Officer Present Ashore, providing commensurate official Navy representation to host government."

Lyle's head began spinning again. He re-read the last sentences. "You think this'll work? Hidalgo slapped his knee and roared with laughter. You need to know that the old man isn't exactly jumping for joy over this, so try curb your enthusiasm. Hand springs down the passageway and laughing hysterically in the wardroom are dead give-aways! Personally, the prospect of several days, who knows—maybe weeks—being my dashing self with the rich and famous and the beautiful people who love them isn't exactly bringing me down!"

Lyle smiled and kept reading. The final paragraphs were the reason that the message was classified HCI, beyond his Top Secret clearance level. *Something else to lie about.*

"TG Seven One to proceed immediately to monitor Soviet Navy transit anticipated vicinity Cape of Good Hope. SOVNAV submarine and surface assets, including trawlers, known to be active since August in Southern Pacific region from Panama south to Cape. SOVNAV assets departed Persian Gulf ports in Iran, transited Indian Ocean and entered South Atlantic. Destinations unknown. Transits not considered routine, possibly connected to SOVNAV submarine active Pacific coast of South America. USS ALDRICH observation of Ivan Class ops vicinity Chile, Peru, pertain. Undetermined missions/unprecedented transits of high strategic/intelligence interest. Assets authorized to confirm/expand foreign national HUMINT that missions include cargo/pax transferred ashore via trawler/small craft in river mouths/inlets."

* * * *

Even if he should not know of the message, he liked seeing it: it offered some sense about what was going on around him; that was a welcome change. In the much broader picture it presented, it did answer at least one question about the long deployment that otherwise seemed like a huge waste of time and money. Who knew? Appearing to get kicked out of Chile was actually cooperation from the Chileans, providing a cover story to confound the Soviet spies in Santiago.

Lyle and every other sailor was aware of Soviet naval activity: the trawlers, actually floating communications stations capable of intercepting U.S. radio signals, had been in nearly every port they visited and often visible at sea. The trawlers had seemed more numerous on the west coast, especially off Colombia and in Manta, Ecuador.

He broke a sanitized version of the news to the band, with predictable reaction. In his stateroom, Lyle packed. Catching his image in the mirror over his little sink, he saw a worried man. Surely, he rationalized, there's more information, maybe even more answers, waiting in Paraguay.

Seventeen

The flight to Asuncion was a party. The venue was a 727 apparently owned by the Great Circle Air Cargo Company, as the round logo on the tail of the silver airplane implied. The bus had hardly stopped rolling before the band followed Captain Hernandez up the stairs and buckled in for take-off in the wide leather seats. Lyle waited to board last, looking for someone to accept the usual passenger manifest, but nobody wanted it. He was the last man up the rolling stairway. The door shut behind him and—within minutes—the airplane was climbing steeply to altitude. The blue Pacific receded steadily behind them, soon replaced with a lush green carpet of vegetation which stretched toward snow-capped mountains on the eastern horizon.

The party started immediately. The pleasantly surprised passengers were escorted aft by two flight attendants in short, red-leather skirts, matching high heels and starched, open-collar tuxedo shirts. Now seated on long, low sofas, platters of bite-sized boiled lobster and grilled beef fillets were served on low tables bolted to the floor. Chilean wines and *chope*, the hearty draft beer brewed by Paraguay's transplanted German population, flowed freely. Except for Lyle nobody wondered about who was hosting the feast, least of all the band and Captain Hidalgo whose idea of a good time after weeks at sea was anything that could not float. In their wildest sailor dreams they hadn't expected this.

The two officers were slightly more circumspect, at least in front of each other, and neither spoke what was obvious: this wasn't the Navy's idea; some source of U.S. taxpayer funds, with much looser accounting oversight, was responsible, and that most likely was the embassy in Asuncion.

Soon, nobody cared. Dog was unburdened by the details, much more interested in sampling the fare, including the eye candy offered by the tall, well-endowed blonde flight attendant who explained that unbuttoning her top buttons was the only way to relieve the tension. Lyle noticed that she later joined Dog into the forward restroom, apparently relieving other stresses.

Nearly three hours later the plane taxied toward the main terminal at Asuncion, a featureless stone-faced building, a South American version of a 1930s WPA project, but with class. Massive concrete eagles stood guard on either side of the long blue canvas-covered walkway which led to wide copper-paneled doors. A black convertible Mercedes, a perfectly maintained museum piece, waited beneath it, complete with Paraguayan flags mounted on the front fenders. An olive-drab bus and canvas-covered cargo truck were parked along the curb behind the stretch limo.

Lyle elbowed Dog to divert his attention from the flight attendant sitting on his knee and pointed out the small window toward a half-dozen men in uniform milling around at the end of a narrow, red carpet. It stretched from their feet and toward the bunting-draped boarding ladder rolling toward the 727. As the door swung open they took the last puffs on cigarettes and flicked the butts on the lawn behind them. A woman smartly dressed in a tailored white suit and heels walked down the covered walk and joined their ranks. She was carrying a clipboard: *Gilbert and Sullivan meet Wall Street,* Lyle mused.

The two officers descended the stairs, faking complete sobriety as they marched in slightly rubbery step down the carpet. Salutes, handshakes and immediately forgotten introductions were made all around. The young woman, Jon Patton, took Lyle's hand, warmly. She began talking to Captain Hidalgo but—perhaps sensing a diminished capacity—discreetly turned her remarks toward Lyle. She was the newly arrived Cultural Attaché, U.S. Embassy, Asuncion, she announced proudly. The Paraguayan officers, both graduates of the Navy War College in Newport, Rhode Island, spoke fluent English, she warned under her breath. The Navy captain, squinting in the bright sun and enraptured by her every word, found Jon's hand and pulled it dreamily to his chest. She smelled wonderful. He leaned forward and clumsily kissed her on cheek; he tried for her lips, but she was too fast.

Dog giggled away the missed advance and refocused his attention on his smiling counterparts. Lyle followed Jon as she marched toward the band, now crowded around the boarding ladder. They followed her aboard the bus where beer was iced down in a tub on the back seats. It was apparent that the party was going to continue. They picked up on Lyle's hesitant nod of approval, then stepped aside as the band served themselves while solders loaded their equipment.

With the formalities and highly efficient logistics complete, Lyle and Jon were seated in rear-facing jump seats; behind them Dog and two other officers sat on the slightly raised rear seat where they could be more visible. She explained that the motorcade would stop first at the Ministry of Defense where they would make officials calls with none other than the Army Chief of Staff and the Chief of Naval Operations. Dog looked at Lyle with an expression varying between boozy confidence and humorous confusion as the limos rolled around the terminal and onto the street to the city center. The look intensified with the appearance of hundreds, maybe thousands, lining the street and waiving wildly at them. *When they're passing out tarts...* Lyle thought, with sad memory.

"In case you're wondering, we have no idea why you're here, but we're going to make the best of it," Jon spoke through her perfect smile as the motorcade picked up speed and roared down the tree-lined boulevard, straddling the yellow lines. "Just smile and wave is all you have to do right now," she instructed, and he followed her example, gazing at the blurred faces, some standing two and three deep in the shade beneath the dense foliage.

"And, what is all this?" Lyle marveled, not sure he'd spoken out loud and turning to study her ivory skin, clipped nose, and her full, red lips. Still waiving, her dark brown eyes flashed, and Lyle was in love, or something like it. "It's all for you and the band. I hope you're good. State run media have been telling them all day that you're American rock stars." She turned to speak directly and sternly at him, "I must admit, you all do look like rock stars: everyone appears to be drunk. The benevolent leader, our friendly, local dictator Mr. Alfredo Stroessner, has decreed that you will be warmly received. Run with it. It's a far better deal than our boss got since he arrived last week. I'll explain later. We have great plans for you."

The crowd began to thin, but only a little. Many more were visible in the blocks ahead. Lyle was still trying to piece together what she was saying and somehow prepare himself for the totally over-the-top audience. But, Jon was disarming. He began to wonder if he, too, wasn't a little drunk. He stole another look at her dark, copper-tinged hair piled high on her head and caught another wisp of her perfume: he was drunk, alright, but it wasn't the booze that was in control.

"The embassy is in total disarray. Normal diplomatic protocol is failing because for some reason known only to them, the old boy and his cronies have decided to play coy with their benefactor," Jon began speaking softly into Lyle's ear. "Our man arrived last week and has been twisting at the end of their rope. For some reason that nobody seems to know, or has shared with me, Mr. Stroessner, our fiercely anti-communist and equally brutal and corrupt former army officer, won't accept the new U.S. ambassador's credentials. Essentially, the U.S. ambassador to Paraguay is a tourist for all they care."

Still trying to figure what any of this had to do with him and the band, Lyle studied the faces of their fellow celebrities in the back of the limo, wondering how much—if any—of Jon's words they'd heard.

"Look at this, these people could give a damn about the band, but here they are," Jon began again, exaggeratedly waiving as though she'd recognized someone in the wall of humanity streaming past. "This whole extravaganza was put together since this morning. We'll talk more later. Bottom line: you and the boys in the band are going to be used by Ambassador James Pillow to break ice with Stroessner government. I may or may not have called the right play, but—either way—you're playing on my team now, lieutenant."

For the next hour Lyle was the perfect mannequin, window dressing on magnificently upholstered chairs in the high-ceilinged, splendidly overdone Victorian chambers of the two service chiefs. Hidalgo chatted inanely and pleasantly in Spanish, little of which Lyle understood. When he wasn't staring at Jon, he simply mirrored whatever expression Dog presented and only made eye contact with anyone when laughter broke out.

Just before dusk they arrived at the *Plaza Uruguaya*, the grand old Spanish Colonial hotel that faced the large park of the same name. A bellman in green trousers, starched white shirt with epaulets and a pith helmet jerked open the limo door and led them toward the wide glass doors to the darkly cool, cavernous lobby. They bypassed the registration desk where two older men in black tie stood at attention as the party began climbing the wide marble staircase. Lyle was peeled off at the second floor and Hidalgo continued up. Just he and a bellman turned and proceeded to the end of the wide, deeply carpeted and darkly paneled hallway. At the end, he threw open wide doors and bowed slightly and stepped back.

The corner suite was enormous, occupying the entire depth of the building. Two sets of French doors were almost as tall as the twelve-foot ceiling. Wide balconies wrapped around the west and south walls. A king size, four-poster mahogany bed, hung with yellow satin contrasted with the red-flocked eastern wall behind it. It stood grandly between two stained glass windows which would diffuse the morning sun in soft green, red, yellow refractions. Gold gilt frames, two he supposed were at least eight feet square, hung on the other walls. Lyle's jaw dropped. The bellman explained in broken English that Captain Hidalgo would occupy the identical suite one floor above. The band, he explained, had been quartered a few more blocks away, in a more modest hotel on the other side of the city's central park.

Lyle splashed water on his face, changed into a fresh uniform and returned downstairs. Dog was faster. He was sitting in a round corner booth with the flight attendants. What a coincidence: they also had rooms at the Plaza. Lyle had barely finished warm greetings before he looked up to see Jon gliding between huge potted ferns flanking the entrance.

The captain filled in names for the awkward introductions. Jon responded coolly, then suggested that she and Lyle needed to talk business. They took chairs around small rattan table on the stone patio beneath a thicket of palms.

"This is the 'later' I spoke about; there's not a lot of time before you go into action."

"Of course not, the United States Navy is at your service."

"Good," she said, pulling papers from her purse. "We've both had quite a day. I'm guessing that your head may still be spinning. I doubt if Elvis ever got a parade like that: thousands of adoring fans, peasants who had absolutely had no idea who you are. I get it, but listen up. I've had all of eight hours to come up with some ideas to work with what's dropped into our laps: you. She smiled, pausing as drinks arrived. "You remember those old Andy Hardy movies with Mickey Rooney? Well, don't laugh, or laugh if you want to because this is pretty off-the-wall. Remember how the solution to every crisis he and his girlfriend faced was 'let's put on a show!'? That's exactly what we have in mind. Don't freak. The ambassador is also a musician, a drummer, and he agrees that throwing a huge garden party—with you as the centerpiece—may be just offbeat enough to break some ice, or at least throw the old boys off balance. So, tomorrow night the U.S. embassy is going to host a party for the diplomatic community, the whole enchilada. It may be a long shot, but we're hoping that it'll be just what's needed to loosening things up, reasoning that it's hard to be a hard ass after everyone has let their hair down. It may work. Let's put on a show!" she laughed and touched Lyle's hand.

"So this is what the mysterious world of diplomacy is all about. I never knew," he lied. Her hand was still on his, and it felt good. "Damsels in distress or ambassadors without credentials, it's the U.S. Navy to the rescue!"

"I've still got a lot to do, sailor boy, like finalizing the guest list. I'm sure there are things on your agenda, too." She looked back inside the bar, "actually, I see that your next appointment is here. That's him there," she said as she stood and shook his hand. "The tall man, there, in the white suit and dark glasses; he showed up sometime last night. Have fun."

She floated away like a ballerina, and he found himself watching her, very closely.

Lyle was still standing as the man approached the little table. His extended hand swallowed Lyle's. Something about him was familiar, but just beyond Lyle's memory. The name he offered was Jim Dunn, a lie, Lyle thought, still struggling to recognize him. The tenor voice didn't seem matched to the rugged, bearded face. Still, something about him, maybe just a bad vibe, was hauntingly familiar.

Lyle studied Dunn as he lied again, this time something about being an assistant to the ambassador for plans and operations. Making no connection he stopped trying. He chided himself: maybe he has become too tightly wrapped in his own imagination, trying too hard to tie the past months together. It is possible, he thinks, that this was the same man who joined his band bus in Colombia. It wasn't likely, besides, he never saw the man's eyes through the wrap-around sunglasses. He was tired and hot and disoriented by the day's Kafkaesque events. He needs to stay in the present, he thinks, not like a child afraid of the dark, seeing a monster in every shadow. He decides not to press but to listen, hoping to learn more from receiving, not transmitting. He was still recovering from Jon's parting peck on the cheek which inspired all kinds of fantasies.

It took a moment for his words to sink in: he was talking about Jones' death. Never mind how or why he knew anything about it. He spoke laterally, almost in clinical terms. Lyle half expected him to produce a flip chart. An investigation, he said, had turned up traces of cocaine on clothing that the ship's master at arms had taken from his locker. After a brief pause to glance around to ensure nobody could hear, he continued. Jones was believed to be some low-level player in a group of rogue DSA agents and others suspected of drug trafficking. This was still speculation, he admitted, but confirmed that—without a doubt—his death was definitely a suicide, a relapse into alcoholism, proven by the missing bottle.

After another pause which Lyle did nothing to fill, the little briefing continued. Now with words kind and oddly sympathetic, Dunn assured him that someone as close as he had been couldn't be blamed for not recognizing signs of desperation and relapse. The unnamed sources, he said, confirm that Jones was in some kind of unexplained financial trouble. He spoke with consolation now, almost pity. He rested his arms on the table and concluded: Jones was a textbook example of a victim ripe for bribery.

The man is lying, he knows it, but he's not sure Lyle does. The effect was to drive Lyle farther inside himself, to his own reality, the one he trusted and knew was true. Hoping his face hadn't betrayed him, he gazed at nothing in the near distance and managed to say, "I see."

Apparently satisfied, Dunn lit another cigarette and in a long breath blew the smoke toward the ceiling. When he spoke again he was relaxed, leaning back into the high-backed chair. Lyle couldn't help looking at his face as Dunn, or whoever he was, expressed his appreciation for his professionalism under the unusual circumstances of the past months. Lyle neither asked for nor received any explanation of exactly what he meant.

The man's mood turned again, too quickly. With sudden joviality, even a broad toothy smile, he explained that everything is going to turn out well in the long run. He assured Lyle that he would soon be rewarded with an early promotion and—to Lyle's astonishment—even mentioned names that only someone familiar with Navy personnel would know. The details included the building and room numbers at the Navy Annex where orders are written.

With great control, Lyle said, "You seem very knowledgeable, Mr. Dunn," embarrassed that his shaky voice might have revealed his astonishment.

Seeming satisfied that his fish was firmly hooked, Dunn finished the green liquid in the tiny glass in his hand and wished him well. He paused at the bar in front of one of the barmen. A moment later he looked back at Lyle, touched the rim of his Panama hat and disappeared in the lobby.

Another in the months-long episodes of odd people and one-sided conversations left him searching, but the exercise—as always—was only frustrating. There were no answers other than what he could imagine, and—after Jones' death—his scenarios were darker. If there was a happy ending, as Mr. Dunn said, at what price, and who was going to pay it? Truth was, he really didn't want to think about it.

He needed to relax. The setting sun felt good on his back. Its low rays now struck the massive brass chandelier suspended from the bar's high ceiling, sending fractured light dancing around the room and into his eyes. He breathed deeply, aware of the warmth, the fresh smells, the sound of birds from the park. No sooner had he begun to unwind than the moment was shattered by drunken laughter. In an instant he was alone again and scared: his mother and someone else were making noises in the next room. Just as quickly he remembered the little party in the corner booth. After weeks at sea with six hundred men, more than anything he craved privacy. He escaped unnoticed and walked slowly through the lobby and up the grand staircase.

His brain was overloaded, in a fog. He fumbled with the door, then clumsily stumbled into a writing table. It held a huge basket of fruit adorned with wide red, white and blue bow and ribbons; a tiny U.S. flag rose in the middle. The note indicated it was from the embassy; this certainly was a first, he thought, more of Jon's work. He looked around; the sheer expanse handball-court-sized room whose creepy Victorian décor made it oddly claustrophobic. He stepped around the table and on to the balcony. The view at tree-top level into the park in the middle of a bustling city was a welcome relief from the solitude at sea. The hustle of evening rush hour high in the South American mountains, even one scented by hearty evergreens and delicate flowers, beat out its rhythm here just like everywhere else in the world. He was a city boy. But, even if it was familiar, the cacophony, the strangers busying by below, only made him more aware of his own strangeness. The flight from Chile, the surreal parade through Asuncion, the mind-boggling reception, the weirdness of the mysterious Mr. Dunn, the calculated enthusiasm of Jon Patton, the disembodied sensation of just being here, was crazy making. It had been a long time, not since the chaos of his childhood in Tampa, that he had felt so vulnerable, or obsessed to understand what was going on around him and—most importantly—escape it all.

He'd survived by studying people—people watching—either indulging their worst instincts or struggling to scam their best. Instinctively looking for clues, he scanned the passing sidewalk parade; it didn't help.

The only thing clearly focused was Dunn's face and voice. *How could he know all that? Who the hell was he really, and could he possibly be right after all about Jones?* Either way, what he said must be the conventional wisdom for the faceless, nameless people who declared it so. The granite railing was cool to the touch. He swayed and caught himself like he was about to fall into a bottomless pit. Opening his eyes he saw happy couples walking below. Would he ever again enjoy such an innocent pleasure? The only thing he knows for sure is that—in the final accounting—he's all he's got. He has always survived. No need to change, especially now. He'll do what has always done: whatever it takes to gain attention and win applause, advance by any means necessary. If it meant sacrificing good people to get what he needed, so be it. *That may change, someday, not now.*

What's the option? Murdered like Jones, addicted and dead like his mother? Discarded like Emma? If he didn't actually kill his mother and Jones he at least enabled. It's too late to change now. *This ain't dress rehearsal.*

The show must go on. Tomorrow night he'll walk on stage and give the audience—whoever that is—what it expects, and more. It is the only way through this. He knows that without this approval he not only is nothing, he also may be dead.

The air in the miles-high city is refreshing. He stood alone until the street lamps along the park's winding paths became brighter. Beneath the ever-darker shadows of trees, the yellow lights traced their routes in the deepening twilight. Overhead the sky is red above vast, empty expanses of forests and jungles stretching to the far-away ocean. It's all beautiful, but he shivers, not sure why. He turned in early, but his night is endless and brings little rest. He wakes often, shaken awake by dreams, faces of dead people, expressionless, staring; their eyes were the worst. Regret and doubt haunt him; cowards know such nights well.

* * * *

"Geez, you look like hell. Have some coffee. Maybe some hair of the dog would even be better," he laughs at the play on his nickname and waives toward a table set with a silver urn, plates of pastries, a split of champagne and decanters of fresh orange juice. He's clad only in a bath towel wrapped around his waist. A stack of papers are piled on his lap. His hairy legs are stretched out on a chase lounge.

The packet arrived only minutes earlier. At first embarrassed to witness a senior naval officer wrapped around the blonde flight attendant, the embassy messenger had wished him a good day, suggesting that the messages would certainly make it so.

"The embassy weenies must have been up all night. Here, start reading this stuff. They're impressed, pissing their pants with joy. They ought to be. You guys were super. Happy endings all 'round. And, you made the news, big guy."

Lyle took the handful of papers from him and pulled up a wicker chair next to the serving cart. Each page was marked "Confidential, No Foreign Release." Each was an account written either by a high-ranking embassy officer, the ambassador himself—Lyle supposed—or intelligence sources. Each went into detail about the event, which—even written in official government prose—hailed it in glowing terms as a complete success.

The paragraphs with the highest classification included deep background intelligence, delivered hours before the party and quoting coded sources only. Minutes after the embassy's couriers had hand-delivered the invitations, every Paraguayan on Jon's guest list had been notified that attendance was mandatory. The intelligence was impressive in its detail; only someone in Mr. Stroessner's close staff must be the source, Lyle thought. The plan was for the despot to arrive fashionably late with his wife and an official party; his mistress would enter separately, but immediately take up her position at his side in the receiving line; this would delight the adoring news crews documenting the North Americans' discomfort with the breach of foolish Anglo protocol and timidity and boost his macho image. Cameras would document his polite greetings; he would continue mugging for them, sitting like a lord surveying his kingdom. After a half-hour at the most, or sooner if he were really bored, he would disdainfully waive away the food and drink. In feigned disgust, he would be overheard expressing his embarrassment at being received not in the embassy but in the appalling inappropriate garden setting; such arrogance typical of the impolite hosts. The kill shot would come on a pre-arranged signal: the entire guest list would rise *en mass* and depart unceremoniously. The disarray of the hosts and the frowns on the faces of Paraguay's elite would be dutifully documented by the news media. The result would ratchet up anxiety and serve as another embarrassment to the United States of America.

The bottom line of the tableau was apparent: after a few more days, perhaps a couple of weeks, of twisting in the wind, the ambassador would receive extortionate demands for greater amounts of economic and military aid and any other itemized whim of fancy that may arise. After all, the old man had for decades been a U.S. owned and operated dictator; it would be a shame, a diplomatic disaster, for the Soviets to supplant Western influence in their own hemisphere.

None of this had been especially disappointing or even unexpected by Ambassador Pillow, only instructional. He had seen similar performances before, most recently in the Philippines where Ferdinand Marcos had perfected a similar act for decades.

In his own after-action, Pillow noted that forewarned is forearmed. His Cultural Affairs officer, Jon Patton, devised a plan. The ambassador, who had worked his way through Princeton in a series of jazz and rock-and-roll bands in New York and Philadelphia, one of a very few drummers who actually could read music, would become part of the entertainment. The sight of him sitting at the drum set, whaling away and jamming with the band, was the last thing his guests and potential spoilers would anticipate. Their plan, it was hoped, would fall apart.

Patton's scheme—based on the intelligence and her creative way to circumvent it—had worked: music surely had soothed the savage breast. Not only did the embarrassing and dramatic exodus not take place, but the cranky old despot soon took to the dance floor, with his wife. The party rocked on into the early morning hours. Just before sunrise a lone black sedan pulled into the embassy's circular driveway and an armed guard delivered a sealed envelope. In it was the signed, official recognition of the new ambassador and an invitation to dinner that evening at the presidential palace. The last guests had departed hardly an hour earlier before the official news arrived.

The papers in Lyle's hands were proof that wires from Asuncion to Washington were abuzz with the news. Best of all, most noted the U.S. Navy's indispensable role in the diplomatic coup. Lieutenant Lyle Rees, USN, was mentioned prominently in several, including those copied to the Pentagon and the Chief of Naval Operations and the Commander-in-Chief, U.S. Atlantic Fleet.

Lyle sat up in the recliner and hooted. The choice of beverage was clear; an hour later he and Dog finished up a pitcher of mimosas. The captain happily concurred that—with little sleep for the previous thirty-six hours and free of appearances for the rest of the day—Lyle would retreat to bed.

This time there were no disturbing dreams. He awoke as low shafts of sunlight began stealing through the French doors to the balcony and into his eyes. Blinking awake, the light brightened his mind and soothed his soul. What a difference a day makes, he thought, as he stretched. He'd done it again. His fortunes, if not guaranteed, were not to be messed with; again, as planned, he was highly visible to some very important people. Who cared what the admiral back aboard the Aldrich thought?

A gentle knock on the door startled him. He was on his feet quickly, cinching the belt around a silk robe and shuffling toward the door. To his surprise, Jon Patton, cultural attaché of renown and lately hostess with the mostest, stood there beaming, thrusting a bottle of champagne at him.

Without invitation, she stepped inside, bubbling with happiness, her eyes sparkling. She didn't see him frantically tidying his bed head hair and wiping sleep from his eyes. She deposited the wine on the writing table, triumphantly surveying the basket of fruit. The kiss was completely unexpected; gentle and lingering as her tongue entered his lips, speaking more than words.

"U.S. Navy to the rescue," she purred, "but, I didn't know you only worked at night. Let's see what else my white knight can do with the sun is still up."

Tilting her head back, Jon surveyed him through half-open eyes. The expression was undeniable. With one hand she pulled at the knot, and with one fluid motion of the other she shook her hair free to tumble below her shoulders. The shift-style dress dropped next; she wore nothing underneath. Pulling him against her small, erect breasts, she kissed him again, this time with more tongue. Lyle's physical response was predictable and obvious. Playfully pushing him away she murmured, "I think you're up for another command performance," she teased, placing his hands on her breasts.

She was warm, and where she was touching him was warmer. Her nipples were long, erect and thick; they pointed up and hardly bent as he fingers slowly strummed them. She closed her eyes and moaned. Her fingernails dug into his forearm as she moved his right hand to explore the curly dark hairs between her thighs. She gasped as his finger entered her. Clutching his head she turned it and gently bit his ear. Seeing that he was completely aroused, she smiled, then turned and tantalized him with the view of her naked back tapering into her narrow hips.

He responded as she planned, measuring her tiny waist with his hands and rubbing against her. With a wry, crooked smile he couldn't see, she bent forward on her knees, spreading her arms across the bed, stretching like a cat. Jon reached back and grasped him, squeezing hard and guiding. At first, she pushed gently, slowly. The tempo rose quickly. Sensing Lyle's loss of control, his thrusts steadily more violent, she arched her back, squeezing, sliding on him, harder and harder.

Her breath came heavy, through her open mouth. A low moan stirred deep in her throat. She stretched, turning her face toward the ceiling. Her guttural sounds grew deeper and louder with each violent thrust, ending with a scream.

* * * *

Loud, persistent knocking woke Lyle. Her sweet scent on the sheets confirmed that he had not been dreaming. The pounding continued until he reached the door. She was inside before he could get it all the way open. She closed it quickly. She was dressed as before, her hair carelessly pulled in a ponytail. Even though her expression was far different now, Lyle didn't focus until she handed him an envelope, commanding, "Read it."

The NIS top-secret message was addressed to Navy-Washington, and it was succinct. Lyle's knees went weak with the first sentence: "Lieutenant Lyle Rees, USN, is the principal suspect in the murder of Chief Mark Jones." Suspected killer and victim, it continued, had been under investigation in connection with illegal drug trafficking during the South American deployment. Evidence, it continued, had been discovered among Jones' possessions aboard the destroyer Aldrich, including documents, cargo manifests of band equipment flown from Venezuela, Panama and Ecuador to Cartagena. Most interesting were video tapes of an unidentified man, presumably an accomplice, speaking with him in Panama. Time signatures on the tape corresponded with the band performance at Fort Amador. The next paragraph stated that his security clearance has been suspended. The final sentence revealed that—to avoid embarrassment to the United States on foreign soil— especially considering his now widespread association with the U.S. Ambassador to Paraguay—his arrest will occur immediately upon return to U.S. property, aboard USS Aldrich.

A lightning bolt could have had no more effect.

Stunned that his and Jones' possessions aboard ship had been searched and confiscated—including a tape that wasn't his—Lyle backed toward a club chair and collapsed into it. Speechless, he looked at her, then buried his face in his hands. He had lost all control.

"Tell me what's going on, Lyle," she speaks, kneeling before him, gently and urgently taking his hands in hers.

He has been a fool, framed by the video tape and some fictional documents. He looked down at the face of the only person in the world who seemed to care or who might be able to help him, and he started talking. He began recalling details, out of sequence, as he tried—for the first time and against all instinct—to create a coherent narrative. He buried his face in hands again. *Was Jones gathering evidence? Why? Had the testing in Ecuador triggered his murder? Why does this woman care?*

"It's my turn for a rescue," Jon said, rising, trying to speak optimistically. "Get dressed, in a uniform. We're going to my office. The Marines will assume we're there on official business, but I've got an idea. I'll meet you," she looked at her wristwatch, "in ten minutes, at the service entrance by the kitchen."

It was Sunday evening, and she had driven her own car to the Plaza. He found the back stairs, and in a few minutes she was driving the reverse route of the previous triumphant parade through Asuncion. He was in shock, and he needed no convincing as she explained her plan: they would use the encrypted secure voice telephone line at the embassy to call Washington and speak with the State Department South American desk. "They may not, probably won't, buy any of this, but that doesn't matter: we've got to get on record."

Lyle stared at her; stuck on "we."

"It was the only chance they had to hear another version of the evidence you and the chief assembled. It doesn't make any sense that you two would have done that. No rational person would believe you two would have gathered evidence, made videos, to convict yourselves. Any idiot knows that's not the way criminals work." She paused, embarrassed at her choice of words. "We'll talk first, it's all recorded, then we'll draft a written account." She looked at clock in the center of her BMW's dash board. "We'll have to work quickly. It's eight; the courier leaves at midnight on a flight to Miami."

With the call and writing completed, they left Jon's office on what once was a second floor drawing room when the mansion was a private residence and took the servant's stairs to the mailroom. As they reached the basement, they stopped in their tracks; Captain Hidalgo was leaving the communications center. He froze when he saw them. There was anger in his face, which instantly turned darker. Through eyes drawn in to narrow slits, he stepped into the stairwell and closed the door. "I've just had a very interesting chat about you. We need to talk, now."

Seeing the hallway empty, she led them to a storage room used as an overflow office for visitors. The little room, farthest from the communications center, was dark, lit only by an exterior security light shining through a window high in the back wall. There was no curtain, only closely-spaced iron bars. Lyle's eyes were riveted on the window as Hidalgo sat in a secretarial chair behind a small table. Jon pulled up metal folding chairs. She had to pull his arm to break his trance and pulled him down to sit beside her.

"Shouldn't she be excused? Oh, wait, I'm guessing she knows more than I do. Maybe we can talk about that, too. I'm so very happy about that." The sarcasm was heavy.

"She showed me the NIS message," Lyle tried to find words to respond, now unsure if he hadn't made another blunder by getting Jon involved, "sir, none of it's true. I've been used. I don't know what to do. She had a good idea. She listened to what I had to say, then brought me here. We just spent a half hour on the secure voice to State in DC. They're expecting a written summary in today's pouch." He looked at Jon, "The courier leaves here in a couple of hours."

Dog sat and said nothing, but his anger seemed to ebb. He looked at her, then said to Lyle, "You know how much trouble you're in, don't you? Let me read it."

They watched Dog's face, now lit by a small lamp Jon moved from atop a file cabinet. His eye twitched and his jaw cinched. He didn't look up until he laid down the papers. He knotted his fingers together and leaned on his elbows. "You've made a bunch of mistakes, but you know that. But, it was a good move getting this to somebody, me included, other than NIS. The two jokers I just met have you on the way to Leavenworth." His features softened as he leaned back and fished something from the breast pocket of his crisp white uniform. He tossed the folder paper across the desk, "Here's a message you haven't seen."

It was an order from the U.S. Commander, Southern Atlantic, for him to take custody of Rees and return with him and the band to re-board Aldrich in Buenos Ares.

As further justification for the arrest, the message continued, NIS suspected that the band director and his assistant, maybe others, were involved in drug and money smuggling. In a self-congratulatory paragraph, the NIS author noted that although suspicions about use of diplomatic pouches and misidentified cargo aboard military aircraft had been suspected for years, it was not until the NIS stepped in that any progress had been made.

"NIS will take you into custody when we land in Argentina." The words stung. Lyle felt like his heart would stop. His face prickled with fear. "I don't like it, but there's nothing I can do about it." He paused to let Lyle gain his composure. "Look, I need this like another hole in my head, but I believe you. There's obviously more to this, much more. Even the NIS pukes know that stuff has been going on down here for years. Everybody knows it." He rubbed his face with both hands before continuing, "No need to preach, but if you'd come to me it would have been better for you now, to say the least. Unfortunately, you're just the latest in what's probably a long line of guys gullible or vain enough to get suckered in. I'll do everything I can for you." He looked tired as he spoke to Jon, "The written summary is a good start, but we need to get you out of the loop." Looking back at Lyle, he continued, "Lyle, I need to hear this from you, if I'm ever going to be a credible witness, I've got to know as much or more than Jon does." He looked at his wristwatch. Managing a gentlemanly smile, he spoke to Jon, "It's getting later, please make sure those papers make it into the pouch. A lot is riding on it, and thanks.

Jon touched Lyle on the shoulder and left for the communications center.

The little room was totally quiet as the door latched shut. "Don't leave anything out. I mean nothing." Neither saw the shadow drift past the high window.

Lyle's memory was sharper this time. He gave more detail about conversations along the deployment route, descriptions—everyone from Maggy Brown to the men who traveled with the band—the drum cases in Ecuador and Chile, everything about Jones' initiative to get the rag tested by men he mistakenly thought were friends.

"I watched the papers go into the pouch. I watched them lock it and hung round to confirm he made the flight," Jon said when she returned.

Dog remained at the embassy to arrange the band's flight to Argentina. After they left for the Plaza he returned to the communications center he called up the one person who might be able to offer some perspective: Capitan Don Jose Vasquez, newly appointed director, Colombia Administrative Department of Security, his roommate at the Naval War College in Newport, Rhode Island.

* * * *

It was nearly daylight when Jon returned. She has spoken again with her contact at the State Department. It was not surprising that the situation in Paraguay was still hot news at Foggy Bottom, but she could not fathom why an undersecretary—Nathan Pierce—was taking personal interest, especially early on a Monday morning. Her source had no idea why, only that years ago he'd been posted in Colombia and was now—when he didn't have a phone in his ear—bouncing off the walls. The most shocking news she saved for last: Jon's summary was not in the pouch or on the inventory of items received.

"It's impossible, Lyle," she spoke, sitting on the bed, agitated, staring at the floor. "I saw it go in, somebody's got it. That probably happened before my friend got there. She said the Pierce character was in his office when she arrived."

For the first time Lyle saw Jon worried and shaken. He knew that she had gone on record, stuck out her neck for him. She didn't have to. *Would she pay a price?* It was his turn to act responsibly. He sat beside her, "You've been wonderful. You've done all you could do, more. Captain Hidalgo is right: we'll take it from here. He knows the whole story now, more than I remembered when I talked with you. He's my friend in court and a good one. He's well connected or he wouldn't have the job he does," he spoke with more confidence than he actually had as he put his arm around her, hoping that he was right. "Whatever happens, it's all going to play out within the Navy. The best thing I can do for you is disappear, let you get on with your career, your life." Forcing a smile, he stood and took his suitcase from the closet. "Just one last request: drive me to the airport and I'll buy a drink next time you're in DC."

Her attempt at a smile was brave but sincere, "Better be more than that, big guy. OK, just one more favor. I'll meet you in the parking garage and drive you in style, top down this time. I hate airport farewells, but I'll make an exception this time. You're more trouble than you're worth, but with at least one redeeming quality."

Minutes later he cleared at the front desk, then walked through the lobby and took the elevator to the basement. The doors parted on a short hallway leading to a pair of glass doors and the dimly lit, low-ceiling garage beyond.

He pushed through and saw the red BMW M3 parked by the far wall, trunk open. She was leaning back, resting on the headrest. *She's got to be tired. Probably wishes we never met. I bet she'll be glad to be rid of me. I hope she will be.*

He walked across the spotless concrete floor, placed his suitcase in the trunk and shut it quietly as not to startle her. *If she has dozed off, she deserves it.* He opened the passenger door. He spoke, almost in a whisper to bring her awake gently, "I can't thank you enough. You're the best, lady. I'll miss you but not Asuncion." She didn't respond.

He touched her shoulder, pushing gently. She rolled off the headrest, face twisting toward him. Her torso slumped toward him. Her head plopped in his lap. The tip of her ponytail was matted and wet with something sticky. He didn't understand, and his brain rationalized: s*he's cut her neck on something, how can she still be asleep?*

With a hand on each shoulder, he sat her up. Her chin was buried in her chest. This time she fell against the door, her eyes staring blankly. She wasn't asleep. Minutes earlier someone had pushed a silenced .22-caliber pistol against the back of her neck and pulled the trigger. The small bullet smashed through her spinal cord and—without enough velocity to exit—had bounced around inside her skull, scrambling her brains. There was little blood. It was a professional job.

He wanted to scream. He could only retch. Something in his head was still denying reality. He clawed at the door handle, and fell out of the sports car. On his hands and knees, immobilized with horror, he emptied his stomach.

On his feet again, Lyle leaned against the fender, he looked around.

Not sure how he got there, he found himself inside, finally finding the elevator "up" button. The trip to the third floor seemed to take hours. He squeezed between the partially open doors and ran to the captain's suite and beat on the door. There was no answer. Trying the latch, he pushed it open. The room was dimly lit by the first pink and grey glow of morning, but in the light from the bathroom he saw that bed was still made, only his packed bag lay on it.

He felt his way across the big room. On the other side of the big bed he saw a mass of white: it was Dog, fully dressed, face down. The carpet was wet. *He can't be drunk!* He kneels near Dog's head and flips on the bed table lamp. In the light he sees a bloody hole the size of his fist just above the captain's right ear, the exit wound from the .45-caliber bullet fired from the Model 1911 pistol lying beside him.

His primal scream was uncontrolled. He slams his palms on the carpet to push away from the horror. He jerks them to his face, realizing that the wet pink goo is the man's brain tissue. He heaves, this time nothing comes. He tries to stand, finally succeeding, staring again in total horror, shaking in disbelief. Gasping for breath, he lunges clumsily toward the balcony.

Tripping on his feet he falls forward, stumbling into the writing table. The momentum carries him on to the balcony. The table clatters noisily against the stone bannister. In the same instant he hears a different, sharper noise. Plaster propels off the back wall; pieces strike him in the back.

Moving takes all his concentration. He jerks his head around and tries to stand. His wet palm slips off the table and he falls again. He is drawn to the striated light from the stained glass windows. Another thwack, more dusty plaster fragments. *Someone's shooting at me!* His body more responsive than his shocked brain, propels him off the balcony. He is scrambling for his life.

On his feet, he realizes that whoever shot Jon and most likely Dog, is trying to kill him. *Something must have scared them away in the garage.* Now the killer or a partner is in the park or a building somewhere on the other side. And, if there are two—or more—shooters, maybe one or more of them is still in the hotel. He races through the open door, down the hallway and careens off a maid loaded with linens. He runs past the wide, marble stair landing to the end of the long hallway, and jerks the door open. Not bothering to check if anyone was on the service stairs, he begins bounding down them until he can descend no farther. He is in a wide basement corridor stacked with furniture. The kitchen is on the left, full of busy people. The only escape is to the right, toward a steel door. Pressing his face against it, he catches his breath, then cracks it open slightly. It opens to a wide loading dock. Seeing nobody, he walks across the platform. The short drop jump to the cobblestone alley below jars him.

Straightening up, he hears sirens, still far away, and walks down the alley, away from the sound. His pace slows as he nears the sidewalk.

Smoothing his uniform, thankful it isn't soiled, he steps onto the palm-lined sidewalk. He hadn't covered more than a half a block before he sees a cab. On the street, in a white uniform, he is an obvious target. The driver looks in the rear view mirror, waiting for instruction.

"Airport; *aero puerto, por favor*." Even if it's a long shot, the airport is the only escape he can imagine.

The cabby glances the side mirror, throws the wheel hard to the left and accelerates across the wide boulevard, finding a split-second gap in the on-coming traffic. Lyle ducks down as the cab passes the hotel. Two green and white police cars skid to stop at the front awning, lights flashing. The cab makes a right turn and heads up the wide boulevard to the airport, ten minutes away.

The futility of his plan quickly becomes apparent. His passport is in the embassy safe with the others. He and Jon were to have picked them up on the way to meet the charter. Now it may as well be on the moon. He's got less than ten minutes of relative safety left in the cab. An Anglo in a white uniform, on the run from the Navy, from the State Department, from whoever killed Jon and the captain, maybe the same people who killed Jones, from whoever is trying to kill him, he has no way out. As the cab neared the airport he was leaning forward to tell the driver to take him to a clothing store. Then he saw it.

He could not believe his eyes. The airplane with U.S. Navy markings was parked behind a chain link fence on the other side of the airfield. A fuel truck is parked beside the Navy P3 submarine hunter, and its crew is rolling the boarding stairs away from the tall aircraft. "*Alli, alli!*" he shouts as they passed between steel towers at the airport entrance and points toward the road to the military hangars.

The section of the low, corrugated aluminum building used as a combination cargo office and flight information center is not much more than a wide hallway. Opposite the entrance, the far end is all windows around a single door to the tarmac. Through the windows he sees that the fuel truck operator is rewinding the fuel line. Men in blue overalls are pushing stairs away from the tall, four-engine aircraft. He is about to run through the door when a Navy pilot steps out of the tiny office. He's carrying large sheets of paper: weather maps and aviation charts. He's absorbed in them, reading while he walks to a long sofa. His back still towards Lyle, he spreads the papers on a low table.

Lyle resists an urge to race up to him, instead takes a breath and pauses. He forces himself to walk slowly and takes a chair opposite the table. "I just saw the P3. You the pilot?"

"Guilty," the pilot still has not seen Lyle, and flips over another chart.

Losing his reserve, he drives straight to the point, and asks collegially, "Got any room for a duty passenger?" The pilot is older. His crew cut is grey at the temples. The green flight suit is baggy on his narrow frame. The interruption is clearly annoying.

"Give me a minute." He finally looks up. His frown is instantly replaced with a look of curiosity. He looks down again. A second later he looks up, this time with a smile. "Hey, you're the band guy! Right? How's it going?" he offers his hand. "Remember? I flew you from Norfolk to Puerto Rico. What was it, about three, four months ago? What in hell are you doing here?"

Lyle could have kissed him.

"Sure, I've got plenty of room. Your timing is perfect 'cause I just got called from the embassy, naval attaché. Told me to hold up. Wouldn't say why. Land of *mañana* down here. Know what I'm saying. Usually it's for a passenger. You it? I wouldn't wander too far. I'll tell 'em you're here, otherwise who knows how long before they get around to calling back."

Lyle could hardly contain his gratitude and turned his nervous energy into a running account of the band's tour. Anticipating that he may be asked for some kind of orders and having none, he created a convincing lie about his dying father in Tampa. The tension in on his face was real.

"Tough break, I'm sorry. My dad passed away while I was on deployment in WestPac. He'd been buried for a month before I made it home from Vietnam." He spoke as he walked across the hall and plunked coins in vending machine. Lyle accepted the offer of a soda. Judging from his pensive expression, Lyle knew the story had worked, and he watched as he gazed across the tarmac. Suddenly he turned and snapped his fingers. "Hey, there may be another option, if we're quick. Come here. See that old C123 out there? It's a long shot, but worth a try," he pointed toward another plane parked about a hundred yards from his. He looked back toward the office and lowered his voice, "Look, this is a 'non-versation,' know what I mean?" He looked at the old plane and continued. "I've seen it and her pilot all over down here. He's a contractor, OK?" he spoke, searching for any sign of recognition from Lyle. Seeing it, he continued, "I heard him earlier. Said he's headed back north, eventually New Orleans, I think. He was checking weather charts for the U.S. Gulf Coast. Look, it might take a day or two, maybe refueling or other stops along the way, but you'd be moving. I'm only going as far as Roosevelt Roads. He may not be much better. Hell, he could change plans in the air and head for Africa. "

Lyle nodded and squinted at the plane in the distance.

"If it were me and my dad were in as bad shape, I'd do it. I'd walk out there and give it a shot. Otherwise, you're welcome to hang out with us."

Lyle's gaze was distracted from the airplane, to the distance beyond it. Two sets of blinking red lights were approaching, about two miles away. In minutes they would turn on to the airport perimeter road, he hoped to the passenger terminal, not the military hangars. "Of course, I'd like to ask. All he can do is say no."

He'd hardly gotten the words out before he was interrupted. "Oh, crap, he's turning up already!" In the still air, a cloud of black smoke shrouded the airplane. "Well, hold on, this isn't exactly kosher, but I might get his attention if he's monitoring U.S. pilot-to-pilot frequency. Here's hoping," he said, pulling a hand-held radio from his a deep thigh pocket in his flight suit. "I'll tell him it's an emergency."

Lyle stepped outside. A set of flashing lights was entering the main access road, racing toward the terminal. As he feared, the other was already speeding down the perimeter road. It would arrive in a couple of minutes. He stepped back inside to search the pilot's face for clues. Plan B: if this doesn't work, maybe he could hide in the P3 until the police left, whenever that may be. Cold sweat clung to his forehead. No Plan C materialized before the pilot dropped the radio away from his face, smiled and shot him a thumbs-up.

"He's cool with it, but you gotta flat-out haul." He grabbed Lyle's arm to keep him from bolting immediately. "Couple of other things you need to know. Technically, you're a stow-away, but nobody's going to care. I don't know how you talked your way aboard, remember?" He looked toward the plane and continued, "A safety note: the props are turning. Give it a wide approach to the nose there, then scoot down the port side. There's little pilot door there. It's open. Step inside. He says pull it shut, then find some place to hold on while he takes off. His only condition is that you leave him alone for a half hour or so, probably so he can talk some spooky stuff on the radio. So, chill out before getting social with him. He's a little strange, but he's a good guy. Actually, he seemed unusually happy to help you out. He's headed for Cartagena. He even volunteered that he'd let you radio ahead for further transport or whatever," were the last words Lyle heard over his shoulder as he began running. He didn't care where he was going.

He looked down at Lyle through the window at his feet and pointed back, past his left knee. Lyle paused only long enough to nod back. The engines roared and the high pitched screech of the port side propeller screamed like a buzz saw and sucked him toward it. Seconds later he neared the little side door. The plane was rolling before he saw how to latch it shut. He fell, then groped a cargo net with both hands. Seconds later the airplane bounced for the last time and broke free.

There wasn't much to see except two cargo pallets stacked with what looked like ice chests, a door in the middle of the forward bulkhead and to the left of it a little ladder. He piled cargo nets between the pallets and stretched out. The noise, the vibration all now seemed oddly soothing. Relief washed over his tired body, and he closed his eyes. Even if he didn't know his next move, at least he now had time to think.

He was alive.

A red light blinking overhead startled him. Sensing there was no alarm, he checked his watch; he had been asleep for nearly an hour. He climbed up the ladder to the flight deck. It looked like an atrium awash in intense sunlight; the whole front of the plane, above and below, was all windows. Unlike the cargo compartment, the roomy cockpit was tidy. He couldn't see much of the pilot's face; his eyes were masked behind dark glasses, but there was a nod and a neutral expression on the round face. His benefactor pointed toward the empty seat to his right. He was an older man, dressed in a light-colored t-shirt with some kind of writing on it and khaki shorts. Discounting a belly, he seemed fit. A red ball cap covered what Lyle assumed was a bald or shaved head. He wore a little towel around his shoulders like a terrycloth shawl. For a spook, Lyle thought, he didn't look very intimidating.

"Buckle up and put it on. It'll be easier to talk," he leaned over and shouted. He reached behind Lyle and pulled headset off a hook and handed it to him.

The first words were stunning. "Hey, sport, if your name's Lyle Rees you might consider changing it. You're in a world of hurt, my friend." He continued, laughing, "You don't look like a murderer. You're wanted for killing some sailor, a full Navy captain, no less, and some embassy babe. Pretty good days work for a blood-thirsty maniac! You can drop the jive about a dying dad, but it's a good cover. The Navy pilot back there bought it all. Congratulations!"

Lyle looked at him in amazement: the man was laughing at him.

"We're about four hours from Cartagena. You a naval aviator? Don't see any wings of gold on your chest. Could of fallen off during the murders!

Staring with wide eyes, Lyle dumbly shakes his head.

"Just my luck. Thought maybe you were pilot since you're pals with the P3 pilot back there. Screw it. If I can't grab a partial charge you're free to finish up your nap. You gotta be tired, killing all those people like that," he laughed again. "Got any friends there? You gonna need them!"

Lyle spoke the name of the Colombian Deputy Naval Attaché, Commander Larry Hart.

"I know his people. I know everybody! I'll ask military ops to patch him through, matter of sensitivity and all that stuff. Don't worry: I'll be urgent but vague. No offense, but you and I will probably part company pretty damned quick when we land."

Lyle looked at the clouds far below and the brilliant sky all around. He saw some sunglasses and put them on. The view was spectacular. For a few moments he nearly forgot about the nightmare back on earth. The voice cracked in the headset, "Here's hoping that, one, he'll call back and, two, that you trust him with your life. You're going to need all the help you can get," he spoke, mopping his face with the towel. It was thick and expensive looking, embroidered in silver and gold: "Mayflower Hotel, Washington, D.C."

"Go on back. Cooling works better back there, out of the sunlight. There's food and beer in the chest in the galley. Help yourself. Bring me a sandwich. It's going to be a rough flight closer to the Caribbean, so hold on." Lyle began to unbuckle, and for the first time stern words were spoken: "And, listen," he grabbed Lyle's forearm in a vice-like grip and pulled him close, "You gotta throw up, hit the head. Don't slash all over my cargo deck; the smell hangs around for weeks down here."

Eighteen

He held the wing strut firmly with both hands and swung his left leg off the aluminum float; it landed with a dead thunk on the wooden dock. Shifting his weight, he pivoted over the gap. On firm footing he took a moment to look around, then laugh at himself. Only a couple of hours ago he'd had second thoughts about climbing aboard the single-engine Beaver, even if it was bigger than others floating nearby. The flight was southwest, down the Cook Inlet and Alaska Peninsula. Two hours later he was smitten by the mind-numbing beauty he had never imagined. And, he was excited: he was about to spring a huge surprise, one he had planned for a long time.

All his gear would be provided, so he traveled light: only one small duffel. He grabbed the straps and limped across the well-kept little lawn. He paused to size-up the zigzag stairs built into the cliff; it was going to be quite a climb for him and his nearly useless left leg. He measured the task from bottom to the top where they passed through the floor of the wide deck. When he saw her he knew the struggle would be worthwhile. It had been nearly seven years.

She shouted a welcome and began descending to assist.

"Wait, please don't trouble yourself." He lifted his cane, "It may take me longer, but I'd rather meet you there. No need for you to make the trip twice." *She looks great*. He smiled from beneath his floppy canvas hat, leaned back and gave an exaggerated salute.

She was more than a little concerned and puzzled to see her latest guest standing at the bottom of the stairs and saluting her. Why a salute?

She didn't recognize the man, but there was something familiar about him, maybe the hint of a dialect she hadn't heard in a while. She looked at the name on the reservation fax in her hand. It didn't ring any bells. The travel agent certainly hadn't mentioned the man used a cane. Lucas Lodge wasn't exactly handicap accessible. Emma made a mental note to mention that in the future. Even if climbing the stairs was going to be a chore for him, it could be done. Emma didn't want to appear overly concerned, so she returned the salute, leaned against the chest-high railing and waited.

The sound of his boots striking the risers began immediately and continued with a steady, syncopated rhythm: the strong leg hit with a hollow chunk; a soft clomp followed a couple of beats later. He made constant progress, pausing only on the three the stair landings. As he turned to start up the last flight, she could see that he was a big man, dressed in a red Pendleton shirt and canvas pants. When his head was nearly level with her feet, she saw his broad, handsome face. She gasped.

She covered her mouth with both hands. An uncharacteristic, girlish squeal followed. Her eyes widened in disbelief, and her arms shot out to embrace Roland Hebert, retired New Orleans chief of detectives, her former landlord, neighbor, friend and mentor.

"I was just in the neighborhood, thought I'd drop in to check on you!" Hebert spoke with mock seriousness, delighted with her reaction. He scooped her up in his strong arms, and she hugged back. She caressed the rugged face in her hands. The years fell away. Only the chiseled features—wide forehead, deep-set eyes, wide nose and square jaw—were older. The kind blue eyes were exactly the same. Tears blinded her. She buried her face in his shoulder.

The Heberts, Avis and Roland, had lived across the alley. She had fed the Lucas girls and their ailing mother at least once a week and appeared with desserts more often than that. They had spent countless evenings and weekends porch-sitting, as they learned to call it, talking and laughing well into the tender nights. The bond of friendship had grown even deeper during her mother's decline. Avis was closer in age and had spent hours just sitting, a tireless companion and nurse to the dying woman.

As the years and sad events had wrenched her from those days in the Garden District, she became even more aware of what a wonderful difference they had made in her and Lucy's lives. In addition to all they did, the Heberts respected her enough, she understood, to leave her alone if she wished. That is precisely what they did after Lyle Rees' sudden marriage had shaken the sisters and after his mean betrayal and all that happened afterwards. Emma had seen the Roland's anger and knew that he easily could have retaliated; planting evidence the least of the tricks at his disposal. It took discipline for him not to make a bigger mess worse. Instead, after Emma's sudden departure for Adak, the Heberts focused even more of their attention—discreetly and often anonymously—on Lucy. He never hinted, or admitted, that it was his connections that landed Lucy's first job with the NOPD.

He followed her around the lodge as she proudly showed off its amenities, including a satellite telephone for her rather impressive—if confidential—guest list. She might be bragging a little, she realized, but knew that—if he thought so—she would soon see a side-long glance and arching left eyebrow to bring her back down to earth. You didn't make it for forty years as a detective, he had told her, without a superbly developed BS detector. She couldn't take her eyes off him. He looked so much older. The curly black hair had gone grey at the temples.

She walked a tray of sandwiches and hot spiced tea to the deck and placed it on a sturdy table between two equally well-built chairs crafted from planks and hardware left over from renovations; Alaskan Adirondacks, Joe called them.

The brilliant sunlight was warm. Emma sat next to him and took in the picture-perfect day. On the distant horizon white clouds lingered above the Kenai Peninsula, a couple of hundred miles to the south, far beyond Lake Illiamna and Cook Inlet that led southwest to the Bering Sea. The endless vastness of Alaska, its brutal beauty molded from earth, sky and water, were awesome, even to the most urbane and sophisticated. The deck of Lucas Lodge offered a perfect place to sit still, to indulge the senses and ponder the timelessness of the breathtaking panorama and—if dared—one's own existence. Emma made sure that her guests, especially first-time visitors to Alaska, had plenty of deck time. Roland would be no exception. She checked the familiar reaction and realized that she had been talking too much. Emma couldn't remember when she'd been so happy just to be near someone. She would let him speak when he wished.

Stories of old friends and good times soon flooded from him. After a while he spoke about the traffic accident nearly two years ago which had crippled him. His wife of thirty five years had not survived it. He retreated into a shell, the reason why Emma hadn't heard about it, he apologized. He credited even more depressing scenes in New Orleans, fueled by crack cocaine and organized crime, for finally bringing him back to reality. The Drug Enforcement Agency contacted him—usual outreach to newly-retired police officers, they claimed—and offered him a job as a consultant. He has been working with them for nearly a year, given a free hand to explore leads—and his theories—about trafficking through the port of New Orleans, Dixie Mafia involvement and the growing influence of even bigger fish in South American cartels. Just describing his work brightened his tired eyes.

"It's great. The task force isn't fooling around with low- or even mid-level criminals. We're actually going after the big guys, at least in the U.S. I feel good about it. We're nailing some real bad guys who've been a blight on New Orleans for a long time. It may do some real good in the long run, and that's about all that interests me anymore," he spoke again, to her and more to towards the intoxicating view, to faces somewhere out in the distance. He paused, and Emma sensed something, at least that she should let him continue.

She was right.

"Everything and everybody is connected. Sometimes what goes around really does come around," he spoke, wrapping his big hands around the mug. "Not as often as we'd like, maybe, but sometimes it does. I guess I wouldn't have been a cop all my life if I didn't think that, that it was worthwhile trying to make it so. He paused and took a deep breath. "What I'm getting at is a name that has come up, only in the past few weeks." He returned his mug to the tray and took Emma's hand. "I've planned this trip for a while, but I'm glad that I can be here with you in person. Emma, the name is Lyle Rees."

The shock on her face confirmed his intuition; her expression moved from shock to concern. He had no doubt why.

He took time to summarize the reports he'd read about Lyle's alleged involvement with drug traffickers on the South American junket. By the time he got to his current status as a murderer and fugitive, Emma had drawn into a fetal position, crying into her knees.

"I don't know what to make of it. I'm sorry to deliver such news. He's in real trouble, maybe beyond help. From what I'm hearing, he's lucky to be alive." He didn't speak what he thought: *it's very likely he isn't.*

"Can it be true?" was all she managed to speak.

"I don't know. After what he did to you, I just don't know. Maybe. If it's any consolation, I don't think he's a killer. I've a pretty good sense of people, even ones I don't like, but I don't see that, Emma. Possibly I can see him stupid enough to go after easy money. The rest?" he shrugged. He spoke cautiously about what he has discovered about Lyle's life: the first marriage had ended quickly, concurrent with her affair with another of Emma's tormentors—Commander Art Jacks—and leading to another quick marriage to a wealthy Texas steel broker, twenty years her senior.

She listened but didn't hear much. This could not be the man she knew, as a friend and—even after all that time—perhaps more. Her mind churned with memories of good and bad times, his awful insensitivity and devastating lies, but also his face and laugh. For years she'd tried to erase those thoughts; but, she hadn't succeeded with that or in hating him. She couldn't even be happy to hear that the marriage had fallen apart, that the shallow, self-centered jerk was getting what he deserved. Her feelings were far different. The old detective read her well.

"In the past couple of years I've learned that our favorite writer was right: the past isn't dead, it's not even the past," he said, continuing to study her face.

Quoting Faulkner brought a smile. The words conjured pleasant memories of the rainy afternoon they had ducked into a little bookshop on Pirates Alley, near Saint Louis Cathedral, once inhabited by Tennessee Williams. It became the unofficial meeting place of an informal book club led by the Heberts.

Memories flooded her consciousness as Roland continued, bringing up the ship-jumping incident. He had theories now about her and Lyle's confidentiality statements, Lyle's sudden and transparently false accusations about Emma's lifestyle, the nearly simultaneous death of their crewmember in Mississippi.

"I may be wrong, but I have been right. I've got a strong feeling about this, Emma. I went back to at least try tie it together, to jog my memory. There's nothing. It's a blank slate. The records of our, the NOPD's, preliminary investigation were loaned to federal agents, and we never got them back. And that's not all: I asked around with the Orleans Parish DA and the Louisiana State Police CID. Got the same story. The feds, it seems, had snatched up everything, every lead, every shred of evidence or anything that looked like it. And, it gets stranger. They, or somebody, breezed through town months later and lifted the DA's draft indictment of a half-dozen big- time operators: a ship chandler, manager of *Monte Verde* Coffee Company and a mobbed up lawyer. They claimed federal jurisdiction, and—times being what they were with the Democrat administration—they never saw the light of day."

He was standing now, his back to the lake, leaning on the railing and focusing only on her.

"Is it possible that the federal investigators, these people, still have the files?"

"Emma, *cher,* you've a trusting soul with a heart of gold. The short answer's no. A couple of months ago I put on my hot shot DEA consultant hat and made some calls and was told to follow up with a written request. Word back from DEA, FBI, State Department was 'sorry, nothing found.' Blah, blah, blah, 'will continue searching files transferred to permanent storage,' blah, blah, blah. A week later I got another letter from DC. Regrettably, those records, including the video tape you turned over that night, were destroyed in a fire at a storage facility somewhere, in Arkansas of all places." He sat beside her again. "The only thing my old friends can remember, that's getting my back up, is that the name of the State guy making the rounds that night and afterwards was bogus. I fired that off to DC, and this time there wasn't a form letter. I got a call—probably from another fictional character—and nothing in writing, only that it was a cover name, part of a sensitive national security investigation. Read between the lines: drop dead. Emma, my BS meter has pegged off the dial."

Sensing that he was beginning to overload, himself and her, he changed the subject, "How is our dear, sweet Lucy?"

Roland had been protective of her, perhaps more than needed. Born with achondroplasia, she was a little person in stature, four-feet six-inches. She progressed in the NOPD job. Two years after Emma left for Alaska, she took a job as a corporate accountant with Deloitte & Touche in their Charleston office. "You'll get a kick out of this. Remember how she was always hamming it up for Lyle's camera? Well, there apparently is a lot of showbiz in her blood. She's gotten into amateur theater in Charleston and sings with a big retro dance band. She's also their accountant!"

"Good grief, I don't think I'll ever forget that party," Roland threw his head back and laughed heartily. "You could have filled the Super Dome if you'd have advertised the musicians who just showed up all night."

Emma picked up, quickly, "Oh, I bet you would have been happier if we did. You were acting so afraid that we'd wreck the house." She lied,

"We invited you over just to put you out of your misery!"

"You remember her singing with the band and cracking jokes, running around with the microphone, interviewing everybody like she was an investigative reporter? What a hoot!"

"Goodness, those tapes. I'd forgotten all about them. They recorded some wonderful, happy times," she spoke sadly. "They may be gone; before I left she was throwing away anything that reminded her of him. Actually, Roland, she may have taken things harder than I did. Maybe, for some reasons you or I can't really know, the disappointments may have been sadder, the fall harder."

"I think I may understand. I've some clue. Sometimes it's better not to look back, just keep looking ahead. But, you can't really forget." He paused again, "As hard as I've tried, there's one night in New Orleans I wish I could."

* * * *

"I want that son-of-a-bitch dead. I want them all dead," Nathan Pierce muttered to himself. He had cradled the phone and turned to look at the National Mall and the Vietnam Memorial out his window.

He tried to calm himself. Interpol was committed. They had issued arrest warrants throughout South America. Deadly force was authorized, and he knew that—with such authorization—it meant most would shoot first and ask questions later. But, the last phone call was shattering that hope. *Would the nightmare ever end?*

The intelligence briefer had no sooner left than his private, secure phone line had lit up. Russell Anderson said the ship-jumping incident has resurfaced; and, the source of the renewed interest was even more disturbing. Now, retired NOPD captain Roland Hebert was nosing around, asking about the police records that Nat had destroyed. He had promised his partners that the episode would end then, now this. And, if that weren't enough, the mole reported that Hebert was working for the DEA and had left two days ago for a fishing trip to Alaska, the guest of none other than Emma Lucas, the Coast Guard officer Nat had argued against eliminating.

Anderson was a cool operator and—like all lawyers—a gambler. Nat had never heard him so agitated, at the very cusp of rage; he was thankful he wasn't in the same room with him, or Menard. He wasn't sure which man scared him more. It was clear that there wasn't one damning source to deal with, there were two more; he'd never been happy with Nat's solution, and now he knew that—in his partners' criminal minds—Nat was the fourth. Trying to mask his terror, he promised fast action with Rees and bargained for more time to deal with the others. That barely mollified. He knew the consequences should he fail; Anderson seemed to calm, if only superficially.

But, what he said next was nearly as perplexing: he began rambling about the Presidential election. Uncharacteristically, he rambled on about Nat's role as mole for Secretary Cotton as the most important job he'd ever have. He had seen everything in DC's political arena, but to his disbelief, the dyed-in-the-wool Democrat, an important donor and even more accomplished illegal supporter of the Democrat party, said it would be better to see Republicans remain in the White House. "Nothing can interfere with a Republican victory in November."

Nat hadn't forgotten his conversation last spring with Secretary Cotton at *Bon Homme*. Her threats were clear, after which he had practically lived in New Orleans, ingratiating her—and himself—with the Administration and its senior advisors, to make that happen. If a newly elected administration stepped up pursuit of the Dixie Mafia, Nat had gathered enough ammunition for Cotton to use—details of creative fund-raising and assignations he had arranged for the Sunday talk show guests—to ensure the matter would be dropped. A democrat victory would ensure four years of benign inattention for all but the most inept organized crime syndicates. He paused before speaking, then cautiously asked why. The answer only raised more questions: Nat didn't need to know. *Didn't need to know!* Nat thought in near rage, but managed not to scream. No words could be more intimidating to a corrupt, paranoid bureaucrat.

He beat his fat fists on the window sill. *What else can I do?*

Two days later three men and two pilots gathered shortly after midnight. They boarded an unmarked Air Force Gulf Stream III. After the Andrews tower cleared the training flight, the jet raced down the runway. Turning slowly and climbing to forty thousand feet, the pilot confirmed a heading of three-one-zero degrees, speed three hundred knots. The tower request for destination was ignored.

* * * *

The old airplane touched down at Rafael Núñez International Airport and rolled smoothly down runway 01/19. A late afternoon shower had just ended. Steam was rising from the freshly paved parking apron.

Now clad in denim overalls much too big for him, sunglasses and a dingy red ball cap pulled low, Lyle waited for the big propellers to jerk to a stop. He made the short step down from the side door, where Cain—as he had promised hours ago—was ignoring him.

The battered Ford F150 pick-up was parked beside the hangar. He walked quickly—barely able to keep from running—and was relieved to see someone behind the wheel. Not until he opened the passenger door did he know for sure that it was Commander Larry Hart, the only person he knew in Colombia, or dared trust.

They first met a year ago during Lyle's European concert tour. Lyle's dedication produced results far beyond expectations, and Hart took creative license to a new level with after-action reports to fleet headquarters, claiming the results were largely his own. He felt only slightly dishonest when he learned that his promotion a few months later was weighted heavily on those exaggerations and out-and-out lies. He owed Lyle, his guilty conscience reminded, as he sat sweating, but this was pushing the limits well past the danger zone. If only he had ignored the unusual request for a radio-telephone return call. Hearing Lyle's voice, his only consolation was that—as requested—he had dialed in on his scrambled line.

"I don't know what to say, other than none of it's true," Lyle spoke first. "I know thank you isn't enough. I'm sorry to drag you into this, but you're my only hope, the only person I know in Colombia. Until only a couple hours ago I didn't even know I was coming here."

"Stop right there. Not another word. The less I know the better. I never saw you or talked to that pilot." He was angry. "I'm sorry, too. Things have gotten worse since then." The truck lurched forward and passed between two hangars and disappeared into the dark neighborhood. "Let me put it this way: officially, I could just shoot you right now and be a real hero. In South America, you are a dead man walking."

Lyle's elation crashed. His meager hope replaced with fresh panic.

"'Deadly force authorized,' is the latest. Down here, sport, that means 'd-e-a-d.' Frankly, I wasn't sure what I was going to do when I saw this," he spoke as he stretched to open the glove box. He pulled out a single sheet of paper. "Read all about it. You're public enemy number one, subject of a hemispheric manhunt. Look, I do owe you, but not this much."

In the light of passing street lights, he struggled to read the message in his trembling hands. It was a who's-who of drug cartel leadership, references to old investigations and conspiracies. Lyle was a key player. The only thing recognizable was a list of dates. Each transaction, each meeting coincided with a band performance. The words were stunning in their effect; his mouth fell open.

"Look, everybody deserves a day in court, but no way are you going to be that lucky. You're a walking target. Did I mention that? And, I am, too, if anyone finds out I'm helping you. I'm not sure what can be done, or how far I'm willing to go. All I can do right now is stash you and get the hell away from you. We're going to safe house, of sorts; Colombian cops and our narco guys use it. It's yours, at least for a few days, at the most. That's the best I can do for now. At least it buys a little time to think." He looked across at Lyle, "They think you're still in Paraguay, most likely dead at the hands of the bad guys. How's that for the best news of the day?"

Lyle was mute, his eyes mindlessly gazing at the cones of headlights piercing the darkness. The street lights were gone. The truck soon left pavement and began bouncing down a dirt road which got narrower with each turn. Twilight faded to moonless night. Soon, the headlights shown beneath a low canopy of trees like a black tunnel. Hart slowed, scanning the underbrush. After stopping twice, he drove slowly, then suddenly turned right onto a muddy trail hardly wider than the truck. Hart said no more as they rocked through the tall grass around them. In sidelong glances, Lyle nervously studied his face in the dashboard's glow; it was expressionless.

The overhead canopy disappeared from the flat landscape, and he drove on, centered on nothing more than a twisting and narrow path; the only sound was the swish the tall grass scratching the fenders. He couldn't see much. His sense of smell revealed more: salt water.

The truck stopped. Lyle turned to Hart. He replied, "Wait here," forced the door open and beat his way in front of the truck and disappeared. Lyle's heart was racing, his chest heaving.

A minute later Hart reappeared and climbed back inside. "It's clear." Rolling slowly forward, the truck soon emerged in a wide clearing, perhaps five or ten acres, Lyle guessed from the little he could see in the headlights. They soon drove over a large "x" painted on the grass. Not far beyond that the lights reflected off a dull yellow building, a handsome Spanish Colonial structure. They drove towards it, turning to park inside a barn to the left of it.

"It's owned by one of our Colombian counterparts," Hart spoke and pulled the sliding barn door shut. Lyle followed him across an overgrown lawn to the front of the house. "Spooks say they're old family, built maybe fifty, sixty years ago. They've been more or less our sponsors down here since we got interested. Beyond that nobody needs to know."

The painted brick walls and red roof tiles were well kept. The tall windows, at least those he could see from the side and front, were shuttered. It was certainly remote. Considering their approach through low jungle, Lyle supposed that most, if not all visitors, must arrive here by air or sea. The compound included several out buildings, some very big. Another barn stood at the far edge of the clearing. Beside it was a tin-roofed shed that protected a large diesel electric generator from the tropical rains. The other major structure, another long, low wooden building, looked like a kitchen or barracks. Beside it was a tall mast with a limp, orange wind sock attached above two large satellite dishes.

The utilitarian interior belied the traditional façade. It was a modern command post, complete with powerful radio transmitters, satellite up-links, surface and air radars and – judging from banks of monitors atop metal racks – cameras that covered each approach from land or sea. Stairs along one wall led to a balcony under the cathedral ceiling and doors to a half dozen bedrooms. Comfortable looking couches and chairs were arranged on the other. The windows in the great room were all covered with black-out curtains.

Hart disappeared and returned soon after the generator started. A computer printer rattled to life, and dials lit on the electronics gear. The bank of monitors awoke. Lyle stepped out the back door onto another wide, roughly planked covered porch. Perpendicular to it was a long wooden dock on tall pilings. It was well maintained and extended nearly a hundred yards, ending at a tall boathouse. The building was atop a twenty-foot sloping embankment surrounding a circular inlet. A narrow channel on the left connected it to the mouth of a river entering into the ocean no more than a half mile distant.

Hart joined him on the porch and handed him a piece of paper. "This is the latest. I'm not sure what it means."

The investigation was widening. The sight of her name paralyzed him, and he couldn't read farther. He hadn't spoken to her in years, but now she and Roland Hebert were investigation targets, apparently based on information from somebody who knew the retired cop had joined her in Alaska. Speculation was that they are in communication with Rees, assuming he was still alive. Federal agents are planning how to set up surveillance at the remote location, and FBI attorneys are preparing a wiretap warrant which will be presented to a Federal District Judge in Anchorage, probably tomorrow. The wiretap, it noted, may be difficult because Lucas Lodge has an encrypted satellite telephone system. Such equipment is typical of the technological advances of organized crime, especially the wealthy drug cartels, the briefing paper noted. The information was credited to DOS protective services division, co-leaders in the investigation.

His eyes again fixed on Emma's name. *This is crazy. What in hell is happening?* Nothing made sense. He had practically destroyed her through his cowardice and ambition. And, she would have been destroyed if she weren't such a strong woman. He tried to shake torturous guilt. He had to, but he was so ashamed of himself. Now somebody was going after her again, and he was part of it, although he didn't know how. *Who? Why?* He sat heavily on a wood bench, holding the paper with both hands. All he could see was Emma's name and phone number.

The satellite uplink directed the call to a relay ground station at the Royal Air Force Station, Mendenhall, England. From there he routed it to the Navy Communications Station San Miguel, Republic of the Philippines. The final bounce was directly to the satellite receiver at Lucas Lodge. Even if a wiretap was in place, there was no way the NSA could trace it. The bounces from earth to satellites took all of ten seconds. Lyle watched Hart's face as he held the telephone receiver to his ear. "Yes, I have a call for Emma Lucas. Stand by," he said and handed the phone to Lyle. He was on the back porch before Lyle could begin speaking.

It was time to act like a man.

"Emma, don't hang up, please. I have some very, very important news for you."

"Lyle?" She recognized the voice immediately; it sounded like he was in the room with her. Hearing the name, Roland turned from the window, stunned.

"If captain Hebert is there you may want to let him listen, it involves him, too. If he has been there for a while he may not know everything. Please, just listen, you both may be in danger."

"We're both on the line. Go ahead."

"I'm glad Roland is there. He'll know what to do." He slumped with both elbows on the console, propped his forehead on his free hand and squeezed his eyes shut. He could hardly believe his own words as he described the past three months, and knew nobody probably did either. He tried to construct logically but found himself wandering. The images were horrific. Aware that this call may be his last chance, he went on, hoping she wouldn't hang up. Federal agents, he wasn't whose by then, threatened him with indictment as a co-conspirator in smuggling if he didn't sign the lies they'd written about Emma.

There was no reply.

Of course not, he realized with more shame: they sound like some kind of justification. "Emma, I didn't mean any of that as an excuse, there is none. I was a coward, an ambitious, self-centered fool. I betrayed the only real friend I ever had. I hurt you, and you've lived with the consequences of my lies. I know that now, and it's about time. I don't know what's going to happen next, but I swear I want to at least try to make things better for you. Maybe what I just said is all that I'll ever be able to do. You've got to be careful."

"I want you to be OK. You've confirmed what Roland has told me. He's working with the government and knows some of the details, but nothing like you just said. The other stuff is ancient history. It isn't important right now." Her stoic words belied her real feelings.

"I don't know what to do next." He looked through the back window and saw Hart pacing. "I'm safe right now, but probably not for long. I'm going to turn myself in."

"Don't you dare do anything like that!" it was Roland's voice. "Do whatever you can, wherever you are, to stay hidden for as long as you can. If you're still in South America and there's a 'by any means' warrant, you've got no choice. Do you hear me? You may be scared and ashamed or whatever, but if I know anything about you, you've got a cool head. Giving up is the worst option. They'll shoot you on sight. You've got to buy time for me to help."

Nineteen

"If this wasn't the only way back I'd never let you do this. You need to get back to the lodge and stay there. You and Joe could hold off an army if you have to." He immediately regretted his choice of words; he wanted her to be vigilant, not paranoid, but he knew he was right about Joe's talents. Somebody was playing for keeps. Hebert had a good idea who: the same people who had caused so much mischief years ago in New Orleans. He suspected that the same people were behind Lyle's problems, and killing their problems, or even potential problems, was a knee-jerk reaction. Kill first, never talk, was the Dixie Mafia's mantra. The bastard had been a stupid fool, he fumed, but he couldn't have known it would turn out involving Emma. "It's absolutely the best place you can be."

Roland had wanted to leave immediately after the call, but she convinced him to rest at least for a few hours. Nobody could really sleep, and a couple of hours later, she had fueled the Cessna 182. She checked Roland's seat harness as Joe pushed the airplane clear of the dock. A moment later she shoved the throttle all the way forward and the two-hundred-thirty horse power Continental O-470-U engine responded with a roar heard for miles across the black, glassy lake. The small airplane began to shake, struggling to move. Slow momentum began raising the torpedo-shaped floats, but only a couple of inches out of the water. Rooster tails kicked up behind them, and the little airplane raced across the surface like a speed boat. Free of water resistance, she pulled steadily back on the wheel.

At 4 a.m. on an Alaskan mid-summer's morning there was plenty of light, but not enough to keep water and sky from blending in a continuous and disorienting grey scrim. The twinkling stars were the only visual reference through the windshield. Emma turned her attention to her instruments; the artificial horizon and altimeter confirmed a steady climb, wings level with the horizon.

The radar screen was blank as she leveled out at two thousand feet and continued straight south. The flight would be only slightly longer this way, but safer over water with no mountains to worry about. Once above Cook Inlet she would turn north by northeast and follow its course to Anchorage. By the time she reached Lake Hood the sun would be peeking over the Chugach Mountains that towered east of the city.

The flight was smooth and uneventful, and most of it passed in silence. Both were absorbed in their thoughts. She had never been complacent about anything, especially flying, but even her attention was interrupted by the weight of Lyle's words. Roland didn't speak much either, but she knew it wasn't unusual for him. He told her at least two more times that he wanted her back at the lodge as soon as possible. The repeated admonition from him wasn't irritating, but endearing in its inference of concern for her safety. She smiled at him and patted his cheek, mouthing "OK" each time.

After tying up at Lake Spenard the trip to the Anchorage International passenger terminal took less than five minutes. Roland was out of the pick-up almost before she had stopped. "I'll call you when I get home. Remember …"

"I know," she interrupted. Nothing's going to happen as long as Joe's around. We'll be OK. You be careful. I know you have work to do. After this is all over, promise you'll come back for a real vacation." He had disappeared through the sliding glass doors before she could get out and hug him.

She didn't go straight back. A quick trip to stock up, even overstock, with groceries was a wise use of her time, she rationalized; she didn't know how long she and Joe would have to remain at Lucas Lodge. Being prepared was always a good idea, especially in Alaska where weather could hold them hostage for days, possibly weeks. Roland's discoveries might stretch the time farther. Besides, something about the Carr-Gottstein store always fascinated her; she was not a superficial woman, but shopping there was therapeutic. To her it epitomized the Alaskan entrepreneurial spirit: meeting a need, taking a risk and making some money in a place where nothing is easy and few are willing to try. She found herself lingering among the rows of fresh produce, enjoying the colors and fragrance; owing to the difficulty of logistics, fresh was always rare and tantalizing this close to the Arctic Circle.

Emma glanced at the clock above the meat counter and was stunned; she had turned a quick stop into nearly two hours.

She backed the truck beside the little dock and transferred the groceries into the airplane's cargo box behind the two passenger seats. Check list completed, she lifted off into the cloudless sky. This time she didn't climb quickly, enjoying a low pass over the little shacks and docks, putting on a little air show for whoever might be looking.

She gently rolled off to her right to avoid air space restricted to commercial traffic at the international airport south and west of the lake. "Sleeping Lady," the locals' name for nine-thousand-foot Mt. Susitna, was in full splendor a hundred miles off the left wing. A year-around snow cover atop its north-south range covered the reclining woman with a white blanket.

The blue Cessna blended into the sky, climbing at a thousand feet a minute, passing through eight hundred feet, rising like a fast express elevator. It's good to be going home again. She rolls gently to her left, to course two-six-five.

Something startles her. She's not sure what. The engine is fine; oil pressure and engine temperature are normal. A slight thermal, she thinks, a convergence, common where land and water meet.

It happens again; it's definitely the engine, the stark reality smacks her. The oil pressure gage wiggles as the sputters come in rapid fire. The engine stops, the nose dips down.

The propeller is stationery, the wind whistling past it. She reacts instantly.

Altitude: one thousand, descending. She can glide for several minutes. If she keeps a cool head, there's no need to panic.

Emma pushes the wheel slightly forward to gain air speed and keep wind beneath the wings as she completes a gentle turn back to the northeast. Lake Spenard is only five miles ahead, she estimates.

She is over Cook Inlet. Option One: set down immediately. It would be difficult and dangerous; the northeasterly wind had risen with the sun; what helped this morning now drove the water to a choppy froth. She may as well try landing on dry land with floats, probably with the same catastrophic result.

Reflexively, she radios an emergency to Anchorage control. Methodically focusing between the altimeter and the near distance, she identifies heading, speed and altitude, surprised to hear the calmness in her voice.

The response is immediate and reassuring: "Emergency, emergency, emergency; all pilots avert or hold positions." The voice from the tower has eliminated Option One, confirming Option Two: "Cessna cleared for emergency approach Lake Hood-Spenard aerodrome."

A threshold thermal pushes her slightly higher as she passes again over land. Ten seconds later the wide commercial runway is only four hundred feet beneath her floats.

The lake shorelines are closer, the longest mile she's ever seen.

Calm and in control, she leans forward scanning ahead, figuring the life-and-death trigonometry of a glide path.

Her altitude is dropping steadily, much too quickly for comfort. *What happened to the tailwind?* Everything is now happening in slow motion. With all her being she wants somehow to lift the airplane. She makes a last effort to start the engine. The radio is squawking with traffic; none of it will help her. Emma Lucas is totally on her own.

Three hundred feet. Her life depends on executing a long glide.

The huge FedEx cargo warehouse is directly below.

The tailwind kicks in again, a blessing beyond compare. It might be just enough, maybe not. Carefully, she noses up slightly to grab even a little more altitude, careful not to catch too much and stall.

Two hundred feet. *Have I overdone it?* Butterflies dance in her guts; she's falling too fast toward acres of parked airplanes; even if she clears them, there's no guarantee she'll miss the stand of trees between them and the lake shore.

She's done her best. With no choice, she pulls the wheel back, fully knowing it may be the last thing she ever does: the floats will either hit the trees or they won't. Even if they do, her life depends on whether the floats toe in or hit flat. She takes a, deep breath. She'll know soon enough.

Both floats slam into the water, jerking her forward violently. The shopping trip has saved her life; the weight near the tail is just enough to keep the floats above the water, preventing a head-over-tail flip she would not survive. *Let's hear for it for the sale on forty-eight ounce cans of fruit juice.*

Only a few onlookers had noticed the little boat towing the Cessna down the lake and to its dock. By late afternoon it was all over but the paperwork.

FAA investigators, interviews completed, departed, replaced by a handful of neighbors and pilots offering congratulations and opinions. There's no doubt in their minds, or Emma's, about what has happened. Why it happened is another matter, and she didn't tell everything to the FAA or her friends.

The official FAA report noted that there had been water in the fuel tank, adding that the tank was topped off shortly before take-off from the fifty-five gallon drum on her porch. Owing to wide fluctuations of temperature and dew point and ventilation, it was duly noted, condensation accumulated, with predictable results. It would be another cautionary tale for all. Emma had been relieved that she didn't have to lie about how long the fuel had been out there. Nobody asked. She had to bite her lip and accept the implied blame, but after what she'd been through it was a little easier to go against her impulse to set the record straight. She knows that fuel was delivered only last week. She had tested it, and there was no water in it. She knew there was another, human, reason for her near fatal accident: someone was trying to kill her. Her long shopping trip had helped them, but, whoever it was hadn't counted on her skill and survival instinct.

With the tank drained and refilled, she ran the engine for fifteen minutes and took-off again. It was nearly six p.m. now. On a late summer afternoon, the sun was still high in the southern sky. Only one thought occupied her all the way home: *where are they, and what's next?*

* * * *

Joe stood on the dock, arms at his side, like a statue, until she came close enough for him to grab the mooring line. Without a word, she stepped across to the dock and buried her face in his shoulder. Both knew that they were the prey.

"Somebody put that water in my tank. Whoever it was must have looked like they belonged. Nobody saw anybody or anything out of place," she said as they mounted the stairs. "Have you heard from Roland?"

Joe didn't respond immediately, trying to choose his words wisely. There was no need to talk at all about the conversation, less than an hour ago, but he could not lie to her. "He called as soon as he got home. I had to tell him. It shook him up. Enough said, OK?"

Emma felt like a fool and nodded.

"Emma, these people are deadly serious; they won't give up. Watering the tank took some sophistication—logistics, appropriate clothing, timing, look-outs—and the smarts to assess the immediate situation and make real-time tactical decisions. Whoever it is, they're professionals."

Joe thought like a warrior because he was one. From the day he first saw what would become Lucas Lodge he saw its advantages. A hundred feet above the lake, burrowed into solid rock beneath a rock outcropping, the lodge could also be a fortress. Like a seventeenth century frontier outpost, it even had a small spring inside the lodge, safe from tampering. The only cover any invader could use was the spruce thicket that shaded the dock. There was nothing but flat ground and grass in the fifty feet between them and the stairs.

He'd been busy while Emma was gone. By the time he heard the Cessna approaching, he was finishing installation of six low-light surveillance cameras: two aimed down from the deck to the dock; two reversing the view. The others covered the views left and right from the balcony and slightly up the mountainside. Even though an assault from above would be practically impossible, he'd put a motion sensor on the overhang above the roof. With unlimited water from the spring, Emma's continuously stocked pantry and plenty of ammunition, they could hold out far longer than it would take to get help from Anchorage.

Rummaging a box of electronics left by the satellite phone installers he had also made a fortuitous discovery in her absence. He handed her cup of hot tea as she collapsed into the sofa, then held up what looked like a book.

"I think you're gonna find this very interesting."

Joe handed it to her. Her puzzled look gave way to a warm smile as she read the hand-lettered label: "Graduation Party, June 1983." It was Lucy's handwriting. She must have brought it last year, when she visited the lodge before it closed for the season. Maybe Lucy had viewed it while Emma was gone and had forgotten about it.

Emma turned the box in her hand, poignantly aware that she and Roland had been talking about the party only yesterday. Something of that time did remain. What a treasure.

"Shall we?" Joe asked, loading the tape in the VCR. He decided to leave her alone; as the first scene flickered on the screen, he remembered that he had more work outside.

The color and resolution were brilliant, shot by Lyle's professional quality camera. Music, dear faces and voices instantly cast a spell. She slid off the sofa and knelt in front of the twenty-one inch monitor. Could this have been only a few years ago? *Was I really there? We were all so happy.*

Everyone was there. Lucy was having the time of her life, clowning with the little band, singing and vamping with every guy in the room. Emma watched, hugging herself with joy.

About midway through the half-hour tape he appeared. The camera jerked then steadied; Lyle must have handed it to someone. He was sitting on that tattered old loveseat on the screened porch. Her vision blurred again. Her face was hot as she wiped her eyes. He looked wonderful, wearing an open collar dress shirt, his feet rakishly propped up on that old ottoman, like he always did. She was sitting beside him slightly elevated on the cushion she used to cover a huge hole in the upholstery. It was about the last time she'd worn a dress, she smiled. It was dark green, a one-piece cotton that Lucy had picked out; Emma never would have bought such a thing. The scoop neck revealed much more cleavage than she ever would have. Her hair was down, tightly curled and draped over her left shoulder. She had resisted make-up, but Lucy must have insisted. As the tape rolled, Emma realized that her eyes hardly left Lyle, and her look was undeniable. *Everyone must have noticed. Had it been so obvious?*

Lucy appeared and they put their heads together singing, *"I Got You, Babe."* Did he know how much those women loved him? She wiped more tears. Lyle kissed Lucy, congratulating her, asking her to do his taxes. Even his words sounded like a song. They always had.

She heard herself praying: *please let him be safe.* There was so much she wanted to say, so much she hoped to hear.

The images and sound faded to black, another professional touch, she realized. She started to stand, but stopped when the screen flashed. *Was there more?* The images were dark, then over exposed, fuzzy and grainy and –finally—sharp, focused and steady. She heard a man's voice, then a woman shouting: it was her.

The screen showed shimmering lights. It took a moment before she realized that the source was a ship, back lit somehow to show its outline. Shaking and blurring stopped abruptly, replaced by a clear, steady image of the ship and men heaving lines. The screen is dark, then her voice booms, "There, in the light, aft!" The screen blurs again with smears of white light which becomes a neatly outlined ellipse in the middle of a black background. There was something moving in the middle. Emma rocks back with stunned recognition. Her mouth drops open and she gasps and speaks to nobody, *"It's the jumper!"* This must be the tape Lyle was making to test the night vision lens, before he ran out of tape and reloaded. She was looking at *SS Maria* at *Monte Verde* dock.

The picture blinks again to black, then to a perfectly focused, clear image: men standing on the ship's after deck. One throws a life ring. One is holding a rifle. The picture zooms in and out, then steadies on two other men standing above on the bridge wing. They're also shouting and pointing down to their left. As their image fills the screen she sees that one is tall, bearded, dressed in a white officer's uniform; it's the captain. The other is wearing a white civilian suit and tie. He's much shorter and fat. Their features become sharp and crisp as the camera closer. The face, she knew it. The smirk was unforgettable. Instantly, Emma's eidetic memory flashed the identity: *the man in the parking lot. He was standing beside the SUV at the hospital!* The tape ends with a loud click, as though the little man is trying to hide from her. *It's him!*

Joe knows exactly what to do.

He retrieves the Polaroid he uses to make instant souvenirs of fishing trophies and snaps a close-up of the man's face frozen on the screen. In New Orleans Roland pulls it off the fax machine and goes to work. In less than an hour he calls back with the news: the face belongs to Nathaniel Pierce, third highest-ranking officer with the United States Department of State. Things are beginning to make sense.

* * * *

Early the following morning Roland enters the Federal Court House and is escorted to the U.S. Attorneys Office. Aaron Frank, U.S. Attorney for the Eastern District of Louisiana is an old friend, and he is not surprised to see his guest. The two had begun talking about Roland's unofficial inquiries shortly after Lyle's name first appeared in the over-classified diplomatic messages. Their last meeting was the day before Roland left for Alaska; the topic had been the latest development: the naming of Emma Lucas and Roland Hebert as targets of investigation. Their attention was centered on the unmanned U.S. State Department source who had made the accusation. Both suspected malfeasance: a secret cable was precisely the place to identify the source, if for no other reason than to avoid confusion among the many players now involved in the deadly manhunt; but, it didn't.

They had already made sensitive inquiries about the unidentified informant, for which there had been no reply, not even an excuse, for the obvious stonewalling. Frank knew there wasn't much he could do beyond that; he most certainly had no influence with the State Department. He heartily agreed with Roland that an answer might shed new light on old questions about missing NOPD records and—their gut instincts told them—on the nefarious recent history of some otherwise esteemed citizens.

The grainy photo was a potential game changer; there was now a direct and identifiable connection between the State Department and Rees. Frank was far from a political appointee, he had worked his way up from beat cop and part-time law student to chief federal prosecutor in a city where underworld connections with the power elite were commonplace. They dashed off yet another request. This one was more direct: they officially requested status to talk with Rees upon his apprehension. It wasn't much, and would probably be ignored, but it might keep him alive, if he could survive long enough to make it into U.S. hands somewhere.

Their conference call to U.S. Attorney, District of Alaska, put the manhunt and dubious link to Emma into perspective; the all-out campaign to locate and isolate Emma was doubtful at best, conspiratorial at worst. Her near crash had been no accident. It confirmed that other, clandestine players were in Alaska, and they were not interested in serving a subpoena or taking a deposition.

Roland ran across Lafayette Square and stopped at the first pay phone he could find. The call woke Emma. It lasted less than a minute: to some very powerful people, her tape was worth more than her life.

* * * *

The Gulf Stream landed at New Orleans international and stopped beside an armored Chevrolet Suburban 1500 LTZ. Nat Pierce disembarked and stepped a few feet through the midday blast furnace and into the black SUV. Escorted by four motorcycle police, it took him to the Cotton Exchange on Canal Street where he had set up his convention liaison office.

He forced a smile as he was waved through the security checkpoint and continued briskly down the cool, high-ceilinged marble corridor. Sure nobody was watching, he turned the corner and out the back door. He walked across North Peters Street to the Westin Hotel parking lot. There he slid behind the wheel of Gene Menard's silver Mercedes 560SL and wheeled into the light traffic headed downriver on St. Peters Street, transiting the Quarter and arriving a few minutes later at the Piety Street Wharf. He drove up the ramp, parked in the vast warehouse and walked through the wide cargo doors to the dock. Menard was waiting for him on the after deck, smiling like he hadn't a care in the world. He had lost weight. The workouts had him looking like a fireplug draped in a red polo and canvas trousers. He threw off the dock line and hurried back inside to join Nat at the wheel as he throttled into the river, pointing the bow for *Bon Homme* Plantation.

"It doesn't get much better than this, Nat. Take a good look," Menard was exuberant, gesturing as Canal Street passing to starboard. "It may not look this peaceful again for a long time." He laughed and slapped Nat on the back, knocking him forward into the wheel. The sweaty little man hadn't a clue what he meant. He had much more to worry about: his own hide.

Nat, annoyed and confused by the urgent summons from DC, began to relax. Somehow he even assumed Menard's inexplicable happiness. "Well, I sure hope so. I've been doing my best." He had done well by his partners and especially Secretary Cotton. He had scored prime blackmail ammunition for her. After the call from Anderson, now seeing Menard so carefree, he hoped that his success was behind Menard's near giddiness. Still, he dared to say, "But, Gene, we've still got a couple of details to clean up, don't we?"

"This is the land of dreams, the Big Easy. Don't worry about a thing. You're my favorite silly old queer, and—in this city—that's saying a lot," Menard laughed, again slapping his back so hard it hurt. "Don't worry. Those two and the old cop aren't going to say or do a thing. Just make sure our party is the best ever. We'll handle this like we should have a long time ago."

* * * *

Joe had tinkered with single side band amateur radio since he was a teenager. It took power, so he had to fire off the generator, but the ability to scramble transmissions was worth it, especially today. He always listened on a headset when he called friends in Anchorage waiting for their daily, official rendezvous and informal bull session. This morning it gave him time to compose his words carefully before he spoke with Emma.

Three men had shown up at the busy float plane base and chartered the biggest plane available, a DeHavilland DHC-2 Beaver. They didn't need a pilot: an up-to-date pilot license and float certificate, including proof of employment and verification contacts at the Great Circle Air Cargo. That was impressive: the old timers knew their reputation as worldwide operators with bottomless pockets. The upfront cash made the lease decision much easier. Regardless, Joe's friend was curious as he watched them load: none of the equipment, all neatly stowed inside watertight cases, looked like fishing gear, at least none he had ever seen.

What Joe heard next from another radio operator, this one in the Anchorage tower, sent chilled water through his veins. The pilot, he said, had filed a flight plan to Bethel, but after they took off he tracked them on radar. They flew nearly straight south and west down Cook Inlet; Bethel was on the other side of the vast frontier state, to the northwest. Unless they were out for a very long sightseeing trip that would take them hundreds of miles out of their way and stretch their fuel to its limits, somebody wasn't telling the real story.

The Anchorage radio operator came on again, chuckling this time. "Yep, they told me they're after rainbows. They sure not going to find them in the Bering Sea! Hell of a lot less expensive to buy fresh at Forty-Niner Sausage and Seafood!"

* * * *

Heavy weather had advanced rapidly up the Aleutian chain, shrouding the Alaska Peninsula, all the way to Anchorage. Low clouds were driven by near gale force winds. When they heard the sound of an engine, at first they assumed a boat was approaching. Nobody would try fly in this. Emma nailed it first: not a boat but an airplane. They looked at each other in disbelief, the sound confirming their worst fears. Joe's thoughts raced. They stood frozen, listening. The engine stopped somewhere to the west, still quite a distance away.

Joe hailed on all the pilot-to-pilot frequencies and emergency Channel 16. Getting no reply, his suspicions were confirmed. Whoever just landed wasn't talkative. As Emma closed the shutters, he returned to the deck and strained for any clue. It came soon: voices of men who don't seem to know that on the water, upwind, their voices carried a very long way.

Back inside, Emma studied the surveillance monitor, split into six images. A dark blur appeared on the west-facing camera. It didn't take much longer before Joe heard the faint putter of an outboard. A small dinghy, an inflatable launch, Joe recognized, was approaching. They made out three men aboard.

From the deck they watched as the trio landed. They were dressed from head to foot in black, and each carried a short rifle slung around their necks, not much more than a long-barreled pistol. Joe knew they were Uzis. In their hands they carried 7.62 mm AK47s and a gas can. There weren't dropping by to clean fish.

Tiptoeing across the deck, he held a finger to his lips and handed her a Winchester 12-gauge pump shotgun. The eight-round magazine was loaded with heavy buck shot. He kept the Winchester .270 for himself and stuffed two boxes of cartridges in his deep pockets.

Moving slowly and quietly, Emma followed him up the 2x4 ladder nailed beside the front door and climbed through a hatch to the roof. Stopping to ease the hatch shut, her hand slipped, slamming it shut with a thunderous clap. She froze in terror and looked at Joe. He was already in the cramped space at the rear where the rock and roof met. Before he could turn to see what happened, a volley of armor-piercing AK rounds exploded through the deck, sending chunks of wood flying. The heavy chunks of lead smacked into the rocky outcrop above them. Stunned but still mobile, she scrambled to his side, vaguely aware that he was pulling a blue tarp off of something: an M1919A4 Browning 30-caliber machine gun.

"Stand back," he whispered before creeping toward the edge of the roof. He fired two short burst toward the dock. He'd barely leaned back before more volleys tore away more pieces of the deck and roof.

"We can hold off for a long time, but I'm not betting on how much ammo they brought." He laid the machine gun down at her feet, "Even with this, we're outgunned, boss. That's the bad news; good news: I planned ahead."

"Where did that come from?" she spoke in astonishment, as though the illegal machine gun was the biggest of their concerns.

"Don't worry about it. Same place I got a kilo of C4 that's gonna come in handy right about now." He pushed her as far as he could under the rock, crouched in front her and fished a hand-held radio from a leg pocket.

"Sorry, it's the only way. Time for some fireworks. Cover your ears." He flipped on the power switch and dialed in a frequency. He waited until he heard footsteps on the stairs, then hit the key button. With one enormous yellow fireball rupturing from beneath, the shaped charges at each stairway landing exploded simultaneously. The lodge shook beneath their feet. Emma thought the whole structure was going to slide down the mountainside. It didn't. Instead, timber and rock landed in the lake and on at least one now-motionless intruder.

The black smoke mingled with the fog. Like thunder the explosion rolled across the lake. The smoke blew away quickly but not before they used its cover to scramble down the ladder and back inside. Two cameras, the ones aimed at the dock, still functioned. They showed only a few stairs still dangling below the deck, twisting in the wind. Joe exposed himself over the railing, just enough to see two figures stumbling with a third toward the boat. Moments later the small motor started.

"Let's give them a nice send off, shall we?"

The trees blocked Joe's view, but—like any special forces veteran— he continued to sight down the barrel where he thought the target most likely would appear. It would save less than a second, but could be the difference between life and death.

He didn't have to wait long to confirm the theory.

The launch drifted into view as it crabbed into the wind and water pushing against it from the west. They weren't giving up. The man controlling the engine had managed to point to windward and steady their position, another in the bow was unarmed and apparently still dazed from the explosion. Joe's attention down the barrel was riveted on the third. He couldn't believe what he was seeing: he was steading himself and beginning to shoulder a Russian RPG7 anti-tank grenade launcher. From a flatter angle farther from shore, even on a bobbing and weaving dingy, they could fire RPG rounds until there was nothing left of the lodge, or them. Joe was now at a disadvantage. He had to land a single round precisely on an unsteady, moving target. Close only counts in horseshoes and hand grenades, he thought grimly, but the grenade launcher needs only to get close for lethal effect. Joe held steady and waited for the shooter to re-enter his sight image. He aimed calmly and squeezed the trigger slowly. It was a direct hit. The round hit in the center of his chest. With a violent twist, the shooter went over the side. The launch shot forward into the fog.

"They're gone," Joe spoke finally, only now thinking about the consequences of a failed shot. They were safe, at least for a while, but they didn't know what the well-armed and apparently extremely motivated killers would try next. With most of the surveillance cameras gone, Emma and Joe stood guard on the deck and waited. What was next? The answer came with the distinct sound of the Beaver's engine coughing to life.

Emma listened with her eyes, "Somebody is still able to fly."

With the stairs gone, Joe began rigging a boatswain's chair in the block and tackle suspended from the peaked overhang above the deck. Emma heard it first. "Listen!" The engine noise was getting louder.

"They're either going to risk a firing pass at us or they're Kamikazes!" Joe yelled over his shoulder as he leapt up the ladder and returned with the machine gun and another ammo belt draped around his shoulders. He lowered the tripod, and Emma wedged it into the deck railing. "Never die with a full clip," he spoke calmly and fed the belt into the chamber. He began firing log bursts aimed at nothing but a steadily increasing roar. When the airplane seemed to be overhead, Emma did the same with the shotgun. Even if Emma's gun was useless, every sixth round Joe fired was a tracer which glowed brilliant yellow as they burned through the low clouds. The pilot could see that and—depending on how close they may or may not have come to the airplane—it apparently had the desired effect. They reloaded for another pass, but none came. The airplane was flying east, toward Anchorage.

Emma leaned on the railing, suddenly tired, breathless as though she'd just run a mile. She breathed deeply and looked at the pile of rubble below. "Do you remember what kind of home-owners we bought?" She started laughing at her black humor.

"Pretty big deductible, I think." Joe fed the levity, also more than happy to lose some stress. "How do you suppose they'll categorize the damage on the claim form!"

"And, oh, by the way, you know this is coming out of your inflated salary."

"Sorry about the stairs. But, look on the bright side, boss: maybe we could charge more now when we replace the stairs with the scenic chair lift!" he chuckled and hugged her. She needed the relief, but felt him tense. She twisted to follow his squint over her shoulder. A strange orange glow flared far off to the east. It brightened. Ten seconds later a muffled roar, more like a moan, reached them, then another. The orange ball brightened. The halo of clouds and fog surrounding it grew rapidly. A long, sustained roar washed over the lake. A tattoo of staccato aftershocks reached them seconds later.

"They've hit the mountain. Looks like a lot of fuel."

"And, no telling what else."

* * * *

There was no moon. Water, jungle and sky were black. Commander Hart had left after first light. As instructed, Lyle stayed inside out of sight and waited two hours after sundown before he began moving. He had used the time to study the maps and charts and to sleep. Aided by the weak beam from a penlight, he walked down the long dock to the boat house. Inside he found the stairs and carefully eased his way down. The boathouse was even darker. In the gloom, Lyle's heart suddenly sank: he didn't see the promised boat or anything else. His hand trembled as he felt his way around the narrow platform built into three sides of the wooden structure. He sighed in relief when he saws it tied beside the wide door to the lagoon. The eight-foot aluminum boat was painted a non-reflective matte green. He stepped aboard and found the oars, slid them into the gunwale locks and pushed off through the door. Once clear of the boathouse, he rowed toward the narrow cut that connected to the river. With no visual orientation and having never tried to row in a straight line, he made three increasingly frenzied approaches before finding it. He hadn't traveled more than fifty yards and he was exhausted.

He pulled on the oars, contorting to look over his shoulder until he made out the outline of tall trees across the estuary, nothing more than a black silhouette outline against a slightly less dark sky. Only now daring to turn on the tiny flashlight, he found the starter rope. Thankfully, it responded with the first pull. He twisted the throttle and steered toward the sound of surf breaking somewhere ahead. The humid night cooled some. Surf-driven wind felt good on his sweat-soaked body. When he felt the waves pitching the boat heel and toe, he increased speed and pushed on farther. Soon he had left the shoreline surf behind and began rocking atop the longer arch of ocean waves. His eyes had adjusted; as he had been told, he made out lights from the tiny fishing village on the bay's north shore. He steered toward them.

The distance was farther than it looked on the chart. The transit was taking longer than he estimated. He still saw nothing on the water around him, but that only confirmed that he was blind. Anyone watching with night vision glasses would know exactly what he was doing; even with no light, his sweating body heat would give a clear signature. Nearer the village he made out the red and white Esso gasoline sign glowing brighter than the rest. Confusion turned to panic: he wasn't getting any closer; the sign kept moving off to the left. A strong ebb tide was pulling him out to sea. He twisted the throttle all the way open. The pitiful little outboard strained; a full minute passed before he knew it would be enough, just enough. He soon was close enough to identify the neon beer signs hung in the front window of the café. His destination was between the two prominent lights. About hundred yards out he reluctantly throttled back, then cut the engine, hoping the surf and the oars were enough to push him silently ashore. The bow bumped on the narrow pebble beach. Exhausted, he rolled over the gunwale and pulled the boat into the undergrowth.

He caught his breath in the low brush. He found the path and crept toward the shanty. The aroma of coffee grew stronger.

He felt exposed but kept moving. He dropped behind an overturned boat only a few feet from the front door. A raggedly dressed old man was seated on the bench out front, smoking, just like he'd been told. He tossed a pebble on the dock. The old man looked into the darkness. He flipped the cigar butt into the water, stood and hobbled around the corner. He climbed into a flatbed truck and started the engine. This was the moment of truth. Lyle's heart raced as he abandoned the cover and walked quickly to the rear. He rolled onto the wide bed and hid beneath a pile of fish nets. The stench of rotting fish was nauseating.

The ride was brief. The truck slowed to a stop and Lyle heard the driver speak to someone. The gears ground noisily and bounced on. He lifted the netting enough to see a tiny guard shack pass by and a cyclone fence gate closing behind. Seconds later the truck stopped again.

"Señor," the voice whispered. Lyle uncovered and dropped to the grass. The old man said no more, but pointed toward into the darkness. It took Lyle only a few steps across the closely mown grass to realize he was approaching an airplane parked a hundred yards away. He walked quickly, his eyes welded on it. Each step brought recognition, then astonishment: it looked like the same plane in which he'd escaped Asuncion. *It can't be.* He was in no position to ask questions.

The little side door was ajar, and he stepped inside. The overhead red light was on. A look around confirmed that this was the same airplane. The red and white ice chests with the little pigs and the words "Go Hogs" were still piled beneath the cargo nets.

"Welcome aboard, buddy. Save me a trip. Close the door, then climb up and take a seat."

Lyle jerked to look up at the flight deck and did as ordered. Chris Cain was busy with the instrument check, but Lyle began, "I, I don't understand…"

"Don't start thinking now, sports fan. I've got work to do. Buckle up and shut up. Just chill."

One huge engine, then the other, coughed noisily to life, followed by the siren whine of the two much smaller jets outboard of them. Cain handed him a headset which Lyle donned with gratitude; the noise was painful in addition to deafening.

The old airplane pitched violently from side to side as it rolled across the grassy strip and splashed through deep puddles. Lyle could see nothing but total darkness through the windshield. Cain seemed to be taxiing by braille. A few seconds later he swung the tail around and the engines revved. He flipped on the landing lights. They showed nothing. The old man made the sign of the cross with his right hand, pulled his head violently left and right, back and forward, and squinted down his nose. The engines roared louder as he pushed the bright red throttle arms all the way forward and released the brake. This time the rapidly increasing jostles over grass and dirt were more than bone rattling, they were horrifying. Lyle gripped the frame on both sides of his seat and clinched his teeth to keep them from chattering. Only then could he see something ahead: a stand of trees, dead ahead. The shaking stopped the instant he squeezed his eyes shut. He left his stomach on the ground. It caught up with him in a minute or two when the C123 leveled out. The few lights he had seen passing below before take-off were all gone. Nothing but darkness replaced them. It took him a few minutes to realize that they were over water, lots of it.

Cain pulled back on the red throttle handles and moved the big orange wheel at his right knee back and forth. The flight smoothed out, and he took his hands off the wheel. He opened a metal door in the compartment at his left elbow and produced a thermos and two tall

Styrofoam cups. "Pour us a couple. The coffee's fantastic."

It tasted like life itself.

"Welcome again, Lyle. Nice to see you're still kicking. I suppose even one of the Navy's best examples of a clueless weenie is beginning to piece things together enough to know that all this isn't a big coincidence," he words sounded jovial, but there was real sarcasm, or something else he couldn't categorize. He was more serious than on the long flight from Paraguay, almost a different personality. Something told Lyle that he didn't have to reply. He paused to sip the coffee before continuing. "I don't know why, but some people who can make things happen have decided to do just that for you. Listen carefully, I don't want to say this again and—even more than that—I sure as hell don't want to answer a bunch of questions. I don't know, and—even if I did—spreading information around is not what I do. You with me?"

Lyle nodded. His crotch was wet.

"Couple of things: first, you're one lucky dude. Second, your friend, Commander Hart, is one super good guy to stick out his neck for you. He's lucky, too. He managed to push all the right buttons: me and a lot of people you'll never meet are the result. Here's all you need to know: even though every cop in the Western Hemisphere has got a license to bag your ass, my job is to keep you alive. Until the elephants stomp this all out, I'm gonna be your daddy." His demeanor changed, the other Chris Cain spoke, "Look. You got no choice. Try to take it on good faith and thank whoever you pray to. Don't try to figure it out, because never in a million years could you get it right. You're on this airplane, and as long as you're with us you're going to be OK, better than OK," he finished with a toothy grin.

Us?

"Thanks. I'll do my best to keep questions to myself. I guess that being here right now means you're telling the truth. But, may I ask where we're going?"

"Fair enough: Managua, Nicaragua. How's that? Got some freight business there. Glad you brought it up. One of your new best friends wants to talk to you." He looked at his wrist watch. The avuncular old Uncle Chris was back. "As a matter of fact, Mickey says it's time to ring them up. Gimme a minute."

Cain turned the radio and Lyle could see, but not hear, that he was talking into the headset microphone. He had finished the coffee before he noticed Cain again moving his lips, then flip a switch. Sound cracked in his headset. Cain said, "Station chief, Managua is on the line."

The voice identified itself as Tony Fox and wasted little time on conversational niceties. He had read the summary Lyle and Jon had written in Asuncion. The narrative, the voice continued, meshes, at least tangentially, with rumors of gold payoffs to crime figures, the Dixie Mafia, it was assumed, primarily in New Orleans. These payoffs, he says, include professional criminals well known to them, including at least one high-ranking U.S. State Department official in their employ. "This, we believe, is the same individual you encountered seven years ago during your encounter at New Orleans. That connection—you and the Lucas woman—is known to our targets. Let's just say they're a little nervous about it. We're certain that your third crewmember was murdered. Your false deposition probably kept you two alive, that and the fact that both of you kept your mouths shut ever since. We believe there must have been some disagreement about you two. That's probably the main reason they didn't kill you then. Bad PR. If all three of you turned up dead, not even they could have shut down the certainty of a full-blown investigation. For what it's worth, your current association with them is pure coincidence, right man, right time. They're regretting the hell out of that now."

For the first time in a very long time, he saw a bigger picture and him in it. Fox didn't pause for questions, and Lyle was too dumbstruck to ask. Alarms went off at CIA when the informant at State drew Lucas in to the manhunt. Lyle felt small and insignificant to hear that the attempts on his life and the other murders in Paraguay were only footnotes until then. The appearance of Pierce on the video tape started the chain reaction.

The call ended as abruptly as it began. "Look, you got to feel like the biggest jerk since Judas. You ought to. I shouldn't tell you this, but maybe you'll feel better knowing that after we rest and refuel in Managua and once again in northern Mexico, we'll land near New Orleans. There's all kind of support there. We'll hide you as long as needed. I don't know details, so don't ask. But, Lucas may be there by then, also under Federal protection. Might give you time to make amends, maybe even rejoin the human race."

The words and all they implied, and more, weighed heavily.

After the stop in Nicaragua, the Provider flew at twenty thousand feet through the vast and empty sky. Somewhere over the Gulf of Mexico, thunder heads formed majestically far off to the right. The green mass of Central America stayed to port and soon faded away, replaced by nothing but the blue water. He was content just to sit, to sort out his life. Emma was going to be safe. He was going to see her again. Amends, Cain had said. He remembered that Chief Jones had used the word to talk about life. Now Lyle understood how much courage it took to overcome fear and live honestly, what it took to drop the mask, to step off the stage and let people see him close up.

There was time now, and Lyle Rees was ready.

Twenty

Isolated thunderstorms swept in from the southwest. Beginning about midnight, they had washed the drunks off the Big Easy's streets with torrents of fresh water. Thunder rumbled farther to the east, promising a slow, soft dawn. Like every other August day on the Gulf Coast, the approaching day would be miserably hot and humid. The cool front lingering overhead had only dropped the pre-dawn temperature to an almost tolerable seventy-five degrees Fahrenheit. Delegates to the Republican National Convention would welcome the relief. Soon thousands would gather to watch the Presidential motorcade make its way down Canal Street to the Super Dome.

The tough old pilot has pushed himself and the C-123 all night after refueling at an uncharted airstrip in northern Mexico. He had been even more cautious than usual, aware that as part of heightened security the FAA had increased radar surveillance surrounding the convention. The left wingtip had nearly touched the calm surface of the Gulf as he rolled north to enter U.S. airspace near Lake Charles, Louisiana. He maintained the dangerously low altitude all the way to a state-of-the-art runway at Vacherie. Chris Cain knew the route above the bayous well, having made the trip many times before. As he anticipated, the passing storm front had further obscured the arrival.

Fat Girl had landed undetected. The passenger was dog tired by the two-day trip from Colombia and everything that he'd been through in the past week. He had asked, but hadn't been told where he was, other than upriver from New Orleans. He was beginning to get it: the less he knew the better. They rolled to a stop about fifty yards in front of a long metal warehouse. A dozen golf carts waited, lit by spotlights above a wide garage door. Behind the warehouse the softly glowing amber footlights traced the narrow asphalt path past the plantation house to the river.

By the time the propellers shuddered to a stop, the electric carts outfitted like small trucks had scurried silently to line up behind the slowly opening cargo door. A dozen men dressed in denim and tennis shoes went to work emptying the two pallets of ice chests. Two men held shotguns in the crooks of their arms and watched. At the warehouse, Cain and Lyle boarded a cart and merged into a steady stream rolling silently toward the river landing. Behind a continuous line of boxwoods, Lyle did not see the plantation house to the right of the path.

Cain dropped away from the others at the brow to a fishing trawler. It had seen better days. To Lyle's nautical eye, the eighty-foot vessel looked like it was held together by rust. It was tied up behind a grain barge, where the other carts were stopping. A frayed and faded U.S. flag stirred slightly from the trawler's jack staff. On the transom below it, barely discernible through streaks of rust and faded paint, were the words "*Nancy Kay, Gulfport, Mississippi.*" Carefully making his way up the equally decrepit brow, he looked farther down the dock.

The only other boat there was quite different: a Chris Craft Commander. Even in the dim lights, Lyle could see it was a floating jewel box. Its white and green paint glistened above polished teak railings and decks, seeming to glow in the dark. Inlaid, foot-tall gold leaf lettering across the teak transom ostentatiously proclaimed: "Bon Homme, Vacherie, La."

"Don't judge a book by its cover. Wait until we're inside." Even before the lights came on, Lyle knew what he meant; air conditioning was the first clue. The passageway was spotless. Judging from the crisp, pungent smell, the haze green paint was fresh. Brass fittings, even the fire axes along the bulkheads, were shined to perfection. Bundles of cable overhead were sealed in steel armored mesh. The slate-grey non-skid on the narrow walkways was newly applied. They turned into a central corridor and walked forward to a polished stainless steel ladder that led to the chart room behind the bridge.

This was no fishing trawler; the small room housed a complete up-to-date combat information center, with radar and sonar repeater scopes, banks of radio and satellite communications and a fire control panel behind a heavy-gauge wire door. The brushed aluminum panel had only four red toggles that looked like light switches. Each was protected beneath a hinged, clear plastic cover.

Up another stainless steel ladder a water-tight door opened on a grimy, rust-covered weather deck. Cain pulled back a filthy canvas crusted with bird droppings. A Browning M2 50-caliber machine gun, disguised to look like a satellite antenna, lay beneath. Looking down one deck, Lyle understood the console; it fired surface-to-surface and surface-to-air missiles on launchers hydraulically raised from inside what appeared to be two large live-hold fish tanks. *Nancy Kay* was a small warship. The rest of the tour revealed an armory stocked with automatic weapons, ammunition and two dozen compact missiles, crew quarters and galley. In the bilge below there was enough fuel to steam for more than three-thousand miles.

The tour ended at a stateroom where Lyle gratefully collapsed into a bunk. He woke briefly, feeling the motions of the small ship getting underway. He assumed somebody, perhaps Cain, must be on the bridge. He didn't care to investigate; gravity seemed to suck him into the soft, clean sheets. He was bone tired; the low, monotonous murmur and vibration of engines far below was hypnotic. But, like the night in Asuncion, the sleep was fitful. It was Emma's face that haunted him. Not long after they'd left Mexico, Cain had told him that she was safely hidden at Elmendorf Air Force Base in downtown Anchorage. She would arrive this afternoon at the Naval Air Station in Belle Chase, about twenty miles downriver from New Orleans, where he was also headed. He was happy that she was safe. But, even with everything that had happened, he dreaded the reunion, but wanted desperately for it to go well. *How will I tell her the truth? Will she believe any of it? Why should she?*

* * * *

She was dressed too warmly, still in the green long-sleeve t-shirt and blue jeans she'd worn this morning when she left Anchorage. When she stepped from the crew transport van she didn't care: she saw him waiting on the main deck. To his immense relief, she smiled, then stepped off to stride across the white crushed-clamshell lot. Somebody had given her a ball cap, and she'd pinned her hair up under it. He couldn't take his eyes off her as she walked straight toward him. She was still trim and fit; the t-shirt was matted to her chest. She was smiling. His heart pounded and his hands shook as he took hers at the end of the narrow brow. The tears surprised him; he'd never wept in front of anyone, at least since he was a child; now he didn't care. He was so happy. Emma was smiling.

With the tenderness of a mother and the touch of a lover, she gently wrapped her arms around him and rested her head on his shoulder. They stood motionless in the broiling sun. The moment was short; Roland and Cain didn't want them seen, least of all together, but they gave them the moment before Cain opened the weather door and hustled them inside.

Roland greeted her in the wardroom, presenting her with a muffuletta, the submarine-style olive salad, cheese and deli meat sandwich favored by early Italian immigrants to the Louisiana coast. It was her favorite treat, and she tucked in with gusto as the briefing began.

"My guy has always had good instinct. He's everywhere, talking with sources I could never approach, who'd never come to me. I can't tell you the number of times his information has led us to solid leads and convictions." He was speaking of the *Times Picayune* West Bank bureau chief, Bobby Lester, a tall Cajun whose slow-talking, phlegmatic persona had lured many into revealing more than they realized. He earned two Pulitzers in a nearly forty-year career. "He's hearing stuff from workers at Gulf Coast Ship and Dry Dock. Nothing that looks criminal *per se*, but enough to get his contacts' radar up," Roland spoke first.

Lyle listened closely but still couldn't take his eyes off of Emma. *She even eats gracefully. How many people could handle that?* He remembered evenings with her at the Port-O-Call; how simple things were then. He wished with all his heart that they were there, that none of this had happened. She sat attentively, splitting her attention between Roland, Lyle, this man Cain who seemed to be the boat's master and the big round sandwich she was sharing with all of them. She had to be reeling from the sub-sonic F-18 flight that delivered her in only a few hours from Alaska. He caught her looking at him. She looked happy, too.

"Emma, you'll remember the place. Right there at Algiers Point. They work on grain barges all the time, but not like they've been doing for months, maybe a year or more. Bobby says his guys have never seen anything like it, but it's the foreign nationals hanging around that got their attention. About the time the regular crews are leaving for the day, they arrive on small boats, then go to work inside barges, always from the Great Circle Tow Boat Company. His sources have peeked inside. They're seeing lots of welding. On one of the barges they've seen some kind of a little room being added inside, on the transom. Conclusion is that they're not being altered for any kind of traditional cargo, like grain or ore. Again, there's nothing illegal about any of this. These barges get finished up, then go upriver. They're not hanging around the port. Rumor is that they wind up at the *Monte Verde* docks up in Vacherie, then they're gone. I've got to think they're going north." He paused and spoke directly to Emma, "MV has been on my scope for a long time."

Vacherie: he remembers the words on the Chris Craft's transom. We must have been close, Lyle surmises.

Emma retrieves the graduation party tape from a canvas tote bag. In the cramped wardroom they huddled around the television screen, freezing the close-up of the short, well-dressed man. The stark terror on his round face had been lost in the fax transmission; now it looked very real.

In response to Lyle's question, Cain spoke rapidly, "There's no way to copy this aboard. Office staff can handle it. It's all we've really got besides these two eye witnesses. It's solid gold."

"It likely will be evidence enough for the USAO Eastern District to file a criminal complaint against Pierce for—at a minimum—obstruction of an investigation." Roland said. "Problem is going to be time; we're well beyond the statute of limitations. There'll need to be something the lawyers can use to pull the incident forward and tie Pierce and others into recent history. When that happens it'll leak, and that may spring the trap, if and when they try to intervene and kill it all over again."

Cain takes the tape from the player and places it inside a steel, magnet-proof box which he places on a shelf inside an armored cabinet.

"It's the kind of stuff the sharp prosecutors are paid for," Roland begins again. His eyes are still on the armored box. "But, it's also a big problem: the really good guys, with career aspirations and families, aren't falling all over each other to get involved. Attorneys are cautious; there'll be hell to pay if the complaint looks like a hunting expedition. They've seen too many attempts to go after these guys fail year after year, sometimes with real consequences for those who tried," he stopped to look at Emma, then settled on Lyle. "A couple years ago one of them disappeared without a trace; speculation is that he had a sweetie and they're now living somewhere in South America. For his sake, I hope so. This we do know: Pierce is mobbed up with these guys. They're all partners in lots of water-front businesses, here and around the mid-south, from Memphis and Little Rock to Mobile and Biloxi. They're rich, and they're dangerous, and they're well connected politically and in the courts with one partner who runs the most powerful admiralty and criminal law practices in Louisiana and the Gulf Coast."

Cain had listened intently, then offered some good news, "This time there's a two-pronged assault. Roland, we've got our guys working, too, and a federal judge is interested. He got his job over the objections of that law firm you mentioned."

Although no name had been given, Roland knew exactly who he was talking about. He was surprised; unless the leopard had changed his spots, the former Orleans District Attorney did not have a good reputation among police. "Don't get me wrong, Chris. Even with your interest and resources, you're still going to have to light a fire under the feds, the locals will be even harder. That process is slow. Bureaucratic foot-dragging is delaying us at DEA. I'm hearing the same from INS. You know better than I do that surveillance turns on equipment and personnel, and they're both hard to come by. I'm new to the feds, but every time we get close, Washington dumps something else of higher priority on us. Preparation for Republican National Convention has been the excuse lately. Agents have spent weeks chasing every nut case who has visited New Orleans in the past six months. Total waste of time."

"You're sitting inside one of the most advanced surveillance platforms in the world. Its night vision cameras and motion sensors are state-of-art, not yet available even to federal law enforcement. Moving upriver will be a good place to hide Emma and Lyle," Cain responded.

Roland agreed that it would be rewarding for Emma and Lyle to be a part of the action, anything that led to the owners of *Monte Verde* and *Bon Homme* who, he believes murdered Emma's crewman and co-opted Lyle. Forgetting the shady federal judge Cain just mentioned, he knew that—finally—this could be the beginning of something far reaching, devastating to organized crime, human and drug trafficking. He had not spoken about leads he had turned that suggested that New Orleans was also beginning to be the center of international trade in fissile material. "If you don't mind, I'll tag along, too. I can probably be better connected here than I can at my office."

"Absolutely, my friend. Let's roll. Lyle, give me a hand topside with the lines. Emma, I could use your help on the bridge. I'll be in the chart house making sure my alligator mouth hasn't overloaded my humming bird ass. It might take a couple of hours, Roland, but by the time we get to Vacherie it ought to be laid on, officially. Got to let the big guys stomp things out on their level, you know what I mean. He pulled several large sheets from a wide drawer and spread them out for Roland. "Until we get the go-ahead, take a look at these. Depending on timing, we could pick up agents along the route. Believe me, there's plenty of firepower down in the armory if they need it." Cain leans over the charts and maps and shakes Roland's hand, "If they try to run, I can't think of a more satisfying way to use it. Welcome to your command center, Operation Tale of the Tape!" Cain pulled the door shut.

* * * *

He woke and stretched like a big old fat cat on the tall four-poster bed. He slid his feet over the side and found the step. He donned the Chinese red silk robe laid out the night before, tied the gold-tasseled belt and opened the tall French doors to the gallery. It was going to be a great day. Nat Pierce was going to spend most of the day and night on the river; just the thought of that made him giddy. At the other end of the oak alley, *Bon Homme* was provisioned, fueled and waiting for his command.

Nat's power will be on full display today. His guests, some of whom dared not accept his invitation, are a who's-who of Washington's corruptible power elite, the kind of people his partners have paid him well to befriend and—whenever possible—to ensnare and exploit. Their power and influence place them well above most gathering in the Super Dome for the RNC kick-off.

With coffee delivered in a Nineteenth Century Limoges cup and saucer, he begins his inspection stroll around the gallery. At the rear of the big house he stopped to view the plantation's working side. He was surprised that the big airplane was still there. He had turned in about the same time it landed. It was unusual that it hadn't taken off right away. He could care less. Whatever his partners were doing back there was of no concern to him. His rewards for the influence greatly outweighed any inconvenience. His only input was the little fleet of electric carts which ensured that he wouldn't be disturbed by their nocturnal activities.

He had wondered, of course. Most recently he saw grain silos appear as did dozens of enormous black cattle enclosed in a two-hundred acre pasture. The worst part of it all had been the smell when the wind was just right in hot, humid seasons along the Mississippi. Periodically he had seen crews loaded huge burlap bags stenciled with the word "manure," filled, he assumed, from huge piles of the filth bulldozed in half a dozen piles around the pasture. He guessed that *Monte Verde* had begun yet another business, this one supplying beef to restaurants and fertilizer for gentlemen planters. Menard dismissed a casual query from a guest at one of Nat's several Mardi Gras bashes with, "there's gold in that manure, it's hot stuff."

Nat pushed the throttles forward gently. The perfectly tuned twin diesels sang in harmony. He caressed the teak-over-walnut wheel and nudged the cruiser into the caramel-colored water. The starched captain's cap was the crowning touch. He'll present quite a vision as his guests watch him step aboard Great Circle's flagship at Green St. Wharf. They and the entire city of New Orleans will thrill at the fireworks that he and the *Monte Verde* Coffee Company of North America are graciously and generously providing to salute the President of the United States of America.

At full throttle, the boat lifts gracefully and flies downriver. This is a great day for Principal Deputy Secretary of State Nathaniel Langsford Pierce.

* * * *

Senior Secret Service agent Lee Parker spoke to four other agents who'll ride in the heavily armored SUV, codenamed 'Halfback." It's his last chance to talk candidly and off-mike with them before they scatter to other vehicles in the motorcade from the New Orleans lakefront to the Super Dome.

"This place may be the city that care forgot, but it just gives me the creeps. New Orleans has always been a cesspool of political intrigue, even before Louisiana was one of the United States. Persons of interest as diverse as Lee Harvey Oswald and Napoleon Bonaparte are prime examples; Oswald to do or be used for whatever purposes he was; Napoleon's cronies to plot a return to power. Nothing in New Orleans is like anywhere else in the United States. The President may as well be descending into the morass of intrigue and concomitant dangers of a third world country. Organized crime used to be called pirates. Now it's the Dixie Mafia, Southern Mob and whatever the bad guys called themselves during the past two hundred years. If there was a command structure like other syndicates it would be easier, but there isn't. It's just too easy to go underground here."

A year ago, when New Orleans landed the convention, he began studying intelligence briefings. They were always interesting but hardly ever definitive; solid investigative leads tended to disappear into the bayous. The Southern Mob was especially difficult; the cast of characters changed constantly, none easily associated with the others. Even flipping, the fed-slang term for leniency in exchange for information, the only really effective tool in going after larger players, didn't work. Nobody talked.

The voice of 'Bone Break', call sign for the President's personal bodyguard, cracks in his earpiece; the luncheon is breaking up, and Parker's team disburses immediately. Wearing a conspicuously out-of-place but necessary raincoat concealing the Uzi slung under his arm, Parker stands beside the 'Stagecoach,' the Presidential limo which will carry President Frank H. Lehman and his special guest, Hays C. Abbott, dean of the Pepperdine School of Law. He slides in the right front seat. 'Spare,' the dummy limo, moves into the lead position, and both black Lincolns merge into a procession of six heavily armored SUVs and two panel trucks. He speaks barely above a whisper, "Go, go, go" into his wrist microphone. The motorcade is hot; vehicles move simultaneously as though they were welded together and drive away from the Southern Yacht Club. Tires squeal as the overweight vehicles pick up speed and turn sharply on the wet cobblestone streets.

President Lehman is in deep conversation with Abbott.

Parker is conducting radio checks with agents along the route and those in 'Halfback.' If he wanted to eavesdrop on the conversation behind him, he wouldn't be able to hear above the voices in his earpiece.

Although air traffic is closed before, during and after the President landed at Louis Armstrong Airport, river traffic on Mississippi is not. The President will not cross the river or get anywhere near it. Still, there are no signs of pirates, today at least, for the Secret Service to monitor. Small relief, Parker thinks.

Coast Guard launches with Secret Service agents aboard have swept the area from Huey P. Long Bridge downriver to Industrial Canal and the Coast Guard Headquarters where it meets the Mississippi River. The Port Captain reports that traffic, both ways, will be light.

Even if Parker thought that shutting down river traffic was remotely necessary, that had to balanced, at least superficially, against the odds and practicality. After thirty years on protective detail, he knew there were limits to expediency; there's only so much that can be done, even in an overabundance of caution. Unlike airports or pubic streets, there is no way to shut down a major American port, especially the Port of New

Orleans, the fourth largest in the United States. Yes, it is within the mile-wide presidential security perimeter, but in his and the Services' calculus, it is also not relevant. Even if an assault were to be mounted from the river, the waterfront is a long way from the Super Dome. There's no clear shot, and even if there were, who could make it? Stop worrying about the river, he concludes, worry about the now moving security bubble.

Still, anything can happen he knows as he sits a couple of feet away from the most powerful man in the world. Because of Parker's unshakable faith in the depravity of man, precautions have been exhausting. Police and federal agents are practically shoulder-to-shoulder on the street and atop buildings along the entire route. Taller buildings on route from the lakefront to the Dome have been swept. Two miles away, a Marine AH-1W Cobra gunship helicopter, 'Mike One,' is turning up in the landscaped infield at the New Orleans Fairgrounds thoroughbred racetrack. He confirms its status, satisfied that should it be needed for additional firepower or—much more likely—to evacuate the President, it can be overhead in seconds. Near the Dome, access is restricted for four blocks in all directions. It is clean—inside and out—and has been for twenty-four hours.

⊕ The motorcade has cleared the lakefront, the lowest threat area of the trip downtown. The motorcade slows only slightly as it swings onto Canal Street. The two limos swap positions. Four more motorcycles pull in ahead of two New Orleans police cruisers; they'll tag-team ahead of the procession to ensure cross traffic is clear at least five blocks ahead of the speeding motorcade.

On the wide boulevard now, the procession picks up speed. Spectators viewing the spectacle have no idea of the firepower rolling by: the two vans with agents armed with MP-5s and two-thousand rounds ammunition for each and eight more agents in the vehicles bracketing the two black, bomb-proof limos.

With the shift completed, the first will transport the President and Dean Abbott. Behind them speed 'Control' and 'Support' with a Navy doctor and the military officer who carries the nuclear football transmitter and launch codes. 'Roadrunner' is next. It carries electronics jamming gear. In 'Halfback' six more agents in body armor are fully locked and loaded. They're carrying an assortment of automatic light and heavy machine guns, riot guns, even a rocket-propelled grenade launcher. For the first time and for reasons not clear, even to Parker, the arsenal also includes shoulder-fired surface-to-air missiles. The press pool rides in the last panel truck, customized with an oversized sun roof to enable photography. An ambulance is last in line, driven by a twenty-year-old who hasn't had so much fun since he drove last Friday night in a demolition derby at the Yellow Belly race track in Slidell.

"Destination?"

"Green."

In an abundance of caution, Parker radios 'November one,' the Navy SH-3 helicopter carrying highly sensitive heat and radiation detectors and a crew of four. It has been patrolling the river for an hour. The Service technician reports that all seems normal; traffic includes two ships northbound, nearing Algiers Point; a twelve-barge lash-up is southbound, approaching the Huey P. Long. At current speed, it will not pass Canal Street by the time the motorcade arrives, well past by the time the President moves again.

The Canal Street Ferry has just left Algiers Landing; agents are also riding it, checking out everyone and every vehicle bound for Canal Street. A large towboat is approaching Coastal Ship and Dry Dock and coming alongside a barge moored there. The most unusual traffic is a trawler making its way up river, approaching Algiers Point. The Navy pilot can't resist providing unwanted levity, "The biggest threat from that trawler is sinking, from the looks of it!"

The reply is terse, "position?"

"Swinging wide in the channel, toward the French Quarter. Estimate opposite Esplanade Street, ten minutes," the technician in the passenger compartment radios. With the same deadpan he adds, "November One tech. Heat signature on towboat approaching Coastal."

The words are barely spoken before the phone rings in the Great Circle operations center at the Green Street dock. Less than a minute later they report the reply from the towboat captain. "Towboat aware. Confirm arrival at Coastal for evaluation and maintenance."

The other hot spots noted today and as far back as a week have all been accounted for. The refineries up river are principal sources. The only other hot spots were newly-fertilized fields, miles upriver, near Vacherie. In Parker's overabundance of caution, agents visited the plantation three days ago. With some amusement, they reported that the heat signatures came from piles of manure, by-products of the bull breeding and manure packaging operation. Their tongue-in-cheek report ended with, "There's a lot of money in BS, and it creates an unusual amount of heat and fragrance!"

Parker is satisfied. The motorcade turns on LaSalle, crosses Tulane and passes by the high-rise Tulane Medical Center where roof-top snipers are stationed.

"Status green."

In thirty seconds the motorcade will turn sharply to the right and travel less than a block up Poydras where it will roll into the shadow of the Super Dome. The environment inside remains sterile, not that anyone can relax, the President will be completely exposed there.

Parker is reassured, but he won't be happy until he's back home in Reston, Virginia. He removes his sunglasses.

He takes nothing for granted. There is never any margin for error: you get what you inspect, not what you expect.

All's well that ends well.

Twenty-One

The barge is two-hundred-fifty feet long, forty-five feet wide and twenty-two feet from top to bottom. It is unremarkable, identical to thousands just like it, scattered the length of the Mississippi and Ohio River waterways and on estuaries snaking throughout the massive North American drainage. It was moved down river last night from Vacherie. A mile away, it and ten others just like it are plainly visible to the tourists across the river strolling or relaxing in the shade along the French Quarter promenade. Even an informed observer would assume number 505907 was awaiting service at the small ship yard adjacent to the Algiers Ferry landing. They would be wrong.

A frail, tired man rides alone in a small room welded to the rear bulkhead. He is spending what precious little energy he has to check, then double check, a control panel beneath bullet-proof windows that slant forward into the dark, cavernous space that houses his killing machine. He is much younger than he looks, unusually thin—practically emaciated—prematurely bald, his skin is yellowing. Everything in the barge is his creation, and he is proud and ashamed of it. His meager satisfaction comes from knowing that it has been his labor and genius that have kept him and his wife alive for the past years.

Now is the moment of truth. With a delicate touch, he pushes a toggle forward. Instantly, the first of four hatches, nested one on top of the other and spanning the width, begins to move. The noise of steel-on-steel rollers rumbles like thunder inside the huge void. For the first time in months, the steadily widening opening allows sunshine to reflect off his creation. The temperature rises inside the little command center and his t-shirt and shorts hang limp on his skinny frame. He wipes his brow with a maroon shop towel pulled from his rear pocket. With the third hatch opening now, he can see the half-dozen gimbaled platforms welded to the keel.

Terrifyingly aware of the consequences of trying to interfere, Alexi Zotkin no longer cares that he is about to commit an unspeakable crime of unprecedented horror. Finishing the task is the only hope for him and Maria. He has long since given up any hope of escaping, and he knows better than trying. Since that first attempt and twice before his sickly wife joined him two years ago, he has adapted to captivity. They have been prisoners, albeit in a gilded cage, with comforts not available to him in the Soviet Union, even as a scientist. Most recently that has included the psychiatric care and drugs Maria has needed, in increasing doses, just to cope with life. She never recovered from the death of her girls in a hit-and-run accident in Moscow. Her memory was a blank until she saw Alexi at Vacherie. She had no idea how she got there. Since then, they have survived in a spacious new quarters surrounded by high walls.

She had made some recovery, busying herself with nurturing the courtyard into an Eden where each day she talks to the plants or just sits vacuously awaiting his return. He leaves her there each morning after a steel door is unlocked. Behind it concrete stairs descend to a tunnel to the laboratory furnished with everything he has ever requested.

Even though he knows what he has accomplished is brilliant, it also is of the worst, twisted, criminal purpose imaginable. He also knows that the radiation to which he is exposed is most likely killing him. He has had no choice. In the year since he completed the first warhead he has produced hundreds more. He has no idea, has never inquired, about where they went after leaving his lab. All he has been told is that random samples of the mortar rounds have worked perfectly. He is not sure what that means exactly, but he has a good idea. What he does know to a certainty is that in a few minutes hundreds of them, each fitted with plutonium tips, will be loaded into the twenty-four 122-mm mortars mounted on the platforms and the computer guidance system he has created.

After the hatches open completely, the radio crackles in the stifling silence. He knows the voice well. It originates from a luxuriously furnished towboat tied up at Robbins St. Wharf, almost directly across the river from him, only a few hundred yards from the place where he first tried to escape his masters, seven long years ago. The caller is pleased to witness the hatches slide open.

The conversation now ends ominously, with words that need not be spoken: any hesitation, any malfunction means he and Maria will never see each other again. Having no other choice, he believes the promise of freedom, perhaps even before this day ends.

The scrambled and encrypted radio transmission finished, he returns the microphone to its hook on the compact radio above his head. He glides steadily downriver, passing the Green St. Wharf. Shortly after noon, as scheduled, the towboat bumps gently against the moored barge; its momentum rocking it, but only slightly.

Alexi climbs up a steel ladder and stands on deck. After years of confinement, the sensation of emerging, seeing the high-rise buildings filled with people inhabiting a free world, stirs strong emotions. He would have run once. His ambitions are much different now. There is work, his only hope is to finish it. He brings his mind back to his task. He takes a line thrown from the towboat and wraps it around a huge cleat. He carefully walks forward on the narrow walkway and secures another to the bow. By the time he returns, six members of the Iranian Republican Guard, who entered the country the same way he did, have boarded with the lead-lined ammunition cases. They must work quickly and efficiently. The helicopter overhead will have detected their heat signature and responded to investigate. Timing is of the essence. Under Alexi's supervision the highly rehearsed Islamists are loading the mortars. Firing will commence, soon. Should any of the first rounds go astray during the initial volley, computers will adjust the gyroscopic platform and ensure that the remainder will punch neatly through the round dome and explode on the floor inside. Hundreds will die instantly. The structure will remain essentially intact, preventing much of the radioactive drift. In the following weeks, those who survive the initial horror will die by the hundreds, perhaps thousands, while New Orleans will be unaffected.

Satisfied that all is in order, Alexi radios the all-ready signal.

Topside again, Alexi throws off the lines. In the pilothouse, a well-dressed man smiles and slowly backs the big towboat into the wide river.

Across the river at Greet St. Wharf, Nat is unaware of the now-loaded killing machine. He spins the wheel, reversing his course and pointing the bow upriver to fight the current. He is a good pilot with years of experience and expertly crabs to starboard, toward the one-hundred foot by twenty-seven foot *Bayou Queen*, Great Circle's immaculately maintained flagship. At precisely the right moment, he throttles back to match the downriver flow and maintains his position. Now almost touching the *Bayou Queen*, he throws a line to two men dressed in starched and pressed cotton khakis.

The maneuver has been flawless. The Chris Craft presses snugly against two huge fenders hanging over the towboat's port side. The gap is quickly spanned with an accommodation ladder. Unaccustomed to the oppressive heat and humidity, most of the guests are gathering in the air-conditioned salon; a few, the men from Arkansas included, are standing on the wide after deck, witnessing his arrival with slightly buzzed admiration.

Nat is wearing yachting regalia of his fussy design: white trousers, blue double-breasted blazer over a frilled tuxedo shirt. Looking like a toad in livery, he makes a grand entrance, snapping his right hand to the brim of his white captain hat, acknowledging his guests. He proudly stretches to his full height and makes his grand entrance. *Show time!* Menard welcomes him aboard, and after several minutes of handshaking and back slapping they step inside to the salon to repeat the spectacle. The décor is classic New Orleans bordello, a tasteless display of Eighteenth Century ketch: brass sconces, crystal chandeliers, velvet red and green draperies above the garish, purple carpet. Nat inwardly winces, but even the consummate host is impressed by the spread of illegally imported Russian caviar, crawfish, giant Gulf shrimp and free-flowing Dom Perignon consumed lustily by some of the most powerful figures of the American political and criminal underworld.

After a few minutes, Menard drifts back to his side. He takes his arm as they walk forward to another brow laid forward of the other, over which two crewmembers are returning to the flagship.

Momentarily alone aboard *Bon Homme*, Nat anxiously awaits while Menard slides the polished-spruce door shut. The room is quiet, nearly soundproof, owing to the salon's double-paned, lead glass windows. The décor is much more tasteful. Nat has decorated his combination pilot house and sitting room with deep walnut paneling, thick blue carpet and leather club chairs. A loveseat faces away from the wheel where Nat pilots during inclement weather. Pale yellow draperies bracket each of the eight windows and the wide glass door to the polished teak rear deck. The room rocks slightly in the wake of a passing freighter.

"Go ahead, take a look," Menard speaks, smiling like Father

Christmas, Nat thinks, and pointing at a polished oak box left on the carpet by the two men who just departed. "I think you'll like what you find."

Nat kneels and touches the shiny brass hasp. The lid swings back on long hinges. He freezes, seeing but not believing. His mouth gapes in wonder and something like depraved ecstasy. The dim light from crystal sconces is magnified off a half-dozen solid gold ingots laid shoulder-to-shoulder, flush to the top of the red velvet-lined box. The light beams around the salon. He touches the precious metal and lifts an ingot, astounded. The sheer heft of the things is sensual. He fondles it with both hands. He looks up at Menard, standing over him and grinning. Fortunately, the face of astonishment and fear are the same.

"There's two more rows underneath, and even more!"

With his heart pounding, Nat—in breathless disbelief—slowly, lovingly empties the box. Eighteen small ingots lay on the deep carpet before he sees a thin cedar plank. In the center of it is a hole the size of a quarter. He inserts a stubby finger and lifts gently, exposing a bed of well-worn fifty-dollar bills bound in to ten bundles of ten-thousand dollars, each.

"We thought you'd like some spending money in addition to the rather solid investment portfolio."

"I'm speechless!"

"Well, that's a first, and a welcome one!"

"Gene, I mean this is unbelievable. Why?"

"Remember? Those who are faithful in small things will be trusted with large affairs. Fetch us a drink. I need to fill you in on our future."

Nat's hands tremble as he fumbles to open the champagne. He manages to withdraw two Irish glass flutes from a glass display cabinet above the sink and not drop them. He nearly drops one of them. He regains composure, turning to face Menard, himself enjoying the spectacle of the chest's startling treasure.

"Nat, in all the time we've been partners you've never taken me for a spin. Fire this thing up and head over toward that barge," he says, pointing toward Gulf Coast.

"Which one?"

"I'll show you when we get close. That's where the action's gonna be. We'll have the best seats in the house when the fireworks begin. Hell, nobody's going to miss us. Our partners can take over. I've never seen the ambulance chaser Anderson so loose. Gordon's running around like a bird dog in heat after some of your classy ladies from DC. Let 'em have some fun.

* * * *

"That one, right there. Number 505905," Menard points through the windshield. Pull up this side of it, turn toward the city. This is going to be fantastic."

Nat maneuvers and throttles to maintain a static position in the swift current. Menard has re-charged their flutes. They climb up the brass-railed ladder and sit side-by-side on the flying bridge. Menard is right: the city lights become more intense as the western sky dims to a crepuscular golden orange. They return waves from tourists on the Canal Street Ferry passing close to starboard.

The deep wake rocks them gently. Menard looks at his Rolex and begins, "Nat, that chest is reward, and it's an investment in our future." He drains the glass. "Your world is going to change in a few minutes, and you and I are going to be a couple of the richest men in the world."

"I love it when you talk like this," Nat says giddily, touching his cheek with his drink-free hand and affecting a feminine blush. "Oh, please go on! You really know how to sweep a guy off his feet." He is petrified.

The response, like much about Nat, irritates Menard, but only a little. Even though he can barely tolerate him, the little fat man is essential, he has way too much invested in him; now the stakes are even higher. "See that barge over there?" Nat leans forward and points to a barge about a quarter mile upriver, halfway between them and the interstate bridge connecting east and west banks. That's where the fireworks are going to come from. They tell me they'll shoot up four, five, as high as six hundred feet. Be seen for forty miles away. All thanks to our great civic pride! But, it's the one behind us that's got the real payload."

"More fireworks?"

"You could say that!" Menard fills his glass and turns to look Nat in the eye, his voice is lower, almost a whisper. His smile is completely vanished, replaced with a nasty snarl. "Inside it are twenty mortars loaded with high explosive, radio-active dirty warheads. And, you've made it all possible. Most of that gold and cash back there is from what you Ivy League guys call radical Muslims. The rest of it is donated by our esteemed associates in the Dixie Mafia. Sounds romantic, doesn't it? I'm French and English, not Italian!" he smiles again. It's thanks to you for making sure that the warhead material, always packed under ingots of gold to throw off detectors, have made it into the country, along with the drug deliveries at *Bon Homme* and lots of places in between. And, certainly not least, it's pay for smuggling Alexi into the country; since his short career as a Mark Spitz wanna-be he's worked out better than we ever hoped. He's inside there to pull the trigger. Boom!" Nat jumped like he'd been shot.

"What are you talking about?" Nat tries to read his expression, then looks back toward the barge.

"A few seconds after the fireworks begin we'll hear the damnedest noise you ever heard. The dirty warheads and explosives will start landing right on top of the Super Dome!"

Nat felt sick. Maybe, he thought, the old thug was playing games, just to see how far he could push him. He liked doing that to prove, in his warped mind, that Nat was dull or just to see if he was listening. "OK, we're going to bomb the Super Dome, killing a few thousand people, including the President of the United States. Maybe nobody will notice. Then what happens, sea monsters climb out of the river and consume the Quarter while we're beamed up to the mother ship?"

"Good guess, college boy. Most of the four thousand people, including the President and his top staff, will be dead or soon dying from the radiation. Old Alexi worked it all out. The effects won't travel far, so most of the casualties will be contained downwind, maybe five or six blocks, max."

Nat could not speak. This had to be a joke. Menard was already drunk. "Are you hosing me; you've got one hell of a sense of humor. You are kidding, aren't you, or you've gone off the deep end? I swear I don't know sometime."

"Serious as cancer, my friend." Menard's tone changed. He spoke not of speculation but of certainty about things over which Nat knew he had no control; at least he didn't think he did until he continued. "After the smoke and radiation clear it won't be very long before we're on top of the world. The political fallout—pardon my pun—will seize Washington and last much longer. With Leman, Abbott, the vice-president, speaker of house and good old-pain-in-the-rear madam secretary Cotton all dead or dying, Nathan Pierce will be one of the most powerful men in Washington. Your bosom buddy, the senate's senior Democrat, President Pro Tempore Arthur Greer, will be chief executive."

The words were beyond fantastic; they were totally insane. The man was calmly discussing mass murder, an unbelievable attempt to overthrow the government of the United States replacing it with a thugocracy with Nat Pierce as its leader. There is no way this could happen, least of all the way Menard was so calmly describing. If they're weren't arrested before they got back to shore, the people who'd piled up that gold and cash in the box would come looking for them all when it failed. He wanted to grab the crazy old man by the lapels and scream. Was what he said really about to happen? He could not process the thought.

"The disgusting little pervert will never recover. You've got plenty on him. He'll do everything we tell him. Orders will be pleasantly and efficiently relayed by old Nat Pierce. Within days, no more than a week, the Soviets will make the first big move. They'll demand, and the United States—still in chaos and vulnerable—will agree, to pull back deployed military personnel from Eastern Europe and Asia. The esteemed Ozark hillbilly, upon whom fate has cast the nation's and the world's destiny, will be a rock of stability and leadership. A gentle reminder about his good times at one of your queer bashes at the big house, his insistence on funding that little airport up in Arkansas like it was LAX, will dispel any righteous indignation. Who knows? If he's as eager a player as I know he'll be, some of the gold we're flying in there might just find its way into that mansion he owns in the Ozark foothills."

It was like a switch had been thrown. Menard was in transmit. He was getting a little drunk, his gaze rubbering from Nat, to the barge, toward the city and nowhere. "He will quickly demonstrate the country's desire to ensure world peace by embracing middle-eastern political overtures. He'll even be believable in his sanctimonious rejection of the previous administration's hostile attitude toward the Arab world. He'll offer reconciliation with Islamic states from Egypt to Jordan, across Saudi Arabia, east through Iraq, Iran, Afghanistan and Pakistan and all the way to Indonesia. The proposal will be written and presented to him by acting secretary of state—you—who has advised him to agree to their demands for the immediate withdrawal of all U.S. military presence from the Mediterranean to the South China Sea. Hell, if we tell him to, he'll jog naked around the White House!"

There was more. "Should there be any hesitation, the secret ultimatum put to Acting President Greer will be a hail of dirty bombs, like the one you're about to see, raining down on major U.S. cities. They'll turn the ports of New York, Baltimore, Los Angeles and Charleston upside down. But, if he's still stupid enough to push, the attacks will begin in St. Louis, right in the heart of mid-America, then Cincinnati, Pittsburgh and Memphis, with a bomb detonation each day in a progression until the Congress and the United Nations fall in line. Our barges are already in place on the Ohio and Mississippi. Here's our payoff: as brokers of the deal, the governments of Iran, Iraq, Syria and the tribal lords in Afghanistan give us exclusive drug source and exclusive, protected trafficking routes into Europe and the U.S. We won't have to suck up to the drug cartels in Colombia; they're history. We'll throw them to the international law enforcement weenies; same thing happens in Italy, Germany, France and England. Bottom line: we get rich, more than that." Menard drunkenly finds Nat's sleeve and pulls himself closer. He practically whispers, "The best part of this, icing on the cake, is elimination of the only people who can possibly screw this up, who can tie you to that pathetic Russian and me. Dead men tell no tales." He laughed, steadying himself before stumbling. He squints downriver. The old trawler is rounding Algiers Point. "Nat, as we speak, they are meeting their just rewards aboard a boat that'll pass by us in a few minutes. We'll get a signal: four short blasts on its horn. You can see the bodies if you want, but I know you don't. My friend, it's all over." He clinks his crystal flue on the one Nat gripped with both hands. "Here's to world peace!"

Twenty-Two

The ambulance had barely cleared the doorway before the heavy steel mesh door slapped into the threshold and locked shut. Twenty Secret Service agents and more plainclothed police stood at the ready along the long, well-guarded interior passageway beneath the south endzone seats. 'Stagecoach's' doors flew open. The two passengers were the last out. They were led a few steps to four black draped partitions arranged as a makeshift greenroom. Seated in two barber chairs, groomers, watched closely by Service agents, apply makeup, fuss with hair, brush shoulders and pull ties and straighten coats. A moment later a smart looking young woman steps inside. She is dressed in a short black sleeveless dress and wearing a radio headset and transmitter clipped to a belt. She leads the two men to a spot marked with yellow tape, center stage, behind a massive U.S. flag. Four Service agents take their positions in the wings ten feet on either side. With one last look, she scans the two men, smiles and steps aside. On her command into her radio lights begin to dim in the massive arena and the crowd hushes. A moment later a deep basso voice booms: "Ladies and gentlemen, President Frank H. Lehman and the next President of the United States…" and with more emphasis on each protracted syllable, "Hayes C. Abbott!"

As the massive U.S. flag, wide enough to span the eighty-foot stage, rises just enough for the two men to walk underneath, they're bathed in blinding glow of four spotlights. The Super Dome erupts. Thunderous applause grows to a frightening roar at the unexpected and unprecedented scene: the President is standing with the man who—technically—has not even been nominated. He grasps Abbott's right forearm and thrusts it straight up over his head. There's no doubt about the President's wishes, nor the convention outcome now. The crowd goes wild.

Cheers and the *Stars and Stripes Forever* overload audio circuits. Outside, television engineers in trailers scramble to adjust settings for the estimated twenty million viewers. The noise grows louder as the two men began a parade around the perimeter of the stage, stopping at the corners to wave to those in the cheap seats high above. The instant they return to center stage, the lights swing stage left to reveal the Secretary of State, Speaker of the House and the Vice President. "Americans—for the past eight years—you have placed our country—the White House, the House of Representatives, the United States Senate—in good hands. We'll do it again in November! And, we're not about to stop now!" The trio joins the two at the podium; all join hands and raise their arms over their heads.

The Super Dome vibrates. Most of Senior Agent Lee Parker's presidential detail have seen it all before, but nothing like this. The sound is literally shaking the plywood platform beneath their feet and pounding on their chests. Parker can now be seen at the rear of the stage, nervously glancing toward the ceiling as if it might begin to fracture; no plan for that other than grabbing the president and dragging him under the bleachers.

"Ladies and gentlemen, patriots, defenders of the constitution, Americans, this is a gathering of eagles, unlike any since our nation's founding." Those words cue the descent of a forty-foot-wide golden eagle, now lit with spotlights and hovering overhead. "This historic gathering of eagles is made possible because of America's return to its rightful role as leader of the free world, a nation that stands up to the Soviet Union, a nation unafraid of tyrants around the world, a nation, under God, dedicated to the proposition that our righteous might will continue an unbroken commitment to peace through strength, and freedom for all!"

Secret Service agents are having trouble hearing the crackling radio transmissions in their ear buds. They, too, crank up volume controls.

A finger to his open ear, Parker strains to hear and talks into his cuff, "Say again?"

The voice in his ear responds, 'Navy Sweep' reports hot spots on the river. Approaching source. Stand by for further traffic."

* * * *

With Cain at the wheel, the *Nancy Kay* has made good time. Everyone is topside; Emma and Lyle lean on the starboard port wing rail and watch the Industrial Canal approach. The perfectly rectangular, lime green Embarcadero Buildings stand where it meets the river. In the silence each is lost in memories, Emma more so. At ten knots, she calculates the trip to Vacherie will take several hours. She could not be happier.

"Seems like it was so long ago," Emma speaks dreamily, and quickly adds, "That's because it was," she smiles and glances at Lyle who is leaning on the high railing watching the canal entrance pass.

Lyle doesn't respond immediately, not sure if this is the time to tell her what he so desperately wants her to know. "I wish I'd made better decisions," he said, dissatisfied with the comment. "What I mean, Emma, is that I regret what I did. I don't expect you to forgive it. Just know that I am so sorry. I hope I wouldn't be that stupid or self-centered ever again." He stumbled on, "I'm not forgiving myself."

She joins him and leans on the rail, "I believe you, Lyle. Whatever happens, I believe this will all work out, for everyone." She smiles and squeezes his hand in hers, "You've always lived a charmed life."

"I'm so sorry, Emma."

The early evening is unseasonably warm. The sunset is unobstructed by high clouds. The delicate light reflects off the water, diffusing it into delicate pink and gold streamers. The trawler is making steady way. Humid air settles like a blanket as the breeze dies with the sunset. Memories of nights just like this fill her consciousness as does the familiar patterns of radio traffic which has begun to intrude on her reverie. Emma pays more attention. It is a lot more radio traffic than she remembered. She can't help notice code names she'd never heard. It has been a long time, she muses. Everything changes. If she was again a young watch officer would she pick it all up again?

"Hey, break it up out there, this isn't exactly the love boat," Cain smiles, seeing them looking toward him. "That's the Secret Service you're hearing. The president's in town, going to the Dome. You two take the con. I need to go below and talk to Roland. You may be old and rusty, but I'll bet you can handle it."

Lyle defers to Emma as they enter the bridge. "You're a civilian, you're senior to everyone!"

She touches the throttles, then checks the river ahead, both hands on the wheel. Cain walks through the door behind them and disappears down the ladder. He opens the wardroom door. Roland is standing, leaning on his hands and studying the maps and charts. "Coffee?" Cain asks.

"Sure, why not."

"Comin' right up," Cain sings in reply and walks behind Roland to a service counter. He opens a drawer below the urn and retrieves a Walther PPK .380 automatic, with silencer attached. He turns, makes a short step toward Hebert, raises the pistol, holds it only inches from the base of his skull and fires. The bullet immediately severs Hebert's cerebral cortex. Death is instant. The thud of his head hitting the table is louder than the muffled snap of the gunshot. Bone fragments and brain tissue fly in a conical pattern down the table's length and splatter on the charts and on the opposite bulkhead. Blood trickles from a bloody hole the size of a half dollar in the top of his forehead.

Cain picks up the gold tipped, ebony walking stick from the chair where Roland had left it. Nice. It might fetch some real bucks at the convent's annual rummage sale. He slips the pistol inside the deep pocket of his shorts, opens the door and pulls himself up the steep ladder to the bridge.

Emma has steered the trawler to mid-river as Piety Street Wharf and the *Monte Verde* Coffee Company passes off to starboard.

"Nice work, lady. I think you've done this before," Cain speaks as he walks on the bridge behind her.

"Thanks," she says and smiles, "That didn't take long. Everything OK down there? "It's Chris, isn't it? Thanks for all you're doing. It's really indescribable to be here again. But, what can we do to help?"

"You're welcome. And, no, the best thing for you two is to just stay low. Nobody knows where you are." Cain looks out toward the port bridge wing, then toward the river and the approaching skyline. "I don't have a crystal ball, but things are going to come together, soon, for both of you. We'll know more later. My colleagues are working the problem. They'll probably want to look at the tape with you, try bring you back to the scene, at least in your mind." He looks at Lyle, " Roland filled me in on a little of your and Emma's history. "Maybe this is a good time for you two to just talk."

"We don't bring much to the table, but is there anything we can do once we get to Vacherie?" Lyle inquires.

"I don't think so, but you're both going to be there to help. Your debriefing will be most the most valuable. Roland really seems to be on top of the charts and maps, really putting his head into it right now." Turning to look at Emma he continues. "Without you two and that tape there wouldn't be much action possible. It is all going to work out," he speaks, touching her shoulder and flashing a charming wink.

He steps out on the bridge wing. Lyle follows him. "Hey, Chris, this is really something. I heard old guys say it, but it's probably true: returning to New Orleans, one sees a lot of ghosts here. Old friends, maybe even yourself, from a long time ago. This place doesn't really change, just the people who wander through."

"Truer words may never have been spoken." The width of the Esplanade Street parkway comes into view. He can see and the orphanage. The light in the bell tower is on. "You're right; we're just moving through. The whole world's a stage; we're just actors playing our parts." He laughs and turns to look inside at Emma behind the wheel, "Or, that's close to what old Billy Shakespeare said." He walks back inside and stands in the doorway behind her. "Hey, Lyle, come here a minute."

As Lyle steps inside, Cain speaks, "I think you've both enjoyed the trip, but all good things must come to an end." Expressionless, he pulls the Glock from his pocket.

They both look across the bridge toward him, no more than four feet away, then at each other. "What are you doing, Chris? If this is a joke it's not very funny, man," Lyle manages to speak first and starts to move in front of Emma."

"Stay where you are. Step away from the wheel." He points the pistol barrel toward the rear door and speaks to Emma, "Move over there." He takes his eyes off them and for a split second makes a quick survey of the river ahead and takes the wheel in his left hand. "You're both dumb as rocks. You don't even understand the problem. Hebert down there was another story: the dumb bastard at least had an idea."

"What about Roland?" Emma shouts, her tone accusatory, her voice shaking.

"Never knew what hit him, m'lady." He was studying the map and charts like there really was gonna be a raid. Silly jerk."

He looks over his left shoulder again, then back at Lyle, then back at Emma in the rear doorway.

"It's been a real romantic pleasure to bring you two together. So romantic, right here where it all began. Nice place for a dramatic stage exit," he laughs at his cleverness. "That's it: you two can die together like Romeo and Juliet," he chuckles, a mocking smirk pulls across his heavy face. "But, with a little twist: this time old Romeo here is going to get to see Juliet die in front of him. No suicides to spin your stupid asses off this mortal coil."

Chris glares at Emma, but she doesn't notice. She is focused on something else. Behind Cain she sees the ferry leaving Algiers Point, heading across the river. Cain has throttled back, and the trawler is barely moving, but the distance between them and the ferry is closing. The bearing is constant.

He points the pistol at Emma.

Stalling for time to think, Emma manages, "Mr. Cain, you're right, I'm very confused. Just who are you? Did you plan all this? Would you do us the honor telling us why you're pointing that gun at me?"

"Well, OK, you deserve that much. Here's the quick and dirty, the Cliff Notes version for you morons. It's all about money. Big surprise! I was like you two. Played the game for years. God and country, all that. Then I got smart."

As Cain looks quickly over his shoulder at the river, Emma makes a plan. Without moving her head, she cuts a glance towards Lyle. She tries to get him to follow her eyes to the fire extinguisher and axe on the bulkhead behind them.. He responds with a confused frown. She scrunches her eyebrows down, stares intently at him and tries again.

"Talent and devotion never earned anybody anything. You ought to know that by now. It takes intelligence." Cain is facing her again. "It took me years to get where I needed to be. When I knew enough about the corrupt bastards running USA black ops and the kinds of friends they had. I played my cards. It took brains and guts. I stayed on as a consultant to old Uncle Sam's corporate intelligence service until I had enough on enough on his spooks to—how should I put it—expand my opportunities"

It's all about him, Emma's mind races. *How can I keep him talking?*

She has guessed right; Cain can't stop. "I never heard of old lover boy here until he started screwing up a simple courier service. Talk about an idiot, you take the cake! He got 'curiouser and curiouser' but he couldn't figure out the next step. You could have set yourself up for life," he shook his head as he turned toward Lyle, who caught Emma's sign. "Far above the feeble brain power of a horn tooter, eh, Lyle old boy? There was hope for you. You blew it, sport. Really stupid: asking questions, writing a really nasty little report down in Paraguay, blabbing to his little girl friend. Hey, Emma, you ought to know about her! How was she, Lyle? Those brainy Ivy League bitches more your style?"

Lyle was looking at Emma, but she was staring at Cain. In her peripheral vision she could see the river churning behind the ferry as it picked up speed, now only yards off the bow. She dared not let Cain see her looking. The distance was closing quickly. She prays that neither notices. The bow will enter the wake in four, three, two…!

"Look!" she shouts and points ahead a split second before the trawler's bow dips deeply into the wake. She and Lyle rush Cain who has lost balance and falls back against the windshield. Lyle reaches him first, but the old man is quick. He hits Lyle on the head with the long silencer. The move makes him squeeze the trigger. The shot misses Lyle only by inches. The bullet ricochets off the ceiling. Lyle lunges as best he can from the deck and grabs Cain's right forearm with both of his hands. He pulls down, enough to spoil Cain's aim on Emma. Cain's reaction is overpowering. Even with Lyle's grip, Cain's response is enough to pull him off the deck. Cain's gun hand is over his head.

The momentum lands both men on the deck. Lyle is on top, but Cain crashes his right knee into his groin. In agony, Lyle rolls off to his left. The exertion winds Cain, at least temporarily, giving Lyle enough time to scramble to his feet and again lunge toward him. Cain is faster. Balanced again, Lyle dodges another swing of the long silencer and barrel. They grapple and spin in a circle, then fall, this time with Cain on top. Lyle's head bounces hard off the steel deck. Dazed, he loses his grip and lies helpless as Cain stands, steadies the gun with both hands and aims it at Lyle's face. His lips curl and his eyes squint nearly shut as he cocks the hammer, "So-long, Skippy."

His face is instantly expressionless. His eyes roll up. His mouth sags open. His grip relaxes. The pistol bounces off the deck and Cain falls to his knees, dead.

Lyle scrambles to his feet. He looks at the bloody head face-down at his feet, then at Emma. She's standing at Cain's feet, frozen. Her eyes are filled with horror. Her arms are extended as though she was still holding the fire axe she has just buried six inches deep in his skull. She's trying to scream, but the heaving sound is stuck in her throat. A moment later it escapes before she clamps both hands over her mouth. Lyle steps over the body and holds her tightly.

Lyle turns her from the dead man, then takes the wheel. The trawler has turned ninety degrees toward the west bank. Not sure why, he corrects the course back toward mid river. "Emma, we've got to get out of here," he shouts, desperately trying to think of just where that could be. He sees the tightly coiled black mike chord swinging a few inches over her head and reaches for it.

She grabs his hand, "Wait. Who do we call? What do we say?"

They jump as the radio cracks to life.

"'Navy Sweep,' 'Navy sweep,' Extremely hot signature on barge at Gulf Coast yard. Signature definitely nuclear. Repeat, definitely nuclear. Closing at hundred feet. No movement observed."

They look through the windshield, now aware that a helicopter is hovering to their left. Emma takes the wheel as Lyle steps outside for a better view.

"'Sweep,' movement detected. Cargo hatches are moving forward. There is no movement inside, but there's something in there. Closing distance. Stand by."

"'Water-Borne,' 'Water-Borne!" The urgency in Parker's voice is as uncharacteristic as it is undeniable.

A thirty-foot Coast Guard patrol boat with a bow-mounted Browning M2 50-caliber machine gun roars under full power as it swings from its station beneath the interstate bridge and heads toward the ship yard. "'Water-Borne' ETA one minute." Simultaneously, the coxswain piloting a twenty-four foot rigid-hull inflatable boat throttles its twin two-hundred-fifty horse power Yamaha four-stroke outboards to full power and races upriver from the Industrial Canal landing. It and the eight NOPD special weapons officers armed with M-16s will reach the shipyard only seconds behind the patrol boat.

"'Marine One,' 'Marine Two,' repeat, 'Marine One,' 'Marine Two,' launch. Rendezvous with Navy One at Canal Street Ferry landing Algiers point. NOLA Coast Guard, belay all traffic. Repeat, belay all traffic Industrial Canal to Huey Long!"

* * * *

"Signature maxed out. Barge doors open. No movement inside." The pitch of the pilot's voice is clearly higher. The words come faster, "Affirmative, affirmative. Artillery tubes present. Repeat, artillery tubes present!"

"Possible bogey off Gulf Coast yard," the Coast Guard patrol boat radios. "Closing to ID."

* * * *

The applause inside the Dome has subsided. Parker has moved his second in command to maintain eye contact with the President while he has ducked outside.

"One vessel immediate, within two hundred yards. Trawler, *Nancy Kay*, approximately eight-zero feet. Location mid-river, possibly disabled or drifting. Estimated range three hundred yards. Additional vessel, a pleasure craft, *Bon Homme,* stationary, adjacent barge, range one-fifty to two-hundred yards, bow upriver."

Emma's face and the deck are covered with blood oozing from the gash in Cain's head. But her shock at the gory sight is being replaced with awareness that something else is happening overhead and at the ship yard and that a heavily armed patrol boat is bearing down on them at flank speed. She is unaware of the other boat speeding from downriver. All she can think to do is point the bow toward the east bank to at least look less threatening. She looks at the VHF mike in her hand, not sure how it got there. She has instinctively grabbed it like a lifeline. Suddenly, as though it had shocked her, she drops it. It swings on its long coiled cord from the ceiling. *Will my voice confirm that Cain didn't finish his murders and bring others who will?*

The speaker cracks to life, jolting her back to reality: "Emergency, emergency, emergency. Coast Guard New Orleans. Emergency, emergency, emergency all vessels vicinity Algiers Point ferry landing, Gulf Coast yard. All units, all stations monitor Channel 16. All vessels vicinity Algiers Point avast, hold positions. Repeat, all vessels avast, hold positions."

Simultaneously from the speaker monitoring the Secret Service frequency, "'Marine One,' 'Marine Two,' copy Navy traffic?"

"Roger, 'Marine One,' 'Navy Sweep' traffic understood."

"Interdict, trawler, pleasure craft, possible bogeys. Immobilization, repeat, immobilization, all deadly authorized non-complying traffic. Weapons hot. Afloat traffic vicinity considered hostile until identified."

Emma looks at Lyle, then Cain's grotesque body face down in the doorway. There's only one option. She retrieves the mike and presses the transmit button "Emergency, emergency, emergency. Trawler *Nancy Kay,* vicinity Algiers Point. Two souls on board. One, possibly two, deceased. Acknowledge declared emergency. Standing by to comply with all directives. Urgently request further instruction."

"Coast Guard New Orleans to *Nancy Kay*: lay off, lay off! *Nancy Kay*, repeat, lay off, clear vicinity, proceed east bank immediately!"

As she eases the throttles forward, the helicopter gunship swoops in a diving approach, barely a hundred feet above the foot of Esplanade Street. It flairs. Lyle sees four orange and white Raytheon-Boeing Joint Air Ground Missiles slung beneath.

In the distance it descends, the JAGMs practically in the water, and circles the Chris Craft. A woman's voice joins the traffic, "Coast Guard New Orleans to all units: *Bon Homme* confirmed friendly, identified by Guard patrol craft as control platform for fireworks show scheduled at 2000 hours. Registered *Monte Verde* Coffee Company, New Orleans. Target is friendly, repeat, friendly."

"Wave off, wave off!" Parker shouts into his wrist microphone.

Emma and Lyle looked at each other. *Monte Verde*? Just a coincidence—a weirdly timed one, at that—nothing but a name from long ago? Intuitively, Emma's eidetic memory knows better. There's no time to react before the gunship has covered the distance from the Chris Craft and is hovering at eye level, staring into the bridge. Barrels of the 20-millimeter cannon spin, then lock in firing position. Emma can see the face through his face shield. He is frowning.

"*Nancy Kay*, heave to immediately. Hold your position," the gunship radios, lining up his shot.

The whine of the twin jet engines is deafening. Barely able to hear her own voice, Emma presses the mike button again and screams, "Emergency, emergency, emergency! *Nancy Kay* complies. Requests immediate assistance. Standing by for further instruction!"

"*Nancy Kay*, heave to, immediately, or you will be destroyed. Do you understand?"

"Comply, comply, comply! *Nancy Kay* repeats: emergency on board!" and pulls back the throttles. The trawler begins to drift backward.

The pilot lowers his darkly tinted blast visor and tilts his head.

"*Nancy Kay* complying. Signal understood!"

"Move!" Lyle grabs her shoulders, spins her around and pushes her toward the rear door.

She stumbles but manages to grasp one of the steel hand rails. She trips but lands on her feet at the bottom of the stairs. Even with wind knocked out of her, she spins and looks up the ladder. Where is he!

The point-blank cannon fire is earsplitting. The huge bullets disintegrate the windshield with a cascade of flying glass. The entire boat vibrates with their impact on the steel bulkhead behind the bridge.

With her heart ripping out of her chest, Emma pulls herself up the ladder. Lyle was there, lying on the port bridge wing. There wasn't a scratch on him. The blood isn't his. Still struggling to breathe, she helps him to his feet. "Look!" Her scream is felt more than heard, drowned out by the roar of the Cobra engine only yards away.

Lyle follows her pointed finger.

"The helicopter is on fire!" Emma shouts.

Behind and closing fast, dense, black smoke is pouring from SH3's high-mounted rotor. It is jerking off balance, beginning to crab sideways, throwing chunks of its rotor blades in all directions, some pieces already violently impacting *Nancy Kay.* The Marine pilot sees it, too. He reacts immediately, jerking back on the stick so rapidly that his tail rotor slices the water before gaining altitude. Within seconds, he knows, there no longer will be any need to disable the trawler.

* * * *

Parker and agent Bone Break stride on the stage. The convention chairman has begun her welcoming remarks. The honored guests are seated a few feet behind.

They approach from his back. Parker gently touches the President's left elbow, leans toward his right ear and whispers, "You must leave now. We have a code, sir."

President Lehman hides his confusion to the five thousand people in front of him, but doesn't have to think about what to do next. Parker has gripped his elbow and is lifting him gently but firmly to his feet and is walking him toward the rear of the stage. A low murmur rises as 'Bone Break' leads the other platform guests behind them. Watching aghast from the wings, angry that she doesn't know what's happening, the woman in the black dress types "continue" which appears on an LED screen imbedded in the lectern.

"Mr. President, we are in a Code Red." Daring not speak the words when Lehman was facing the crowd, he speaks calmly as he would have repeated a weather report. Confused and concerned for the visual image of his rapid departure, he is also aware that his face is still visible to scores of others back stage. He even manages a pleasant smile as Parker throws him inside the limo and lands against him. "We've picked up nuclear signatures. 'Navy Sweep' has crashed into the river, apparently shot down. We believe the gunfire came from the same source, a barge, about a mile from here. Before he went in, the pilot reported seeing what looked like artillery tubes. We are well within range. We are interdicting to verify and take appropriate action. Until the river is secure, we're going to the hole, the City of New Orleans command bunker at City Hall. That's just around the corner. The First Lady and the other official party are right behind. The decoy motorcade is headed to the Coast Guard Headquarters." His next words were the hardest. "Best case, Mr. President, is a false alarm caused by faulty calibration." If that was true, both knew, the career of Senior Special Agent Lee Parker was officially finished.

The tiny motorcade of one limo and three SUVs careen from beneath the Super Dome and fishtail into the sunlight on Poydras Street. At City Hall the limo's left rear passenger door flew open. The President and 'Bone Break' scurried across the sidewalk, blast through the main entrance and fast walk down service stairs to the basement vault. At street level outside, the entire contingent of twelve Secret Service agents stand with weapons drawn, rounds chambered and safeties off. Curious, then startled, crowds seeing the motorcade and show of weapons were herded off the sidewalks by uniformed police as the agents spread and laid down firing lanes in all directions. Parker radioed the FAA to declare an emergency and to alert them to inbound traffic at City Hall's rooftop helo pad. The Bell UH-1 Huey would land in five minutes, departing immediately for the Belle Chase Naval Air Station where Air Force One's crew had scrambled to start engines. It is no comfort to Parker to know that the mysterious barge, which some junior—perhaps now dead—Navy pilot thinks is full of mortar tubes, lies in a direct line between the two points.

He takes a situational inventory. Good news: The president is safe. A new green zone is established. Evacuation is underway. Bad news: the sensors are wrong. *I have just sent the entire free world into panic over some new way to unload grain.*

* * * *

Emma throws the wheel over and rams the throttles forward. The over powered trawler spins in place. It is enough: the tail section of the burning SH-3 glances off the stern and slides off into the muddy river. The aviation fuel burns off rapidly. Trying to move down the long central passageway below on the main deck, Lyle bounces off the walls like a rag doll. He bursts through the door to the aft working deck. As the flames disappear into the water, he throws a life ring. The gesture is symbolic, but it is all he can do. Nothing but debris bobs to the surface.

On the bridge, Emma hears the radio traffic on Channel 16 and the police VHF frequencies increasing frantically. She cannot believe what she hears next. Someone reports that *Nancy Kay* is hostile! The gunship is back, dropping in front of the slowly turning trawler. Emma has no choice but to join the confusion, hoping that somebody believes her. She keys the mike, "*Nancy Kay* searching for crash survivors."

"Coast Guard acknowledges. Proceed." *Finally!* She palms more blood off her face.

The radio traffic is constant and chaotic. She doesn't understand the code names, but their near hysterical words are unmistakable. Both radio channels mention gunfire, believed coming from the barge at Gulf Coast. That, at least, makes sense. *That's where the bad guys are!* Knowing that the Marine can see her, she points toward the ship yard, as though it might get him back in the game. *Over there, stupid!*

Lyle knows that the swift current has already pushed the wreckage and crewmen hundreds of yards downriver. It would be a miracle if anyone made it to the surface. Emma knows this, too. Even so, she makes one more circular pass, drifting down river, then throttles forward to hold a position where she had been told to go.

From the radios she knows that NOPD officers and agents dispatched to Gulf Coast Steel have not boarded the barge because they can't get to it. It's tied to pilings away from the bank, and it's not nested with others boats that would create a walkway from shore. That's the way Alexi wanted it. Neither have they seen the rope ladder, painted black like the barge, dangling from the transom.

Agents in the inflatable boat have arrived at the shipyard. She hears instructions for them to stand off while the patrol boat comes alongside with boarding hooks. To her relief, the gunship has backed off, now heading upriver toward the fireworks barge.

Lyle rejoins Emma in what was left of the little bridge. Action seems to be focusing on boarding and searching the barge. With no continuing confirmation from 'Navy Sweep' that the barge is indeed hot, one voice on the radio, the one which seems to be in charge, suggests that—

although unlikely—the nuclear signature may have been inaccurate.

Monitoring the Secret Service frequency, they're relieved to hear their emergency call acknowledged. But, it's only a passing comfort. She is surprised that—even under the circumstances—nobody is hurrying aboard the *Nancy Kay* or even asking what kind of emergency they've declared. *It is New Orleans after all; too hot for more than one crisis at a time.* Looking at the grizzly mess on the deck beside her, she also knows that eventually she and Lyle have quite a tale to tell, one that makes no sense to them, nor will it – she fears – to anyone else. *Time for that, later.* Looking back at the ladder to the wardroom she knows that the one man who might make sense of it all is lying dead down there.

The Cobra is back from upriver. This time it makes a fast, low pass over the barge. The pilot reports no movement inside. Maybe the shots weren't fired from there. No one has noticed the tiny room hung on the rear bulkhead and the two bodies inside. No one—certainly not Alexi— saw six men, each armed with an AK-47, pull themselves up the rope ladder from a paint skiff. The round tore through his chest; another was pumped into his head as he slid down the control panel. Maria, so over medicated in the past two years that she could not comprehend what was going on around her, stood, detached, arms at her side. When the gunman jabbed the muzzle between her breasts her last expression was a sweet smile. They hid inside until the SH-3 crossed from the river bank, directly overhead and hovered over the water about a hundred feet away. In unison, they jumped to the narrow catwalk above the mortars, aimed and put more than a hundred armor-piercing titanium rounds into the cockpit and rotor assembly.

* * * *

The Coast Guard boats arrived together and held positions while the boarding lines were rigged. The inflatable turned, its stern facing the barge as it moved to a better cover position. Seeing the mistake, six men dressed in black jeans and hoodies, exposed their position and opened fire. Most of the seven-hundred rounds of 7.62mm rounds are direct hits. Five agents died instantly. Both boats are sinking. To shield two wounded men in the water, the patrol boat helmsman drifted back into the river. On the bow, the gunner aims its 50-caliber gun, now at nothing. Sighting down the barrel, he also knows that—should the shooters reappear—the huge incendiary rounds would tear into a row of buildings and bystanders on the bank beyond.

Only 'Mike One' is left to attack. Seeing the boatswain's predicament, he crabs to gain an oblique angle from which he could fire from above and slightly forward of the Coast Guardsmen. He releases two M65 TOW missiles that blast two massive holes at the waterline.

The concussion rocks the patrol boat and sends steel fragments into it, wounding four men on deck. Emma witnessed the effective but foolish attack with horror. She had to do something, if only get close enough to pick up even more bodies from the river. She throttles forward, but before the trawler has covered a hundred yards, the patrol boat gunner has swung the big gun around and found his target: her. Panicked, he fires two long bursts.

The tall bow shields them. Most of the rounds pass overhead, landing miles away; from the direction of fire, she hopes in Lake Ponchatrain. Then all hell breaks loose; columns of smoke and sparks streak skyward; huge explosions thunder across the river. They cover their eyes. The fireworks show has begun, joined by another burst of 50-caliber rounds bouncing off the bow. The lightning flashes of green, purple, gold, silver surrealistically paint the water brighter than noonday.

The gunfire almost seems insignificant. Emma and Lyle are shaken to their toes, both cover their ears. The effect is the same on the patrol boat crew, who—sensing that the trawler is not attacking—return to rescuing. Prepared for the chaos with earplugs and dark glasses, the six gunmen continue firing, calmly picking off two in the water and two in the boat.

A quarter mile away, the two men aboard the Chris Craft watch in horror. The fat little man has fallen to his knees and has crawled under the bridge console.

Impossibly, the noise grows more intense. The sound is different, coming from ahead, not from above, it takes Emma a second or to comprehend. Like the steady beat of a giant bass drum, the mortars are firing in unison; the rounds are tearing into the sky in groups of five. In the glow of falling sparks, Emma sees the patrol boat disappear below the surface. The intense white light also reveals two large holes in the barge that are allowing water to rush in. The barge is slowly, imperceptibly beginning to list. Inside, the gimbaled platforms keep the mortars on target, level and still dry. Emma is struck with two thoughts: the barge will sink, but only eventually; the top of Nancy Kay's bow is now higher than the barge. The Cobra has recovered and has returned to fire more

20mm cannon rounds; but, nothing is stopping the mortar fire. The *Nancy Kay* is the only effective weapon left. It's up to her.

"Lyle, we're going to ram it," she screams. "Hold on!" Emma shoves the throttles until they can move no farther, and the over-powered trawler practically leaps out of the water. Confident the bow will not veer off course, they jump down the stairs and flatten in the passageway, holding on to the stair railing where it was welded to the deck.

Their bodies flail forward with the impact. The collision is followed by the scraping scream of the reinforced bow slicing through more steel. Finding their feet and climbing back to the bridge, they can see the tactic has worked: their bow is now at least ten feet inside the barge; there's a gash all the way to the water line. Water is rushing in, but the mortars are still firing. She reverses the engines and prays that the trawler can disengage before it, too, sinks. *Where are the shells landing?*

At first nothing happens, but then the deck shifts. Under full reverse, the trawler slides free. Reversing stern-first into the channel to gain distance and speed for another attack, she notices a boat speeding toward them. *Now what?* She's too busy to care. By the time she's free of the barge, the Chris Craft is laying no more than ten feet off her starboard. Lyle steps on the bridge wing to try wave them away. He sees two men. The response is immediate and unexpected: one of them levels a pistol and begins firing at him. He tumbles backward into the pilot house and lands at Emma's feet. "Lyle!" she screams.

She sees, but does not hear, two more long tongues of fire burst from the pistol; one round strikes the bill of her ball cap, kicking it off her head. It lands between the two blood-spattered bodies at her feet. Rage replaces terror. She sees Cain's Glock. A bullet jerks the dead man's leg inches from her hand reaching for the pistol.

By the time she has straightened to stand, Menard has grabbed the trawler's railing with his left hand and is swinging aboard. The other man at the helm is steadying the boat. Emma aims and begins firing. The first shot misses Menard but tears a hole in the Commander's deck beside Nat's left foot. The next shatters the windshield in front of him. Menard falls backward, managing to land back beside Nat. Looking at his empty pistol, shoves in another clip and begins firing rapidly. This time his aim is better; sparks spit off the steel behind her while the boat falls away, turns into the current and begins to pick up speed. Enough, damn it! She spins the wheel and throttles forward in pursuit.

The Commander is no match for the powerful trawler's acceleration.

The panicked men can only look back in horror as the mass of steel begins to tower over them. They jump overboard as it smashes through the teak transom and begins grinding the boat to splinters. The powerful current sucks them down, into the vortex created by the trawler's massive propellers. They emerge two hundred yards down river as unrecognizable chunks of meat.

Emma's senses are numb. Her last act was one of instinct, not rationality. The body of Lyle Rees lay still at her feet.

At the center of the enormous orange fireball the barge becomes nothing more than chunks of shrapnel. Pieces, some the size of billboards, flip into the sky. Others slice horizontally across the water like cards tossed at a hat. The biggest slab shaves off the bridge house like it was made of paper. Emma Lucas smashes against the rear bulkhead, then forward into the wheel, breaking her ribs at the sternum.

Time had stopped. There is no pain, no pleasure, no hope, no dreams. Three bodies lie together on the cold, bloody deck. The show is over. This wasn't dress rehearsal. Silence returned to the face of the water.

Where they once fleetingly shared their time, their disappointments and dreams, the dark river rolls past. Its muddy waters still flow between those two banks, as they have since time immemorial: powerful, serene, with eternal indifference to the folly of man.

Epilogue

The two-story building was solid, even in its run-down condition. It was a rare find.

The flat roof over brick walls had withstood years of heavy snows and punishing winds. Lucy knew that it was expensive to build in 1967 and still would be. Bricks are still costly and hard to come by; there is no local source for them or any other heavy building material. Everything from bricks and mortar to carpet and paint still comes by sea.

On the other hand—as she thought when she first saw the place— respectable night clubs were even rarer. With reasonable attention to detail, the kind available from a proprietor who lived upstairs, she also knew that nobody ever went broke selling booze in Alaska.

The structure sat empty for more than a decade in the city's seedy-to-eclectic Spenard neighborhood, the city's first—and still-reigning champion—red-light district. In recent years the reputation of the neighborhood between Lake Spenard and downtown Anchorage had improved, but only slightly. A constant rotation of ethnic restaurants, the occasional health-food store, yoga studio, adult book store and a few store-front churches added an Alaskan-grown, mostly garish gentrification. For a wise entrepreneur, one like Lucy Lucas, it was all irresistible. It provided an opportunity to act on ideas first born back in New Orleans.

In those years she had been a frequent companion of Lyle Rees, Emma's shipmate. He lived nearby in the Garden District. The relationships grew from neighbors to close friendships. The part-time but professional musician began inviting them along to his gigs and exclusive backroom parties. With entre to places respectable young women never visit, they encountered a world of colorful characters.

She sensed that Emma was blossoming around Lyle's charm. Lucy's interests grew, too, but toward the people who owned the cash registers. She quickly realized that theirs was a business like any other. Shunned, sidelined, pigeon-holed as not quite real as she was by many as a dwarf—a joke or object of pity—she knew they were no different than any other successful business investors. Whether drawn by her business sense or driving ambition—most likely both—many of the proprietors became clients of her part-time accounting business.

During her last year at Tulane, counselor and client learned from each other.

The lesson that she took away was fundamental, intuitive for her: she had everything she needed to ensure independence and success; height had nothing to do with it.

Immediately after graduating, she landed a job with the New Orleans Police Department. Shortly afterwards, Deloitte and Touche recruited her for their Charleston, South Carolina, office. The transfer to their Anchorage office was tantalizing; she never told her sister about the offer, believing it would be bad luck. The move came through. She planned her arrival as a surprise, but only days before she landed in Anchorage, Emma had been whisked away to a mysterious rendezvous in New Orleans.

A year ago it was. That tragic night, memories of betrayals, the people and institutions that enabled them, still troubled her. She knew that corporate politics would be no better, and it made her transition to private practice easy. She never looked back.

She paid cash for the old building.

She painted it a brilliant, almost phosphorescent yellow. The unfinished, raw brick interior was perfect. She installed a state-of-the-art kitchen and built a tiered stage, surrounding it on three sides with café table seating. The finishing touch was a long walnut antique back bar that spanned the back wall opposite the stage.

The roof-top embellishment was the capper, literally.

What started as an inside joke between her and friends in Anchorage, turned into an unforgettable icon. She found the ten-foot-tall pair of fiberglass mukluks in a trash heap. They'd been discarded by a boot store. She painted them metallic red. Mounted on a twenty-foot tower on the roof, they gleamed in the morning and evening sun. During the long Alaska winter nights, spotlights on them cast a warm glow on the snow-covered neighborhood.

The Yellow Brick Bistro and its Ruby Mukluks were Anchorage landmarks, an unofficial beacon for pilots, in more ways than one. From the beginning the transplanted Louisianan and her business maintained first-class reputations: hers as an entrepreneur and consultant; her creation as a must-see destination for locals and tourists hungry for Southern cooking and the hottest live jazz north—much farther north—of the Crescent City.

* * * *

It was another early morning after a late night. There was work to do and no time to rest. She tromped downstairs and opened the wide front doors, knowing panhandlers and ecobums weren't awake to intrude at this time of day. The reward was immediate and therapeutic: the cool, crisp breeze off the inlet.

The Bistro's previous night had been a huge success. Tonight, Saturday, may even be better. The U.S. Navy Pacific Fleet Show Band, touring the West Coast from California to Alaska, had packed the bar to capacity. Proceeds above their expenses were earmarked to fund a jazz program in the Anchorage public schools. Seeing the sailors in Cracker Jack white jumpers was bittersweet. They had played three sets, and until the last note the cash registers had practically rung in rhythm with their music.

Today Lucy and her partner, in town to help with the special weekend, began their routine slowly. They sat, silently savoring the rich coffee. The previous evening's afterglow lingered, making it strange to gaze at the empty stage.

Both were aware of the day's significance. Neither would ever forget the events, exactly one year ago. The silence ended when Lucy spoke, "Those were two good people confronting the very worst of humanity. It's still hard to believe," she paused to gain composure and to change the narrative, if only slightly. "Amazing, really. It was all hushed up in the press. An accident, is all that was ever reported. I'm still in awe of the Russian. Too bad we'll never know his story, why he did what he did. I wonder what I would have done under the same circumstances. I wonder if the world will ever know what nearly happened."

The coffee was ready. Her words had been directed toward the antique copper urn. She filled two mugs, slid them across the bar and climbed up on a tall stool beside her partner. "Cheers. The death, the destruction, could have been horrendous. He knew that. I've thought about it every day, and I still can't even begin to imagine why or how he did what he did. He ensured that the rounds would always fire the dirty warheads nearly straight up, never with enough trajectory to strike the Super Dome. They all landed in the river. Think about it: he was literally in hell, a slave for years, emotionally tortured by the loss of his girls, his wife's descent into insanity. Somehow, from somewhere, he found the courage to sabotage it. The fact that nobody, other than those on the river that night, lost their lives is a miracle."

Lucy's eyes moistened. There was so much ahead, so much to live for; she tried not to look back, instead to appreciate the moment. Even so, she spoke softer, "There were a couple of other heroes, too. You know who I'm talking about. They didn't have years to plan and plot; they hardly had time to think. Those two were thrown into the middle of chaos and reacted instantly, instinctively. They could have run away, could have made all kinds of excuses, but they didn't. They could have given up. I probably would have." Lucy took her eyes off her and looked again at the stage. "The world ought to know it was Emma Lucas and Lyle Rees who got the bad guys. They were heroes." She wiped her eyes with the back of her hand. "But, tell you what. I do a fist pump every time I hear about another conviction of some scumbag in DC or New Orleans!"

"There was somebody else, too. Let's hear it for pack rats!" Lucy's smile widened at the unexpected reply. "Nobody's going to know that it was you who unleashed the tale of the tape. Think about it, kiddo, your hoarding habits outwitted the most brilliant criminal minds in the world!"

Lucy clinked her mug, "OK, I guess. When they're passing out tarts…"

"I'm watching all the cases, too. I think the count so far is more than twenty organized crime convictions, everything from human and drug trafficking, smuggling, extortion and murder to selling nuclear material. And, they haven't stopped. The INS, Customs, the Coast Guard and Navy, police departments from New Orleans to New York, are still digging. I can't help hear my guests talking, but I can say that even the Secret Service is changing some procedures. Who knows what effect that could have for a future president? And, even better, I've heard that the State Department was nearly out of business for months while they cleaned house. The rats scurried in every direction, mostly into jail!"

"So many players, people who never met each other, some who did. I guess life's like that. It came with a huge price tag, costs paid by people as different and—in some ways—as similar as Roland and Alexi.

Mentioning the two names brought another silence. "I've got to believe that—somehow—they know the good they did; I hope you do, too," Lucy said.

A man approached the open front doors. Hearing the voices, he stopped, only a little ashamed to be eavesdropping. In the past year he realized how much he cared about both of them. Just seeing them sitting with the backs toward him, sharing their feelings, was exhilarating in a way he had never imagined. Their words soothed deep scars. They had forgiven him, even if he hadn't. How long had he been so ignorant, so blind? Their voices affirmed that he had been handed a gift, a second chance to pursue real joy, to make the best of every single day. *It's more than a second chance, more like a third or fourth or four thousandth.* The thought was silly; but, he did know that he never again needed to fear anything, especially himself.

He stepped quietly into the doorway. The sight of them, the spruce-scented ocean breeze, the warmth of the sun on his back, were joys he once would not have savored with such simple pleasure. What a gift. Even the struggles, however great or small, are their own reward. For the musician the metaphor was obvious: it is the difference in hearing music and creating it, even performing. The reward, the real joy, the soaring freedom, was in the honesty behind it all: the sweat to learn, the discipline to perfect, rehearse, the passion to make magic with every fiber of being and to share.

He had to look no farther that this pair to see the kind of courage that endures all and conquers all.

* * * *

They hadn't noticed the long shadow on the plank floor, now sliding toward them. Lucy saw him first as he rounded the end of the bar and stopped between their stools. He wrapped his arms around each of them and pulled their faces close to his. He kissed each on the cheek. "Good morning, ladies, got another cup for an old shipmate?"

"Aye, aye," Lucy spoke with a salute and hopped off her stool.

"Ladies, we do have a lot to celebrate today. Sad or happy memories, they're ours. It is quite an anniversary." Lucy handed him a mug, and he raised it, "Here's to those who are no longer with us and to those who are. May we never forget either." He saw the faces plainly, and he knew she did, too. He placed the mug on the bar and took Emma's hands in his. "May I?"

She didn't speak, pulled a crooked smile and nodded.

He placed his hands gently on her shoulders and squeezed. She lifted her face to his and softly returned the kiss. Old memories, indeed, he thought, just like remembering how shallow he had been, how hard he must have worked to be so stupid.

"Lucy, give me an F chord."

The old upright looked much better than it sounded, but it didn't matter. He hummed the note, closed his eyes. The words sprang from his heart. With a fine Welsh tenor he sang:

"Should old acquaintance be forgot, and never brought to mind? Should old acquaintance be forgot, and *auld lang syne?* For *auld lang syne,* my dears, for *auld lang syne*, we'll take a cup of kindness yet, for *auld lang syne.*"

Lucy had sounded out four more chords to fill in the accompaniment. She picked up on his head cue and played lowly beneath his voice, louder and stronger now.

"We two have run about the slopes, and picked the daisies fine; but we've wandered many a weary foot, since *auld lang syne*. We two have paddled in the stream, from morning sun till dine; but seas between us broad have roared since *auld lang syne*."

Tenderly cradling her hands in his, he brought them to his chest. She felt his heartbeat. His hard hands covered hers, protecting them.

His voice cracked, "And there's a hand my trusty friend! And give us a hand o' thine! And we'll take a right good-will draught, for *auld lang syne.*"

She kissed his tears.

"Thanks, ladies. What a day this is!" He smiled at Lucy, then back to the brown eyes adoring him. "You know, it might have taken me a long time to get it, but I do: this isn't dress rehearsal." Lyle Rees knew all that mattered, ever did or ever would, had heard his confession and all it implied. "My dear, fearless ladies, let's go live it!"

END

CPSIA information can be obtained at www.ICGtesting.com
Printed in the USA
LVOW08s1358050614

388773LV00001B/20/P